silk
fire

First published 2022 by Solaris
an imprint of Rebellion Publishing Ltd,
Riverside House, Osney Mead,
Oxford, OX2 0ES, UK

www.solarisbooks.com

ISBN: 978-1-78108-976-7

10 9 8 7 6 5 4 3 2 1

A CIP catalogue record for this book is available from the
British Library.

Designed & typeset by Rebellion Publishing

Printed in the UK

silk
fire

ZABÉ ELLOR

SOLARIS

Names and Pronunciation

The honorific 'dzaxa,' commonly applied to the ruling class of the War District, is correctly pronounced 'dza-HUA'

Koreshiza Brightstar (koh-REI-shi-zah), called Koré (koh-REI)

Riapáná Żutruro (RIA-paa-naa ZHU-true-row), called Ria

Faziz (fa-ZEES)

Vashathke (va-sha-THI-kay) Faraakshgé (fa-rock-SHE-gay)

Dzaxashigé (dza-hua-SHI-gay)

Dzaroshardze (dza-ROSH-ards-EY) Faraakshgé (fa-rock-SHE-gay) Dzaxashigé (dza-hua-SHI-gay), called Dzaro (dza-ROW)

Akizeké (acki-zeh-KEI) Shikishashir (she-key-SHA-sheer) Dzaxashigé (dza-hua-SHI-gay)

Rarafashi (rah-rah-FA-shi) Akéakireze (ah-key-AH-key-rez-eh) Dzaxashigé (dza-hua-SHI-gay)

Geshge (gesh-GAY) Akéakireze (ah-key-AH-key-rez-eh) Dzaxashigé (dza-hua-SHI-gay)

Eprue Zucho (EP-rue-ey ZU-cho)

Żeposháru Rena (zyeh-POSH-a-rue REI-na)

Tożätupé (TOH-zyah-TWO-pey)

The Megabuildings of Victory Street and their Owners

An Incomplete List

Skygarden, property of Judge Rarafashi
The Palace of Ten Billion Swords, property of Magistrate Vashathke
The Surrender, property of Lady Dzaroshardze
The Slatepile, currently unincorporated
The Archive, property of Lady Xezkavodz
Towergarden, property of Lord Rezadzere
The Prizeheron, property of Lady Fidzjakovik
Old Dread, property of Lady Jeshethize

The Elemental Substances
To support the vast architecture of Jadzia, the eleven elemental substances allow skilled artisans to manipulate the laws of physics. The scholars of Victory Street sort them as follows:

The Four Principals
Holdstone, source of all Jadzia's minerals
Holdmetal, source of ores and alloys
Holdlife, universal substrate for growing all vegetation
Holdwater, source of Jadzia's oceans, rain, and plumbing

The Three Ethereals
Holdair, to bind and control atmosphere
Holdweight, to manipulate and redirect gravity
Holdlight, to cast and shape illumination

The Three Powers
Holdice, to maintain superconductors and craft weapons
Holdspark, to power electronics and craft weapons
Holdfire, to fuel engines and craft weapons

The Grand Prime
Holdfast, to bind all things physical and immaterial, in service of construction

To all who yearn for the light.

CHAPTER ONE
Atop the statue of the stone dragon

19th *Zxo*, Year 92 Rarafashi

"Above all, a wedding is a financial transaction. Dress as richly as if you own a bank and behave as politely as if you owe that bank money."—Men's Life Magazine: "Ask Jasper." Published and distributed in the Palace of Ten Billion Swords

"A good boy is a jeweled chalice. A stupid boy is a leaky sieve. A bad boy is a water pistol. I'm a bad boy."—Hishura, Blood and Stone 3: The Bloodletting (Modern Jiké subtitles)

THE FATHER OF the groom stopped halfway up the aisle to spit in my face.

With the bright store of essence tied to my soul, I could have dodged. But I didn't believe another man would behave so crudely in public until the hot, wet missile struck my cheek. The guests – mostly wealthy *dzaxa*, with a few Engineers for added prestige – tittered and laughed. My pale skin went scarlet. I yearned for the pavilion to collapse on my head.

"Whore," the groom's father growled. "You humiliate chaste men and rob essence from our marriages. Behind that pretty face, your soul is shit and worms."

I said nothing. I couldn't deny the charge. All Victory Street knew Koreshiza Brightstar, courtesan and proprietor of the High Kiss brothel. And I stood out starkly beside this man, who, though dressed in rich purple velvet, had the lined face and prominent pores of a dull. He'd invested most of his essence in his child, leaving him weak and worn. I'd gathered essence from my patrons in their pleasure, brightening myself with flawless skin, racing wits, and the strength to shatter steel.

Small wonder this man's wife had hired me to warm her bed tonight.

The groom's father marched on, to the dais, where his wife and the bride ceremonially haggled over dowry goods. The groom stood between them, silent in a skirt of translucent white. Staring at me like his eyes could dagger an unwelcome guest. Spit was sliding down my neck, and I'd brought nothing to wipe it away with. I couldn't move. Couldn't act.

I deserved this shame. I'd accepted a contract for a wedding and invaded the most important day of the young groom's life. I'd done it not for money, not even for essence, but for an excuse to get in and introduce myself to the woman I hoped to place on the imperial throne.

My long and winding path to vengeance, sundering another family.

"It's okay," whispered a serving man with long, dark hair, passing me a tissue. "Your client made the mess, not you."

I wiped my cheek and neck as the ceremony began.

The groom's father trembled as he touched his son's temples. Space fluttered around them, a flock of soundless starlings. The lines on the father's cheeks deepened, cracking through his makeup. Silver furrowed through dark hair, and the skin of his chin sank low. Light bloomed in the boy's eyes, turning his red irises deep as wine, tightening pale curls and deepening muscle lines. Shaping alluring beauty from a merely pleasing smile.

The last tithe. I hoped the groom enjoyed this part of the ceremony, if nothing else. He'd surrender most of his essence to his wife before she chose to conceive. He'd never shine so bright again. But Victory Street would know him for a good *dzaxa* husband, a respectable member of the ruling class. Most men found that a worthy trade.

The groom's mother gave the wedding speech, detailing the goods she'd exchanged with her son. She and the bride signed the contract; then, fashionably progressive, let the groom sign too. The bride nicked her finger, and the groom's, on a ceremonial razor, and pressed both together.

As the cheering crowd pressed forward to congratulate her, I sought my mark.

Akizeké Shikishashir Dzaxashigé, Magistrate of Armory Street, pushed to the head of the receiving line and embraced the bride. Her eyes were the stewing hue of old blood; her white-blond hair fell neatly to her chin. Crow's feet and stretchmarks lent her maturity and wisdom, and the wedding pavilion shook in echo of her laugh. The picture of a traditional politician—albeit one with little traction so far in her campaign to succeed our dying judge.

If she chose me as one of her campaign strategists, I'd have every notable from southmost Coldwater District to the blighted border of the Lost District demanding her ascension. Every wealthy lip on Victory Street would endorse her for the throne with the same eagerness as they begged me for private sins. I'd spent years preparing for this moment. Building connections. Collecting debts. I would flip the succession contest over as easily as I'd dangle downward on the dancing pole.

That was what I'd told myself this morning. Now a *dzaxa* magistrate was walking past me on her way to the bar, draped in gold and sparkling steel. Her stagnant campaign needed help, but suddenly, it seemed I'd have an easier time restoring the gods to life than convincing Akizeké to put her political future in the hands of a sex worker.

"Pardon me, Magistrate," I said as she passed, lifting a hand. "If I may have a word—"

"A photograph? Of course!" Akizeké flashed me a toothy smile, a politician's grin even dull eyes could pick out from miles away. She slung an arm around my hip and pulled me in, closer than I normally let strangers come without charging. The serving man who'd given me a tissue—one of her personal staff, perhaps?—shouldered a camera. "Think how pissed off your father will be if he sees his bastard making nice with his chief rival."

His only remaining rival. I smiled as the orange holdlight bulb flashed. A piece of photo-paper spat out below the lens, slowly resolving. The glare off Akizeké's gold-trimmed pauldrons had wiped my face from the image. "Actually, Magistrate, I'd love to speak with you about my father and the campaign—"

She patted my shoulder and tucked the blurred-out photos into my sash. "Hold onto those. Tell your future children how you met me just months before I ascended to judgeship."

"Thank you, and I will." I tried to sound gracious, grateful, but I had to make my proposal before someone more important stole her away. "You're my political role model. How you defended Armory Street's salvage rights in the border ruins. How you've funded the War District's museums. I only wanted to know… are you looking to hire more campaign strategists? I have excellent references."

Akizeké considered me. I shivered under her clotted gaze. "You're young. Pretty. Well-connected. But there's a hundred million other boys in that exact same position. If you want a job on my campaign, earn it."

My cheeks flamed. Venomous whispers in the pit of my stomach hissed *fool* and *imposter.* But I hadn't come empty-handed. I spoke for my aunt, and her allies. I could offer Akizeké a powerful block of supporters—

"Magistrate Akizeké!" A young man clad in green and white, like a living lily on the stem, shouldered in between us. "Have you scheduled a date for your concession speech? I need to file permits for my candidate's coronation parade."

She laughed. "Announcing six foreign endorsements in one day was an excellent trick, Zegakadze Kzagé. Your boss scared half the candidates into dropping out. But tricks won't keep me from my throne. And when I rule as judge, I won't need parades and parties to prove I have power."

Shaking her head, still chuckling, Akizeké set off toward the bourbon fountain with the hungry purpose of a stalking raptor.

Well. She certainly had an ego sized for the judge's throne.

"You're looking for a campaign job, Koré?" Zegakadze Kzagé—Zega, as he'd bid me call him when we'd been a couple—turned to me, faint humor playing around his lips. Brown curls framed his fair face in casual disarray. "A natural progression from sex work. Only in politics, you don't get to wear a condom when someone fucks you over."

"I hardly bother with prophylactics. Getting a prescription costs a fortune. Quite a few inappropriate itches plagued me when I entered the industry, but I gained immunity when I brightened."

"I'm sorry to hear that," he said. I wished I could believe him. His pillow-soft words too often concealed slaps. "You don't want to work for Akizeké. She's too far behind to win. Join us. Magistrate Vashathke will find you a place on his campaign staff."

"As a pretty party favor?"

"As his *son*. He loves you, underneath everything. He's always asking me to tell stories about you."

"How convenient. He becomes a caring father the moment a visible bastard can hurt his career most. Who does he plan to marry me to in exchange for their support? It can't be anyone too important. I'm used goods."

"I would never let him marry you off against your will. Because I still care for you." He declared that like a gambler revealing a winning hand. But I knew what was written on the back of his cards. *You didn't protect me from my marriage, Koré. You didn't care enough. And you owe me yourself for that.*

I was done being someone else's tool. Even if they said they loved me. Even if they were my own skin and bone. If it meant I had a heart of stone, so be it. Only stone survived Victory Street untouched.

My client was posing for photographs with her new daughter-in-law. Akizeké was circling the pavilion shaking hands. I had more than enough time to learn how far Zega would play this.

"How kind of you," I purred to my ex, offering him my arm. "Shall we go for a walk and discuss?"

He slid his elbow through mine. The lily perfume drenching him flooded my nose, blooming from the lace choker at his throat. My skin tingled where his delicate blue veins brushed my inner wrist. *A dead reflex.* My brain, not my heart, led me now in the great and small games I played. Careful to keep my smile vapid and my steps directionless and light, I led us outside the tent and onto a granite walking-path.

The wedding pavilion ran along the top of the stone dragon, a massive, ancient sculpture carved to mark some pointless, bloody victory. Its hollow body held only seventy thousand apartments, making it one of Victory Street's smaller buildings—and one of the quietest. Even my bright, sensitive ears couldn't find the background din of hallway traffic, arguing voices and clashing jazz harmonies that rang out life on Victory Street. The *dzaxa* landlady who owned this building had raised rents and driven folk from apartments they'd rented for generations, turning her building into a luxury address for the rich and bright.

All because Magistrate Vashathke had undone the old rent-control laws. *Dzaxa* who'd sworn a man couldn't rule Victory Street now praised him as an innovator while stuffing their bank accounts. The dull children begging on the yellow, brontosaurus-sized cobblestones of Victory Street—their ranks swollen from mass evictions—knew Magistrate Vashathke by cruder names. "Bully" was the tamest I'd heard.

My father had picked wrong when he'd bullied me.

"This is such a boring building," Zega moaned. "Forget my cousin's wedding. Let's jump down to the crossway and find a jazz bar. With how bright we both shine, we could be dancing together in minutes, and the whole place would queue up to buy us drinks."

"You're a respectably employed widow. You can show off your essence. People get upset if I remind them a bastard sex worker can punch through sheet metal."

"What's the point of power if you can't have a little fun?" He pulled a compact from his purse and flipped it open. Red powder flashed inside. Zega grinned, then ducked into the sheltering nook of the stone dragon's carved, empty eye socket. I slipped in after him, bending my tall head to fit the space.

"Power isn't a toy," I said as he snorted the firepowder. "What's left of the War District's influence could also fit up your nose. We all must use what little we have strategically."

"Or—" He held out the compact. I shook my head. "—or we could simply accept the slow death of our world and enjoy the fall on our way down. Be as tiresome as you wish, Koreshiza, you'll never bore these beacons to burn bright." He tapped the side of the socket.

Once, everlasting ruby fire had burned in the great statue's eyes, reflecting the glory of our massive neighborhood's dragons. But the dragons had died with the gods, and the supply of fresh essence they breathed had dwindled to drought. The Temple District had crumbled into the Lost District, from which no explorers returned. The survivors of the cataclysm, and the wars that preceded it, had brokered a city-wide peace, ensuring no district would lose valuable essence in the battlefield dead. They'd created the playing field Zega and I stood on today.

No battles. Fewer bombings. Higher stakes.

"Zega," I hissed. My ex shivered at the first brush of a high. "Listen to me. I can't work for Vashathke, but that doesn't mean there's no hope for us. You're no longer a boy trapped in a bad marriage. Don't keep following Vashathke's bloody path to power. Take your skills and connections. Help me get on Akizeké's good side. We can raise her to the judgeship. Together." My heart stuttered on the final word. *Reckless.* Bidding so plainly for his loyalties was a gamble, even if all I stood to lose was the faint flickering hope I could fix our relationship if we tried again.

"Elevate Akizeké and share half the credit with you?" he scoffed. "You've grown more selfish since you left. Or perhaps you've just grown more like your father."

The comparison ground into me like broken glass. My parentage was an open secret, and people often compared my looks and manner to Vashathke's. But Zega knew my history, and saw the deeper tie—I, like my father, wove plots and treacheries behind gold-lined scarlet eyes. "I was born with Vashathke's face stamped on mine. You chose to serve him." My voice rose, half-hysterical, slipping beyond my control. "Have you forgotten how he had me and my mother thrown out on the streets?"

"Have you forgotten that I saved you?" Steel flickered behind his soft blue eyes. "I follow Vashathke because he's strong. Not because he's good. Strength will put him on the throne. Kindness and charity have brought me nothing but your dagger in my soul."

I flinched. Had my leaving really made him this ruthless?

Or perhaps I'd been so greedy for love I'd overlooked his darkness. *My loves turn to ash in my fingers.* A bastard, a whore, a monster's son. Maybe only cruel, fetid hearts could safely love me. True hearts, I devoured.

"Wine, gentle *dzaxa?*" came the meek, rough-edged voice of a dull.

Akizeké's serving man, the one who'd given me a tissue, clambered clumsily into the socket I'd easily leapt inside. Wine glasses rattled on his tray. His long, dark eyes peered out beneath a low brow, capping a thin, straight-nosed face. He stood shorter than me, broad shoulders corded thick with muscle. Knife scars laced the gold-brown canvas of his chest. With his long, tied-back hair and his untrimmed goatee, he painted a portrait of trouble.

Zega snatched a glass, swirling sunlight-pale wine below his nose. "The bouquet's off," he snapped. "Are your senses so dull you can't spot a bad wine?"

"Zega!" My eyebrows arched. I turned to the serving man, whose smile masked any anger at Zega's slight, and took a glass for myself. "I'm sorry for my friend's rudeness. You walked far to bring us these, and you were so kind to me at the ceremony. Let me tip you."

"No need, *dzaxa*. Please, enjoy your drink."

Of course there's a need. Little luxuries meant everything when living dull. I grabbed a gold *thera* and reached for the sash of his black uniform skirt. He tried to dodge, but I was brighter. Quicker. I tucked the coin in the band—

My fingers licked the edge of a blade.

The sash spilled its jangling contents as my bloody hand pulled free. Grappling hooks, wire cables, throwing stars, lockpicks—and, exposed atop his skirt, the hilt of a sword. A long, single-edged blade in the Scholarly District tradition.

Lethal weapons had been illegal since the fall of the gods.

"Assassin," I whispered, and his placid servant's simper cracked into a wicked grin.

Fear washed out my propriety. Awakened my abominable anger. My motion blurred as the flat of my wrist slammed into his throat. My wine glass fell to shatter with the others as his tray dropped. I pinned him in a shadowed, rain-worn crevasse in the marble, my bare chest pressed to his. "Who hired you? Am I your mark, or are you after Zega?"

He struggled. But body-to-body, only brightness mattered in this contest. The knot of his throat trembled as his breathing sped. His steel bracers drummed helplessly against stone. But his eyes—dark brown bleeding black—refused to flicker wide in fear. They slipped over me and found Zega, rapid as a racing hovercraft.

"No one hired me. Your friend bought my enmity himself." With a defiant grin, he shrugged off the *thevé* cloth covering his shoulder. A poem in Old Jiké glyphs, shaped like a bell, tattooed the broad muscle beneath. *Ash and ruins,* it read.

"Faziz of the Slatepile." Zega sniffed, then poured out his swirling wine. A green film clung to the glass. "Shouldn't a gang leader have people to do his poisoning for him?"

Faziz of the Slatepile. A name cursed by *dzaxa*, merchants, guards and lawyers. A dull immigrant man who controlled fifty thousand illegal apartments in Victory Street's Slatepile ruin, offering cheap housing the law couldn't reach. A legend bringing hope to naïve dulls. *In flesh, this legend smells of sweat and ashes.*

"I have people in places that'll scare you shitless," Faziz said. "This is personal, Zega. Under your orders, Vashathke's guards evicted six hundred of my apartments last week and collapsed a cavern with holdfire charges. People of mine are sleeping on the street. Seventy-two have died. Mostly children."

"Killing me won't bring back their essence." Zega yawned. "It'll only destroy my essence store alongside theirs—and mine's a million times brighter."

Faziz thrashed. His dark eyes locked on my hand with

murderous intent. Would he bite free? "It's not about essence, you reeking shit. It's about people!"

"Everything's about essence," Zega said. "Or money. Or power. You're as foolish as Koreshiza here if you think the world is any different."

Faziz's eyes flickered to me. "Koreshiza Brightstar. The courtesan." He named my occupation without the customary twist of judgement. "Let me go. The whispers below Victory Street say you want to keep your father from inheriting the judge's throne. Zegakadze is your father's dirty right hand. Let me cut him off, and neither man rises."

Let me cut him off. I shivered, not slacking my grip. Did Faziz know how spite had kept me alive, my early years of sex work? Dreams of Zega's shattered skull and my fists painted red? *Three young men, alone, body to body.* The *dzaxa* at the wedding would cluck their tongues at the promised indecency of us. They'd lean in to glimpse the lewd spectacle, unbelieving it could turn to murder.

We three all had bloody fingers in our hearts.

"Did you order mass evictions?" I asked Zega, my voice thin as strangling wire.

"Vashathke isn't afraid to protect Victory Street from criminals." Zega drew his baton. "I'm not afraid to protect myself."

Silver flashed off the weapon's scalloped sides. I recognized it. "You still carry the baton I gave you?" Strange hope fluttered in my heart.

"Of course." He pressed a hand to my bare back, drawing in close. Beneath me, Faziz cursed in a language I didn't know. "I haven't forgotten you, Koré. Maybe we can start again. Maybe I'll leave your father's campaign for you. If you kill this dull."

"Manipulative asshole," Faziz gasped as I pushed harder. "Come on, Red Eyes. This steaming shit isn't worth my blood on your manicure."

"This isn't you," I told Zega, because he wouldn't care if I said *I don't want this to be me again.* "That's my father's bloodlust you cry."

"Faziz would have poisoned you, too!"

"I deserve it." I met Faziz's eyes. Tried to make my point over the hammering of my heart. "No one dies today."

I flung the outlaw over my hip and out into open air.

Zega cursed and leant out into space. Gravity's light tug had already pulled Faziz five stories down. My ex seemed to consider leaping after, but, while our world's natural gravity wouldn't kill a falling human, giving chase meant missing the reception. "I could have you arrested as his accomplice, Koré!"

"Try." My words came curt. I had no energy left to please him.

Zega had driven children from their homes. Had urged me to murder on the promise of a kiss. I'd been foolish, appealing to his good nature, believing something genuine lingered between us. I'd been arrogant, hoping Akizeké would see me as a potential ally, someone worth her time. The tears blurring my eyes stung with more frustration than sorrow. Even how I broke down was ugly and wrong.

What was I doing with my life? Believing a sex worker could bring down Vashathke, who reached to rule one-twentieth of the planet? But I'd sacrificed too much for revenge—safety, purity, eight years of my life—to stop fighting. My world had revolved around Vashathke's ambition since before my conception. If I wasn't his enemy, I'd be his pawn. And, with his minions driving the poor from their apartments, I wanted to be his enemy.

As I stared at my ex, trying to decide between choking him or asking him to hold me, gravity flexed like a fist on the back of my neck. A frozen wind billowed down from the north. Zega's eyes widened, and he pointed over my shoulder. "Do you see that too, Koré?"

I turned. On the edge of my bright vision, between hovering clock bells and spires rising from the sea, a floating black bar shadowed the foot of Victory Street.

A *hovership*. The dark iron craft was long and narrow, tapered to a wedge on the ventral side. Silver swirls of holdweight substance, its sheen and texture between plastic and metal, traced faces on its flanks: women, men, and children, screaming in agony. White-gold figureheads lifted axes and smiled cruel grins. Not a whisp of exhaust escaped as it rose, soundlessly, to float as a black bar against the sun.

"I see it," I said. "It's... uninviting."

"I've only seen pictures of those craft in schoolbooks," Zega whispered. A tangled mix of awe and terror had pressed the guile from his voice. "That ship is Temple District work. From the age of the gods."

A shiver spider-stepped down my spine. "That's impossible. Nothing and no one has left the Lost District in ten thousand years." I'd sooner expect to meet my mother's shade than travelers from that ruined neighborhood.

We stood silent for a breath, watching it hover and hum. Shadows that might have been crew or my imaginings crawled over the silver faces. All down Victory Street, windows dropped open and whispers of awe rose high. From one sill, a very-illegal antique rifle pointed up at the craft, until a steel-ringed hand pushed it back inside. Even the cobblestones seemed to hold their breath.

Nothing drew my street together like the prospect of conflict.

"Maybe they've come to witness this historic occasion?" Zega suggested. "Me elevating the first male judge to the throne of War?"

A tiny, bitter laugh fluttered up in my throat—and died when I realized he meant it. Legends didn't rise to mark the deeds of upjumped commoners and bastards. Zega and I had swept fragments of power together to build our lives on Victory Street, but history and majesty belonged to trueblooded *dzaxa*. The years that transformed the Lost District into legend would crush us smaller than footnotes.

But my own insignificance gave me freedom. I feared no fabled nightmare more than my father winning the power to shatter my life.

Again.

"They've come to support Akizeké," I said. "They only don't know it yet." Traveling diplomats all sought the same comforts, whether they came from neighboring districts or the ancient mists of time. Once they fell into my arms, I'd collect their endorsements for Akizeké before anyone could lure them to my father's cause.

She'd have to appoint me a strategist then. And I'd ruin Vashathke's dreams of power as neatly as he'd ruined my dreams of a father's love.

CHAPTER TWO
Upper Victory Street

2nd *Kafi*, Year 92 Rarafashi

"Those who dwell in light forget shadow wove the universe"—inscription on Lost District artifact salvaged by Fire Weavers 5728 Post-Liberation

"Some power is too great for any one woman to wield unquestioned. We have seen the destruction caused by unrestrained war. On this day of hope, we lay the foundations our children will build into a perfect, peaceful, and just future."—remarks by Judge Dzefik-eké II (also known as the Traitor Judge) upon the signing of the Treaty of Inversions and the formal conclusion of The Brass War

DEEP-FRIED MEAT sizzled and hissed beneath clanging bells. *Coconut. Chilies. Nutmeg.* Bobbing tissue-paper lanterns lit the chef's pale brow as she passed me snake fillets. Each stretched two hands long, the breading packed with red

25

onion and black peppercorn. Nutmeg pâté spread down each strip in a dripping line. I balanced six scorching fillets on my outstretched left arm.

"Two *thera*," said the chef.

"Are you trying to cheat me?"

"Whores cheat essence from the marriage bed. Hurry, you're holding up the line."

I sighed and handed over my gold. It seemed half of Victory Street waited behind me.

My father had thrown a parade to welcome the Lost District envoys—and, hopefully, secure their endorsement. The Treaty of Inversions specified that seventeen international endorsements were required to qualify for the judgeship of War. After its codification, our magistrates and ladies had swiftly demanded their own say in the process. Seventeen international and thirty-eight domestic endorsements: numbers weighted in ten thousand years of custom and lore, a target every candidate had to strike before receiving the essence store and throne of the dying judge. A mark Akizeké had to hit before my father.

A curtain of sound rose around me as I pressed through the crowds. Merchants sold souvenirs in five languages. Brontosauruses called, low and trumpeting, as butcher teams pulled their leads. Protestors with the smooth accents of Engineers shouted, "No welcome!" and "The Fire Weavers warned us!"

Banners flew the names of favored candidates for the judgeship, glyphed into elaborate sigils. Akizeké's snowflake topped several tall poles, and one fool still flew Kirakaneri's mushroom, though she'd dropped out of contention. But Vashathke's dagger-petaled lily marked a sea of handheld white pennants. His guards stood on every street corner, offering his flag free to passers-by. To the envoys, it would appear every soul on Victory Street demanded Vashathke's ascension.

This was why Akizeké needed me. I understood optics. How making oneself appear desirable invited desire in.

The courtesans of the High Kiss had been pushed against a steel guard barrier. My poor employees had successfully protected their white silk-and-metal finery from pushy spectators, but beneath their crowns of steel flowers, their expressions were as unappealing as balance sheets.

"Eat up!" I said. Kge and Stonefire took one fillet apiece; the boys tore theirs into neat portions. "You might have two or three clients before your next break. We want to get the ambassador into our party and make her leave happy. The High Kiss should be her home on Victory Street."

"Are you after something besides her money?" Bero asked, flicking crumbs from his painted lips. "When the envoys from the Husbandry District wanted to schedule a private party, you made me tell them we were booked solid."

Their judge already endorsed my father. I might as well host an open house for spies. I licked grease from my fingers and shrugged. "I plan to franchise the High Kiss and open a location in the far north. I suppose the staff will need to wear shirts."

Bero lowered his voice. "If you're going to be sarcastic, I'd prefer no answer at all."

"Really? My sarcasm is delightful."

"But hardly appropriate. I'm your assistant manager. I can't help implement your business plans if I don't know what they are."

I bit my tongue. *This goes beyond business.* If my employees knew I was interfering with the judge's succession, they'd decry me as a dangerous fool and run screaming from the High Kiss.

Thankfully, from further down Victory Street—at the foot of the great stone dragon sculpture—a horn sounded and cut off conversation.

War's trumpets played brass defiance. This deeper,

slower note rose from the planet's heart, from the ancient foundations of the world-sized city of Jadzia. Ruin stacked atop ruin, all the way down.

I smiled to hide the shiver in my soul. "Look lively, boys! We have guests!"

Raptors shrieked as a fleet of guard *reja* swept the street. Batons flashed, steel and shards of green holdspark. Drumbeats rolled through air and bone, their players advancing in neat formation. Men in translucent skirts spun to the horn's ceaseless call.

"Are those dogs?" whispered young Opal, his eyes wide with fear.

"They're direwolves," I said. Five dozen of the beasts, white-furred and wide-shouldered, towed a hoverplatform up Victory Street. Amber and iron flashed as envoys flung tokens to the cheering crowd. Singers chanted in an ear-stinging, twisting language. All the party wore fur cloaks and skin leggings, even the gold-crowned ambassador, who sat atop the massive bone horn.

A foreign fashion. That didn't bother me. All districts of the city-planet valued my goods. But War simmered with resentment of other, wealthier districts. Vashathke had made a name for himself, early in his political career, by denouncing the neighboring Engineering District's ownership of Victory Street's crossways, threatening tariffs that never became more real than words. He'd quieted his blowhardery now he needed international endorsements to rise to the throne, but the world outside War would never count him a friend.

I could offer these envoys more than his thin-lipped smiles and backhanded insults.

The endless note wavered and died. The horn's player winked at me. Pale, dark-haired, and commanding, she shone every inch as bright as the ambassador.

"They look like they can afford us," I told my employees. "Let's go."

We slid past the barrier in a perfumed tide. Bero slipped a purse to the guards, who turned their backs on our trespass. I leapt atop the hoverplatform and bowed to the ambassador. "The beauties of War, for your pleasure!"

"We have fucking at home," said the horn-blower, accent clipping her words. "I am Tamadza of the Twelfth River. Why should I buy flesh when I can love at my leisure?"

I smirked up from under lowered brows. "Flesh is cheap. Do you know decadence? Wine, spirits, games and dance? Come to the High Kiss, where no rules bind the bright."

Tamadza groped up the cup of Stonefire's *fajix*, pushing through the garment to fondle her breast. Stonefire grabbed the diplomat's arm, and the women held steady. Pinned by lust and anger alike.

I bowed. "Welcome, Envoy Tamadza."

Opal let an older guard sweep him into her plump arms. Neza posed for a wolf-driver, flexing powerful arms as she giggled and stared greedily. Ruby and Bero clambered up the bone horn, whispering to the ambassador about a delightful game for three.

I scanned the crowd for my own mark. But only one or two of the visitors looked my way. Had I gone dull? My eyes shone Dzaxashigé red, a scarlet as wicked as bloodshed and lust. The skirt I'd worn, white satin patterned with pink roses, drew out the famous color. My *thevé*, pauldron-cut cloth covered with silk petals, perfumed my left shoulder. *You can only get this in War.*

At last, familiar eyes held mine. Carmine, beneath a bristly brow. Their gaze drank the hard muscle of my chest and back, the low fall of my skirt. *Hello again, Jasho-eshe.* Instinct pulled me toward the *dzaxa* man like a hunting raptor, noting weak points to hook my claws. *He's lonely. He'll buy your touch with gold, essence and secrets.*

I leapt off the Lost District's vehicle, brightness speeding me across the fifteen-meter gap. Jasho caught me and pulled me onto his *reja*. "You cut your hair." He stroked my close-cropped blond locks as a servant refilled his wine glass. "I liked it long and messy."

I eased into his embrace. The perfume of aster oil and raptor stables washed me as I nuzzled the sunny curls of his beard. "I have other clients to please. It's not every day an ambassador from a lost civilization crosses your doorstep."

Jasho-eshe Phfigezava Dzaxashigé reclined on his pillows, pulling me down beside him. His gold brocade skirt shifted low beneath his round belly. "The Engineers at the university complained about the welcome parade. My mother's busy meeting with Magistrate Vashathke—for the third time this week!—but she sent us here to monitor the envoys."

Lady Xezkavodz met him three times? The owner of the vast Archive building might meet with my father on innocuous business. As the ruler of all Victory Street, Vashathke arbitrated conflicts between landladies and oversaw Victory Street's economy. He had innocent reasons to meet Xezkavodz—but three times said he was angling for her endorsement.

My pulse quickened. Maybe I could still win her away.

"Technically, I'm the one monitoring the envoys," said a bright girl. Dark curls spilled down her rich brown shoulders as she gulped from a whiskey flask. Drunk mischief filled her short, round features. She shook my hand. "Riapáná Żutruro, Initiate Fire Weaver. Call me Ria."

A Fire Weaver. Her gold bracer, the mark of her order, brushed the inside of my wrist, hot as if it had drunk down sunlight.

"Our very own hero-in-residence," Jasho said dryly. "The High Master of their order sent his daughter to visit my mother's building. We're honored."

Movies framed the Fire Weavers, the Engineering District's society of technological archeologists, as altruistic protectors of Jadzia, defusing ancient fission bombs and incinerating giant worms that roamed the city-planet's core. But heroes only lived onscreen. Ria, with her honey-oak whiskey breath, was likely no more than a pleasure-seeking idle. An idle whose father commanded the ancient, deeply respected order.

Every time in War's history where the judgeship was disputed between candidates, the one endorsed by the High Master of the Fire Weavers had won.

"Ria," Jasho said, "this is Magistrate Vashathke's bastard."

"I've heard about this custom of yours!" Ria rubbed her hands together, excited. "That means his parents didn't swear marriage oaths before conceiving him, right? So he can't call himself a *dzaxa* or claim a family name?"

"It gives *dzaxa* men dangerous ideas if their bastards thrive." Jasho rolled his eyes. "Your district has plenty of essence. You don't need to control what people do in bed. But the *dzaxa* believe, if War doesn't control its men, they'll surrender their essence to the first untrustworthy who fucks them. Apparently, we can't help it."

No one could help it. True sexual pleasure made one slip essence to their partners. Skilled courtesans like I shone, our bodies the War District's ultimate luxury, because our clients paid in essence and in gold. A fact of nature for which men were ever blamed.

"I'm Koré," I said, sweet as iced apple wine. "Nice to meet you, Ria. Are you enjoying the parade?"

She shrugged. "Honestly, it's weird. Weird as a triceratops with two frills. The Lost District lies in ruins. Where'd all this fancy shit come from?"

And if you're revealing yourself to the world, why start with a poor, backwards district like War? "Has Engineering ever sent diplomats or explorers there? The Dzaxashigé family used to fund salvage expeditions every few centuries, but the women never came home."

She laughed. "Engineering doesn't need to hunt down legends to make friends. The other districts love us! Of course, it helps we Fire Weavers single-handedly retrieved millions of their cultural relics after the conquests."

"You speak like you found all those yourself, Ria," said Jasho. "How mighty of you. Traveling the world centuries before your own conception." He snorted a mocking laugh, then turned to bellow orders at his poor driver.

"Ignore Jasho," I murmured to her. "He tears someone down whenever he's in a poor mood. Approximately eight times an hour. Now, if I need to smile, I simply behold myself in a mirror."

"Come to think of it, I've seen your advertisements in the herald pamphlets," Ria mused. "Captioned 'The Loveliest Bastard in War.'"

"Did you see the all-audiences version, or the one for adult distribution only?"

"The one where you hang a silk scarf on your erect penis."

"I'm gorgeous *and* a marketing expert. What more could you ask for in a man?"

"I prefer my men with brains." Her brown-diamond eyes studied me with focused intent. The first hint of fear brushed the back of my neck. "Men who ask interesting questions. Do you know much of the Lost District's history? The Fire Weavers map and survey the Lost District—my mentor's traveled there several times—but I'm just an initiate. I won't learn more about them until I earn my second bracer."

I shrugged. "I only know children's stories. My education ended at age fourteen. Kneeling and sucking doesn't require an advanced degree."

"But understanding the present world requires scholarship and critical thought! I'm sorry you lack that."

Dzkegé's tits, not pity. Nothing upended a seduction faster. I neither wanted nor needed a stranger looking past my eyeshadow and boyish silliness, so I smiled and flattered her. "You'll earn your second bracer soon. The Fire Weavers must see your obvious talent."

She nodded, took a second whiskey flask from a servant, and drank deep. "I'll get promoted when I make my big discovery." A brass-and-wire chip flashed between her fingers. "I'm remotely monitoring energy signals in the Archive's lower levels. One reading matches the signature of Dzkegé. The war god."

"Our... *thigakazifi?*" I had to dip into Old Jiké for the phrase. *The god to whom we kneel. The god of the War District and its people.* Nineteen deities had laid the foundation of Jadzia, the planet-sized city, each choosing a neighborhood to represent their sacred trades: civil engineering, urban gardening, research and scholarship, medical manufacturing... and the violence through which great cities suppressed disorder. But modern languages didn't need religious terms, and my modern mind couldn't fit the concept. Why would a god hide below the Archive? "That would be impressive indeed."

Impossible, indeed. If Dzkegé still existed, my *dzaxa* ancestors would have forced her to invest a new herald generations ago. Even one of her dragons could have solved our essence woes. Opened the way for us to dominate Jadzia's economy once more.

"If I find Dzkegé's shade, she could transform our knowledge of history and science," Ria said. "Which would impress my nerd friends back home and usher in a new era of utopia." She grinned like she could fix the world with a wine glass in one hand and a whiskey flask in the other.

"Not even a god can change Victory Street," I warned her.

"Well then, pretty boy, how does anything get done here?" Ria took a step closer. "Let me guess: do you pull all the strings?"

I bit my tongue before I could answer. Even half-jesting, I dared not speak aloud of all the *dzaxa* in my fist. *What is this stranger doing to me?* I hadn't felt true confidence since age six. But Ria believed she could do the impossible, in a way that whispered I could, too. Without a sip of alcohol, I was drunk on her.

A cry rang up from the street. A guard knocked a dull child's hand from her sash. A purse flew from the child's fingers as another guard struck her with the sparking *shiki* end of a baton.

"Barbarians." Ria flicked a switch on her bracer. Gold façade slid off its carvings of triceratops-horned giants. Orange holdfire shimmered beneath, blocks of hammered, molten color. Flames gathered in her palm, rising and stretching like a cat, drawing eyes and worried whispers from the crowd. She gave her flask—and the monitoring chip—to me. "Put that on ice for me, pretty boy."

Bright essence fueled her speed as she leapt into the fray and flung a guard over her hip. Her bracer blocked a descending baton. Her fist caught the steel shaft and bent it backward.

"Go!" she shouted to the child. "I've got this."

The child fled. Ria flung herself into the growing brawl. My eyebrows lifted. *We could have driven past and done nothing.* I knew such vulnerability in my bones, and I'd grown used to turning away. Searching for kindness on Victory Street was like asking to be broken.

Ria moved like a hero. Bolder than the crushing world. Fire flashed. Her dark cheeks and red skirts danced through the pale, duller guards in the melee. The watching crowd pressed tight against the parade barrier, shouting, placing bets.

As Ria sent three guards sprawling with a kick, her chip buzzed in my palm.

"Her sensors found something." Jasho plucked the chip from me. "Dzkegé's shade? Ridiculous story. She wants the Nojof-era genetic recoders."

That made more sense than hidden gods. Jasho's soldier ancestors had robbed the Warmwater District dry and the Fire Weavers were sworn to help our world recover from those ancient wars. "Can you make the recoders work?"

"We keep them to celebrate our family history. Every time the Fire Weavers demand them, we move them somewhere new." Jasho sighed. "First they take our money, then they come for our pride."

You're in debt to Engineers because your family didn't invest in civic infrastructure until half your pipes exploded. The septic recovery company had charged his mother a fortune, the arduous work exacerbated by centuries of neglect. Many of the *dzaxa* blamed the Engineering District for our economic woes, even though their skills alone kept our district standing. *We built War on weak foundations. Our district was always doomed to crumble.*

"Come and help me find them, Koré. The abandoned lower levels of the Archive are quite private." His fingers slid across the nape of my neck. "You wouldn't be chatting with me if you had a client booked."

I almost refused. Stonefire had already led Tamadza off her horn; the ambassador was answering Ruby's smiles. Powerful guests would flood the High Kiss. I had to prepare.

But my employees could start a party themselves. If I put Jasho in a good mood, he might tell me how his mother's support could be won.

And if I could discover where his family kept their plundered artifacts, and slip that location to Ria, she might be grateful enough to secure me an audience with her High Master.

"Let's go," I breathed in Jasho's ear.

Jasho muttered to his driver. The *reja* changed course, its six gold-plumed raptors tossing their heads, the hoverplatform—wide enough to hold Jasho's reclining bed—knocking over guards as it spun. Jasho pulled me onto his lap. Spectators dove from our path as we abandoned the parade's train and raced toward the Archive's squatting shadow.

Two hours later, we arrived at the first alcove out of ten million.

I dismounted, squinting off into the evershade, where sunlight would never seep. Even my bright eyes couldn't see where the line of alcoves ended. *An abandoned storage floor.* I knelt and touched up my makeup by the *reja*'s low holdlights. The bronze powder on my left eyelid had smudged. I wiped off the old coat and swept fresh powder out in the traditional shape of a dragon's wing.

"Jasho-eshe, you dishonor your wife with this… improper friendship," said Jasho's driver, tossing a pigeon to a raptor. The beast caught it in serrated reptilian teeth. Blood and feathers flew.

"Rank and raging queer sexual yearning," was how I'd describe Jasho's feelings for me. *Improper friendship my ass.* But War used that euphemism for feelings it ignored. Homosexual affairs weren't illegal, but frowned upon as a waste of essence. Happiness meant nothing when propriety demanded one raise children and pass on their store.

"I've done everything for my wife," Jasho said. "I built our salvage company. I raised our child. I won't be slut-shamed by some dull!"

I walked to the *reja*'s front and caught the driver's eye. "Could you please send a herald to the High Kiss? Have Stonefire pick me up at the sixth bell. Thank you." Her fist curled around the silver *vodz* I tossed her. *A courtesan's coin is as true as a judge's.* Raptors chirped as she reclaimed the driver's seat and whipped them back towards the stairs.

Jasho and I were alone.

He passed me a holdlight. Warm yellow illumination shone from the fist-sized, cool lump, an unset chunk of one of the eleven substances transmutationists teased from the bodies of the dead. The elemental building blocks enabling a city Jadzia's size to defy physics and remain standing.

"My mother showed me the hidden recoders as a child," Jasho said. "Hopefully, my bright brain remembers where they are. Keep an eye out for Fire Weaver instruments."

I bowed to him. "Lead on."

He steered me into the guts of his family's building. My fingers ran along the cool jet-green feldspar of the lined-up alcoves. I lost count at six hundred of the waist-high, identical cylinders. The scent of old parchment rose from the worn floor. The air sat choking still. Jasho's grip on my shoulder weighed me down like an anchor.

"My ancestors brought the Archive to War by boat," he said. "The founders of the Phfigezava line."

Phfigezava, Readers of Knowledge. One of the many lines within the sprawling, knotted Dzaxashigé family tree. I recalled my childhood history lessons. "The Phfigezava fought alongside Varjthosheri the Dragon-Blessed in the Warmwater–Scholars War." Half a million souls had drowned in the final battle. But I'd focus on the glory to flatter him. "Tell me more about your family's victories."

History spilled into the surrounding dark. A story of warriors conquering the Archive, soldiers dragging the building up Victory Street, and indebted merchants selling back its contents to the Scholars, scroll by scroll. The only ancestor I couldn't make Jasho talk about was his mother.

Disturbed dust swirled about our hems and sandals as we walked. Deep crimson parchment winked in our footsteps. The line of alcoves ran out beneath my fingers. I stretched out my holdlight, but saw no next row. "How much further?"

"Not much." Open space swallowed his deep, musical voice. The lack of an echo sent needles pricking up my spine. "But we can rest if you'd like."

I knew what he wanted. Stepping forward, I kissed him.

The curls of his beard slid smooth over my shaven chin. He moaned, deep in his throat, and leant into me. *Slowly. Slowly.* His teeth nipped my cheek. A quick gasp escaped me, and, encouraged, he wrapped his hands across the small of my back. Fingers hooked under the lip of my skirt.

"How are you?" he said. I knew what he meant. I wasn't

hard yet—but he was. I could feel him through his gold brocade.

"Get me there," I commanded. Essence tuned my voice true. He obeyed. His lips brushed my neck, my collarbone, my nipple. His teeth pressed. Biting. *Lower. Lower.* Potential gathered in my loins. My breath hitched.

Stay focused, I told myself. *Be hard. Please him. Learn secrets. Win allies. Get revenge.*

His brushing lips provoked me. My fists tightened on his curls, steering him. I woke inside him. All vanished but his breath on my thighs and the sweet tightness at the core of me.

I recalled a memory. *Scarlet eyes, twin to my own, washing over me like garbage.* Bitterness balanced the demanding need between my legs. *If my own father can look at me so, no one will ever love me. Jasho cares for me only as an object of lust.*

As my peak rolled through me, no essence leapt from my skin.

The floor trembled. A light flared deep below us, ghostly and half-smothered by stacked floors.

Are the planet's foundations resettling? Is the Archive collapsing? Fear tensed me. Jasho gasped. Essence fluttered like wings as it leapt from him and settled into my flesh. The rattling pulse stilled.

Only when I was completely limp did he pull away. I re-tied my skirt with finer-seeming hands. My light tan smoothed into a warm gold dusting. My nails were thicker and more even. A papercut on my knuckle had vanished.

So had the light from below.

"Drink," I commanded, offering a flask. Jasho gulped down whiskey as amber drops flooded his beard. When he ran empty, I brushed a chaste kiss to his forehead. Another drop of essence flashed into me. "How's your thirst?"

"Sated, for now." Jasho lifted his holdlight. His fingers

fluttered as they closed, a heartbeat less quick, an inch less graceful. We both still burned bright as stars. But when he'd drunk his pleasure, he'd lessened and I'd gained. "You're the most beautiful creature I've ever seen."

"I know."

His hand, unbidden, cracked on my ass. I bit my tongue.

"Learn modesty, boy!"

I'd never be modest. But I'd play anything for the right price.

Onward we went. The line of alcoves resumed under my fingertips. Jasho's spirits lifted into song. An old husband's lay for his soldier-wife drifted off into coiling evershade.

"How is your mother feeling about the succession?" I asked when I couldn't take another verse. "She and Judge Rarafashi are old friends. It must be hard, watching the judge's health decline."

Jasho broke off mid-line. "She visits her in Skygarden whenever she can. Still, Rarafashi has ruled for ninety-two years, and War has only grown poorer. It's time for new blood."

War would only ever grow poorer. Such was the truth of a world without fresh essence. But wishing for new blood—I could use that. My father was young, but, as Rarafashi's husband, hardly the fresh face Xezkavodz might crave.

Electronics beeped. Light flashed near my sandal—a cherry-red diode wired atop a canister of dials and antennae. *A sensor. Did Ria leave it?* Precise scorch lines marked the hexagonal red parchment tile, like she'd tried burning her way through.

What lay below the Archive? If Ria sought Jasho's stolen relics, why weave tales about a god's shade? She hadn't struck me as someone who liked—or needed—to lie. *If she's not after the artifacts, what else can I gift her for her favor?* I needed time to think. To plan. "Jasho, could you forget your lovely voice and sing to me with your body?"

"Bend over!" he bellowed across three octaves.

I braced my wrists against the cool stone of an alcove. My nipples stiffened as he lifted the back of my skirt.

"It's my turn," he grunted. It had been his turn all afternoon. I braced myself for the flex of pain and pleasure as he stepped forward. *Ria. If I was the daughter of the High Master, all the respect and prestige in Jadzia, what more might I want?*

With a quiet rip, the parchment floor gave beneath our weights.

The light fist of gravity tugged me down. I glimpsed another floor of identical alcoves—then punched through another parchment layer. A third. A fourth. My fingers grazed a wooden strut. It snapped. *Alcove. Alcove. Reach!* The last support strut fell away. The alcoves vanished. I fell into empty air and darkness.

Impact punched air from my lungs. Stones ripped skin and fabric as I rolled. The spark of my holdlight bounced in and out of view. *Stop. Stop. Stop!* Cold water washed over me. A bitter, chemical taste filled my mouth. Jasho splashed into my side.

"Are you hurt, love?" I asked as we stood. My nerves howled like I'd taken an electric *shiki* blow. I'd have an apple-sized bruise where the small of my back had hit stone.

"No," Jasho said, and my concentration fell from him as I looked around. We'd fallen under the Archive, into the ruin that sat here ten thousand years ago, when Jasho's ancestors had dragged their prize up Victory Street. A pyramid, once. Now, with dark waters flooding the chamber, only its top tier could be seen.

Sickly orange light radiated from the altar at the small island's heart. Electrum and aluminum etchings twined its sides: dragons swooping over battlefields, dragons investing Dzaxashigé judges to rule all the War District, male dragons cradling winged infants. Heralds of our god. Living sources of essence whose deaths had plunged us into millennia of drought.

From a holy place to a candle in the dark.

"The old temple," Jasho said. His last word echoed, high and strange. *Temple. Temple.*

"Hear that?" I asked. "Something's wrong. This isn't safe. I don't think Ria's after your relics. She's after... this." *The ghost of a god.*

Part of me considered bending my bright strength to rip up the altar and carry it back to her. But that would be unseemly—and blasphemous. The strange mirror-sheen of the metal seemed to promise any damage done to it would rebound on my own soul.

"You trust an Engineer?" Jasho swam to the island in a few bright strokes and poked the altar. "I hear nothing."

"We have to climb out." Fear wavered in my voice. "Let's go. It's not like we can fly—"

Fly. Fly. Fly.

A woman's voice echoed from the altar. Jasho didn't react, but the hairs on my nape prickled like thorns. *Dzkegé's mercy. It's alive.*

"Come here." Jasho's erection pressed the wet brocade of his skirt. "You're under contract."

I bit my lip, fighting to shake my gut-knotting, superstitious dread. Dzkegé was gone. Our god was as powerful as a dull, as real as a courtesan's love, and she'd never address a bastard whore before a lady's trueborn son. She couldn't be here—and gods and ghosts didn't concern me. I'd been hired to break taboos. I'd come to steal treasures and secrets. The business of gods rose higher than skyscrapers above me.

Bitter water slowed my stirring as I swam to join him.

Jasho stumbled into my arms, resting his drunk weight on my shoulders. "You should tell your mother about this," I said, tracing kisses down his collarbone. "She should hire an architect to inspect these foundations."

"My mother won't be concerned with the Archive much longer." His fingers drummed an offbeat rhythm on my ass. "She and Vashathke have a deal. In exchange for her endorsement, when he's the judge, he'll name my mother the next magistrate of Victory Street. Both get promoted, and Vashathke doesn't have to give the Palace to his disappointing sons."

Only disappointing? I'd never been in line to inherit—my half-brothers lost here—but still. My father didn't fear me at all?

I stepped backwards. My hand brushed the electrum dragon. *Fly!* called the echo. *Dead!*

Jasho turned me over and pushed up my skirt. I braced my forearms on the altar, pressed my chin to cold metal, and lifted my hips. *Vashathke. Another endorsement for the magistrate of Victory Street. Another voice elevating my father.*

Another, called the woman's voice, close as a whisper in my ear. *Fly! Fly!*

"Jasho," I gasped as his finger explored my lower opening. "This is—ah!"

Orange light rolled through the altar, shining behind my closed eyelids. *Fly, sons, fly!* A soldier made of stars blazed against the night, her blade cutting swathes through the charging shadows. Darkness swarmed up her armored skirt and twined about her arms. Eyes like planets met my own.

Dzkegé's shade. Her body like the sky. Her presence the weight of the universe. The last fragment of a god wrapped about the trembling speck of me.

Your skin will be my standard. Your bones will be my weapons. Your soul will be my light. She tore her hand free of the shadows and reached out. *Stand against shadow, my dragon.*

Her touch struck my heart like lightning. Jasho pierced me, punched me, split me in two. The world flashed white.

Orange cords anchored themselves in my trembling soul.

I sobbed, wounded by bliss, pinned by Jasho's motion. The altar went dark. The echoing voice screamed in distant rage.

My client moaned as his peak hit. My courtesan's trained instincts mastered me. I twisted to kiss him—

The heat in my throat sprang to new, strange life, alive as spiced honey. Molten silk poured from my lips to his as I exhaled, relief as sweet as the seed I'd spilled on the altar. Unfamiliar. Revelatory. Welcome.

As the kiss ended, I pled once more. "Let's go. It's not safe—"

Then I saw him.

The essence tied to his soul had doubled between heartbeats. His pale skin lay alabaster-smooth and solid. Hammered gold filled the curls of his brow and beard. His belly hung in a near-perfect globe. His lips—full, pink, swollen from kissing— spread in a paternal smile. "Koré? You're staring."

My cheeks turned scarlet as I stammered, "You're so bright. Essence like diamonds." Eloquence had deserted me. I wanted to crawl and kiss his beautiful feet. Hear him say he loved me and he'd shelter me from harm. *If only he'd take my hand!*

Jasho examined his reflection in the rippling water. "They said it's never been done." He laughed like a booming parade drum. "But I've made Koreshiza Brightstar tithe me essence."

Fear slapped me like a frozen wave. "I did?" My voice sounded no different. I felt no weaker, though my hands trembled. Where else could all his new essence have come from? How much had I given him? *Don't let me be dull. Don't let me be broken.*

"Let's end this session early. Don't worry, you'll get your full payment." In a flash of gold, he leapt across the cavern and flung himself ten meters up into the air. His hand caught a strut of the Archive's foundation. He vanished back into the shadowed hall.

I waited too long for him, face on fire, hating myself. *He's not coming back. He's your client, not your boyfriend. A flicker of attraction can't create a bond between you. You'll never bond with anyone.* I was a puzzle to be solved, a prize to be won. I'd forgotten that truth, and invited this storm inside me. In a moment of shock, I'd let myself want.

Again.

It's best if no one wants a monster like me. My emotions collapsed into a rough wash of self-loathing anger. I had to act. If I didn't get myself out, not a soul would come find me.

I swam back to the pile of scree, holdlight clamped between my teeth, and ripped off my ruined *thevé* to free my left shoulder. I lacked essence to jump as high as Jasho, but my legs carried me three meters up, where my feet found purchase on a broken steel beam. Pushing hard with my thighs, I flung myself high enough to grab Jasho's strut. Wood slipped under my wet fingers. I squeezed until my palms tore.

Stories rose above me in a twisting tunnel. Holdlight darted wildly around as I tossed my head back, lighting shattered struts and torn parchment. I leapt, grabbing hold of the next floor's roof. Something ripped. The torn edge of my skirt flapped loose against my calf.

Fuck you, Jasho, for ruining my outfit. At least I had the knowledge I'd sought. *The lady of the Archive will endorse Vashathke.* That gave him eleven out of thirty-eight, only mere weeks after announcing his campaign. *He's gaining momentum.* I wanted to scream at Lady Xezkavodz her greed had blinded her. She'd raise a monster to be judge of us all. But no one would believe the truth about my father. I could only play pleasant and cross her name off my list. *One less supporter to bring Akizeké. One reason fewer she should trust me, or even listen to me.*

I pulled myself back onto the floor I'd fallen from and limped past the empty alcoves. My anger subsided into its constant, seething knot below my breastbone. Now I felt the sting of a hundred fresh cuts, the clammy clasp of shredded satin on my legs. Grime clinging to my feet like a badge of humiliation.

Somehow, I'd let myself feel pleasure with Jasho, and a vast portion of my essence had slipped into him. If I made such mistakes, I'd be better off wearing Zega's collar.

"Koré?" Stonefire asked when I struggled up to my *reja*. "You look—"

"Laugh if you want." I grimaced. "I'm a dull fool. I deserve it."

"What? Are you drunk? Dzkegé's tits, sulky skinny boys shouldn't drink whiskey!"

Hopeful embers lit in my breast. My fingers trembled as I opened my compact mirror. *Dzkegé's mercy.* Luring fire still danced in my eyes. My cheekbones shone sharp. *Bright, lovely, and valuable to my targets.* Giddy joy swept me, sweeter than crisp white wine on a hot day. "Never mind. Let's go."

"Traffic's bad," Stonefire warned me as I slipped into the *reja*. "The eyes of the stone dragon sculpture lit up. The parade spectators went to gawk and gossip about the rebirth of dragons."

A dragon, reborn? I'd normally laugh. But after what I'd just witnessed, my courtesan's detachment threatened to slip my face and shatter. *Play the game. Manipulate. Hide. Be the boy no one loves and no one leaves. Be the safe you.*

I closed the curtains and finally let myself exhale. The cushioned bench on my *reja*'s hoverplatform hadn't been built for a tall frame, and my ass burned as I tried to get comfortable. An unopened vial of flaxseed oil pressed against my leg. *Further proof Jasho is an inconsiderate little cock.*

Of course I hadn't gone dull. A dull couldn't have climbed that height. I'd gained essence as I'd drunk Jasho's bliss. But my client's store had shone doubled.

Where had that essence come from? We'd been alone, save for the altar. It had beat like a living heart, whispering to me, waking my skin with electric potential. Potential Jasho didn't feel. Voices he didn't hear.

The question wasn't what had happened to Jasho. It was what had happened to me.

Nothing happened, I told myself, fighting a tremor in my chest. *The gods' age ended. Their bodies fell. Dzkegé's dragons died with her.* Heat prickled inside my thigh, faint but insistent, like a lizard's footsteps. *It's a bruise,* I told myself unconvincingly. *Just a bruise.*

Minutes passed before I found the courage to roll up my skirt and see.

Silver glinted inside of my thigh. *Scales.* Rippling and reptilian, dotted with ruby flecks. *I'm dreaming. I'm sick.* My fingers stroked their tender edges. Smooth and hot as sun-kissed snakeskin. And real.

Silver light rippled through the patch. Scales vanished, leaving my skin bare, gold-dusted. But I couldn't trust my humanity would stay. I trusted nothing. Why wouldn't my own body betray me?

"By Dzkegé's fucking tits," I whispered, and bit my tongue. Stonefire couldn't hear me. No one could know. My whole life, I'd been used by people who'd turned my feelings and body against me. I'd barely escaped that cycle alive. My freedom would vanish as soon as someone painted a target on my back.

Dzkegé's dragons had once stood equal to the rulers of the War District. The power to make fresh essence lay in their breath, as much a part of them as their skin and souls, and they bore children who carried the god's fire in their flesh. Their death had shifted Jadzia's power balance against us for the whole modern era of history.

And their rebirth would leave me vulnerable, at the mercy of judges, magistrates, and any great power who sought to claim an era for their own.

CHAPTER THREE
The Archive, North Exit

3rd *Kafi*, Year 92 Rarafashi

"As the fist of law, I preserve the essence of War."—motto of the Old Dread guard academy

"Watch your clients with a raptor's eye. Search for emotional manipulation, reluctance to pay, possessive behavior. You're providing a service, not a relationship. If you're scared, come to me. No client matters more than your safety."—High Kiss employee handbook

As Stonefire drove us from the Archive's entry bridge to the crossway, I pulled back the curtain. Clean night air washed over me, laced with sweat and piss. Holdlight veins beamed down from the edges of the Archive's tiered roofs, the great hovering clock bells flashing against the stars. Riotous sound rose around us as we merged lanes: pounding talons, rattling wheels, humming hoverplatforms, their holdweight cores breaking gravity's light grip. *Reja*, runners, and raptor-drawn carts journeying across Victory Street.

Stonefire cursed the slow pace, cracking her whip at rubberneckers. "The stone dragon!" one cried. "What does it mean?"

Flames blossomed in its carved stone eye sockets, marking where our city-planet curved. *A dragon, awake and breathing. And me.* How could this be? We were nothing to the wider world. Even the arching iron crossway we drove on, a marvel that let us cross Victory Street in three hours, belonged to Engineers. War's miracles had dried up and died.

We deserve no favors from the gods. I certainly don't. I was a manipulative slut like my father, with bloody hands and heart. *Why choose me?* Had Dzkegé seen my sweet mask and yearned to save my shattered innocence? A god should know my secret crimes stranded me past all redemption.

Corrosive anger festered inside me. *It doesn't matter. I won't let the scales appear again.* I pushed the truth—*I don't know how to stop them*—into the pit of my stomach. I had work to do.

"We'll take the Slatepile crossway," Stonefire said, turning onto an off-ramp. "It's near deserted at this hour."

That route was always deserted. Once, a carved green slate bell had stood between the Palace and the Surrender: a festival instrument from the Scholarly District, tall among Victory Street's trophies. Two millennia ago, it had collapsed and crushed its ten million tenants. The magistrate had ordered the debris stacked into an ever-shifting, fifty-square-kilometer pile, and condemned it as a ruin. Unsafe to enter. Prohibitively expensive to fix.

Rents in the Slatepile's caverns and crannies were the lowest on Victory Street. But you paid to a gang, and you lived by their rules.

The raptors yipped and fussed as Stonefire drove across uneven slate. Though their nimble talons balanced well and the hoverplatform smoothed our ride, animals held no essence to supplement their ability, and the *reja* braked before a collapsed trash chute too wide to jump. Before we could back up, a low thrum rumbled through the road. White rose against the night sky—a helicopter, sides inland with snowflakes picked out in diamonds. The symbol of Armory Street. A gaudy jewel amidst dark and fallen stones.

Understanding struck me like a spark through a wire. Faziz hadn't merely disguised himself as Akizeké's manservant to sneak into the wedding. He was working for her.

Which meant he knew how to rise in her favor.

"What are you doing?" Stonefire asked as I climbed down. "It's dangerous here."

So am I. "Wait for me," I commanded her, and leapt. My essence tore me free of gravity and carried me toward the pale blue light of a helipad.

Watching guards flinched as my feet cracked down.

"It's Vashathke!" gasped the youngest, drawing her baton. "Protect the Slatepile! Don't let him in!"

My hands flashed up. "I'm not my father. Koreshiza Brightstar, here to see your leader. Faziz. I know it's late. But if he can receive Akizeké, he can speak to me too."

"It's the courtesan," an older guard told the younger. "Pity. I bet three *vodz* he'd be too scared to come, but Lord Faziz assured me he'd visit within the month."

"He styles himself a lord?" As if he owned the ruin he squatted in. "I suppose I should charge him for this visit."

The guards laughed and led me into a green slate tunnel. Eighty meters underground, it opened on an atrium cavern shaped like a knife blade through the world. Scattered illumination from a million salvaged holdlights divided it into pockets: market stalls and apartments bunched together in the best light, construction and salvage sites on the outskirts. High above, strings of winking sparks lit a network of iron walkways, rusted control panels, and holdsound speakers—a ruined nightclub. Children laughed and called. Vegetables withered in sunken heat. Green pallor tainted every face, more than a few branded with the open circles of the Unrepentant.

It could have been any poor building. But the air lacked the reek of fluids and sickness that marked low stories abandoned by their landladies, cheap apartments only ten or twenty stories from the simmering street. Here, men strolled alone in and out of evershade. The guards ringing the cavern stood mostly unarmed. When we passed a dull beggar, murmuring feverishly into her cupped hands, one of my escorts carried her to a tent infirmary. Despite the shifting slate whispers of the world threatening to collapse, Faziz's domain felt safe.

Which meant I'd missed the true threat.

"Faziz is aloft," said a guard, pointing at the abandoned club. My bright eyes caught the broad-shouldered silhouette on a catwalk. "Doing his evening sword drills."

Did they expect me to go to him? A dull would need hours to climb down.

A spring hissed. Steel cable hummed through gears. A bucket of rags shot upwards. Faziz dropped like a spider on a line, gold muscles tensing through his arms and back as he slid into a back handspring on the unspooling winch. *Show-off.*

Scandalously dressed, in black leather leggings and vest, he dropped down before me and grinned. "I'm glad you stopped in, Red Eyes."

"You dare a great deal of familiarity," I said. "What in Dzkegé's name are you wearing?"

"Clothing." He grinned. "It's in better shape than yours. You should take off your skirt before climbing in the bath."

At least my wet hems weren't a spectacle with him around. *Dzkegé's mercy. He's me at eighteen.* The unconventional, irreverent queer I'd have grown into if I'd never left Zega, entirely unwelcome in polite society. *Maybe it works for him. Other criminals wouldn't respect a traditional man.*

Faziz clipped his winch to another cable and offered me his arm. "May I?"

I eyed his waistband for hidden needles and knives. "Can I trust you?"

"You saved my life after I tried to poison you. You already trust me more than you should."

Dzkegé's tits, I'm such a fool. I nodded, and let him wrap his arm under my shoulders. A spring snapped. Counterweights shifted. The ground dropped away. His grip pinned me, so tight against my diaphragm I couldn't breathe. He laughed as force and gravity spit us up.

"Very clever," I said as we landed atop a catwalk in the nightclub above. No one below was bright enough to hear or see us. I could speak freely here. "You've built a world for dulls. You don't have to stay one. Ever thought to make tenants pay rent in essence?"

"They're my people." A provoked nerve purred in his throat. "I don't rob them. I serve them. I'm the only power on Victory Street looking out for their needs. And when a sentient genital wart like Zegakadze Kzagé makes war against them, harasses them, to prove his boss is just as violent as his bloodthirsty Dzaxashigé ancestors, I stop him at all costs. Don't think you can charm me into sparing him, Red Eyes. I won't abandon half a million lives for your smile."

"You think I came just to beg for Zega's life?"

"I sent my spies to investigate you, following your... interruption. They discovered you and he were lovers for several years."

I snorted. "They didn't even find the good stuff. I came because I need an in with Magistrate Akizeké. There's a great deal more to me than the fool I dated as a teenager."

"Apparently so." Faziz paced shallow circles on the catwalk. "Unlike your friend Zega, I limit my violent impulses. Keeping my neck intact means surrounding myself with people I understand. Now a red-eyed man—with a habit of extravagant tipping and hip-checks—wants me to introduce him to my most powerful ally. Hardly what I'd expect of a courtesan famed for his beauty and sweetness."

"I cultivated that reputation." I donned a sly smile. "A gang leader should understand a sex worker offering the public a benign fantasy of himself."

"Of course. Plenty of sex workers rent from me. But they don't fuck with politics. You should understand my hesitancy to trust, Red Eyes. I do you a favor, and the real you stabs me in the spine."

The real me. My father's hereditary monstrosity, driving everyone I loved away. The holy sweep of dragon wings grafted to my soul, a gift from a dead god who never should have touched me. Two strangenesses running against the deep truths of my world—how boys should behave, how our dead gods left us futureless—blasphemy shared in my body. Like bright Dzkegé had draped a diamond mantle on a barrel of burning bronto shit.

"I won't betray you," I answered, softly. "I know what it's like, to be dull and broke with nowhere safe to go. I'm not sure how much your spies uncovered about me—" Dzkegé willing, not the worst truths "—but I've suffered dearly at my father's hands. For the pain he's brought Victory Street, I plan to shatter his glorious future." Cold honesty crept into my voice. I dug my nails into my palms, where they pressed sharp as talons. "Faziz, you're the hope of souls far more vulnerable than I. I'd sooner shatter a priceless vase than give you away to Zega. We're on the same side."

Faziz plucked a scrap of foil from his sash and began folding it. His eyebrow arched thoughtfully as he weighed my words. "You come to me draped in shredded silk, your scarlet eyes powdered up like coins. Loathe the Dzaxashigé rule you might, but part of you craves your kin's approval and love. That's a weakness."

"Are you strengthened, that the *dzaxa* want you dead?

Neither of us can pick and choose our allies. I lack the leverage even to bid you shave your thatched pits."

Faziz sniffed at his clavicle. Lifted his arm and thrust the reeking dark hair toward me. "Does this bother you?"

"Thoroughly."

"Good." He tucked the folded foil back in his sash, and laced his hands together behind his head, flashing both. Mocking me. "What help do you need with Akizeké?"

"She said I had to prove my worth before she'll appoint me a strategist. Five ladies and a magistrate have already pledged themselves to me, and I'm in the process of securing several key international endorsements. How many will I need for—"

"No." Faziz shook his head. "That's not what she meant by 'prove yourself.' It's not about endorsements. She wants to fuck you."

"Well," I said, my cheeks reddening as the air seemed to leak from my lungs. How had I missed it? "That's easy enough. Does she ever hire escorts? Can you recommend me to her?"

"She's more dangerous than a flash flood. Once she sleeps with you, even if you set clear terms, she expects you to fall in love with her. She grows entitled to a foothold in your life."

"I've had clients with boundary issues before." They thought their own lusts love, they thought their love a deed of ownership, and they grew incensed when their property misbehaved. "Rarafashi is hosting a state banquet to welcome the envoys. Half the War District has already written me to schedule dates. Pass her my name. Join me and my allies. In return, I'll help remove Zega from his position." I paused. "Without bloodshed."

"You really do still care for him."

"No," I said, my heart whispering *lie*. "It's been eight years since I ended things, and he treated me terribly all that while.

But Zega provided for me when I had nowhere else to go. I owe him a debt."

His eyes still lingered on me. Reading my dishonesty? Something like pity flashed in his eyes. "I've never been in love. I won't name myself an expert in disposing of it. His life, I can't promise. But I'll help you bring your father down. If he falls soon—and takes Zega with him—the boy can walk away with his long throat unslit. Is that enough?"

Not a promise. A tenuous thread of reassurance. This might only postpone Zega's murder.

But I could work with postponement. "You're in," I said, and shook his hand. When I pulled it away, I held a pinky-sized folded foil dragon.

"For luck," he said, and I bit my lip lest scales wash my skin.

I flung the token down a garbage chute as I left—holding it made me feel like his eyes still tracked me, daggering out my secrets— and hiked back across the slate. Stonefire raised an eyebrow as I slid wordless into the *reja*, but said nothing as she whipped the team on. Vashathke's guards had dispersed the knotted traffic. Smooth as satin, we slid back onto the main crossway.

The sparkling yellow sandstone building called the Surrender rose five hundred stories above Victory Street. Two hollowed-out sculptures held its bulk: the western half a soldier, tall and proud, the eastern a kneeling, defeated man, his lips meters from her armored thighs. Ramps and crossways slotted into them at all angles, traffic pouring down onto Victory Street and surging towards the austere steel façade of the Palace of Ten Billion Swords.

The wind howled around our *reja* as we climbed the ramp to the Surrender's mid-levels, past the sculpted bent knees and pleading sandstone arms. Stonefire drove us through the kneeling man's lips, up a staircase to a high corridor, and to the holdlight-embroidered violet curtains sectioning off the High Kiss. Brass jazz played low seduction as I stepped down.

"Swap skirts with me," I commanded Stonefire. She rolled her eyes, but obliged. Her sturdy, red-and-gold painted leather ran a touch more aggressive than my normal style, but I couldn't attend a High Kiss party in the skirt I'd just been fucked in.

This is going to work, I told myself, cinching the borrowed sash tighter as I ducked through the curtains. I may not have captured Lady Xezkavodz's endorsement, but I would win the favor of the Lost District envoys, and I'd made the acquaintance of a powerful Engineer. When next I spoke with Akizeké, I'd earn her favor with my body and more.

What had happened under the Archive would roll off me like mist evaporating from hot garbage at noon. I didn't deserve a god's blessing, and I certainly had no idea what to do with it.

The Lost District envoys had divested themselves of their furs; pale breasts and dark eyes flashed under neon-filtered holdlight. A blue-painted Bero spun on the pole, suspended by his taut, strong legs. Ambassador Sadza, draped in amber chains, grabbed for my ass. I took a wine glass from the bar and sat on her lap. Her thigh was ice-cold; her eyes a bottomless dark purple. An exhausted beauty, compelling in its threat to fade.

"What brings you to Victory Street?" I said. "It's a long trip for my company."

"Our district has changed greatly in recent months. So will War, soon enough. Your judge, Rarafashi, has only young sons, unfit as heirs. She struggles to choose if her husband Vashathke, or some other, will succeed her to lead War. We've come to offer our aid."

Had no one explained to them how this worked in the modern era? The final choice of heir was Rarafashi's, yes. Only her hand could bestow her vast essence store, the treasure of War, on her successor. But she wouldn't invest her heir—and close out her own life—until a candidate had secured the required number of endorsements.

The Treaty of Inversions left who might give endorsements purposefully vague; the spirit of the law primarily ensured the international community approved of War's leaders. Judges, of course, could give their say, and their heirs, who would have to deal with the new ruler of War once they inherited themselves. Magistrates of other districts generally refrained from endorsing, so as not to displease their judges, but a few had been known to enter the ring. Cultural leaders, high-ranking priests back when organized religion still existed, could all choose a side. And an ambassador could pledge her district on her judge's behalf.

"A toast. To 'some other.'" I drank. Dark wine, ripe with cherries and cloves, tannins nettling the roof of my mouth.

The ambassador frowned when I offered the glass. "I don't drink."

Had I broken a cultural taboo? But the other envoys were drinking. I studied Sadza's sallow, bony, bright face. *Something's off.* "What's your home district like, Ambassador? We've only heard of it through movies and folktales. Are the ruined temples as grand as legends say?"

She snorted, like the back of her throat had gone centuries dry. "Our neighborhood is cold and poor, desolate and empty. Your *dzaxa* see themselves as the chief victims of the gods' fall. Forced into a disadvantageous treaty. Can't afford to build their own bridges or salvage their own ruins. But they only have to sign paperwork. We spent five hundred generations ravaging the temples our ancestors built to feed our children spoiled frozen meat."

Well. That killed the mood. Shame flushed unflattering red into my cheeks. I'd envisioned the Lost District, with its great furred beasts and marvelous hovership, as a neighborhood full of lost secrets and ancient glory. But their tech meant little if it couldn't feed, house and support their own people. Whatever had survived the fall and come to visit bore the thick-hide scars of survival even deeper than I did.

And survival tinted strangely everything you saw thereafter.

Bourbon breath crept up my nose. Hands snaked over my collarbone. A hot gold bracer brushed my shoulder. "Hello, bright boy."

"Ria?" I rose and turned to face her. The Fire Weaver wore War's style: a white skirt with armored scales, a *fajix* overlain with ruby beads cupping her breasts. "What are you doing?"

"Learning if the notorious Koreshiza Brightstar can dance." A drunk smile slunk across her lips. She pressed her soft thighs against mine.

She's not part of the plan. I should have her removed. But drum and saxophone called rhythm, neon purple and red turned her rich brown curls to fire. The roll of her pelvis and shuffling slippers drew me into dance.

I'm attracted to her, I realized, suddenly amused. Women, men, and all folk could stir me, but I ignored my lusts. My clients might hurt me if they suspected I would rather bed another. Still, this was a private party. And if Ria could get me to her father's ear, I could justify a dance. "Specifically, who let you in? I only invited our Lost District friends."

"A Fire Weaver can get in anywhere." She leapt. Her thighs locked about my waist. For a heartbeat, her breath washed my neck; then she flipped away, tucking into a tight ball before landing on the flashing floor. "And can get anything inside her." Her eyebrows waggled in ridiculous, dramatic lines.

I laughed. "The truth! Or I'll have your drunk ass escorted out!"

"You can escort me anywhere!" She grinned. "Fine. My old mentor was traveling with the Lost District delegation and she invited me. Päreshi. Back at the bar."

She pointed at an older woman drinking from an arm-length horn of beer. Heavy furs and goggles concealed her form. Two gold bracers shone on her light brown wrists. The holdfire *opesero* and the holdice *riasero,* two to Ria's one *opesero,* marked her a full Fire Weaver. "Has Päreshi learned what brought the Lost District out of seclusion and onto Magistrate Vashathke's doorstep?"

"Let me ask some questions." She spun tight against my chest. "Do you have any siblings, Koré? Pets? Hobbies?"

"Three half-brothers, no, and sewing." *Politics* and *revenge* didn't count.

"How old are you? Did you always want to be a courtesan growing up?"

"Twenty-six, and no. I wanted to be…" I paused. I hadn't been allowed to want anything. "Married. But sex work isn't bad when you run your own business."

"That's right." Her breath rolled against the crook of my elbow. She leant her weight on me, twisting us in time with the brass beat. Could she stand on her own? "Men don't commonly own businesses in War."

"It's not that rare. We even have a male magistrate now. Vashathke of Victory Street."

"You sound like you hate him." She laughed. "Men! Put two in a locked room and they'll scratch each other bloody. Women were built to talk, plan, and work together."

I froze. Her tone hadn't been patronizing—she'd spoken like she merely spoke facts. But I hated someone seeing my history with my father as a boyish spat. Quickly, I turned the subject. "The monitoring chip you handed me at the parade—I lost it. I'm so sorry."

"Don't be." She sighed. "I checked the readings directly. Dzkegé's shade is gone. She might have never existed at all."

"I'm sorry," I said, and meant it. If Ria had stumbled across the altar first, Dzkegé would have given her the dragon's power. With her courage, passion and charm, she was a movie-perfect picture of a hero. She could handle anything. "It's not your fault. Don't be hard on yourself. It was amazing, how you saved that child from the guards."

"Really?" Light winked in her eyes. Reflecting the neon back brighter. "Päreshi yelled at me. She thinks helping people in the War District wastes my energy. I need to focus on neighborhoods willing to change."

"You changed today for someone in War. Fuck Päreshi." I paused. "Or don't. She strikes me as someone who gives notes to her lovers after the act."

Ria's deep, rolling laugh rang off the walls. She nuzzled her face against my breastbone, and, guided by the warmth of her, I cupped my hands to the back of her head. Thick curls spilled through my fingers.

The base of my spine pricked. *Lizard footsteps. Flesh rebelling inhuman.* Scales spread beneath my sash. *Did Ria wake this in me?* I was a fool for dancing with her. She hungered for promotion, and nothing would impress the Fire Weavers like a caged dragon. My fears and wishes were spilling through my courtesan's persona, and every slip gave Ria a wedge to crack me open.

"Koreshiza Brightstar?" called a herald, her tongue tripping through the mangled Old Jiké and Modern of my name. "I carry an official statement from Lady Dzaroshardze Faraakshgé Dzaxashigé!"

"For public release?" She'd have better luck shouting it down in Mouthmarket, or even printing it in a pamphlet, not that she'd want my notes on her job. Unlike the divine servants for whom they were named, modern heralds disseminated news, messages and *dzaxa* opinions with more speed and precision than the material often deserved.

"For you directly. She demands to meet you in your chambers. She's angry you don't have her pinot!"

I smiled at Ria, and let her go. The prickling scales faded to nothing. *I've escaped. For now.* "The Lady of the Surrender calls me, honored Fire Weaver. Amuse yourself at the bar." *Revel and drink until you forget Dzkegé's shade.*

Gracefully as I could, I disentangled from her and climbed the grand staircase to my personal room.

Green velvet draped the sandstone interiors, covering centuries-broken control panels. Couches and cushioned mahogany stools lined the walls. Night wind poured through arched windows, washing the room with scent from the lavender oil pots on each sill. The great bed was headed by a pillar rising nearly to the ceiling, curtains spiraling from its apex down the walls. Heart-shaped poems embroidered the silk sheets.

The perfect chamber for a boy with nothing to hide.

Lady Dzaroshardze—my aunt, Dzaro—sat at my table, wearing an older, shrewder version of my own face. Her skirt and *fajix* were silver-studded black cotton. An iron dog's-head pendant hung from her throat. Scarlet fire in her eyes hinted mischief; the thin line of her lips promised a building avalanche.

"I dined with Lady Xezkavodz," Dzaro said, her voice a deep rumble. "Jasho-eshe walked in, bright as the judge herself, bragging he'd mastered you. I went straight to my helicopter to come see. You don't look duller. Is there anything you'd like to tell me?"

Did she want to know why I still shone? Hurled slurs rose to mind. *Essence-stealing whore.* Was this a criminal investigation? Sex work had always been legal in War, but courtesans were arrested every year for "improper essence extortion." Just because Dzaro was my ally and kin didn't mean she'd believe me. "*Dzaxa.*" I leant into the honorific. *Placate her. Her order keeps the High Kiss rent-free. Her protection shields me from Vashathke's wrath.* "Please, I didn't…"

"Did Jasho extort you?" Dzaro continued. "You excel at checking your desire. You've never lost a drop of essence in the time I've known you. Did Jasho threaten or blackmail you into tithing essence to him? I don't care whose son he is. I'll have him dragged before Judge Rarafashi and branded Unrepentant if he won't pay back what he stole."

For a moment, I didn't understand. Then the tightness in my chest slackened. "You're offering to protect me. At the cost of Lady Xezkavodz's friendship."

Her hand curled about my wrist. "Family first. Vashathke excepted."

I flushed. Was she playing a game, or was this true affection? I didn't have time to speculate. My life depended on concealing I'd breathed Jasho's new essence. "Please don't worry. Jasho brought a second courtesan, an untrained boy who spilled his whole store. Sad, really. Only exceptional men succeed in this profession. I'm fine."

"Are you certain? That must have been upsetting to see."

Had my lie not convinced her? "I've seen worse. I'm no pampered *dzaxa* boy. I chose this life and I'm strong enough to handle it. Please don't pry. I can't discuss a client's bedroom secrets."

"You can come to me with anything, at any time, and I'll help you." Her grip on my wrist tightened. "Okay?"

"Okay," I muttered. I had to change the subject before her care sank deeper inside me. I wouldn't let myself be hurt when she inevitably pulled her love away. What mattered was she saw in me a good, sweet, pleasant young nephew she'd want to protect. A hard-enough image to maintain as a sex worker. "I'm glad you took the helicopter. Street traffic is awful tonight."

"Did you see the stone dragon? I flew past the eye sockets. They're glowing like Voro's sacred forges. Lady Xezkavodz thinks the fire signals the creation of a new dragon. She suggested we buy nets."

Dragons. I summoned my bedchamber detachment, commanding my skin *human.* "Let's talk strategy. How are your friends?"

"Don't worry about my friends. Focus on your work and leave the rest to me."

"Please. If I don't know where they stand, I'll just get more anxious."

She sighed. "Well. Right now, they're happy to endorse whoever I decide on. But no one wants to risk making an enemy of a judge. If we can't connect them with Akizeké soon, they might choose Vashathke just to save trouble. Maybe I should approach her—"

"I've set up a private meeting with Akizeké," I said, hoping Faziz would come through. So what if the magistrate had boundary issues? I had to forge the alliance between her and Dzaro myself. I had no title or obscene vault of wealth. My value was bringing the right people together, and if I couldn't do that much, my co-conspirators had every reason to shut me out for good. "I'll be her date at the state banquet."

"You're going? Are you sure that's wise?"

"She's a widow. It's not like her jealous husband will pour acid in my shampoo."

"She'll be seated at the high table. Beside Rarafashi and your father."

I sucked in my lower lip. Dinner with the judge and my father. Their lying red eyes on my chest while the blood on their hands clogged my throat.

"You don't have to do this." Dzaro's gaze weighed me up. "You look… unsettled."

Unsettled. One word for a man's anger. The seething pulse in my chest like the beat of a second heart. The distant echo of my mother's sobs. The sizzle of a brand on flesh. Scarlet eyes flickering past me in a crowd. *I will punish you. I will do the justice law ignores.*

Yet my aunt wouldn't understand if I voiced my frustrations. Under the customs of War, gender was as much a public performance as a facet of the soul. When Dzaro had declared herself female, she'd swept off to Warmwater where the *jegiseij* had knit the change in her flesh and returned with a blazing force of presence. None could challenge her as a true daughter of War.

Judge Rarafashi had embraced her as a sister, and brought

her into the imperial household as an advisor. Vashathke had grown strange, bitter toward her. Accused her of betraying a brotherhood they'd never truly shared. All had culminated in a shouting match between my father and his wife that shook the hovering palace of Skygarden and echoed onto the streets below.

For once in his marriage, my father had won. Dzaro had been evicted, and her wound still festered. She and Vashathke had been each other's worlds as children—rich, but lonely, merchant mother ever traveling, father lost in an opiate haze. She didn't understand how the truth of herself would turn her little brother against her.

I knew my father better than anyone. He'd rejected Dzaro because it served his game. If any of Rarafashi's sons revealed a feminine facet in their own souls, decided to transition genders—no doubt something the judge had encouraged—they would almost instantly secure enough support to inherit the throne. Vashathke's heart would have delighted in wreaking this practical misery: disowning his sister to terrify his sons.

"I'm fine, Dzaro. Truly." My lips twisted into a false smile. What more lies could convince her to stop prying at my weak points? "I just need a plan to get the Lost District on Akizeké's side."

She shook her head, but didn't push further. "Tell them Akizeké can offer a trade deal when she inherits. What goods can the Lost District sell? Salvage from their ruins, meat from their massive beasts, maybe lumber…" She tapped her cheek with a long, elegant finger.

Unconsciously, I copied her gesture, doing sums in my head.

"I love it when you do that. You're like the mirror of myself who has fun," she said.

I laughed. "You're like the mirror of myself who owns twenty dogs."

"Eighteen. I sold Buzzy's last litter. I still have collie puppies if you're interested."

No. Pets were too good at making you love them. "Offer one to Sadza. Free with her endorsement. Puppies make the best bribes."

"Dzkegé willing, I'll never sink that low."

"Excuse me, *dzaxa*." Kge bowed as she opened the door. Vomit streaked the yellow-and-blue bronto leather of her skirt. The imprints of bright hands covered her bent baton. "Boss, there's drunk trouble."

"My favorite kind," Dzaro said, and we ran for the stairs.

Ria stood, swaying, in a puddle of wine. Red soaked up her skirt. Anger roiled in her topaz-brown eyes. Päreshi, the Fire Weaver who'd come with the envoys, offered a supportive hand. Ria slapped it away.

"How dare you insult my father?" she shouted, slurring the round vowels of the common Engineering tongue.

"Listen to me," Päreshi answered in the same language. "Your father is a slut who hides behind his beard. He'll never promote you because he knows me and my allies, all us real, skilled Fire Weavers, threaten his leadership. Yet you hunger for his approval like a fledgling bird. Stop wasting time in naivety. Come with me and the envoys. Learn what we can teach you. Claim your place in history."

"Do you think I'm not good enough to succeed without shortcuts? I'll earn my second bracer myself, I swear in Voro's name—" Ria punched her fist against her own breastbone. The gesture shifted her momentum. She stumbled backwards and sprawled across Sadza's lap.

Dzkegé's tits. The ambassador. A heartbeat later, I was at Sadza's side, mumbling apologies as I rolled a drunk Ria into my arms.

"Koré?" Her eyes pled, wide and vulnerable. "I'm not a complete dumbass, right?"

Then she threw up on my skirt.

Damage control, I mouthed to Dzaro. She moved to pacify the ambassador as I dragged a trembling Ria toward a couch, hoping to salvage the evening and the alliances it promised.

"By the bar," Bero whispered from the pole—and I looked up to see Tamadza slap Stonefire across the face.

Stonefire reeled, pinned between bar and wall. One Lost District visitor had an arm around her waist. Tamadza pulled her hair, shouting, "Disloyal whore! How dare you go off with her?"

"Enough!" said Stonefire. "She bought my next hour. I don't belong to you!"

My heart dropped. "Order! Order!" I needed to intervene, but Ria weighed me dead. I couldn't—

Red-faced and raging, Tamadza brought a pitcher down on Stonefire's head. Blood flashed under violet light.

Dzaro screamed and raced forward. I dropped Ria on a couch. The world blurred neon as I cradled Stonefire to my chest. She lolled like a doll. I didn't dare look at the back of her head.

"You dried-up shriveled hole!" Dzaro slammed her knee into the envoy's face. With one fluid twist of her torso, she had Tamadza in a headlock. "Guards! Murder!"

INTERLUDE: AGE SIX
The Prizeheron

27th Thzejezxo, Year 72 Rarafashi

"Once upon a time, a rich merchant remarried to give her young son a father. But the evil stepfather envied the boy's bright beauty and banished him to the stables."—'The Straw Boy', *a traditional children's story of lower Victory Street*

THE LAST DAY of my childhood began with a bucket of slops-water flung across my chest.

Bodzi clutched his hands to his belly and laughed. "Got you!"

I'd been cornered by a grocer's stall. Bodzi and his friends tightened around me. The grocer reached for my arm.

They moved too slow.

I flung a ripe plum into Bodzi's face. My feet blurred as I escaped, laughing like mad. Shoppers cursed as I weaved starling-nimble around their skirts. I snatched a fistful of chocolates from the confectioner's and leapt atop a pillar to enjoy my prize in secret.

The market guard nabbed Bodzi and my pursuers. I sucked nougat from my fingers and watched their ears get twisted.

Three gave up my name. I marked them for more plums tomorrow.

"Koreshiza." Boots landed on the pillar's top. "Starting trouble again?"

My mother, dressed in her bank guard's uniform, towered over me. Her grey curls fell loose around her face; her sneer alone could stop a thief. I spoke true. "The girls were playing with me. But Bodzi said they were his friends, not mine, and chased me—"

"Six years old, and every boy already wants to rip your face off." She sighed. "Better too friendly with girls than improper with boys. But I'm not looking forward to fighting off your rivals the next ten years."

"I got him with a plum," I said. That struck me as the most important part. But my mother didn't smile, and I wilted. I'd done wrong.

"No more plums. Let's get you presentable for the Chosen Heir's festival."

My mother dragged me back to our apartment: an ancient bubble in the green glass of the Prizeheron. She dropped me into a tub, dressed me in a new skirt and sandals, and called the man next door to cut my hair.

He set his two-year-old daughter on our floor as he took up shears. "It must be hard, raising a boy alone. You're a hero, Briza."

"He's difficult, but I try my best." My mother let the toddler fondle her baton.

She'd never let me hold it, no matter how I begged. Like every true baton, the green holdspark knob of a punishing *shiki* hummed at one end, and the sedative *njiji* darts pricked free at the other. Scallop shell patterns imprinted the shaft. Her boss had gifted her the weapon after she'd caught her fifth thief.

She was a hero, as a guard and as a mother. She'd raised me after my father had died. I'd never known him, but I didn't care. My mother was all I needed, and all I needed was to please her.

When my hair was neat, my mother gave me a packet. "You're old enough now." Inside lay nickel-alloy bracers, set with garnet chips and embossed with dragon scale patterns. *Real jewelry.* What boys wore in tales when ladies dueled for their hands.

This Chosen Heir's festival had to be important.

"You'll do, though I wish you'd outgrown this baby fat." She tweaked the skin hanging over the hem of my skirt. I winced. "You like your gift, Koré?"

"They're beautiful. Thank you, Mama." I reached out for a hug.

She sidestepped. "Don't get sentimental, boy. Do as I say."

With a few quick instructions, she sent me off.

The stair of the Neck rose from the Prizeheron's gizzard high into the giant glass bird's brain, where Lady Fidzjakovik held court. Ripples of emerald and gold light poured through the fifteen-foot-thick feathers. *Reja* ran through the inner lanes, raptors snapping as they passed. People climbed the outer lanes on foot, some imposing and lovely, most stooped under heavy burdens. I darted through their maze in a nimble blur.

Familiar whispers rose behind me. *Bright. Ge-imigo. Thothasha.*

At the summit of the stairs, guards waved me forward. The doors to Lady Fidzjakovik's apartment lay wide open. The owner of the Prizeheron sat atop a blue jade throne, her lip curled in boredom, a picture-book in hand. A crowd of children stretched out the door.

Chosen Heir's festival honors ties between War's *dzaxa* and its common children. Once, a general's only daughter was captured by Entertainment District spies, who demanded she negotiate peace with their neighborhood as ransom. Instead, she adopted a dull girl as her heir, watched her daughter's execution on live television, and burned three buildings to the ground. The ladies of War commemorate her charity by welcoming in tenant children for sweets and blessings.

Admiring eyes picked me out as I joined the throng. Green eyes. Brown. Blue. No reds among them. I, as ever, was exceptional.

The landlady's strong voice carried a story to the crowd. "And still, the wandering gods found no place to call home. So bright Dzkegé, their leader, called them together and declared, 'We will build the grandest city in the universe, large as a planet. We will call it Jadzia, and we will fill it with humans worthy to worship our names.'"

She told the story of Jadzia's creation—but incorrectly. The marketplace storyteller, an elderly man who wore his locks stacked in a tall spiral bun, said the gods built our world as equals, hand-in-hand. Why didn't such a powerful person know the truth?

"To bend the laws of physics and lay Jadzia's foundations, the gods needed eleven arcane substances, from lowly holdstone to priceless holdfast. Yet only the brightest of mortals, the Shapers, could grow substance from their souls on command. The gods' cleverest servants, the dragons, stepped forward and—"

"It was the giants!" I said, reading ahead on the page she held the book open to. "The giants discovered how to draw substance from the dead, not the dragons. That's the right story!"

I didn't realize how loud I'd spoken.

"Come, boy!" A strong hand dragged me through the crowd. A tall, pale girl with ruddy blond curls and strawberry eyes kin to mine. "Don't struggle! I'm helping you!"

I could break away. But my instinct urged me to be polite, to please her. I let her drag me to the throne and didn't cry out as she twisted my arm.

"Let the boy go, Iradz," said Lady Fidzjakovik, not looking

up from her book. "You can't torment every mouthy brat in the building. You've homework to do."

Iradz shoved me forward. "See how bright he shines!"

I shivered at how she said *bright*. That word followed me whenever I stepped outside. A name for the fineness marking me unique among the slow and ugly children in my hall. *Brightness*. Something people wanted. Something people envied.

Iradz spoke like it made me a target.

The lady gripped my chin, tugging me into the light. I made myself smile as she studied me—my mother liked my smile, and a boy in a story would be honored by a lady's attention. "You shine brighter than my daughters. What's your name?"

"Koreshiza. Just Koreshiza."

"A mistranslation if I ever heard one. Where's your mother?"

I told her of our apartment. Lady Fidzjakovik nodded. "Iradz, have your tutor evaluate his essence. I want answers from this Briza." Fast as lightning, she ran across the room. Children stared disappointedly at her wake.

Iradz grabbed my arm. "You have to obey your landlady. And I'm the heir to the Prizeheron, so you have to obey me, too. Everything in it will be mine."

She pulled me down an interior corridor, past hanging tapestries, etched poems, and priceless holdlight tablets flashing family photographs. A thin-faced tutor met us in a schoolroom twice the size of my apartment. I stumbled through math problems, needlework, and a poem written in Old Jiké glyphs. The tutor's stone expression gave no feedback, but Iradz laughed at my every mistake. The joy I'd felt at being chosen melted to a terrifying churn in my guts.

"Don't let Iradz bother you," the tutor said. "She has a crush on you, that's all." With a smile, she swept up her armored skirts and left us alone.

"Why are you so bright, Koreshiza?" Iradz said, yawning

as she plopped down on a pillow puff. I remained standing, watching her for a cue. "Are you a slut?"

"What does that mean?"

"Let me tell you a story. Once, an evil whore stole essence from the families of honest women. He hid his crimes by tithing extra essence to his son. The boy grew strong, smart and beautiful. Like you."

"I don't have a father!" I didn't know half the words she'd used, but the bile in her voice still splashed me.

"I didn't mean it like that, stupid. Listen. The boy thought his essence made him equal to a Dzaxashigé. So he fucked the guards protecting the judge's betrothed. They let him in the boy's chamber. He strangled the groom and replaced him at the wedding. But when the judge bound their blood with the sacred dragon's sword, she saw his eyes were blue. Not Dzaxashigé red. She couldn't break a vow sworn on the sword, so she ran the blade through his chest to end the marriage he'd tricked her into. What's the moral of the story?"

"Don't murder people?"

She laughed. "You're stupid. All essence comes from somewhere. If you find it somewhere strange, even behind a pretty face—something's wrong."

Lady Fidzjakovik entered, followed by the tutor and my mother. "Wine to celebrate a bargain well-struck," the lady called. "Iradz, join us. You're ten. That's old enough."

"A moment alone with my son, *dzaxa*?" asked my mother. The lady nodded and drew her people away, leaving us. My mother beamed. "My bright, beautiful boy. Well done."

I said nothing, rubbing the red marks Iradz had left on my wrist. My mother had told me to climb the stair and follow the crowd. Had she wanted the lady's heir to befriend me?

My mother hugged me tight. "I'm now a captain in our lady's guard. We're moving to the top floor. We're rich. You've done it, Koré."

I still didn't understand. I wanted to be rich, and see my mother honored. But what had I done?

She cupped my face in her hands. Framing it like a picture. "You're going to marry *dzaxa* Iradz. Your wife will inherit a building!"

"But I don't love Iradz. I just met her." Boys in stories only married their true loves, though wicked merchants and generals threatened to steal them away. *Though in some stories, the boys are the wicked ones.*

"You'll grow to love her, and she'll love your store. You're the brightest boy in the Prizeheron. Your children will shine like stars."

I wanted to weep, though I knew it wasn't allowed. I wanted to capture my mother's rare smile forever. I wanted a hundred contradictory things, and my wants didn't matter.

I'd just been sold for the first time.

CHAPTER FOUR

The High Kiss, within the eastern sculpture of the Surrender

3rd *Kafi*, Year 92 Rarafashi

"Shadow lingered in their flesh and poisoned their love, for the priests could not deny their pleasure"—untitled book in the Archive's university library, categorized as fiction

"Wearing a condom tells your wife you don't trust her to choose wisely when to conceive. You're poisoning your marriage. If she rips it off, blame your own selfishness."—Sexual Education for Boys, Armory Street Civic University Press

HOURS RACED BY in the wake of Stonefire's murder. Dzaro screamed and shouted. Ruby and Kge rolled Ria into a spare bedroom as a shamed Päreshi slunk away. Sadza argued for her diplomat's release and met my aunt's obstinacy. Heralds returned with cleaners and a transmutationist.

"You're next of kin?" asked the transmutationist, a somber, hooded Engineer.

"I was her employer." She'd never mentioned family to me. And in War, *boss* ranked next to *blood*.

"Would you like us to attempt a higher-order transmutation of the body?"

"Holdspark," I forced through numb lips. "Stonefire was a guard, once. She would have wanted the essence in her soul to fuel batons."

I'd ordered my employees to their rooms, but they hadn't listened. Ruby wept in Kge's arms, and Bero was speaking quietly with both. Opal watched me, his brown eyes haunted, questioning. I had no answers for him, save violence had always been part of our trade, and I couldn't summon those cold words. My soul felt like a poured-out cask.

Possessive. Controlling. Faziz's description of Akizeké lingered in my ears, quivering in a distant corner of what was left of my heart. I'd told myself one bad client was a small price for the magistrate's attention. But bad clients could go off like bombs.

"I witnessed the murder myself." Dzaro glared hatefully at Tamadza. "As the Lady of the Surrender, I find you guilty. You've slain a woman with her essence store intact, forever depriving the world of the power she carried. I sentence you to tithe threefold Stonefire's essence to her next of kin. Refuse, and be branded Unrepentant."

"She means it, you bloodthirsty fuck!" shouted a guard. A holdfast brand shimmered in her hand. A circle to mar those withholding essence from the law.

The anger in my breast leapt with crazed joy. I wanted Tamadza to say no. I wanted to watch her flesh sizzle as every eye in the High Kiss forever turned from her.

"I'll tithe," Tamadza said, turning to me. "Will you take your price now? I'd like to clear up this disgusting matter promptly."

Propriety dictated I give her my hand and accept the tithe. Stonefire had worked for me, after all. With no family to recompense, I was due payment for the end of her labor. But I wanted Tamadza's sentence to hang heavy on her. To make murder nag at her conscience, not quickly paid off with a touch.

"Now that I think of it," I said, "she may have had a cousin in the Prizeheron. I'll write and see if they'll collect the tithe. The journey downstreet should only take you a few days, gracious envoy."

Her nostrils flared. But I'd gambled correctly—she couldn't risk ignoring me and incurring more of Dzaro's ire.

"I'll handle the rest of this." My aunt placed a soft hand on my shoulder. I didn't let myself take comfort from her. "Go to bed, Koré. Please."

Strain cracked her voice. Exhausted and soul-worn, I turned and dragged myself up to my chambers.

The great bed was only a prop. I leapt into the nook hidden by the tall bedcurtain, maneuvering past my desk and filing cabinet. My pallet here was lumpy, but I didn't care. Sleeping in the wide bed built for lovers reminded me of Zega's absence. I flung off my ruined skirt and dropped it into the messy pile of blankets.

At the fourth bell, I woke from dreams awash in shadow. After privately weeping on my pallet, I donned an old leather shortskirt, and my boss's face, and joined my people in the gym.

"How are you doing, Koré?" asked Kge. She and Ruby, who spotted each other as they hoisted barbells, lowered their weights and hurried to my side. "You missed breakfast. Cook made triceratops bacon."

"We're doing fifty sit-ups for each strip," Bero said. The jest rang hollow. But at least he was here. Providing leadership while I slept in and moaned. "How are you feeling? We cried at breakfast."

"I'm fine," I spat. Too aggressive. Too angry. Ugly traits in a man, even in a boss. *Be soft.* "Would you like the day off? Two days?" Their eyes were raw from tears. My offer did nothing to stir them. *How can I make you feel better?* Bero should have this job, not me. He had the leadership experience—he'd run his wife's businesses in the Warmwater District, before divorcing her and moving back to Victory Street to start a career of his own. All I knew was how to tally a balance sheet and get fucked.

"I'd like to keep working," Opal murmured. "I want a distraction."

A distraction. Something I could do. "Good. Check the angle of those core twists. Your chest won't define if you don't throw your shoulder into the upstroke."

"Right. Sorry." He twisted harder, spine stiff with fear. I flinched. I'd forgotten how my youngest employee feared my wrath. I would never fire him or endanger his livelihood, but he wouldn't believe me if I told him so. Victory Street leached away the soul's power to trust.

I knelt beside him on the woven mat, pushing his dark shoulder across his body to his knee. "Thorough and smooth. Concentrate."

"I'm trying. But... what if I fail and I'm not pretty enough? What if a client hurts me?" Tears streaked the white lines of his makeup.

"You don't need definition." Neza's own arms bulged as he patted Opal's shoulder. "You have a sweet smile, and you listen well to people. We have our own strengths."

Opal sobbed. His fear recalled memories of phantom slaps and cutting bonds. My jaw tightened. If I spoke to reassure him, tears would spill with my words. No one respected a crying man.

I turned away, a storm in my chest. *Better separate myself from friendship. Stay in total control.* I had a dragon to hide.

Running my hands along the free weights, I felt out my own. How much one could lift varied with the essence one carried, and my weights were two and a quarter times heavier than the other boys'. But today, I felt weaker than a cooked noodle.

"Do people still want to go out tomorrow?" Ruby asked. Her sapphire earrings flashed, a match to the deep-blue skirt she wore. "For the Seven Crows Festival?"

"Celebration is the High Kiss's sacred art!" Neza hugged her. She kissed his cheek, and soon the boys were naming bars and clubs. Bero pulled Kge over to join in the preparations. Ruby wrote a schedule on the mirror in lipstick. Even Opal was smiling by the time they'd picked their destinations.

"Would you like to come, boss?" Bero asked. "It would make you feel better. A nice team-building exercise."

They'd stopped asking me to join them years ago. I never let myself say yes. "I've sewing to do. Enjoy yourselves."

Thank you, I nearly added, but didn't.

After lifting, I bathed, shaved clean, and returned to my room to dress for the afternoon: a skirt of cream-colored silk, cloth-of-aluminum rays slicing the front into wedges of stylized armor, my silver bracers inlaid with electrum starbursts. I left my shoulders bare, brushed gold around my eyes, and sat at my table feeling like me again. Desirable. In control.

Tragedy couldn't throw me off for long.

As I sorted through escort requests for the state banquet, Ria barged through the door.

The Engineer wore sheer green silk, her *fajix* straining to hold her breasts, her skirt stretched tight about her wide hips and plump belly. She nearly tripped over the too-long hem. *Ruby's clothes.* Gold nuggets winked at her earlobes; her unbound hair fell in a charming mess, no doubt fresh from just rolling off the bed where we'd tossed her drunk ass.

"Honored Teacher Riapáná Żutruro," I gave the Engineers' honorific in their round, open-voweled common tongue. "I hope you slept well."

"Worrying about me? Poor Stonefire was murdered!"

My heart twisted. "An occupational hazard. Fire Weavers shouldn't concern themselves with the lives of courtesans."

"The Fire Weavers protect everyone on the city-planet. Including courtesans. Or at least, we're supposed to. Mostly from ancient abominations and hungering magmaworms and whatever weird shit ancient civilizations buried near the planet core, but, you know. I like to think we generally look out for everyone." She sighed, and winced. Essence could cure hangovers, but not shame. "And don't 'Fire Weaver' this and 'Honored Teacher' that. I'm just Ria. It's weird hearing you act formal after I threw up on you."

A smile crept across my lips, despite everything. "Okay, Ria. How can I help you?"

"I'm here to apologize." She stared down at the floor, where her foot traced a pattern on sandstone. "If I hadn't made a scene, you would have been free to stop Tamadza. She used me as a distraction to grab Stonefire. It's my fault."

My jaw dropped. *Ria, all light, blames herself for this evil?* "Say no more. Trying to cheer me is kind, but it's my fault. I invited the envoys. I left to talk with my aunt. I own the venue. It's my fault."

"That's foolish. You couldn't have predicted your customer was a murderer!"

"And you could have predicted murder from a stranger at a party?" I folded my arms. "I forbid you to blame yourself under my roof."

"Forbid me?" Her lips melted into a confused squiggle, quirked up at the ends. "From thinking? While you stand there and loathe yourself? Hardly a generous host."

"I can also loathe myself for being a poor host. Or we can both blame Envoy Tamadza." A weight slid from my shoulders. Tamadza had struck the blow. I'd had no power to predict or stop it. If I could absolve Ria of Stonefire's death, I could absolve myself, and miss my friend without making her death about my pain. "Fuck Tamadza."

Ria gave me a thoughtful grin. "You're right. Thank you. And fuck Tamadza. My mentor, Päreshi, likes her—but Päreshi likes everyone who badmouths my father, murderer or no. She and Dad argued so much at this one feast, I asked the judge to move them to separate tables."

"You're acquainted with the Judge of Engineering?"

"Yeah! No big deal. I'm good at making friends. But Fire Weavers are supposed to be good at languages and history. So everyone back home is like 'oh, Ria, you're so smart' and I'm like 'thanks,' and then it's 'let me explain why you're not living up to your potential, because every little thing you do is wrong!'" She mimed the second speaker's mouth movements on her hand, tapping her fingers to her thumb like she held a sock puppet.

"It sounds like they owe you considerably less advice and many more expensive fruity drinks." I considered. "Perhaps non-alcoholic ones. But you can certainly figure out how to be yourself on your own."

She sighed. "I'm sure doing a great job so far. Like, how do I even start? Being an adult? Being my own person?"

I shrugged. I didn't like considering myself deeply. It reminded me how little I'd accomplished in life beyond scheming. "Let me know when you learn. Shall we return to discussing murder? That's simpler."

"Agreed," Ria said. "It can't be a coincidence Tamadza shows up the day Dzkegé's shade disappears. She's after something darker than diplomacy. If I can tell the Fire Weavers what Tamadza is up to, they'll have to give me my second bracer." She stepped closer. I bit my lip, remembering how easily she'd provoked dangerous scales down my spine. "But I need your help to expose her. Let's get some answers, and some real revenge for Stonefire."

"I don't care for revenge," I said. "It breaks more than it heals." A normal man would say that. Normal men didn't know the trick of revenge—*already be broken*. "But as for

81

answers... I wouldn't mind learning how to keep my employees safe." And how to make Sadza endorse Akizeké. *Forgive me, Stonefire.* Tamadza stood at Sadza's right hand. I'd have to keep dealing with her until the endorsement was pledged. I needed to show Akizeké I could bring her power, along with my flesh. And if I could also bring her Ria's powerful connections... "What do you need from me?"

"An invitation to Rarafashi's welcome banquet. Päreshi refused to use her connections to get me in. My best option is taking Stonefire's place."

My jaw dropped. Impersonate an essence-thieving courtesan? "The stain... to your reputation..."

"Oh, no. People might learn I enjoy fucking." Ria rolled her eyes. "The shame."

"The stain to my reputation," I said. "If I send someone a poorly trained escort. I could sneak you in as a caterer, perhaps..."

"What? How hard can your job possibly be?"

Despite my hesitation, calculations spiraled through my mind. Thick, muscular limbs, curves in her hips and bust... every lesbian in War would stare at her ass. Did she have what it took? "You're bright, funny and bold. Boys likely throw themselves at you. But posing as a courtesan will require more than fucking. Your client will likely be a woman. She'll want to dominate you, because you're short and adorable. If you have any problem with that, you'll have to hide it well."

"Sounds like an adventure. Not a problem."

The arrogant smile hadn't budged from her cherry-red lips. I'd have to test her with more than words. Blood pounded in my ears, foolish and heavy as a down comforter. "Pretend I'm a client. What do you do?"

"Pretend you're a woman, or show you how I'd take a man?"

"Whatever you'd like."

"I'd like you, Koré. I'd like you very much." Her fingers

locked about my wrist. Firm calluses brushed the tender skin above my veins. "Might I kiss you? You're so…"

I bent down and pressed my lips to hers. She stiffened, then stretched onto her toes, wrapping firm hands around my neck. She tasted like the heat of the noon sun, light flashing off Victory Street, fire and smoke in some enormous machine. Her tongue teased mine. Her teeth closed on my lower lip. I gasped before pulling away.

"Not bad," I panted, pulse racing. "You were about to call me beautiful, weren't you? Don't. Clients expect more effort from lies. 'I can't look away from you.' Sound surprised. You weren't expecting to like this job—now, despite everything, you're enjoying yourself."

"But you are beautiful." Her hands traced the line of pale hair down my stomach. "And I'm very much enjoying myself."

She tugged the front of my skirt, and I fell into her arms. Her legs wrapped around my hips. She levered herself up. Her weight steered me backwards until I tumbled onto the bed.

"Careful, boss!" she said, fumbling with the knot of my skirt. I unlatched her *fajix*. Her breasts slid into my hands, heavy and riper than melons, tipped with coin-sized dark nipples. *Very beautiful indeed.*

I nursed the tender, swollen flesh. Ria moaned a blasphemous invocation. She abandoned the knot and flung my skirt up over my chest. My shaft slid free. She ran her lips over the tip, and, while shivers still danced down my chest, changed her mind and slid on top of me.

It was wet and easy, like some strange homecoming. She steered me inside her, holding and controlling me until she clenched with pleasure. Her lips parted in a silent howl. Essence flooded my senses like the tide.

Resisting pleasure was easy. I was still hard when she dismounted and dropped onto the bed beside me. A sleepy smile washed her face, but her nipples stayed taut. I yearned to kiss them.

"You didn't hold back," I said. "But your essence slipped. Does that always happen?"

"With men? No. Take it as a compliment."

"Compliment your client all you wish. Don't complain to me if you're half dull by sunrise."

"I won't—" Anger flared in her eyes. "I... no. You're right, Koré. Teach me how to hold back. I couldn't tell my father I lost my essence store in bed."

Something slipped in her demeanor. I'd first taken her for a cocky partner who, absent evidence, believed herself a god of the mattress. But Ria weighed her actions against other's perceptions just as heavily as I did. We both hid secret anxieties behind bright smiles, and I wanted to hold her to my chest until she saw the light pouring from each inch of her clearly as I. *Dzkegé's tits, I'd sound so foolish if I voiced that. Naïve. Uncool. Infatuated.* All I could do was teach her what she wished to learn.

I tossed my skirt aside and straddled her. Her eyes widened in surprise. Her unbound hair sprawled like a storm cloud. "Lay there. Let me show you what a client does." My fists bunched around her thick curls. My tongue pressed her, wet and commanding. "People say essence transfers at orgasm. But pleasure and orgasm aren't the same. You can make someone orgasm by force, and you can fuck someone enjoyably without making them come." I pointed down at the proof. "I've made people tithe to me with a kiss. Essence flows when you surrender to desire. When you love, with your skin, bones, and soul."

My lips lapped her nipple. She squirmed, impatient, below me. "*Sakri*, that feels good! How do you keep from loving, when you're surrounded by bright, beautiful people?"

"Remind yourself what's at stake. You want to prove yourself to the Fire Weavers, and so you need essence.

Essence is surer than love. It won't hurt you. It won't lie. It won't fail you."

Staring into deep, endless brown eyes, I slid myself inside her.

Her hands clenched tight around my ass. This time, I had control. My hips pushed forward, thrusting deep and fast. "My turn," I grunted, dragging on her hair. Her neck arched. Her lips parted in a perfect circle. She twisted against me as she climaxed, her breasts heaving with every gasp.

"More! *Sakriu su riu*, dead gods and living, give me more!"

"No." A tide of pressure built in my groin. I dropped her hair, grabbed her hips, and pulled her sure against me. Her pleas faded into unimportance as I used her, stabbing hard, intent on nothing but my own release. *This is a lesson, Ria, one rarely taught for free. Your pleasure only matters to yourself.*

I enjoyed fucking, but work was all it was.

Ria screamed—in frustration, not relief—as I came inside her. My hips shuddered. My fingernails dug into her tender cheeks. I wanted to ride the wave cresting inside me, to lose myself in the crash and flow. *Trust her. Love her. Only her.*

Cruel red eyes, high above me. The smell of stables and silk flowers pricked with blood. A bitter memory, locking down my entire essence store.

"That's the job," I said, lying back down beside her. "You serve the client. Even if you beg, they won't grant your wishes unless it pleases them."

Ria laughed, all powder and flash once more. "You enjoyed my begging." She slid a hand between her legs, releasing her pleasure with a final squeak. "You like controlling a woman?"

"I enjoy getting a job done." I touched her bracer, the marching gold giants atop the holdfire core. "The heralds of your god, Voro. Her giants. They were shapeshifters, weren't they?"

"All the heralds were human shapeshifters, including War's dragons." She rolled over and nuzzled against my side. "As she built the city-planet of Jadzia, Voro elevated the greatest civic engineers to serve as her giants. They discovered how to transmute all eleven substances, from holdstone to holdfast, from dead bodies, without needing Shapers to make them. Some of their name-lines continue to this day."

"In Engineering, you name yourselves after your mentors, right? Family lineage isn't so important?"

She nodded. "My formal name is Riapáná Żutruro *reru* Päreshi."

"Riafana Zothroro rero..." I blushed at the mangled words. "Sorry. I don't speak Engineering regularly. Your Modern Jiké is excellent."

"Modern is easy, once you wrap your lips around 'dz' and 'th' and 'x'." She pronounced the final consonant oddly—more of a 'ha' than the strong 'hua' in the back of the throat. "Your grammar is simple, easy for a conquered people to learn. Engineers learned many Jiké languages in the age of the gods."

I blushed. "The Brass War. The genocide. Right. Sorry."

"Don't apologize for your dead ancestors." She rolled her eyes. "I can see blaming yourself for Stonefire, but that age ended millennia ago. How much evil can a sweet boy take responsibility for?"

I am not a sweet boy. Despite how safe I felt in her arms, I couldn't speak those words. I wanted to be who she saw when she looked at me. "Go tell Bero you're hired," I said, turning the subject. "Ask for the handbook and read your legal rights. Dinner's at the sixth bell. Tell the kitchen to send food to my room; I have paperwork to do."

"Do you need help? I'm good at paperwork. And I'm good company."

Her words offered so much. Scales knotted tight at the base of my spine as "Stay" almost rose to my lips. I rolled back against the bed and let years of hiding steel me. "My time—and my essence—is my own." Cold words cut the prickling transformation short.

"You do the trick you showed me all the time? No lovers? No partners? Are you interested in relationships?"

The short lines of Zega's profile flashed through my head. His curls brushing my chest, his lips puckered when he laughed. Iradz and her bullying brass. Gei-dzeo fruitlessly trying to drag me away. *All gone behind me. Some further away than others.* "I'm interested, but unlucky. Who'd date a courtesan?"

"Dating you would be an adventure. There's forty billion people on the city-planet. You could find one or two willing."

I rolled my eyes. Maybe one or two in billions would date a fallen man. But anyone who'd stay once they'd discovered the depths of my perversions was likely more monstrous than Zega. "Thanks, Ria. Anyone would be honored to be your chosen. You're brash, bold, and as brave as fire. But if I want love, I'll buy it."

When she'd left, I retreated to the desk in my nook. My thumbprint opened my holdfast-locked safe. I pulled out the scroll where I tallied endorsements and checked Lady Xezkavodz of the Archive into my father's column. *Eight international endorsements, eleven domestic.* Even in this modern era, the *dzaxa* of War were slow to rally around a man. *Akizeké. Two international*—her lavish investments in the Entertainment District had secured the favor of their judge and her heir—*seven domestic.* What sort of trade deal could she offer Ambassador Sadza to capture the Lost District's support before my father could?

A chattering noise rose near my foot.

"Out!" I'd opened the curtains onto my private balcony, and starlings had flooded in. One cheeky yearling pecked my ankle, her down fluffed into a ball. She quirked her head up at me and cheeped.

I grabbed the jar off my desk, scooped up the yearling, and waded onto the balcony. The flock dissolved into a pecking frenzy as I flung seed. The yearling pecked at my hand.

"Someone thinks she's the lady of the Surrender." I spilled a thumbnail-sized portion at her feet. "You should fly up and bother my aunt." She fidgeted her wings as she ate. I stroked the back of her head, and curls of childhood down came away on dew-damp skin. "Don't grow up too fast. It's awful. Believe me."

Distant thunder rolled through the air. The clouds coalescing on the downstreet rooftops flashed bright. The flock took flight. Wings beat against my hand.

"Stay close!" I shouted as the starlings swirled away. My bright eyes let me track my own bird across the evening. *Beautiful.* Cool wind stirred my cheek. Rising planets sparkled like gemstones against sunset's blush.

This evening begged me to enter it. I fetched a dismantled dancer's pole, raised it like a baton, and ran through the drills my mother had taught me. A stabbing lunge with the *shiki* tip, to immobilize a target with electric pain. Rolling my wrists as I struck from right to left. Darting through footsteps as I struck and blocked imaginary foes.

My muscles hummed with soft, glowing satisfaction. A fine sheen of sweat built on my brow. I was glad the tangled curls of the Surrender granted my balcony privacy. My rusty skills would embarrass me if seen. To improve, I'd need a real baton, and a sparring partner I could trust not to judge me.

For a heartbeat, I let myself want. Let myself be. Not the scheming plotter I'd shown Faziz, or the pleasuring courtesan for Ria, but the true self they'd both, in their own ways, pulled to the surface of my soul.

Delicate silver frills fanned from my neck. Wind tugged at my back, unfolding new muscle and bone. Foreign sensations teased my tender skin as my wings unfurled, and I gasped.

Silver fire leapt from my throat, shimmering like oil before dissolving into the breeze.

So beautiful. My thoughts spun, half-drunk, half-dreaming. My new limbs stretched, testing the air. *But how do I use them?* Crackling lines of silver foil, alien as a god's eyes, folded over my brain. Instructions, instinct: *cup hot air below, displace mass, downflap—*

No. I couldn't dare. Not just because the sight of me would throw all Jadzia into upheaval. My own beauty was a false thing, crafted through silks, jewels and paints. Ugliness lurked in my soul, a stain I hadn't invited but forever drove people from me. *If I'd been a more dutiful boy, my mother would still be alive. And maybe my father would have spared us if I'd presented a sweet face to him sixteen years ago, instead of the scheming smirk of his true heir.*

I didn't deserve beauty, flight, or magic.

I recalled the part of me that lied. My weapon and my tool. *You aren't a person. You're a dagger aimed at Vashathke's soul. Your wants don't matter. You don't matter. You please others, challenge nothing, and survive.* My scales shimmered back into flesh. My wings vanished into evening air.

The knowledge of flight—and the wish for it—still tugged my heart skyward.

I tossed the pole away and chewed my lip, thinking hard. I was a dragon. Part of me yearned to fly and breathe brilliant life into my dying world. But all I touched bred disaster. I could never be what Dzkegé wanted me to be. I'd set out to shape history, with whispers and a soft touch. Not overturn it with wings and dragon fire.

I could force my desires back inside me. Make myself a fancy toy, not a breathing person. I could protect myself from my dark, wrong soul.

CHAPTER FIVE

The High Kiss, within the eastern sculpture of the Surrender

12th *Kafi,* Year 92 Rarafashi

"The Dzaxashigé general invited the besieged Engineers to a state banquet. While discussing the terms for her surrender, Lady Trochäná Efuä reru Uäźa requested her tenants be spared from assigned labor in the slaughter camps. When denied, she requested and received a twenty-percent share in profit from their manufactured weapons, which she insisted (before her murder) would pay to support vulnerable elders and children the laborers left behind"—The Liberation Wars, by High Master Sonuafi reru Nori of the Fire Weavers (text banned in War District)

"Whomever holds the deed to the Laboratory of Choking Waters shall be responsible for the medical costs of all victims of the blightburn plague and shall open the building for inspection by impartial observers twice yearly." Appendix

Five of the Treaty of Inversions, "Reparative Clauses"

MAGISTRATE AKIZEKÉ HAD sent me a costume for the state banquet. Platinum-thread snowflakes shimmered on the white silk skirt as I painted frost beneath my eyes. The cape-styled *thevé* cloth laced across my chest and draped down both my shoulders; tiny white-gold rings studding its satin mantle all the way to my feet. With dots of glue, I pinned faux snowy owl wings to my lids and forehead.

White and pure. Akizeké wanted to play 'teach the virgin.' Not the most creative game, but if she'd let me join her campaign, I'd blush and stammer all she pleased.

My employees awaited me in the front hall, draped over stair rails, lounging by flowerpots. Neza nursed whiskey. Opal stared at his jewel-netted hands. Ria and Ruby sat by the fountain of two embracing women, Ria's jokes pulling smiles to Ruby's painted lips.

My people. Alive and beautiful. The ultimate luxury for the *dzaxa* of War, but priceless to me. *I need them to know it.*

"Stick together and be vigilant," I said. "If a client threatens you, or if you feel uncomfortable, come to me. No business is more important than your safety. I'm not afraid to feed dead *dzaxa* to the raptors."

An uneasy laugh spread through the crowd. My heart twisted. I wished I had more than words to offer. *Power. Inspiration. Safety.* What I hadn't felt since I'd strayed from my mother's set path.

"We're a team," I continued, fumbling for perfection. "We look amazing. Your clients aren't worthy to kiss your feet—but if they do, it's a ten percent gratuity. Remember how Bero couldn't open a *fajix* when he started? How Neza used to snore like a bronto? Now you're almost all as good as I am. We can do anything."

"Thanks, boss." Opal smiled. "That helped."

I pivoted to hide my blush. It wasn't enough. I needed them safe. That I couldn't guarantee such was acid to my skin.

Tonight, the judge's flying palace of Skygarden hung over upper Victory Street. The countless tons of steel worked into the great hovering dragon sculpture winked and flickered, chrome-bright, in the afternoon sun. Terraced gardens slotted out from its sides. A tight maze of gold and electrum spikes pointed skyward from its arching spine. Though it only housed six million souls, Rarafashi's domain could cast whole worlds in shadow.

We passed through a security queue below the giant-grown garnets of the sculpture's eyes. Though five times taller than a standing woman, the orbs seemed to focus their accusing gaze at me.

You're the most desired man in War. Not a dragon. Never a dragon.

The guard at the metal detector waved me to the side. I rolled my eyes. *They call it a pat-down when they're sneaking free samples of my ass.* Into the screening tent I walked, already unlacing my *thevé* for inspection.

"Keep that on," Faziz said as I entered, lounging atop a confiscated hoverplatform, weaving beads of slate into a cord bracelet. "Set that sparkly cape where I can reach, and you'll never see them again."

Outrage bubbled in my throat. "You're robbing the guests?"

"Rarafashi's security staff take luxury goods for inspection and slip them into her treasury. I'm skimming off her thieving. There's more money to be made skulking around a party's edge than waltzing through the doors."

"It's more fun inside," I said. "And you'll certainly profit when I put your sweet friend Akizeké on the judge's throne."

"Call her 'sweet' to her face and you'll taste her slap." All humor fled him. "I wish I could go in with you."

"Thanks for your concern, but I can handle the *dzaxa*."

"I'm not concerned for you, Red Eyes." He turned, long,

dark hair whipping off his neck, and pried a ruby from a gold tiara. "I have a mission for you. Find Zegakadze when your conversation with Akizeké is done. Tell him to resign his post."

"I tried that."

"With a bribe. Now try a threat. Tell him my next assassin comes in a month's time."

This is his postponement. A month for Zega to shift his stubborn heart. The thought of trying to reason with my ex felt heavy as raw flax in my mouth. "What if I can't?"

"What are you? A cold-hearted conspirator caring for naught but revenge? Or a soft-boned pleasurer, seeking to save the love of his life?"

"Neither. I'm complicated. Didn't your spies tell you that?"

"Maybe I want to hear the answer from you. Speaking business partner to business partner. This fabled 'love' too-wealthy poets praise—how likely will it overshadow your good sense?"

"Extremely likely. But more than love lies between him and I. When we were together, he'd turn his hurts against me. I'd do the punishment chores his mother gave him. I'd say cruel things to the servants who offended him. If I ever told him no, he'd accuse me of not caring for him as I should." I bit my lip. "Maybe I'm silly, but I'm scared he'll refuse your offer and endanger himself, all to yank on my feelings like a raptor on a lead."

"Zega sounds like an abusive asshole," Faziz said. "He treated you as poorly as he treats Slatepile folk now. I'm sorry to make you speak with him. It's clearly not healthy for you."

"Don't apologize. Like you said, it's just business for you. And I'm done loving monsters." *I'm done loving anyone or anything. I've lost more loves than a proper son of War should take.*

"Your passionate romances sound exhausting," Faziz said. Soft wistfulness filled his voice, oddly youthful for the veteran of a dozen underground turf wars. "And terrifying."

"You don't sound frightened." I laughed. "If we're exchanging business information, we should trade note for note. Are you seeking a particular passion, Faziz? I can arrange anything, for a fee."

Faziz coughed hard into his elbow, breaking my gaze. I'd struck gold and left him quailing like a virgin.

"You're not supposed to be here!" A uniformed guard pushed through the curtains. "There's no men on this shift!"

Faziz pressed a hand to his breast. His other slipped the ruby into his sash. "I'm looking for my wife, Nadzo. Have you seen her?"

"There's no Nadzo in this company!"

His face fell. "She said she'd found work!" He gripped a table, as if to steady himself. An ornamental gold compact vanished into his broad palm.

I wrapped an arm around his shoulders, wrinkling my nose at his sweat and stone-dust scent. An odor to seep through my dreams. "Excuse us. My friend's distraught about his wife leaving."

"Off with you, then." She dismissed us with a flick of the wrist.

"You left your slate beads behind," I hissed in Faziz's ear as we left.

"I want them to know I was here." He grinned at me, tugging my own lips into a wicked smile. I hadn't broken rules for the joy of it since I was six. *Stolen plums and* dzaxa *rubies.*

The monster that was me, smirking as it fed.

MAGISTRATE AKIZEKÉ RECEIVED me in her private Skygarden apartment. She wore black to match my white—silver-tipped steel feathers of armor, spaced in diamonds on her skirt and in sprays off her pauldrons. Dark paint cut her eyelids long and dark.

"Kneel."

Essence saturated her commanding voice. I dropped at her feet.

She grabbed my ear and turned my head sideways, studying me through narrowed eyes. "You come quite highly recommended, Koreshiza Brightstar. Faziz tells me you're the boldest harlot in War."

"Faziz strikes me as an expert in boldness."

Her fingernail flicked, jarring my ear. "I hate bold men. For the length of our contract, you speak to no one without my permission."

A challenge. My blood stirred. This would make introducing Akizeké to Ambassador Sadza difficult, especially when I'd have to nudge their conversation toward the trade contracts Akizeké could offer for her support. But the boldest harlot in War could do anything. "Yes, *dzaxa*."

"If you break that rule, you'll be punished. If you offend me, you'll be punished. If you at any point appear less than overjoyed to stand beside me, you'll be punished."

"And if I sing bawdy songs atop the banquet table with a *fajix* on my head?"

Her hand cracked against my ass. A sharp, delicious pain sang through my midsection. "Beg the dead gods you never learn the answer, boy."

Woman-sized flowers bloomed beneath the banquet hall's glass floor. Blossom-shaped holdlight veins sent sparkles dancing through the white sandstone benches. Ambassadors in tiered robes and holdweight-levitated finery sampled smoke from curled glass pipes. The judge's counselors, waving matched fans of red and purple feathers, settled the fates of billions in murmured conversations.

Akizeké pulled me down on a bench near the high archway. Ambassador Sadza sat across from us, dressed in ivory-trimmed furs, dark circles blooming beneath her eyes. Tamadza sat with her, even brighter than when she'd killed

Stonefire. Anger flared in my breast. I gave her a shy, false smile.

"It's a pity you've come with Akizeké." Tamadza leered at me, eyes flint-sharp. "I'd love to get to know you better."

"Akizeké," I said. "Do you have the honor to be acquainted with the noble envoy Tamadza? I met her at a party where she murdered one of my employees. I do believe Lady Dzaroshardze might issue an arrest warrant for her soon, as she hasn't paid her essence-fine."

"Because you sent me chasing non-existent cousins through a giant glass bird." Quick as a lash, Tamadza's hand darted out and closed around my wrist. "Here. Threefold your whore's essence."

Before I could cry out or turn to Akizeké for aid, the pressure of a thousand harsh wingbeats sliced up my arm. Essence never held flavor, but hers tasted of the air above an avalanche and the ancient ruins below the street. A cold fire slipping invasive fingers under my skin.

Strength gathered in my limbs, and I slipped my wrist free. Tamadza, only slightly dulled from her tithe, bowed mockingly. I glimpsed my reflection in a wine glass and bit back a surprised gasp.

I looked as pretty as Jasho below the Archives. Upturned nose sculpted by a master's hand. Scarlet eyes glinting with wicked fire. Pale skin almost glowing with peachy light. Slender, long-necked figure arched like a drawn bow. *Temptation incarnate.* Under the table, my foot found a dropped steel corkscrew and crushed it under my heel. *Dangerous temptation.*

Purple rings budded beneath my eyes, peeking out from my silver makeup, as if I hadn't slept in days. Tamadza's essence flexed like a worm in my guts. *Hello, boy,* it whispered in a seducer's voice. *Let me offer you planets.*

The back of my neck prickled. What had this murderer passed me? Essence had no will of its own. *It's nothing. I'm just tired. I'm making it up from my own darkness.* Perhaps these last few stressful weeks had shattered something in my mind. Essence could blunt illnesses of the brain and body, but it had no mind to shape brights toward some arbitrary perfection. A bright woman without legs could punch through steel, but would still need a hoverchair to carry her. A bright man could charm thousands with his beauty and quietly lose his mind. *I need more sleep. I need to burn everything I've ever built to ashes so no one else is killed on my account.*

"There," Tamadza said. "We'll have no more trouble over dead whores and debts."

"We'll have whole skyscrapers of trouble," Akizeké growled, "if you lay another hand on him."

Her clotted-blood gaze must have convinced Tamadza she meant it, because the envoy turned to murmur with a passing servant. "Thank you," I whispered to Akizeké. "I needed that."

She kissed my cheek. "The men of War wield cutting words. Sometimes, you just talk yourselves into trouble and need a strong fist to back you up."

Her hand was halfway down my skirt when the heralds announced Rarafashi with a trumpet call-to-arms. The guests stood in a scraping of benches. I hastily adjusted my skirt, grateful all eyes rested on the high arch.

Rarafashi entered, ablaze in metal and light. Her cloth-of-platinum skirt flourished a thousand swords embroidered in geometric blocks. Gold-plated steel flashed across her *fajix*; her crown was billowing Engineering bronzework. My knees quaked as her garnet gaze swept over me. The floor rattled with each slow, deliberate step she took.

"Sit!" Her voice filled the hall. Gladly, I obeyed, blinking as my eyes adjusted to her presence.

At two hundred and fifty-two, Rarafashi remained as imposing as the day she'd inherited her throne. Should she pound her fist on her bench, it would shatter. But her flawless skin had gone thin as tissue, her hair fragile as glass. *Time topples thrones.* Soon she'd need to invest an heir with her store, go dull, and embrace death.

If I failed, that heir would be the man whose arm she leant on.

Vashathke, Rarafashi's husband and the magistrate of Victory Street, had gathered essence from a thousand secret sources, and his beauty remained the callous confidence of youth. The upturned nose, the high line of his eyes, the carved cheekbones. *Me. All me.* A neat mirror to set my skin crawling. Small wonder my mother hated me as much as she loved me. It would be weeks before I could glimpse my reflection without recalling my twin monster.

Servants in diamond-studded *fajixa* laid delicacies before us. The first course was pickled snake embryo, served atop cubes of rock salt, which cut like a knife on my tongue. Next came a diluted lime soup, in which floated thumbnail-sized roses carved from red chilies. Starling breasts cloaked in caramelized sugar atop sliced plantains. Rare brontosaurus fillets dressed in black peppercorns. A Lost District delicacy: thick, pâté-like paste with sharp flavor and smooth texture.

Ambassador Sadza saw the question in my raised eyebrow. "We call it *cheese.*"

"Truly a marvel, Sadza." Rarafashi's gaze turned to me. I shivered. "You're that Koreshiza boy. We've never been formally introduced. Do you like my palace?"

If I had a death wish, I might have laughed in her face. She'd spoken like she wasn't my stepmother and hadn't nearly killed me once. I gave the safe response: batting my eyelashes and gazing demurely down.

"You're not mute. Answer me."

The power in her voice pressed me. Akizeké's hand clamped tight about my shoulder. My breath caught at her magnificent trap. "Don't be shy, Koré. Tell our judge how much you appreciate her hospitality."

"I'm most grateful for your welcome, *dzaxa* Rarafashi." I bowed my head low as I could without getting cheese on my face. Akizeké's nails dug into my flesh. *Too low. Oops.*

Vashathke smirked at me. *Laugh all you want, Father. You sold your body and soul to become Rarafashi's third husband. I lease my flesh by the hour. We're the same. Pleasing silk wrappings over cruel-hearted deeds.*

The moment Rarafashi turned to him, his face fixed back into an insipid smile.

Dishes and wine paraded on. Whenever Akizeké was occupied with a solicitor, I studied Sadza over my goblet. She didn't respond to my questing gaze. Her food went untouched; her lips only murmured occasional niceties. My father brushed her knee, and asked gently about her home district, but her passions went unaroused. Where smirking, subordinate Tamadza held fire, the ambassador was smoke.

After the fifteenth course, Rarafashi clapped her hands, and the servants dragged the benches away. Holdlights flashed inside the glass tiles, lighting a thousand-colored dance floor. Musicians assembled instruments. Akizeké went to track down a business partner. Forbidden to mingle, I leant against the far wall and watched Sadza progress. Each *dzaxa* who spoke to her mouthed, "endorsement," and each she waved away. Zega greeted her with an obsequious bow. She never met his eyes.

Ria came up at my elbow, gold hairbands flashing red in the floor lights. "You're quiet. Feeling okay?"

I smiled, and flourished my hand in Akizeké's direction.

"Power exchange? I haven't played that game in ages."

I nodded. I wanted to warn her not to mention my name if Tamadza caught her snooping about, but that could wait. All my plots would fail if I couldn't persuade Akizeké to appoint me a campaign strategist. I had to please my client.

"Is everything a game to you?" She locked her arm around my shoulders, planted her feet back against the wall, and walked up it until she braced level with my ear. "My client has the greyest mound I've ever seen. I'll picture you between her thighs tonight."

My cheeks flushed. I bit my lip to choke off laughter, hoping she could feel how funny I found her.

"You're not the only one enjoying themself. When my client falls asleep, I'm going to sneak into the envoys' apartments through the maintenance shafts. I'll let you know what I find."

She pushed off my shoulder and flipped forward into a neat crouch. Applause rolled through the crowd. Sadza and Tamadza ducked into a curtained room near the hall's entrance.

Hiding secret meetings in plain sight? They could fool pampered *dzaxa*, but not a sex worker with basement grime in his bones. With a courteous smile for everyone I passed, I crossed the floor and lounged outside the curtains. My bright ears snatched up conversation within.

"I could be wrong," said a man, "but I feel this arrangement will benefit us all."

"We want this contract," Tamadza said. "But on our terms. If your patron disagrees, she can meet us herself."

Listen to Tamadza, her essence hissed my gut. *She knows the truth of power.*

Hushed negotiation continued. The man's patron wished to lease Lost District machines the envoys would fly to the Engineering border. In return, she promised unrestricted use of key shipping and air traffic routes, fishing and salvage rights, ten thousand tons of holdwater, and unlimited 'peacekeeping support'. A trade contract only a future judge could keep.

"A pity we can't make this alliance public," the man mused. "I imagine your endorsement would shock the War District to its heart."

"You think the Treaty of Inversions will matter when our

work is done?" Tamadza laughed. "There was a time before other districts ruled War. There will be a time after."

A time after the treaty? Might as well say a time after air, a time after history. Maybe I'd misheard. Only one sound was certain—the scratch of pen on paper. My blood pounded hot. I'd been pre-empted.

Footsteps clicked. I slid into the curtains' shadow—but not fast enough. The departing man caught my arm and hissed, "You!"

So this mysterious patron isn't a 'she.'

I'd imagined this moment for years. Vashathke was a monster, but my younger half-brothers were unknowns. Their lives tied to my father's rise. Their vulnerability born of his sins. Geshge had reasons to hate me, but he could also embrace me as kin. *Please, brother. Love me, and I'll return a thousandfold—*

"What are you doing, you damned bastard whore?"

Three words brought the Slatepile down on my hopes. The gold rings on my *thevé* jingled as my shoulders slumped. *Don't react,* I told myself. *You've felt this rejection before. If you can't please him, you can at least please your client.* Habit pinned on my slipping smile, and I held it steady, some petty corner of me gloating I'd inherited Vashathke's fine-carved striking looks. Geshge's stubborn brow and chin were shared by neither our father nor the judge.

"I've sealed an important contract! I won't let some little slut ruin the night for me!" Geshge's face went redder than his eyes. "You should be ashamed of yourself, marching into Skygarden like a true Dzaxashigé. Do you have anything to say in your defense?"

I spread my skirts, bowed low, and stayed quiet. I'd show this *dzaxa* respect. Not my wounds.

"Geshge!" his wife shouted, breaking off her dice game with a gold-clad Engineer. "Leave him alone before he rubs off on you!"

I met her eyes. *Hello, Iradz.*

She sneered at me like she had when I was six. A look screaming *whore.*

"The dancing's started." Akizeké took my arm. "Stay close."

She spun me onto the floor. I drove my boiling anger into footwork. Horns and drums built a fast, brassy rhythm. We swung in dazzling arcs, faster than dull eyes could follow, our bodies tucked low, our feet locked in a complex six-step.

"You hold your tongue well," she muttered, spinning into my chest. "I thought your brother would provoke you."

Bile filled my throat. "I have nothing to say to him."

An important contract. I tried to push through anger and see strategy. Vashathke must have been working on the trade deal since the welcome parade, using Geshge as his agent. But why keep it secret? What could the Lost District offer him worth more than their public endorsement? Tamadza may have denounced the Treaty of Inversions, but Vashathke had to follow its restrictions if he wanted to rule. He could gripe all he wanted about its perceived unfairness—but for ten thousand years, that framework had kept the world from violence.

"Stop frowning. Be pretty." Akizeké squeezed my ass. I forced on an insipid smile.

"Dzaxashigé of War!" Every atom of air hummed as Rarafashi spoke. Musicians froze. Dancers spun to stillness as the last note died. "Many of you wonder what brings the Lost District to War after ten thousand years' absence. I rarely entertain wild tales, but the eyes of the stone dragon burn, and my great house should hear Envoy Tamadza's story."

Tamadza smiled. "My thanks, Rarafashi. Our district didn't forsake the world by choice. The dying gods placed an intangible barrier around our lands. Penning us in like meat animals. We've been isolated for millennia. But recently, we found a way through."

"Due to the Fire Weaver you travel with?" Vashathke asked. "Trusting them is unwise. They cross borders without visas, wield unsafe holdfire weapons, and hoard essence. They steal treasures from those who rightfully won them in battle under the guise of mending wrongs. I wouldn't be surprised if their ancestors construed the fall of the gods. Judge Źeposháru Rena is unwise to tolerate them in Engineering."

"Suck your own cock," shouted Päreshi, squinting from behind her heavy goggles. She and another, male, Fire Weaver sat with the Engineering District ambassador and a dozen of her party. Despite the differences in their dress and towering hairstyles, all wore identical disdaining frowns. "I don't have time to teach your sorry ass a history lesson. You'll need to sing a sweeter song if you want us to support your rise to Rarafashi's ass-freezing steel throne."

"Have some imagination, dear Vasha," Akizeké said. "Why shouldn't the Fire Weavers chase history's secrets? The past was greater than our present."

"Thank you, Magistrate," Tamadza said, chuckling contemptuously as my father purpled. *Irrational xenophobe. He deserves the shaming.* "The barrier was powered by a shade of Dzkegé lingering in the world. It fled when we broke through, and our instruments can no longer detect it. We believe Dzkegé exhausted herself by creating a new dragon."

A shiver ran down my spine.

"I swear on my life," Sadza finished. "The last god has fallen. A new dragon has been unleashed. If not caught and restrained, she threatens to change everything."

No. No. I forced my smile wider, trying to look uninterested in burning. *Dzkegé's shade. Fleeing her shattered wall. Appointing a courtesan to fuck the world back together.*

"Ridiculous," Vashathke said. "If I had a coin for every rumor about dragons—"

"The essence drought has restrained War too long," Rarafashi said. "Forced us into treaties that benefit us naught. Turned our lovely glaives and swords to soft batons. A dragon could restore our fallen glory. The *dzaxa* who brings it to me will be invested as my successor."

My guts wrenched. *The crown of War. She would shatter the treaty that keeps the peace. For a dragon.* She couldn't mean it. It had to be a mistake, a senile outburst from a bright light fading. In the conquests, soldiers kissed by dragon fire had torn down buildings and bare-handed, shattered ships. Killing billions. Crushing skyscrapers to rubble. All so our Dzaxashigé ancestors could wring gold from the wreckage and live richer than the incarnate gods.

That age had ended. We simply couldn't return. But magistrates and ladies, councilors and wealthy merchants, all the *dzaxa* would stretch fortunes toward my capture. Every dull eye would flicker skyward, seeking high favors for reporting glimpses of me. If anyone glimpsed the truth behind my false smiles and flattery, the world would go to war for my body. And I'd live out my days on a judge's chain.

I'm not Dzkegé's chosen. I'm the cruel joke of dead gods. My chest tightened. *Forget. Escape.* I grabbed a flute of sparkling wine from a server's tray and tossed it down.

Akizeké laughed and commanded the servants to bring spirits from her own store. "If you vomit," she warned me, "I'll shove a shot glass inside you."

I downed alcohols with lightning intent. Clear raspberry vodka. Bronze rum. Yellow elderberry liqueur. Light spun from the glass floor. Metal music rang in my ears. Akizeké's hand on my waist anchored my spinning head. *She's happy with me. She enjoys watching me do this. She's fine. I'm fine.*

The Engineers clustered in tight, worried knots, whispering, "violation" and "what else did you expect in Skygarden?" Even Ria, laughing with her client, smiled with an uneasy edge. The very palace atmosphere seemed to thicken. *A palace crafted by Engineer prisoners of war, in the age before the gods fell.* No one from our neighboring district could ever feel completely at ease behind these walls.

I mistook my approaching father for my reflection.

"Koreshiza. Dear. Let's make peace. It's not right to have such distance between father and son." Vashathke stroked my cheek.

Did he sound like that when he told my mother he loved her? My mask shattered. My knotted anger flared to red life and every careful courtesy escaped me. "Fuck off," I growled, and spat at his feet.

Well said, dragon boy. Tamadza's shadow essence purred cruel approval in my soul. I flinched at its frozen-velvet touch.

Akizeké grabbed the throat-lace of my *thevé* and, one-handed, dragged me from the hall. Choking and deserving to struggle for air.

CHAPTER SIX

The apartment of the Magistrate of Armory Street,
Skygarden

12th *Kafi,* Year 92 Rarafashi

"The Defendant said, in our video footage, 'eighty million thera is only a number, come collect your debts with whatever army your dry ovaries can pump loose.' We hold the Defendant in contempt."—transcript of court hearing, common Engineering tongue

"I would cut off my balls again if it would make me a father. I can't have biological children. I'm a sexy monster."—Hishura, Blood and Stone 2: Crimson Crush (Modern Jiké subtitles)

AKIZEKÉ'S PRIVATE APARTMENT was one of Skygarden's largest. Holdair filters hummed near the balcony arch, keeping the atmosphere balanced. Black hangings draped steel walls, embroidered in white, snowflake-shaped poems. *Rise and dominate. Rise and make bright war.* Her bedroom was bare

save for a massive four-poster and a leather-padded bench—
which I lay across, face-down and naked.

"Did you enjoy the party?" she asked from the balcony,
facing away from me. With her hands on her hips, her
helmet of grey hair stirring in the wind, she resembled an
ancient general. If she'd lived ten thousand years ago, she
might have saved the gods from whatever had toppled their
thrones. "Aside from your father's idiot prattle, of course."

"I enjoyed you. Quite a lot." Akizeké made sense to me.
She gave orders, I obeyed, and predictable results ensued.
My blood kin made for a knot of senseless, random pain.

"Rarafashi, Vashathke, the wealthy *dzaxa*... they speak
of glory like they know what that word means. Yet ever
since the gods fell, people like them have devoted their petty
lives to maintaining War's essence store. Keeping the status
quo, even if it means writing foolish laws, diving into debt,
leaving developable ruins empty. Hypocrites, all of them.
You're different, Koré. Modest, bright, and beautiful. You
exemplify a man of War from a brighter age, and yet you
make a living on your back. That bothers me."

Tonight, I'm making my living on my front. Some *dzaxa*
assuaged their discomfort at seeing a red-eyed man in my
trade by trying to rescue me from my own career. It made
me feel like a patronized child. But it helped hearing Akizeké
also loathed my kin. "We need new leaders. Better leaders."
Alcohol slipped honesty into my words, stronger than the
magic of the dragon's sword for compelling truth. Silver
scales unfurled down my wrists. My heart skipped. *Not here.
Not now.* "We need you."

"You're trying to seduce me."

"You hired me to seduce you." I flipped to the harsh
language of business, dragging plots and strategy across my
soul. Scales vanished in a wink of silver light. "My Aunt
Dzaroshardze could put four Victory Street ladies and
Magistrate Kirakaneri of Shadowcoin Street behind you. My

father is gaining momentum in the endorsement count. If you don't announce major gains soon—"

"He'll secure War for himself and his idiot sons. Engineering and Warmwater will fuck us for centuries. The deficit will triple." She shook her head. "I'm not running for my ego. I'm running because I'm the best candidate to lead the War District. And I'm happy to work with Dzaro. I like her. Vashathke's ungrateful treatment of her is just further proof he's unqualified. But why do I need you, Koreshiza? Shouldn't I just approach your aunt directly?"

Why me indeed? I couldn't bring her names and influence like Dzaro. I couldn't reveal my past and all the twisted choices that led to me begging before her. The truth was, simply, I wanted to be my father's undoing more than I wanted to keep breathing air. But what I wanted didn't matter. Only what I could provide.

"The High Kiss is an excellent location for campaign meetings. Central, discreet, and no one questions what notable *dzaxa* do in brothels." It wouldn't be enough. I forged ahead. "And because I can bring you the Engineering District."

She froze. "You lie."

"You saw how they reacted to my father. He's lost them. I know powerful Engineers. I can bring them to your side." I bit my lip, hesistated, and continued. "One of the High Kiss's newest patrons is the High Master's daughter."

"The Fire Weavers? Well, then. Welcome to my campaign staff. Unpaid. Tell Dzaro I'm her candidate."

"Done." I hid my triumphant smile, suddenly lighter than air. "And now, *dzaxa*?"

"I punish you for acting above your station." She stalked inside. Starlight shone on her heavy steel bracers. Her thighs pressed against mine as she straddled me. "How dare a little boy involve himself in politics? You should be in the nursery with a toddler on your hip."

Her slap echoed. The lean muscles of my ass clenched at the blow.

"Forgive my insolence," I panted, hard and eager with desire. "I'm a poor bastard from the lower street. What do I know of the *feshi ka* and their *dzeitho*?"

I'd slid into my native Lower to finish. After so long, the words felt strange and clumsy on my tongue. But they proved fetish to Akizeké. Her next slap rang my body. The third knocked loose my cry of pain.

"I'll fill your foolish mouth." She came to my front. Her hand locked around my chin, forcing my head to her clitoris. Platinum stubble pricked my lips as I kissed her. *Slowly. Slowly.* My tongue slipped across her vulva, teasing her apart. Her fists squeezed my shoulders as I pressed the sweetest part.

At her first shudder, she scooped me up and flung me across the bed. Hunger tightened her grasp on my hipbones as she pulled herself up and took me. Wet and virile, she rode as a hawk striking prey. Silk tore as my bright fingers clawed the sheets. I craned back and gasped her name as my pleasure crested. *Akizeké. My weapon. My answer.*

She didn't know she was a tool in my hands.

"You have a musical voice." Akizeké lay down beside me as her orgasm ebbed. "Perhaps I'll make a singing little son with you. An ornament for a judge's court."

"Please don't!" Terror gripped me as I watched for the silent thunderclap of conception. I'd been taken by a hundred women, but never considered— "We aren't married, I'm dishonored, I—"

"I was joking. Don't be so jumpy."

She tucked a thick arm around me and dropped into snores.

Her weight at my back felt secure and constant as the planets shimmering low over the horizon. In a night of humiliations, she'd given me victory. But my spine remained tensed in her embrace.

We'd only been playing a game. But my body still feared her.

After a sleepless hour, I dressed and walked out onto the balcony. My feet found scale-shaped ridges in the steel dragon's side. I let myself climb.

Concealed handholds crisscrossed Skygarden, a pathway for the bright. Soldiers had once used them to ready the steel dragon for battle. Tonight, they made my lovely, lonely road.

Reflected stars and planets swam in Skygarden's electrum plating. Where time had worn handholds flat, my fingers pressed new ones in steel. Night air whipped around me, numbing my burning shoulders, if not my trickling unease. I shouldn't be here. Good boys didn't climb, especially not up the judge's palace, and I was on the clock with Akizeké until dawn.

"It's not your authority they doubt, Vasha." Rarafashi's voice echoed from barely half a kilometer away. I froze.

"Then what is it? I threw them a parade. They still won't speak with me as an equal!"

Vashathke. The knot of anger in my breastbone spurred me forward. A heartbeat later, I balanced atop the steel dragon's spine. Gold-lined spikes rose like pillars around me. My hands and feet sank into the soft metal as I climbed, gaining meters every second. Skygarden lay open to me.

The judge stood on a narrow terrace atop the dragon's left shoulder. Vashathke paced near its edge, chewing his lip.

"Emotional displays, like your rant about the Fire Weavers, do you no favors," Rarafashi told my father. "They're less closely tied to the Judge of Engineering than they once were, but we can't risk our economic partnership with their district over conspiracy theories. The leader of War must prove herself—or himself—to be strong. Even-tempered. Disciplined."

"Strong and disciplined, like you? Offering the throne for a dragon? Even when appointing a candidate outside the formal endorsement process would violate the Treaty of Inversions?"

Rarafashi changed the subject. "So eager for power. So eager for my death." She squeezed his hand. Bones moved. He gasped. "I married you. Mentored you in politics. Named you a magistrate. Still you don't love me?"

"We didn't marry for love. You wanted children. I wanted a crown. My heart was never in the bargain."

"I wanted daughters." She gave his hand one last twist and dropped it. "You gave me three boys. Don't say that's beyond your control, with your clever answers to everything. Here's me being clever. I'll be remembered as the judge who brought dragons back. Maybe the judge who appointed the first male to rule in her stead. You'll be remembered for building off me, if you're remembered at all." Rarafashi cocked her head. "A spy."

She leapt. White blazed up the golden spike and struck my chest. I fell. Metal crunched under my back as I hit the terrace, Rarafashi landing soundly beside me. I flipped onto my feet, my fists curling before my good sense caught my body. *She's the sovereign judge of War. Be a good boy. Please her. Comply.*

I knelt before my judge, pressing my forehead to the cool steel.

"Did you see, Vasha? He looked like he wanted to claw my eyes out!" Rarafashi laughed. "What are you doing, boy?"

"Forgive me. I went walking and lost my way."

"Don't lie," Vashathke said. "You've been poking your nose into my business since childhood, Koreshiza. Your obsession with me has brought you nothing but heartbreak."

You chose to break my heart. Only family here. Pretense could vanish into wind. "What obsession, Father? You mean less than nothing to me."

Vashathke dragged me to my feet, his eyes scarlet daggers as he studied me. If our shared faces invoked paternal sentiment, his trained expression hid it well. "I apologize for how clumsily I approached you at dinner. I want to claim you as my child. You should carry the name of the Faraakshgé Dzaxashigé and be a joy to your brothers. I should be a dutiful comfort to you."

My breath caught. My head spun. I wanted to spit at him, but the warm, welcome beauty of his words drew me, skin, bones, and soul. *Foolish. So foolish.* He had never so much as offered me a warm word. Why would he start now? But Faziz had been right about me: I did crave love and approval from the *dzaxa*. At least, from my father. Too many years had passed since I'd tasted it from anyone. I'd take what I could get. *If he loves me this time—*

"When I'm judge, I'll outlaw prostitution, confiscate your brothel, and marry you to the first merchant who'll take damaged goods for the Dzaxashigé name. Such is a parent's right. Or you can stay the fuck away from my campaign, you poxy little cock."

His words struck hard as cracking whips. I reeled back. If the railing hadn't stopped me, I might have stepped off Skygarden. *Of course he doesn't love me. He knows the evil in me better than anyone. He sired it.*

"Such a soft-hearted boy," Rarafashi mused. "You're certain he's yours, Vasha?"

"Dearest." Vashathke's eyes skipped over me as he turned to the judge. Like I was garbage to him. "He'll stay away now."

"What a selfish heart you have." The judge sighed. "Even our boys, you only love as extensions of yourself. I mourn the day Geshge rebels and you cast him out like your sister."

"Geshge is a good son."

"Believe what you will. But if you want my throne, dearest, stop moaning and capture me a dragon."

Everything comes back to ruling my flesh. Tamadza's dark essence ignited inside me. Caustic and sharp, like burning trash and toxic fume. Violent visions washed me: Rarafashi's teeth cracking under my fist. Vashathke's face purpling as I wrung his neck. *Perfect and sweet.* The hunger in me gloried at a promise better than sex, better than love. An anger to burn down the world that raised me. *I'll show them I'm alive. I'll carve my name on their bones.*

But, as always, my need to please screamed I couldn't let any perverse current show.

Get away. I slid over the balcony, ripping handholds into metal. My feet found a hole in the steel dragon's side. With a kick, it tore wide enough for me to swing through. I sank to my knees on the holdair-lined floor of a maintenance shaft.

The world sees you as a trade good, called Tamadza's dark, high whisper. *Show them the monster that's always lived inside you.* Behind my eyelids, a silver-and-violet dragon blew shadows on a fleeing crowd. People dropped, clawing at their chests. Some opened their breasts with their fingernails; some were trampled to a bloody pulp. All bodies rose, blank-faced, bruise-eyed, and beautiful. *Let me have you. It won't matter how they see you once I set you free.*

My body seized. My feet drummed a twisted rhythm. Gas hissed as holdair cracked beneath my blows. In the distance, footsteps echoed up the shaft's side—but I had no attention to spare as my enemy consumed me. *Tamadza. So tempting.* My essence wavered like a dying candle, warping strange and powerful. Coating my soul in an armor of tar. *This isn't freedom. Only Tamadza's chain.* Worse, part of me longed to be caught on it. I sought Vashathke's destruction for the joy I imagined in seeing his fall. Watching everything he ruled charred to ashes promised pleasure so dark it would devour me.

The echoing footsteps reached me. "*Rodi Voroná!*" Ria's voice. Her warm brown arms held me steady. "Are you okay?"

My self-control shattered. The transformation seized me, spikes rolling down my spine, wings battering dead air. "Ria!"

I gasped. Silver fire washed around her. She must have been on her way to the envoys' quarters when I forced my way into the shafts. "Help!"

"*Ah jonuä, p'betru, biaru juro*—shit, fuck, you're a dragon!"

"I know," I gasped. "I'm sorry." What else could I say?

"What's going on?" Her breathing sped. "What do you need? Tell me." Her voice, even panicked, rang as clear as a brass trumpet. Her earnest concern battered past my defenses. I needed someone to hold me more than I needed to breathe.

"Don't let me be alone."

Her embrace tightened as the shadow sliced at my soul. I grounded myself with her breath on my neck and the double rhythm of our hearts. Scales wrapped me. Lightness settled through my gut and limbs. A long tail coiled around us both.

You bloodthirsty monster, whispered the shadow. *Be mine and feast on Vashathke's flesh.* But with Ria's warmth close, I could almost believe there was more to me than spite and violence, something a caring hand could touch. A self that *was*. A self to fight for. *No,* I told the shadow. *I'm not the little queer boy you get to control.* I wanted to hold myself intact more than I wanted to burn the world.

The shadow withered and died like a starved candle. The voice vanished. My head quieted into foggy dim. Night air pieced my shivering core.

"Relax. Breathe. I'll get you warm." Ria helped me stand. Her sweaty, trembling palms revealed an agitation she'd kept from her voice. "Want to turn off the... special effects?"

Hungry magistrates, I reminded my sluggish self. *The throne... for my body.* Light winked across my skin, leaving it human once more.

But something was wrong.

"Cool trick." Ria patted my side. I gasped in pain. "Sorry! Be quiet."

She dragged me from the vent and into a side room of a *dzaxa* apartment. Skirts and metal bracers hung from racks around us. Ria helped me onto a cushioned bench, her arms still tight around my waist. "My client's a heavy sleeper. We'll be fine if we keep quiet."

I didn't answer. I was lost contemplating the horror in the closet's mirror.

My pale gold skin had gone blotchy, bruised and uneven. My hair hung limp. My slim form seemed skeletal; my slender arms as weak as spun sugar. Only embers flickered in my puffy-lidded eyes. Ugly. Vulnerable. Dull. *Again.*

I'd fought free, but Tamadza's shadow essence had eaten most of my store in the battle.

How could Ria hold me? Wit curled in her plump smile. The roots of calm, steady wisdom filled her brown-diamond eyes. Her finely crafted bangles and gold hairbands paled beside her beauty. *My breath did that.* I wanted to kneel at her feet and confess my troubles. I wanted to flee before my dullness offended her. *I have no value like this. She could fling me out the window and none would blame her.*

Ria stroked my hair. "How long have you been a dragon?"

"Since the parade."

"Did you see Dzkegé's shade?"

"Yes. Beneath the Archive."

"I knew it!" She grinned. "What triggered your first shapeshift?"

My dull brain remembered fear. "Why do you want to know?"

"This is what I needed! I've found a dragon. A new source of essence for the city-planet. Forget just me getting promoted—we'll be world-famous heroes. My dad will finally stop doing those little head-shakes when I tell him what I did with my day!"

"No," I croaked. My eloquence had fled. Fear ruled me, knotting my tongue, winding my dull guts tight. "Please. It's not... safe for me." The emptiness in my soul was the essence drought that mattered. Only the bright could play politics. Dull, I had nothing. "Tithe me some of your new essence, and you'll get answers in a week." *Buy time. Escape. Please her.*

"Oh. Okay?" She sounded confused. Didn't she know her rise would render me a trapped pawn in Skygarden's steel halls? Her fingers brushed tears from my eyes. Essence pulsed into me, sweet as rose perfume. "How's that?"

"More," I gasped. My embarrassment peaked, driving me beyond decency. She hugged my head close to her chest. Fluttering wingbeats of magic churned the air. Filling me. Suffusing me. Making me whole. *A gift. At the cost of exposing myself to the Fire Weavers.*

"Imagine a world where everyone shines," she said. "New buildings. New technology. No customs ruining people's lives to control their essence. Think of the future we could build!"

My cracking laugh smoothed as essence filled my throat. "It sounds lovely. It'll never be." Tamadza had woven a shadowy curse to destroy me—by accident, on purpose, or for simple fun. Monsters from fables could come to life and walk among us. But the high halls of Skygarden ever brimmed with monsters. Utopia could never bloom as easily as despair. "If I could change the future—for my employees, at least—I would. But nothing gets better on Victory Street. I won't make things worse."

"Don't worry," Ria said. "I'll make something good. For you. For us. I won't let you down. I swear."

Her smile dimmed as I grunted in reply. The world felt small and far away. Her arms, her essence, her quiet breath on my ear... even with fear dancing up my spine, I couldn't break away. I wanted to let myself be held, like back in the corridor. Where she'd gently embraced the creature who put the world's future in her hands.

Ria and I were alike in the worst possible way: wanting things so bad they ate us from the inside out. Of course she'd choose power over me. Wouldn't I do the same in her place?

"I'll get you back to Akizeké's bed," Ria said, once we'd balanced out. "I don't have time to spy on Tamadza. But remember our bargain. One week, and I get the truth. You won't drive me off with your icy courtesan act." She grinned. "You care. Deeply. That's good."

Spoken like someone who's never had her care turned against her. The sickest irony was I might have confided in her freely. The Fire Weavers had knowledge, and no love for War's politics. With a few decades to safely befriend her, I could have trusted her enough to confess my secret and seek aid.

But the truth had slipped free. The crown of War hung at stake. And Ria, who said she cared for me, had chosen to wrap a collar round my neck.

CHAPTER SEVEN
Skygarden

13th *Kafi,* Year 92 Rarafashi

"I have never met anyone who feels as sharply as Koreshiza Brightstar. His hates rule him, his loves undo him, his needs blind him. Our plot needs drama to conceal it, and drama he'll endlessly supply."—letter to Tamadza of the Twelfth River, written in Old Jana, the Shadow Tongue

"The hormone testosterone makes men moody and prone to discord. This is evolution's design to keep boys from wasting essence among themselves. As puberty can be lonely, young boys are encouraged to keep cats instead of risking improper friendship with other boys."— Sexual Education for Boys, Armory Street Civic University Press

"Do you think Magistrate Vashathke means it?" said a servant to her fellow as I passed in the corridor. "One million *thera* for a captive dragon?"

"He must have bought stock in some netmaking business," mused the other. "But if Rarafashi believes the envoys, I'll keep my eyes open for scales."

Ria knows. My options slip away like rain to the sea. I forced on a harmless smile and fought to focus as I slunk through the thin, twisted corridors of the judge's husband's apartments within the steel dragon's neck. *Get Faziz his results. Save Zega's life.* My ex wouldn't step down for essence or virtue, but fear for his skin might stir him to resign.

"Koré?" said the guard at Zega's door. "Good to see you. Zegakadze isn't in fit shape for company."

"I'm here on business," I said. "Tell Ironwhite I said hello."

How could one ever be in fit shape to receive an ex-lover? I wondered, shutting the door behind me as I slipped inside. The smell of whiskey and deadly-sweet firepowder hit me hard. Crystal liquor flasks sparkled and flashed before the sunlit balcony. Electrum-plated steel walls, painting human bodies tumbling before a giant hand's blow. *Anticipating legal power to control and break bodies when Vashathke is enthroned.*

The familiar crack of a baton on bony flesh—and a boy's low cry—flung me back through memories. *The Bold Blades brothel. Spinning, thighs locked, on a silver pole. Metal strikes on my back. My client, laughing, as I fell.* My heart raced. Sweat prickled in my palms. I froze, caught seven years back, shame and hot self-loathing washing my cheeks. *I should have used the safe word. She would have respected it. I shouldn't have frozen—*

"*Kejaxo!*" Opal gasped, straining against the shackles binding him to Zega's bedpost. The High Kiss's signal to slow. "That's too hard, *dzaxa!*"

"So are you." Zega reached around to grope him, his other hand lifting his baton for a second blow. "Hungry whore. You enjoy this."

Bruises ran down the backs of Opal's thighs. A red scrape

bloomed on his cheek; threadlike *shiki* burns—an unsafe voltage for pleasure—laced his teak-brown nipple. Wounds made too fresh and rapid for essence to heal.

Zega smashed the baton down against his lower back. Light flashed down its familiar scalloped steel sides. Opal curled up, cheek pressed tight to the silk sheets. His dark blue eyes stared all the way to the sea, a look saying *please don't make me have a body any longer.*

I hated living in a world of broken boys.

Zega flexed his wrist. The world snapped red. I lunged. His lips parted in a confused *O* as I twisted the baton—my mother's baton—from his hands. *My childhood. My inheritance.* It fit small in my fist, but I held it high between Zega and the door.

"How dare you?" I hissed, trembling with the force of my fury.

Zega flushed rosé-wine pink. "What are you doing here?"

I couldn't remember. "Let Opal go. Now." I jabbed the sparking, electric *shiki* end of the weapon toward him.

He rolled his eyes at my threat. "You're making skyscrapers from street shit. Opal brought this on himself. He's no good in bed. He cried when I struck him with the *shiki*. You would have begged for its kiss."

"You would have made me beg. You taught me love meant suffering for you." Acid boiled in my throat. "You killed love for me."

"As my marriage tore my heart to tatters. You left me alone with my wife. It's all your fault. At least, when I fuck like this, I feel free of her."

"So freedom means someone else suffers? This is wrong." The knot of anger pulsed in my breast, sweeping me from cool strategy to foolish, lovely fire. If I'd still carried Tamadza's shadow essence, I would have surrendered to its darkness and ripped him in two. Instead, I lifted the baton. "Untie him."

"I don't take orders from whores." His full lips pouted. His bright arm blurred as he flung a whiskey bottle at my head.

I ducked. Crystal shattered on the wall. Shards laced pain up my arm. A copper blood-scent rose as I stabbed the *shiki* at his stomach. Electricity flashed from the holdspark knob. Zega convulsed, grunted, and twisted away.

"Guards!" Zega shouted. "Help!"

"Mercy, *dzaxa!*" Opal screamed, low in his throat. Covering Zega's sound.

I grinned. "Your guards won't disturb your pleasure, Zega. It's my mercy you need."

"I need nothing from you." Hatred lit his sapphire eyes. "You hold that baton like a smarter whore would hold a breast. I was wrong to offer you a job in Vashathke's campaign. Only an exceptional man makes it in this world. You're common, slutty trash."

I stabbed at him again. He danced around me, knocking me back with a cheek-cracking slap. My injured arm stung as I lifted the baton two-handed. Sunlight, smooth and focused, rolled down the shaft of my reclaimed weapon. "What will be your excuse for losing to common, slutty trash?"

He charged. His shoulder slammed into my gut, emptying my lungs. I wrapped my legs around his waist, summoned my strength, and twisted. The bedframe shattered as he hit. Opal wrenched sideways, still bound.

"Beg mercy, Zega," I mouthed through my stinging jaw. My skin tingled warm where he'd touched me.

"Go fuck yourself!"

The baton flew up to my shoulder. I fired a *njiji* dart. Zega slumped. All was still.

My racing heartbeat swelled to fill the room. My face and side ached deliciously. *Better than sex.* From the strange and bastard nature of my conception, to the bloody vengeance of my dreams, I knew I was no kind and normal man. But I'd forgotten how deep my stain went. An eerie reflection stared back from a broken crystal shard: harsh and unsmiling, lipstick smeared from Zega's blow, silver scales winking down my cheek. I recognized myself too easily.

"Koré?" Opal gasped. Red shame flushed scales from my skin.

"Careful," I said, and punched through Zega's bedpost. Priceless cedar shattered further. Opal sagged back into me. I wriggled the silk tie from his wrists.

"I'm sorry," I whispered. "You shouldn't have had to see that."

"Sorry? You saved me."

My worst self saved you. And I'd failed my mission. I couldn't deliver Faziz's threat to the unconscious man at my feet. *A letter. Later.* We'd communicate better from separate buildings. *I'll save Zega. Somehow.* His cruelty still hurt. Something real lay between us.

"How'd you get here?" I asked Opal. I'd assigned him to the elderly Lady of the Old Dread, who'd sooner confuse him with her grandson than remember she'd paid to touch him. I wouldn't contract a courtesan with Zega for all the essence in War.

"He offered me double pay for a session. I was stupid." He blew his streaming nose on Zega's sky-blue brocade sheets. "I wanted a secret hoard of money in case you fired me. I fear I'm not working hard enough and you'll fling me to the street if I make a mistake. But you saved me. You struck a *dzaxa* for me."

"The High Kiss is your home," I said. "Lady Dzaroshardze protects us. I try my best to make it a good place."

"I want to believe you," he murmured. "So many people have turned their backs on me."

"The world breaks us." My voice cracked. I hugged him closer. "I know."

With my mother's baton hidden in my sash, I hailed us a *reja* and returned to the Surrender—dropping Opal at the High Kiss, then riding to Dzaro's apartment, where Faziz and Ria couldn't reach me. I bathed, scrawled a report on

Geshge's deal with the envoys, and dropped my lunch—cored peppers holding cucumber salad—on the dining room floor as my sleepless night caught me.

I woke in the bedroom Dzaro kept for me, the sixth bell pealing in the evening sky. As I pushed through the entry curtains into her salon, a raptor-sized black hound planted paws on my shoulders and lavished me with unpracticed kisses.

"Down, Lady," Dzaro called, then turned back to her guard captain. "Thirty thousand *thera* now, a million if you succeed. If you catch the dragon, you bring her to Akizeké, not my brother. Down, Lady!"

The hound had gone to the captain. At Dzaro's command, she dropped to all fours and whined. Slayer, a curly-haired terrier, leapt off his cushion and attacked the captain's skirt. The captain clenched her jaw, bowed to her lady, and left.

I pulled Slayer off her skirt as she passed and let him gnaw at my finger. "Dzaro, you're too wise to waste fortunes chasing dragons." Thirty thousand was five times my profit on the holdspark transmuted from Stonefire's body.

"A dragon might enthrone my brother." She tossed Slayer a dead skink from a golden bowl. "A dragon might break the Treaty of Inversions. We can't ignore these rumors. Our gods died. Their bodies toppled. Their age ended. I learned that as a child, though my teachers didn't explain why and how. Ancient history, I've always thought. A quirky little mystery to fuel conspiracy theories and films. But history draws the blueprint for the skyscrapers we live in today. If myths can turn this succession contest, better it be our hand spinning the wheel."

I'd never been much of a student, in history class or elsewhere. *The dying gods sealed off their district. What were they keeping inside?* The memory of Tamadza's shadow traced shivers up my spine. "I'll leave magical threats to the Fire Weavers." *If only they'd leave me alone.* "Did you read my report? Something big is happening with Geshge. He made a deal with the Lost District envoys—but on the condition it be kept secret. He bought technology, not their public endorsement, for Vashathke's campaign. What technology is worth that much?"

"Maybe he had no choice but to agree. The envoys could be hedging their bets so they can take a better deal if it's offered. We might still have a chance to convince Sadza to endorse Akizeké." She paused. "If you still want Sadza's support. After Stonefire."

"What I want." My fingernails drove into my palms as I fought to stay cool. "I want to keep Vashathke off the throne." All it was safe for me to want. "If we get a copy of the contract, we can see how things stand."

Dzaro sighed. "Geshge ran it through a shell corporation, Ten Staves Holdings. They're incorporated on Armory Street; the paperwork is halfway across War. But there's other ways to find answers. Ten Staves has applied to Rarafashi's visa office for permission to import Lost District technology. Transport it across War, to the Engineering border. There's a public demonstration of the tech tomorrow for the office's approval. We can go see what he's bought, steal a copy of the contract, and sabotage the event to keep Sazdza from leaving until she's on our side."

I grinned, some of the fear draining out of me. I loved a good scheme. "You can get us in as the Lady of the Surrender. But you're far too honest for sabotage, dearest aunt."

"I'm not." The scent of crude soap and ashes hit me as Faziz pushed through the curtains, a basket of gleaming holdfire charges under his arm. *Dzkegé's mercy. He's already found me.*

"Are you stalking me?" I demanded.

"Stalking implies I'm enjoying myself. Posing as Lady Dzaroshardze's manservant to smuggle bombs into a *dzaxa* event is just another day's work."

"An excellent plan." Blood pulsed hot in my neck. His gaze cut like chipped quartz. "So you won't be needing me."

"We might need a good-looking diversion. What if valuable information hides up a *dzaxa* skirt?"

Dzaro chuckled. "Faziz, you made my nephew blush."

I bit my lip. *This isn't a cute blush, aunt.* I'd thought myself clever, bringing Faziz into the conspiracy. But he already knew me too well. Worse, he knew the parts of me I'd hidden away.

Just because I respected his mission to protect Victory Street's poor didn't mean I could trust him. Faziz did his protecting with an unsheathed and undiscriminating blade.

But here he was. To keep him from asking about Zega, I insisted Dusklily, Dzaro's concubine, join us for dinner. He was a shy, pretty boy, more at ease cradling the new collie litter than discussing politics, and his presence kept conversation light. We drank and dined on wild oysters until late in the evening. I barely escaped without adopting a puppy.

The next morning, Dzaro's personal *reja* waited to receive us. I wore a salmon skirt patterned with brown daisies. My hair was combed neat, my trashy makeup swapped for natural blush pinks. "I'll still be recognized for what I am," I told my co-conspirators, who'd chosen the outfit for me. "Who wears florals this century?"

"You look nice," Faziz said, sliding into the driver's seat. He wore his modest black servant's uniform, steel bracers holding knives, thick wool sash hiding an assassin's kit. Mischief lit his elsewise-dull eyes. "The pattern disguises the line of the bombs."

Six holdfire charges, loosely stitched into the fabric of my hem. Light, but heavy with meaning. "I don't need reminding."

"I have the detonator," Dzaro reminded me. "And they're not large bombs. Just diversion-sized."

I bit my tongue and drew the *reja* curtains around me and

my aunt. At least worrying about bombs kept my mind off dragon hunters.

The Lost District's black wedge hovership hung over the Archive's roof. Wispy threads of cloud draped it like a cloak, threatening storm. The carved holdweight faces on its side screamed frozen agony, their sprawled jaws shimmering through the fog, the silver substance itself as adamant as a vault of secrets. I shivered as we drove into its shadow.

A chain winch lifted us into a darkened hallway, where fur-clad servants awaited us. Blue-flamed braziers burned along the walls, washing faces with unearthly pallor. A silent man stepped from the attendant line and waved us forward. Chemical flavor tinted the air.

Be polite. Dzaro's watching. You can't embarrass your patron. I cast down my eyes and donned an insipid smile as we entered the audience hall. Its high, round walls cupped us like the bottom of a pit. A lattice of silver snowflakes glimmered in the dark iron floor. Investors and inspectors whispered nervously among themselves.

"Good morning, Koreshiza," said a *dzaxa* who called me by her son's name as she fucked me. "You're a pleasant sight in these dark halls."

"So thoughtful of your aunt, bringing your bright smile here," said another, who wore raptor teeth in bed. I nodded and let them pat my shoulder as they passed.

With no client buying my time, my aunt and our supposed manservant at my side, I could almost pass as an innocent young *dzaxa* man. Red eyes opened doors. Was this how Geshge lived, an ornament of a different sort? A judge's son, too young to have proven his value, too male to earn automatic regard, too married to draw interest. Welcomed in the highest circles as a curiosity. What I might have been. What my mother had wanted me to be.

From the walls, Ria's mentor Päreshi studied me. *Trying to remember my name?* I smiled at her, switching my language to the common Engineering tongue. "How are you, Honored Teacher? Did you enjoy the state banquet?"

"The one where your father slandered my order and your judge threatened the peace?" She laughed. The flickering blue light painted her bracers green.

"I'm sorry you witnessed that. I greatly respect the Fire Weavers." I widened my eyes and tried to look innocent. I needed to learn more of Ria, who held my secret and my fate in her hands. "Especially Riapáná Żutruro. As her mentor, you must be proud of her achievements and character."

"Ria?" Päreshi snorted. "Too much character. Too much integrity. Not enough discipline or study. Defending her father's leadership of the Fire Weavers, when I'm better qualified for the post. Don't you think so?"

Equivocate. Take no sides and don't anger her. "I think a boy born and raised on Victory Street knows nothing of Engineering's high affairs."

"So pleasant." She flicked my temple with a gloved finger. "So boring."

"Koré!" Ria pulled away from the grey skirts of the judge's visa officials. "I didn't know you were interested in technology commerce."

"He's advertising his own goods. Don't fall for it." Päreshi rolled her eyes. "I should go. Tamadza wants me."

Ria sighed as she left. "I'd swear those two were dating. But Päreshi only likes men."

"Considering how she speaks of your father," I said, "*liking* isn't what she feels for us."

"The last High Master of the Fire Weavers trained Päreshi and my father together. They were like family once. But Päreshi can't forgive my father for earning the leadership, even after he offered amends by letting her mentor me."

Entitlement. I understood that well. "Does Päreshi know my secret?"

"No! She'd take credit for my discovery." She drew out

a flask and drank deep. "Don't worry about her. Once we reveal you, judges and magistrates will lay fortunes at our feet."

Judges and magistrates will send killers to abduct me in the night. I flinched and turned away from her.

Broad, worn hands caught me firmly by the shoulders.

Faziz calmly adjusted my *thevé,* setting the tails of the simple wrap even on either side of my shoulder. His knife-loaded bracer brushed my throat. "Your brooch is loose. Come where the light is better so I can fix it." He pulled me to the rippled iron wall, where blue flame braziers crackled heatless. Not a speck of dust or oil rested on the iron-and-silver floor, as if servants without fingerprints swept the craft nightly. As we ducked free of *dzaxa* attentions, he murmured, "How did Zega take my warning?"

"He's terrified." I pulled on a smile. "He'll resign the end of the month."

"I'm glad to hear that. I hope confronting your ex wasn't too hard. You deserve better than someone who hurts others to make himself feel powerful."

I laughed, hard and bitter. "I deserve nothing. I hurt people. I'm a literal walking bomb."

"I'm not saying you're a good boy." He met my eyes. Past his kohl, I couldn't help noticing how thick his lashes grew. "I'm sure not. It matters what you're bad for." He leant in. His lips brushed my ear; his goatee pricked my bare neck as he whispered, "I know about Opal."

I froze. "You know I failed? And you're not stabbing me?"

"You failed at your goal, not mine. I'll see your ex removed somehow. I like the choice you made."

"I lost my temper," I admitted. "It was a mistake."

"You can only work with what's inside you, Red Eyes," he said, still fiddling with my brooch. He'd shifted its position three times now. "What's in you is fire. Your feelings—even anger—are natural and good. This street needs more anger."

I wished I could believe him. But I'd seen what destruction my anger and want wreaked. "I'm not you," I said. "And I won't become my father."

"I know. It's incredibly annoying. I still can't completely pin you down. At least the *dzaxa* can't either. You look on them with open scorn and all they see are those scarlet Dzaxashigé eyes they've learned to trust."

"The glitter of money and lust can be doubly blinding."

"Glad I'm that much wiser."

"Says the man who's been adjusting my brooch for two whole minutes."

He stared at his hand on my chest, then pulled it back like I'd stung him. I might have laughed, were it not for the shock in his eyes. Like the sudden realization of my beauty had upended gravity beneath him. *That's right, you tattooed hellion. You're not the only one of us with power.*

A wooden staff banged loud on the silver lattice floor. "Gather for the demonstration," called Tamadza. I ducked from Faziz and his danger, murmuring pleasantries as I slid through *dzaxa* crowds.

"Is that their invention?" Dzaroshardze scoffed as I drew near, pointing to the device in the room's center. "Of course Geshge and Vasha would put their hopes in a flower."

Atop a waist-high pedestal sat a lotus blossom carved from a deep purple substance. *But none of the eleven substances are purple.* Two wicked-sharp iron horns rose from the blossom's heart, bringing the odd machine to a woman's height.

"The *Pa-ajgusukisa*," declared Tamadza, lifting a gnarled white wood staff. "The Reclaimer, in your language. These machines let our district survive millennia isolated with only a small store of essence. They can aid War—"

"Sorry I'm late!" Geshge gasped as he entered. Two ranks of Iradz's guards filed in behind him. "First we had to nab a test subject, then—"

His eyes found me. He froze. I held my breath until a stranger's laughter broke the silence.

"This is a public event." I tried to smile. Forestall a dramatic scene. "Our aunt brought me. We're family."

"Only by our father's stupidity." Uneven pink blotches spread across his cheeks. "I'm the judge's son. You're a whore who eats ass for breakfast. There's no true kinship between us."

"You're right. How silly of me, to believe we could be brothers." My anger boiled free. He had every reason to hate me—but he called me "whore" like it branded me. "I'm hotter than you. Smarter than you. Brighter than you. And your wife enjoyed fucking me."

"Take him!" Geshge hissed at his guard. "In Iradz's name, throw him over the edge!"

My spine tensed. The guards drew their batons. Dzaro stepped before me.

"What is this?" Tamadza shouted. "You may be my guest of honor, Geshge—an agent of your respected magistrate—but I decide who gets thrown off the ship. Forget your petty quarrel. You and your brother are family. Soon, you'll realize the importance of what binds you." She smiled at me. "Koreshiza Brightstar. Welcome."

I smiled at Stonefire's killer. Guilt at my faithlessness twisted my stomach.

Iradz's guards dragged a chained prisoner up to the machine. A circular brand glittered on her cheek. *Unrepentant.* Guests turned their heads from her. Dzaro spat on the floor. *Convicted of an essence-destroying crime. Sentenced to tithe. Refused.*

You didn't speak with the Unrepentant. You didn't acknowledge their existence. Across the city-planet, the crude circle marked those who withheld their essence from justice. Total isolation torturing convicts into tithing their fines.

"This wine merchant sold a poisoned cask to a rival,"

Tamadza said. "Murdered her entire family. When sentenced to titles the threefold essence of the victims, she refused. And yet she lives, debt unpaid, because she hoards essence too precious to destroy."

"The plague killed them," shouted the prisoner. "Eighty people died in the outbreak!"

Her anger rang a chord in my bones. *A street-broken soul, guilt decided by a thousand factors, none of them truth. The justice of War.* To stop myself from meeting her eyes, I bit my lip until I tasted blood.

"My district was not the only victim when the gods fell," Tamadza continued. "War lowered her weapons. Sacrificed her glory to preserve the world's essence store. Now convicts live to mock you. The districts you conquered hold you in debt."

The guards flung the Unrepentant forward. Tamadza spun her staff. A purple haze of living shadow rose from the substance flower and launched itself into the prisoner's chest. She convulsed, thrashing violently—then brightened. Wild hope filled her eyes.

Tamadza drove the point of her staff through the prisoner's spine.

Screams echoed off metal walls, my own among them. Dzaro's fingers tightened around my wrist. Päreshi dragged Ria back before the young Fire Weaver could leap in.

"How dare you?" shouted a *dzaxa*. "She still held essence!"

"You'll have your due." Tamadza circled her staff once more. The metal horns atop the blossom vibrated, a high, keening note.

I stared at the dead woman in her pool of blood. *Essence. All that matters.* I wanted to flee, scream in Tamadza's face, tell the whole world this was wrong. *You murderous little hypocrite.* How could I judge Tamadza with blood on my own hands?

Behind me, Faziz tensed like iron and reached for his

sword. I grabbed his arm and pinned him safe beside me.

"You can't help her," I whispered. "You'll be killed."

"I hate being part of this," he growled.

I shook his arm, harder than I should, and felt him wince. "Go while they're distracted." I pulled the false lining from inside my skirt and draped silk-wrapped bombs in his hands. "Plant the charges. I'll have Dzaro blow them in ten minutes. While everyone panics, look for a copy of Geshge's contract."

Something flashed in his eyes—murder, fear, self-loathing. Emotions I recognized but didn't understand. Faziz, more than any of us, was a bystander here. "You're still trying to ally with them?"

"I'm going to figure out what they plotted with Geshge," I said. "And then I'm going to ruin their whole motherfucking day."

A grin played in the corners of his lips and died. "Right," he said, and vanished down a hall, the corner of his black wool skirt flowing away like neat midnight.

I felt colder without him. The vibrating Reclaimer twisted shadow around it. The humming note reached its peak.

The dead hand lifted.

Dzaro cursed and dragged me toward the wall. My heart skipped. The dead woman's fingers fluttered like butterfly wings.

"Geshge Akéakireze Dzaxashigé!" Tamadza said. "Step forward!"

My brother took a single, shaking step towards the body. "*Dzuchab!*"

The hand locked around my brother's ankle. The air fluttered with the pressure of a thousand beating hearts. Darkness swam over Geshge's skin. He gasped, in ecstasy or pain.

The hand dropped. The crowd gasped and murmured as the prisoner's body fell, still and dull.

I stared at my brother. Fresh essence lent his round chin a

childlike charm, and his beige skirt now seemed attractively simple. But the purple circles beneath his eyes set my spine prickling. Those hadn't been there when he'd arrived.

"Once the target is revived," Tamadza said, "the operator has complete control and can make them tithe to anyone. With Reclaimers, essence can be harvested from a battlefield. Peace becomes unnecessary. You see, *dzaxa*? Our districts are natural allies. As partners, we can both return to greatness."

"Dzkegé's mercy," Dzaro said. "This is wrong."

Ten thousand years of peace. Five hundred thousand people had drowned when Varjthosheri the Dragon-Blessed had broken the Scholar fleet. We'd executed eight million prisoners while we'd held the Engineering District. I didn't idolize my genocidal Dzaxashigé ancestors, but I'd never seen their atrocities beyond in the abstract.

But Dzaro spoke true. The wrongs of the past lived in the flesh of today.

"This is necromancy!" Päreshi declared. "The magic that slew the gods. Friends we may be, Tamadza, but I won't stand for this!"

"I'm sorry to hear—" Tamadza started, but Päreshi cut her off.

"Come, Ria. We're leaving. Fire Weavers must stand against darkness." She spun on a booted heel and marched out.

"See you soon," Ria mouthed at me as she followed her mentor. Her easy confidence had dimmed. Her grip left fingerprints in her metal flask.

I winced, fighting to swallow my fear. *Maybe if the other Fire Weavers knew how much she drank, they wouldn't believe her report about a dragon...* But my problems felt small beside a second murder and a growing storm. "Dzaro?" I pressed close to her elbow. "Wait ten minutes, then detonate the bombs."

"Shit." Dzaro fumbled in her sash. "The detonator is missing."

It must have fallen in the *reja*. My stomach dropped. "We can't let them leave—can't let them get what they want. This is bad, this is very bad and wrong—"

"I know." She laid a steady hand on my arm. "Fuck Sadza's endorsement. Let's go show the ambassador that our family is a bad investment. Follow my lead."

We pushed to the front of the crowd. Geshge turned from the visa officials to fix us with a dead stare. "You should be ashamed of yourselves. Embarrassing our family with this display."

"I know you feel I robbed you of the Surrender, Geshge, but you should blame your wife." Dzaro sighed. "I took the opportunity I needed to rise. I'm sorry it hurt you."

"I'm not," I added. *Snap at the bait, Geshge.* If he lost control of his emotions, he'd show the envoys he couldn't be relied on. The chemical, cool stillness of the hovership's recycled air filled my lungs and made dredging up venom easy. "No one ever spared me pain, Geshge. Why should they spare you? Because you're such a good boy? Because you're a judge's son?"

His voice trembled. "You think it's easy, being Rarafashi's son?"

"Easier than being the son of her rival," I said, "with all her power bent against you. I don't know what Vashathke's told you about me and our family, but you must have realized he lies."

"I grew up with our father. Every morning, he'd tell me what I'd done wrong. Paired the wrong *thevé* with my skirt, danced with the wrong *dzaxa,* smiled too much or too little. Even as a child, I forever failed him. Even though nothing truly makes him smile." He lowered his crimson eyes. "He compares me to you. Always asking why I don't have your looks, confidence and business sense. 'Koreshiza would get this right,' he tells me. Every day. So yes, I know he lies. I am not your lesser shadow."

Father likes me better. Some sick part of me leapt in joy—but I wouldn't fall for Vashathke's ruse again. "It's a game, Geshge. He loves neither of us. He wants us divided and hungry for his approval."

Geshge said nothing. Bit his lip for a heartbeat, deep in thought. Then he said, "I don't know if I hate you or him more. But I do agree Father will do anything to control us."

Us. My heart leapt at that note of kinship, his essence-rich voice in natural harmony with mine, our eyes and curling lips a match. *Sharp, monstrous minds behind silken courtesy. Brothers in truth.* "You had an Unrepentant killed for your demonstration. To help the Lost District import their machines for Vashathke's purposes. Why?"

"For Vashathke?" Geshge's lips parted in a confused ring.

"Honored guests!" Tamadza banged her staff on the floor. All turned to her—and the charges blew.

Concussions swam through the silver-snowflake-engraved floor. Servants gasped and tumbled. Geshge and I locked arms, holding each other balanced, as blue-tinted smoke blasted out of a corridor. The scent of burnt amber washed the chemical air.

"Engine malfunction!" Dzaro shouted, clearly inspired, to the visa officials. "Deny the import application. The ship's unsafe to fly across the district."

"No!" My brother pulled away from me and scuttled to Tamadza's side. "We have to send the shipment quickly!"

I'm so fast forgotten. My brother's absence felt like a hole in the air beside me. *Faziz,* I thought, heart sinking. Whoever had found the detonator—*found, and not announced it?*—had pulled the trigger at least a minute before ten. Had he cleared the blast radius in time? Where was he?

"It's no engine malfunction," Tamadza said. "The ship runs on holdspark, not holdfire! I'll investigate, and—"

"You'll investigate in a holding pattern," said the ancient head official, glaring through steel-trimmed glasses. "Your

Reclaimer may be safe to import, but your ship isn't."

"The Reclaimer is safe?" I gasped. No one heard my outrage.

"Welcome to the War District, *dzaxa* Tamadza," said another bureaucrat. "*Dzaxa* Geshge is most fortunate to do business with you."

My brother beamed at the compliment. My stomach churned as the bloody pool brushed his hems. Was I so love-hungry I'd embrace a brother who slaughtered prisoners in the name of War?

"Evacuate the ship!" the head official declared. "Honorable envoys, please do make repairs. We can revisit our ruling if you show the ship is skyworthy."

"Please!" Geshge's voice sank deep with fear. "I need to get the envoys cleared. Everything depends on me!"

Dzaro took my elbow. "Let's go. Before we're questioned. I'll write to my Warmwater friends and see if I can get their ambassador for Akizeké. All she cares about is patent law, not murder machines."

"Faziz," I insisted, digging in my heels. "He's—"

A wall panel dissolved open. Faziz stepped through, carrying a thick folder. I bit down a relieved sigh as his dark eyes met mine. *Stupidly* relieved. I'd told him things about myself I'd never told anyone, but that didn't make us close. He'd just asked the right questions to unlock my secret selves.

"You're not hurt?" I asked. "Dzaro lost the detonator. Something—or someone—else triggered the bombs."

He shrugged. "I asked for ten minutes as cushion. I didn't plan to use them all. I stacked the charges and went snooping."

"And?"

"I couldn't find the contract, but I grabbed this off a table. Check it out."

Papers. Mostly meaningless, covered in script from a language I didn't know. One held a map of the ship, though, with arrows illustrating various paths. A single phrase, seven glyphs long, had been copied many times in a shaking hand. *A password?*

"Let's not discuss this in public." Dzaro pushed us both down the hall toward the lift. "But well done, both of you."

We've only come halfway. We'd uncovered the device Geshge—and, through him, my father—sought to buy from the envoys. We'd prevented them from bringing it to the border, and hopefully sown enough discord to stave off Sadza publicly endorsing Vashathke for the judgeship. But their ultimate goal eluded me like the rumble of some great beast in the city-planet's foundation, weaving through Jadzia's ancient depths.

And I'd given up seeking an alliance with those murderers. Which meant I had a line I wouldn't cross, and Vashathke could shape even the finest of lines into spears pointed against me.

INTERLUDE: AGE TWENTY-TWO
The Bold Blades, Subbasement, The Palace of Ten Billion
Swords

12th *Thze,* Year 88 Rarafashi

*"Whores lie to steal your essence and gold.
Approach with open eyes: trust them with
nothing. Save affection for your husband."—
Sexual Education for Girls, Armory Street Civic
University Press*

MY CLIENT ROLLED off me with a satisfied grunt. She didn't look at me as she dressed. I lay panting on the mattress, trying to disappear into the tangled sheets.

When she was gone, I checked myself in the tarnished mirror. My bruises were already fading. Fresh fire in my eyes said I'd taken extra essence. I'd pleased her well. *Worth it. Brightness will let me enter Vashathke's world and bring him down.*

But I wasn't brightening fast enough, and my heart ached at waiting to rise. Once I'd washed and composed myself, I went to my pimp's office.

"You're done early," Fi-ththako said. "Was your client left dry?"

"It's fine." I bit back a gasp as I sat. She didn't care for my pains. "I was only contracted to the seventh bell."

Fi-ththako glared at me. She was a beautiful woman, copper curls long, frame as thin as a baton. She'd worked at the Bold Blades before purchasing the brothel, and had the essence to show for it, but none of the sympathy one might expect from a fellow sex worker.

I gave her my scrawled calculations. Leant forward and tried to look assertive. "I earn twenty percent more than the other boys. The income I bring is comparable with the women, and I take the clients everyone refuses."

"You're a greedy whore. What's your point?"

"I want the VIP clients." For the next step of my plan, I needed bedside gossip from the floors above.

She considered. "I have a VIP client scheduled next week. She's sensitive about her new body. Normally, I'd take her myself, but she requested a man. Show me I can trust you."

My heart leapt. "Thank you. I won't let you down."

For a week, I took no clients who'd leave visible marks and slept full nights instead of slinking through drug dens for thirdhand court gossip. The afternoon of the VIP appointment, I painted silver spirals round my eyes, washed my chest and ass with vanilla oil, and donned a flimsy, replaceable skirt of wine red, in case my client tore it off.

But I hadn't learned her name.

The stairs outside my bedchamber creaked under her weight. The smell of grapefruit and orange blossom hit hard as she entered: a tall figure, her *fajix* torn, a glass of wine in each hand. Scarlet eyes, drunk and laughing, washed me over. Her high cheekbones and upturned nose matched mine.

I pressed back against the pillows, jaw agape. A full minute passed before recognition clicked in her eyes. "Oh, shit," she slurred. "Shit, shit, shit."

"You're the magistrate's sister." The trans one. The one Vashathke had just cruelly disowned. Everyone in the Palace of Ten Billion Swords knew the gossip—Vashathke owned the building, after all—but I'd never expected to meet Dzaroshardze Faraakshigé Dzaxashigé. Certainly not like this. *I have family. I'm not alone.*

"Who are you?" Dzaro demanded. "How do you exist?"

My cheeks lit aflame. My breath caught. Right. My family would only see me as living shame. Twisted evidence of corrupt choices. "Remember Briza? Guard captain in your household, older woman, grey-brown curls?"

"Dzkegé's tits. My brother's an idiot." She kicked a chair. "Now who will I fuck?"

"What's wrong, *dzaxa?*" Fi-ththako stormed in. "Koré! Attend our guest!"

"She's my aunt. My father's sister."

"Dzkegé's tits," Fi-ththako said. "I suspected, but... gods. You're Vashathke's bastard."

"I'm sorry." I cringed away. Not far enough.

"Selfish slut!" Her hand cracked across my face. "This brothel is my livelihood! You think the magistrate won't learn I'd sold his seed? You've jeopardized me and the boys!"

My heart dropped. *You monster. You didn't consider that. It's good you drive everyone away before your presence poisons them.*

"How dare you strike my kin?" Dzaro shouted, and punched Fi-ththako in the jaw. The pimp stood unmoved, bright as a rising planet. Dzaro cursed, shaking out her hand—she only shone as bright as I. "Come, nephew. I'll help you from this trashheap."

You could have helped more by not making a scene. Anger like concrete filled Fi-ththako's eyes. *I'm fired. And I'm bleeding from her rings.*

I knew better than to resist a *dzaxa.* I let Dzaro take my hand, and she didn't let go until we reached her *reja.* Her whip cracked across the raptors' backs. Brass music chased us up the stairs, from the Palace's scrap metal undercellars

141

to ground-floor market atriums lined by hundred-meter-high windows.

People stared at me as we rode down a hall. Servants swept red-eyed children from my path. Young couples pointed and laughed as they strolled the steel-blade floor. *Stranger. Outsider. Harlot.* My aunt didn't slow until we had passed the hall's sparring courts, when she stopped the *reja* and stabled the raptors in stalls divided by electrum mesh. It was a wealthy corridor she'd brought me to, but not a welcoming one.

"Fucking Vashathke," Dzaro fumed as we entered her apartment. Furniture, styled from simple plush cushions to elaborate scorpion-shaped recliners in Warmwater fashion, packed tight the room. I perched on a stool and nodded. "Playing the perfect, pure, pretty son whilst you ran about below."

Anger. She could be a useful ally. I fished. "He never told you about me?"

"Not a word." She passed me a mug of dark, hoppy beer. "Drink. It'll help."

With unemployment and homelessness? But I drank. I couldn't insult her, and I didn't want to be sober.

"Where are you from?" Dzaro sat in a high-backed chair carved like a bronto's neck. "You have a Lower accent. Briza raised you downstreet?"

She'd noticed? I winced. To infiltrate my father's world, I needed Modern Jiké to peak harsh from my tongue.

Drinking deep, I reached for a plausible story. Enough truth to be verified. Enough falsehood so she'd like me. My safety depended on showing what she wanted to see. "My mother loved Vashathke once. He wounded her deeply when he married Rarafashi." All true. "I grew up in Lady Fidzjakovik's Prizeheron household. She betrothed me to her heir, Iradz. But my father learned of me..."

Dzaro rubbed her chin. "And conspired to end the betrothal."

Close enough. I nodded.

"He's a shit." She squeezed my hand. "Stay here as long as you need. There's a bedroom—"

"Thank you, but I won't fuck my aunt!" The words leapt free in a fearful, jumbled mess.

She pulled back. "Dzkegé's mercy! A spare bedroom, I meant. I wouldn't... I know what it's like when a woman feels... entitled."

"What do you want from me?"

Dzaro cuddled an elderly, short-legged dog. The steel walls wrapped too tight about us. Two months had passed since her brother ousted her from Skygarden, and she hadn't discarded her extra furniture. Still waiting for her brother to call her home. "I want a family again."

Another wound carved at my father's hands. I'd empathize—but I was too vulnerable to risk that. Dzaro was *dzaxa*. She couldn't understand my life and struggles. I had to note her still-aching heartbreak as a weak point I could strike to protect myself. "Okay. I'll stay."

So began my time in Dzaro's household. The next day, after she left for work, I discovered she'd given me the only bedroom. Eager to prove useful, I organized her library, polished her armor, and brushed dog hair from cushions. To buy dinner, I went to the atrium market.

Merchants hawked skull-sized oranges. Giant onions perfumed the air. I passed ices carved like tree leaves, bronto marinades in fist-shaped jars, and raw sashimi twined up crystalized ginger sticks. My neck prickled as skeptical eyes tracked me.

"If you're going to skulk, whore, buy something." A guard flicked her baton at me. I leapt away and nearly knocked down a serving boy.

Quietly, I cursed my own foolishness. If I wanted Dzaro's protection, I had to play a perfect demure *dzaxa*, fallen in circumstance but not in soul. Pleasing her like I pleased my clients, playing a different role and playing it every hour. *The perfect nephew. The boy from the Prizeheron.* A boy who'd cook and make his beloved aunt smile.

Dzaro came home to burnt squash and half-breaded chicken. She washed it down with rosé and pronounced my effort excellent.

Over the next few weeks, I built a domestic routine and carefully explored the hall. The boys who frequented the sparring courts adopted me, eager to hear my downstairs gossip while their girlfriends sparred. Some silly part of me longed to join the women and practice the baton skills I'd abandoned, even if doing so would raise painful red memories of my mother and Gei-dzeo. I wanted to feel strong and capable of protecting myself. But to fit into this world, I had to break the habit of wanting.

My father does this, I told myself, fighting to follow conversations on movies I'd missed, pet tigers and cheetahs I couldn't care for, fabrics I couldn't afford. *So must I. Every hour of my life, every word I speak, needs to please these people. I'll get vengeance—I'll be safe—once I make this part of my soul.*

Then, one morning, a visitor knocked on Dzaro's door.

Iradz Akéakireze Dzaxashigé had grown into adulthood as sharp as a knife. The gold of her tanned brow matched the *fajix* holding her small breasts. Mischief glinted in her strawberry eyes; brass-blond hair fell to her shoulders. Beside her, I felt pale and unkempt, a whore who hadn't stepped outside in years.

"*Dzaxa.*" I bowed.

"Lady Iradz," she corrected. "I won the deed to the Surrender in a card game. My new husband and I move in tomorrow. But I heard you were here, and I couldn't leave the Palace without visiting my first love."

Your first toy. "I'm honored by your visit." I stilled my trembling fingers by pouring wine. "Tell me about this card game."

144

Iradz drank deep, spinning a tale of illegal swords and high-stakes gambling. I feigned interest, planning my reaction when she inevitably propositioned me. I'd have to give her what she wanted. I'd need to make that work for me.

"How's sex work going? Not well, it seems. You're duller than when I last saw you."

Zega's scar tugged on my heart. "I paid to learn my craft. Now I never let my own essence escape. I'm the best sex worker on Victory Street."

She laughed. "The best? Let's wager. If you make me give up essence, I'll deed you a rent-free suite in the Surrender. If I make you give me essence, you'll become my concubine."

Adulthood hadn't made her subtle. Iradz hated other people playing with her toys. Our parents had promised her my body, and she'd come to claim it. Better to gift her an hour of me than risk *dzaxa* anger.

Staking my freedom risked everything. But I didn't trust Dzaro's charity. My aunt, like any *dzaxa,* would withdraw her shelter once she glimpsed the true wrongness inside me. I needed my own place to live and work. And I'd never desire Iradz enough to tithe to her. "Done."

She grinned and kissed me. "Let's roll dice."

We retreated to my borrowed bedroom. Iradz pulled toys from her sash, gold-dusted and finished with meticulous skill. Some I'd used. Some I'd never dared touch.

"My weakling husband froze when I showed him these." She licked an anal plug. "He's not like you."

"*Dzaxa* boys don't speak of these." I stripped, rolling over onto black silk bedsheets. "They're supposed to be sexy but naïve. Unaware they can control War's women with charm."

"Are you charming me now?" She trailed the wet plug down my back. Holdspark buzzed. My eyes flew wide as she forced it in. My world narrowed to a sharp, pressing point beneath my tailbone.

"You're here, aren't you?" I tried to play light. In control. Fearless.

"I'm here because I want my stubborn boy back." Her hands pinioned my hips. Her mouth closed on the sparking plug's base. Every press of her tongue sent it spinning, tracing lines of fire through my core. "What happened to you and your mother was awful. I'm sorry. I should have protected you."

"What?" I gasped. Iradz, *apologizing?*

She flipped me over, meeting my eyes. "I still love you. Give me your body and I'll make you whole."

It's a game, I told myself. But what I said was a soft, questioning "Really?"

"You trust me?" When I nodded, she bound my wrists and eyes. "Pretend you're back in the Prizeheron. You're mine, you have babies of your own, and your mother is alive beside you. See what might have been. See yourself as normal and safe. No stain inside you. Only joy."

The image needed nothing more to seduce me. Her arms secured me like warm blankets, her kiss a soothing promise. My world pinched into short, sharp nothings. I could believe.

"Mine." A blade licked my nipple. I gasped as the blood ran free. "You're mine, I love you, and all's well." A hot curtain rolled down my chest as she mounted me. Our hips thrust together in perfect slow rhythm. "It's okay, dearest. We have all the time in the world."

Pressure built in my groin. My tangled, monstrous self floated away. *Good.* My self had never brought me much happiness. Better to let her guide me, even into a lie. Into the fantasy of being good, of doing right, like my mother had wanted. Pleasing others as my true nature, not my sick game.

Not aching from the inside out.

"Easy. You're almost there. Let's come together." The blade kissed my stomach. My peak slammed me like a crashing wave. Iradz moaned, clenching tight. Holding me limp between her legs. Whispering my name like a trophy.

You can't trust her, said some small part of me. *She abandoned you once.*

"Don't cry, sweetheart." She gently brushed tears from my cheeks. "I'm here. I won't ever leave you. You're perfect."

Such compassion. Love undid me. Essence slipped from my raw and naked skin. I curled in a ball, weeping like my spine would shatter.

"You little fool." She stroked my hair like I'd pet Dzaro's dog. "It's okay. You're mine now. I'll get you a collar and we can do this every night."

Her voice held no joke. No possible escape. *Dzkegé, have mercy!* Iradz owned a building. Dzaro wouldn't challenge a lady for me.

Iradz could and would drag me out.

A sick, desperate laugh escaped me. There were so many lives worth wanting, happy, wonderful lives, though they felt miles from me. Life as Iradz's property wasn't one of them. *I can't deserve that, no matter what's wrong with me.* I had revenge before me, the locus of my soul. I couldn't destroy my father from Iradz's leash.

"Double or nothing." I pulled the plug free, covering my wounded nipple with my hand. "A high-risk game. Don't offer a suite in the Surrender—offer the whole deed."

"Wager my position?" Intrigue sparked in her gaze. "What do you stake in return?"

"My heart." I drew myself up to my full, lovely height. "You've won my servitude. Not my love. You'll always look in my eyes and see a thousand women had me first."

The mention of competition inflamed her. "Done. But we'll battle on my field." Her baton flashed free. "To the sparring courts."

I had no other choice. We dressed and marched down the hall, my worried, wounded soul running through my short list of options. I hadn't held a baton in years. Iradz was a small target, had professional training, and knew my weaknesses.

But she didn't know the monster I concealed.

The three training *dzaxa* graciously stepped aside for Iradz, although I earned concerned looks. "I'm consenting," I murmured, and one handed me her baton as she left. It didn't feel strong, like my mother's had. I'd left that—and most of myself—with Zega.

Spectators murmured. Iradz grinned, both murderous and warm.

"It's hard to make you fall in love," she said, and charged.

Our batons cracked together, fierce and furious. My wrist stung from the impact. I stumbled away, blocking her blows at awkward, unnatural angles. My back hit the court wall. I crouched. Instinct drove my baton up to block a downward stoke.

Instead, Iradz stabbed. The electric *shiki* cracked on my wounded nipple. My spine went rigid. My scream became a gasped sob. With a foot on my chest, Iradz knocked me into the dust.

Disbelieving whispers rose from the stands.

"I like your whimper." She leant in close, breathing on my ear. "We'll bring a *shiki* into bed once I tame you."

The knife I'd palmed from her toy kit winked into my hand. I swung. Flesh split.

Iradz reeled backwards, clutching her stomach. Her breath hissed sharp and short. I'd hit a lung. "You fucking whore!"

My battered body screamed as I flung myself at her, hammering blows with soul-desperate fury. Her chest heaved, arms fluttering, as she blocked. I felt no remorse at the proof of her pain. The monster in me struck until her breath ran out.

Iradz collapsed. Her hands flashed up in surrender. I levied two swift kicks into her ribcage. Victory's flush burned my cheeks. "We had a bet. I'm owed a deed."

"Fuck you," she gasped. "The bet doesn't stand."

The gathered boys murmured. A woman spoke near the court's edge, looking up from the companion she bandaged. "Don't complain, *dzaxa*. Bright as you are, that hole will heal in a day. We see the marks you left on the boy. Pay up."

"It was a joke!" Iradz stood, swaying. "I staked the deed to the Surrender on it."

"You're the Lady of the Surrender," said another woman. "The deed is yours to stake. You'd cheat a boy you beat half to death? I wouldn't stand to see my sons so poorly treated."

"He's a whore!" Iradz bellowed. "You'd have me name him a lady's equal?"

"Lord Whore," one woman joked. "Why not? He'd brighten up the street."

"Bad enough you'd beat a boy," called another. "But breaking your word?"

"Women like you are why men don't feel safe on the street." A curly-haired *dzaxa* cracked her knuckles. "We won't stand for women like you among us."

The women blockaded Iradz, their sparking *shiki* pointing in at her chest. Iradz looked from face to face and found no friendly eye. Grimacing poison, she drew parchment from her skirt and scribbled a writ.

"Welcome, Lord Whore." A woman passed me the scrawled deed. "Find us if you need witnesses to push this through court."

I clutched the parchment tight. They'd forget this gesture when their boyfriends and husbands weren't watching. When they stopped and considered the wrongness of the anger I'd unleashed. I couldn't hold what they'd given me.

But I could make their chivalrous impulse matter.

"A building for me?" Dzaro said when I presented her with the deed.

"I'll need my own suite and investment funds. I want to start a business, not rule. You're more fit for the post." She was Dzaxashigé. Legitimate and known. No one would deny a magistrate's sister. And I gained a base—and an ally—to move against Vashathke.

"I'll take it, but... did Iradz say why she was at the Palace? She married Geshge. Your brother."

"What?" I whispered, not bright enough to quickly tally gains and losses. I imagined a brother I'd never met. A wedding I should have celebrated.

"Lady Fidzjakovik has disinherited Iradz for her recklessness. She's gone from the future owner of two buildings, a candidate for judgeship, to... nothing. They'll live off Rarafashi's charity."

That struck deep. I yearned to apologize to my unknown brother, but nothing could fix this. Fucking his wife. Stealing his future. *I'm sorry, Geshge. There's a monster in me, driving all from my mind but vengeance and selfish gain. It's good you don't know me. I'd certainly hurt you worse.*

"You look upset," my aunt said. "You know you can tell me anything, right?"

Zega had once promised me the same. "I'm fine, Lady Dzaroshardze." I donned an easy smile, the sort belonging to a passive, friendly, fuckable whore. A mask and a shield. I needed its protection more than anything.

CHAPTER EIGHT
Lower markets of the Surrender

18th Kafi, Year 92 Rarafashi

"The Jedzge Principle states no compensation is legally required to a victim of sexual assault, as the transfer of the assailant's essence is compensation enough. Undoing this precedent is my life's work."—Vashethshareki Tharazadzji Dzaxashigé, first male chair of the Armory Street bar

"Some Dzaxashigé use the cloistering of Scholar men to counter our pro-equality arguments. 'They can't freely walk the streets! Be glad you're allowed to be educated and own property.' But a whole building dying in fire does not argue you should let the small rag on your oven burn."— Lord Rezadzeré of Towergarden, commencement address at Towergarden Men's College

LIQUOR SALES WERE strictly controlled in the Surrender, and we'd lost our vendor after Stonefire's murder. To find a replacement, I endured the two-hour *reja* trip to the import market in the Surrender's bent knee—an exhausting venture that would nevertheless keep me away from the High Kiss long enough to miss another of Ria's daily visits.

She's ever earnest, honest-eyed, but I can't trust her. Yet when she came to ask about dragons, the words "fuck off" froze anxious in my throat. I had no skill for confrontation. Worse, I needed her if I was to keep my promise to Akizeké. My instincts to please warred with my dark urge to scream in faces. I went too soft until I snapped and went dangerously hard.

Maybe the letter I'd written Zega would save him. I'd informed him of Faziz's threat in my most pointed prose. But threats only mattered from a position of power. Against Ria, I had no power at all.

The first liquor merchant ordered me out, but the second happily sold to scandal-ridden brothels. Her price was high, but she offered free returns on unopened casks, and I paid with a wink and a smile.

Daylight still filtered through sparkling sandstone windowslits when I stepped back into the bell atrium of the kneeling man's skirt. The beats of a drum symphony boomed off twisted plastic ramps. Children darted up and down ten stories of stalls. I crossed the ground floor, tried on a stack of chunky necklaces, palmed a plum off a grocer's stall, and, behind my back, flung it at a child tormenting a puppy. *Dzaxa* unfairly shunned the poorer, lower stories of great buildings as dangerous, but even though my current address sat above the 300th story, the bustle and woven music of this place made it feel like home.

The greatest danger lay in what the *dzaxa* sent here.

I was debating how my employees would react if I bought them nailpolish—would I accidentally invite them to be my friends if I picked special colors for each one?—when I caught the scent of chili-rubbed bronto flank, promising grease, fat, and all my favorite sins. Even better, no one I knew could judge my self-indulgence. I ducked into the maze of plastic slats, looking for the restaurant.

Food. Food. They had to be spit-roasting it, for the scent to carry so far. *Is that bourbon I smell?* The subtle salt of fried crab balls joined the medley. *There!* I slid into a narrow alley. Garbage bins and a locked door greeted me. A large white cat looked up from grooming its paw. The scent wafted through wall slats. *Wrong entrance,* I realized, and turned.

"If it isn't the stupidest whore on Victory Street!"

I froze. Three pale, compact guards blocked the alley entrance. The one who'd spoken flourished her baton in a mock bow. Zega's personal insignia marked the left breast of her *fajixa.*

Dzkegé's mercy. I'd known Zega had grown monstrous past childhood cruelty. He'd driven people from their homes, sundered families, and ruined thousands of lives. But I'd never charted his violence onto me.

I'd been a fool, thinking myself immune. And I'd bitterly pay.

"Sorry." I tried to sound agreeable. "Enquiries about my schedule and rates should be sent to the High Kiss. Unless you also came for dinner?"

"Shut up! Nothing pisses me off like a chatty slut!" The speaker darted forward. Her baton slammed into my abdomen. The world flashed red. I doubled over, gasping for air.

"I'm sorry!" My hands flew up in submission. "What I did after the banquet was wrong. Tell Zega I got his message!"

"If you knew it was wrong, why'd you send another letter to threaten him?" She laughed. "Stupid boy. The message is just starting."

She lunged. My instincts alight, I spun into her swing,

knocking back her *shiki* with my wrist. Foolish exhilaration twined with fear. As the other guards darted forward, I glimpsed an opening and dove towards the alley's mouth, essence fueling my speed—

Fists of lighting caught my shoulder and side. Electricity arched, forcing back my head, squeezing my heart. My jaw locked against pain.

"Cry, whore!" Heavy arms flung me against the wall. I reeled, thoughts skipping, fingers twitching for the baton I didn't carry. My blind kick sank into a guard's hip. She staggered, cursed—and drove her *shiki* into my groin.

A biting tide of fear and humiliation seized me. I screamed. My eyes rolled backwards. My knees buckled.

"Teach him his place, Crusher. Break that pretty face."

A booted foot flew. I rolled, taking it on the side of my head. Bile churned in my throat.

"He's hard! Take him! It's the cheapest you'll ever have him for!"

They're going to beat and rape me. My thoughts swam with stars, but that much was painfully clear. *Go away inside. Get it over with.*

A *shiki* punched my chest. Lighting lanced. A rib cracked.

You're mine. You belong to me. Iradz's old promise echoed in my ears. *My beautiful Koré,* Gei-dzeo had sworn. *I'll protect you.* But even my mother wasn't here for me any longer. I was the only one who could protect Opal. Stonefire. Myself. *Dzkegé's mercy, I want to protect myself. I want to be selfish, even if only abominable men fight back!*

Anger ignited. Talons rippled into existence. I sank them into the nearest guard's thigh.

Pale flesh parted under my fingertips. She stiffened. Screamed. *There!* My fist tightened. With all my strength, I tore. Blood burst.

"Gods!" She collapsed against the wall, fumbling to hold shut the wound. I dove for the next guard. She swung for my head. Frantic strength let me catch her baton. My free hand opened her throat.

A whistle. A numbing sting on my wrist, and my head swam. Scales armored my breast and abdomen in living silver. The second *njiji* dart bounced off.

"You'll pay for that!" The last guard pulled a rusty bronto cleaver from the kitchen trash. "I'll cut off those pretty hands and drag you to Vashathke in chains! I'll rape you and make a dragon child of my own!"

Ice jolted down my spine. She stood between me and the alley's exit. My limbs were already stiffening from the *njiji* sedative. *A baton*—but the batons lay by her feet, and she was advancing, weaving loops with the rusty blade. I couldn't get the height of me around her in this cramped alley, and my scales couldn't stop a blade. "Fuck you," I spat, ready to go down defiant. "Now and forever, fuck you and your ilk!"

The cleaver flashed. I hoisted a bin lid like a shield—and then the guard froze. Blood spurted from her gasping mouth. She fell, eyes staring at nothing.

A familiar voice shouted my name. I listened to nothing but my pounding heart as I ran.

Faster. Faster. My sandals pounded on plastic. Shouts rose. Arms reached for me. I shied, clasping bloody talons to my chest. My stomach roiled as the sedative swept on.

A hundred meters through the maze, strong hands seized my neck and dragged me backwards.

"Hello, big brother," said Geshge. Then he slammed my head into the wall.

Wood shattered. The world flashed black. Tight, terrible pressure built in my throat. Talons carved bloody rents in his wrists as I pulled desperately at them.

My brother stood unmoved, fierce and deadly as a hunting cat. His eyes simmered, molten fury above purple rings. "The shadow promised anything I wanted. The throne of Victory Street. Iradz's buildings restored. Babies and a loving wife.

155

Everything you took from me. But I wanted to see you beg."

"Still... brothers," I gasped. My lungs screamed for air. The sedative towed me toward darkness. "I didn't know she'd married you... never meant to hurt you... Geshge, please!"

He answered with a wild, triumphant grin.

Then his eyebrows lifted. His lips parted in an O of surprise. His hands fell away.

A familiar sword protruded from the center of his chest.

Faziz pivoted and flung Geshge's body down. Dark steel rippled red down his blade.

"You're fast, Red Eyes. I almost lost you." He shook his head. "I've been following Geshge for hours. Had a feeling he'd try this."

Dzkegé's mercy. What is this? What's happening? My brother's blood stained my sandals. This couldn't be real.

I pinched my wrist and felt bloody scales.

Faziz grinned. "You're the dragon. I knew there was something special about you."

My blood ran cold. Silver light rolled down my arms, winking scales into flesh. "Please. You can't tell anyone."

"Relax. You can beat me in a footrace to Rarafashi, even *njiji*-shot."

Right. My selfish instincts kicked in, cool and calculating. With him, I had options I didn't with Ria. He was dull, male, with a bounty on his head. If I wanted to eliminate his threat, I could call for aid. Caught crimson-handed, few guards would hesitate to pay the paltry essence-fine for killing him.

He needs my help as much as I need his. The sheer unfairness of how War valued lives shook loose my gripping worry. I took his hand. "We have to go."

There was a bathhouse two minutes away. My trembling fingers slipped gold to the attending boy. He escorted us to a side chamber, brought clean skirts, and left without a word.

The blue strip of holdwater beneath the tub's lip activated, and, as the basin slowly filled, orange holdfire strips glowed in concert. Water steamed. Faziz cleaned his sword, dropped his ragged, bloody skirt on the tiles, and slid into the bath with a contented sigh.

My congenial assassin. I studied his weapon. A curved blade of rippled dark steel, handle bound with ruby leather—a *huduv dagun,* a general's sword, in the tradition of the Street of Singing Artisans. He must have acquired the blade, and the training to use it, in another land and life. "You grew up in the Scholarly District?"

"*Miran nah mumiru,*" Faziz invoked the Scholars' god with a wry smile. "*Nik heve chen Tsetso chetsutse.*"

"But your name, 'Faziz,' is Old Jiké for 'ash.'" I switched to the Tongue of Seven Cranes. My bright brain eased the phrases' flows, though I did dance around some harder concepts. I'd only studied the Scholars' tongues on trade documents. "Is there another name you prefer?"

He shook his head. "I'm fine being ash, Red Eyes. It's better than being on fire."

Fire. I thought of the burning, unmanly anger in Geshge's eyes as he'd strangled me. Most men spoke fondly of their little brothers: shared secrets, favorite games, swapped makeup—but I'd only known Geshge these scattered, vile days. Slurs and exploitation built our relationship. Maybe our shared blood made that inevitable.

I scrubbed my gore-flecked hands in the washbasin, drenching them in cheap vanilla oil. Then I flung off my stained skirt and slid into the bath. My broken rib traced red pain through my chest. Knowing my essence would restore me soon was cold comfort when I felt every inch the ache.

"Were those the first people you killed?" Faziz asked, switching to Modern Jiké.

"No," I blurted, unthinking. Then I clapped my hands to my mouth. *You fool!* Just because Faziz hadn't already unmasked me to my father didn't mean he couldn't hurt me. I'd trusted Zega with less, and he'd ripped my heart out.

Zega attacked me instead of following my warning. What will Faziz do to him?

"How do you feel?"

"Good." The word hung between us, surprising us both. I tried to be a perfect man of War. My weapons should be words and looks. Engaging in violent messiness, like Faziz did, was unseemly. Deviant. Monstrous.

As delicious as a kiss in cool rain.

"Now I've got you figured out, Red Eyes." Faziz stretched his arms with a contented sigh. Green Slatepile dust littered his unshaven pits. "We're the same shade of soul, you and I. Fighters. Rebels. Bleeding out our lives to make Victory Street just one heartbeat better. Must be exhausting, destroying your father's campaign while working this hard to suppress your true form."

"I've spent my life pleasing others." I scrubbed hard at a red fleck on my shoulder, like I could rub off my skin and reveal my angry-beating heart. "My mother, my partners, the worst of the *dzaxa*—not because I liked them, but because they might hurt me. The judge has already said she'll break the Treaty of Inversions to invest whoever captures me as her successor. We'll lose a fortune in international investments. The *dzaxa* will cut costs, meaning they'll cut jobs, and evict more families to boost their balances. So I placate people like Rarafashi whenever I can. If they see me for what I really am, all Victory Street could suffer."

"You're no longer a powerless child. You have allies, myself included. Have you considered becoming so strong the *dzaxa* can't abuse you, dragon or no?" Faziz sized me up, like a butcher estimating the meat weight of a bronto. "You're a good fighter."

"What, for a boy?"

"No. Just... good. It's not about gender. Women are quicker, balanced, more resilient, sure. But a man can be stronger if he works for it. And with the right weapon, in the right circumstances, longer reach can be an advantage. I could teach you to fight."

"Teach me?" I practiced baton drills occasionally, but Faziz possessed skills no honest guard knew. Tricks and tactics to guard myself, even if I doubted I could fend off a horde of greedy *dzaxa*. A baton couldn't defend me from the women who owned the ground I walked on. "In exchange for what?"

"The pleasure of your company."

The pleasure of my flesh? No. Faziz didn't have essence to waste on sex. "How kind. Keeping me close until you've found a buyer for a dragon?"

"Koreshiza. Listen to me." My name rang deep and true on his lips. His dark gaze pushed aside my lies and hit my soul. My instincts screamed I should hide, but I couldn't look away. He touched something I'd buried. "When I first came to the Slatepile, as a trash salvager, a gang leader tried to assault me. I killed her and took her place—but if not for my sword, I don't even like to think what she and her guards would have done. I would never endanger anyone else that way. Especially not you."

He's passionate. Kind. But I'd read those same qualities in Zega, once, and suffered for it. Worse, he knew me far better than my ex-boyfriend ever had. At least Zega's ambivalence made it easier to walk away at the end. How could I gain leverage over Faziz? "I owe you my life. Let me tithe you some essence." *Let me put you in debt to me. Hook you on my power like a drug.*

"No thanks. I'm good." A smile tugged at his lips during the long, slow drop of my jaw. He pulled gold foil from the ruin of his skirt and twisted it into a flower.

"No one refuses essence," I spat. "It's the most valuable thing on the city-planet."

"No. That's happiness."

"Dzkegé's fucking tits." My courtly manners slipped. I splashed water across his face. Surprise danced in his dark eyes as he looked up at me. My heart leapt. I'd made him react. "You're a gang leader. Wanted by every *dzaxa* in War. You have half a million people relying on you and everything you've built could crumble if a bronto steps wrong. Don't tell me you're happy. If we're anything alike, you're also burning inside."

"I wouldn't count myself as overjoyed," he admitted. "The responsibility wears me down, and it's lonely work. I'm always watching to make sure my lieutenants don't slit my throat, and Zega's guards target anyone I speak to twice—"

"Thank the dead gods, they're already after me."

Faziz smiled. "I'm content. I know who I am, I live as I please, and anyone who thinks I'm a deviant can argue with my sword. That's worth achieving, even if I can't be happy just yet. Happiness starts with opening up to people." He slapped the pool and sent a wave my way. I dodged. "My offer stands. Come find me, Red Eyes. Let me train you."

Seized by the madness of the moment, I whispered, "I will."

When we re-entered the plastic maze of the marketplace, people with nets and ropes prowled the walkways. One grabbed me by the chin, turned my face towards her, and muttered, "Not pretty enough for a dragon," before letting me go.

"If you're going to grab me in public, at least compliment me!" I shouted at her back. Faziz dragged me to the *reja* stand. I paid three *vodz* to skip to the head of the line.

"Better leave before Vashathke's guard snarls traffic," the driver warned me as I climbed into my taxi. Faziz took the *reja* behind us. "Someone spotted the dragon. It's a boy. A cute blond."

They've marked me. I could feel the chill of Vashathke's shadow. Sardonic laughter bubbled from me. "A boy? Don't be silly. You can't put makeup on a dragon."

Back in the High Kiss, I returned to my private nook,

opened my safe, and spent a long time staring at the scroll labeled 'Geshge.' Part of me wanted to shred it. Instead, hand shaking, I wrote, *Murdered in the low markets of the Surrender.*

Dzaro will mourn him. I'll have to cry. I tried to summon a sad memory, to make me feel as awful as I should. Instead, I found Iradz, her lips on my skin, her soft words tempting me past distraction. A love that should have belonged to Geshge. But it hadn't. I wouldn't loathe myself to please the dead. Dzaro could call me unnatural if she wished.

"Found you!" Ria said, swinging up the bedpost into my nook.

I dropped the scroll into the safe and slammed it shut. "How'd you get in?"

"Climbed the silks hanging from the bedpost. You like your privacy, don't you? That fancy room down there is just for appearances."

"It's for other people. This is for me. I keep those things separate."

"You're hiding. You've been hiding from me all week. Avoiding me on the hovership, and when I visit every morning. I don't understand. I can help you." She folded her arms. Her gold bracer flashed. "Is something wrong?"

"Everything's wrong," I said. "For one, a tiny stalker climbed into my private space and started interrogating me."

"No. Really. You look upset." I could hear her scrambling for the right reaction. "Did your girlfriend dump you? Did a client hurt you?"

Such concern in her voice. For me, or for her precious dragon? "Ask me about magic. I'd rather talk about that than my personal life."

"Koré—"

"There's a temple beneath the Archive." I spoke quickly; I wanted this done. "A client and I found it. I touched the altar, and Dzkegé's shade invested me."

Her eyes widened. "I knew something lay beneath the Archive! Is it magnificent, being touched by a god?"

"I came on the altar."

"Close enough. What triggers the shapeshift? Is it hard? Are there multiple steps?"

"When I relax... when I stop worrying about things... it flows over me." *When I embrace my dangerous desires.* "It wants to get out and make essence. The challenge is keeping it in."

"But you're keeping it in now."

"I'm not relaxed. Can you imagine why?"

"I'm trying!" she shouted. "I don't understand any of this! We get along well, you helped me investigate Tamadza, and in Skygarden, I tithed you half my store! I thought we were friends, but you're acting like you're scared of me. What have I done?"

A new source of essence for the city-planet. That's what she'd called me. If I could snap my fingers and end the essence drought, I would. But Ria had to know fixing the world would cost me everything while she prospered. "Don't speak to me like I'm stupid."

"What? No, I—*Rodi Vorona*, clearly, I'm the dumbass here!"

Stone crunched on my balcony. Ria and I spun as a bright blaze sprinted through the curtains and knocked me flat. My head cracked against the floor.

This time, my body knew better than to hesitate. I drove my finger into my attacker's eye socket. Jelly popped. Congealing fluid ran down my wrist.

Geshge leered down at me. Purple light coiled in the socket of his ruined eye. "Did you think it would be easy, brother?" Slender hands skittered toward my neck. On his chest, clotted blood shone where Faziz had stabbed him dead. *Dead. He's dead, he's dead—*

"Get back!" Ria grabbed Geshge's torso and flung him

over her hip. He sprawled back onto the balcony. "Fuck off, or I'll—"

He lunged at her. I screamed her name.

Ria lifted her wrist.

A wave of fire poured from her bracer and caught my brother in the chest. His burning hands reached through the inferno as he came on. She angled the stream into his face. His last eye popped and melted. With a graceful kick, she knocked him over the balcony rail.

Smoke billowed in his wake as he fell.

"Oh, shit. I set a boy on fire! Koré, are you hurt?" The holdfire panels on her bracer shone bright orange. She twisted the lower cuff, and the gold façade swung back into place.

The true power of a Fire Weaver. Their technology. Their force. Movies and newspaper articles mixed with Tamadza's speech and my father's ravings. *This is bigger than a throne. This is older, dangerous, and it won't take no for an answer.* "Hurt?" Hysterical laughter burst from my aching chest. "I've never been better! Fire Weavers, dragons, gods, the living dead. Legends come to life and seeking to undo me. I'm losing control of everything I've worked eight years to build!"

"I'm sorry—"

"You're part of the problem! I'm not your toy. You can't march me back to Engineering and demand your second bracer. I have my own life. It doesn't involve being a dragon or anything you want from me!"

"I want to help you," Ria stuttered. For a moment, she was only twenty-three. Vulnerable. Scared.

A normal boy, a boy in a story, would let her embrace and kiss him for saving his life. But my hammering heart drummed up pain and terror instead of gratitude. *Alone in a classroom with Iradz. Begging for Vashathke's love before blows broke the air. A crimson beast of anger leaping free from my soul.* The part of me forced to grow up too fast now screamed like a crying child.

No good came from me. No good came from trusting. My storm of fear, relief and lonely longing howled high, more than I could bear. I stood on the brink of oblivion, and I wouldn't fall, for Ria, anyone, or anything. It didn't matter I needed her to fufil my promise to Akizeké. It didn't matter she'd saved my life. My heart had shattered too many times. If I didn't cut her away, she'd cut me open.

I brushed eye jelly from my hand and set my face hard. "Get. Out."

CHAPTER NINE
Upper Victory Street

1st *Dzeri*, Year 92 Rarafashi

"The shadow promises consistency. In our war-torn world, many exhausted victims will trade their souls to escape the unfurling catastrophes. But the only true constant in life is death."—Third Teaching of Miran, Scholar oral tradition

"Baby, my good soul chases the gods."—"Wanderer", by Fezeof, popular song of Year 82 Rarafashi

SHEETS OF LIGHTNING crackled across the Palace of Ten Billion Swords. Clouds cloaked the Surrender's victorious soldier in grey. The Slatepile ran with a dozen rivers. Carts, stalls and shacks swept down Victory Street towards the sea.

Skygarden had flown low to shelter the plaza before the Palace during my brother's funeral. Perching atop one of the steel dragon's curved talons, in the ancient mount where a cannon had once rested, my bright eyes had the best view in War.

Roses spilled over my brother's shroud, a swathe of flowers fifty meters long, their perfume choking the humid morning air. Mourners pressed tight around the bouquets, bowing to the bier before dispersing to gossip on the crowd's edges. Even Jasho-eshe paid his respects, returned to the average brightness of a lady's son—his wife had invested my gift in a second pregnancy. Rarafashi watched from a hovering throne, pale hair a broken halo round her face, unfocused eyes full of crystal tears.

Vashathke sat by Geshge's head, face a blank mask. To his left sat my two youngest brothers, both dark of hair as the young Rarafashi, the older not yet even sixteen. Neither would inherit anything good from this debacle. *The best they can hope for is wives who don't gamble and a father who ignores them.* To Vashathke's right sat Dzaro, who reached for his hand. He pulled it away. Zega lurked behind him, his twitching nose giving away his high. If my letter had spurred him to protect himself—to consider resigning—he'd shown no sign of it yet.

I'd snuck here to lay my foolish dreams of a whole, happy, loving family to rest—and to drink in Iradz's pain.

The frowning widow sat at the bier's foot, ignoring my male relatives. She looked like she couldn't wait for this to end. *Be fair. It was an arranged marriage. Neither wanted it.* But for Geshge, it had been prison. For Iradz, it had only ever been an inconvenience.

Vashathke smoothed his black lace *thevé* and stepped up to the podium.

"As his soul chases after the gods, let us celebrate the life of my beloved son, Geshge Akéakireze Dzaxashigé. A bright ornament of so many lives. Few were honored to know him as I did." Stories spilled out: Geshge dazzling tutors with his intelligence, driving his first *reja*, shining like a star on his wedding day. Tears dimmed Vashathke's blazing eyes. "We won't forget his loss. Nor will we forget who killed him.

My son was murdered by an Engineer's weapon. Any with a hand in his killing will pay."

The transmutationists—Engineers, like most in that profession—traded wary looks as they approached the bier. The crowd whispered as their instruments flashed and beeped.

My brother's vast essence store had died with him—*died twice*—and Iradz would have ordered a holdfast transmutation, to recoup some of her loss. The transmutationists would draw the dead soul's store into the rarest and most valuable of the eleven substances; the one to bind any two things together, physical and immaterial alike. The raw stuff of miracles.

The body shivered beneath the shroud. The air tightened and stilled. I held my breath, waiting for flesh to warp into dazzling spires of substance.

Nothing happened.

"Try again!" Vashathke shouted. The transmutationists twisted the dials downward—a holdspark or holdice transmutation would be almost as respectable—the air fell dead with each attempt. The essence in my brother's corpse remained inert. By the time the dials reached holdstone, mourners were slipping away.

"Enough," Rarafashi commanded. "I won't subject my family to this public indignity. We'll schedule a private transmutation." She rolled onto her feet like a rising mountain, swaying as she stepped off the throne. Vashathke reached to steady her. She swatted him away so hard his wrist snapped.

Then she fell.

Her guards blurred bright and closed ranks around her. The crowd screamed—*she's gone. Her store!* My guts knotted like cowering snakes, electric instinct screaming *flee!* If the judge died before investing an heir with her essence store, every minor *dzaxa*'s private guards would riot for control of

Skygarden. Three thousand years ago, the Pleasure District died as magisterial police slew protestors following the assassination of their judge—

A flurry of motion. From inside the knot of protectors, Rarafashi's fist was lifted high. *Still bright. Still vital.* But the voices didn't stop. War had seen.

"We're stronger than this!" Vashathke called, voice cracking, broken arm cradled to his chest. "If the Engineers keep insulting our district—sheltering the dangerous Fire Weavers, killing our children, poisoning the bodies of the dead—they'll face the ancient fury of War! They think they have us bound by the Treaty of Inversions? Chains of ink cannot hold a district with a soul forged from our ancestors' bright swords!"

The voices paused. Changed. Instead of fearful murmurs, the crowd took up his name. *Vashathke. Honest. Beautiful. Strong. Judge Vashathke.*

Nausea added to my stirring panic. Could War really miss the monster in his sweet pink smile? Invoking the fury that had devastated districts? *I can't watch this.* I turned and leapt.

The back of my neck prickled all the way back to the Surrender.

I FLED TO Mouthmarket, where a thousand stalls dotted the wide corridor like teeth. High above, wind roiled and flocks of starlings weaved through the statue's lips. Holdair pumps hissed in the gap.

The line for Greenwolf's bakery stretched past three stalls. I didn't mind waiting. The narrow, crowded market teemed with sights: a bassoonist playing Warmwater-style, children riding a rickety hoverplatform eight meters up, cage fights between feathered theropods. But today, a thick, pale arm waved me to the front of the line.

"Koré!" Neza said. "Is the funeral already over? I wanted to cheer you up with your favorite bread. How are you feeling?"

Blood rushed to my cheeks. My employees worried about me? A creeping terror insisted he'd put faith in the wrong person. I almost went to the back of the line, to escape him, but that would look strange. "Thanks," I muttered. "This means a lot to me." *This means everyone I love will die.*

"Six loaves, fresh from the oven." Greenwolf handed me gold-crusted, oven-warm bread. "Eat it all, skinny boy. Your friend's already too big to fit up a... pipe." She winked.

Neza rolled his eyes and passed her silver. "What do they think that line achieves?" he said as we threaded back through the crowd, self-consciously rubbing his broad forearms. "Like I'll drop to my knees and give a free lick?"

"They like your reaction. My mother told me to take it as a compliment."

"Did she learn parenting from a porn pamphlet?"

My stomach churned, queasy. "She did the best she could." Why was I defending her? I turned my back on Neza and bit into a loaf. Crust crunched under my teeth, a melody like harpsong. An edge of sour yeast lent signature flavor. *Dzkegé's mercy, that's good.*

"Give it up, you stupid slut!"

I wheeled. My first thought was, *Oh, good, it's not about me.*

A guard held Neza's wrist, shouting, "Your hand flashed silver! Like a dragon's talon!"

"I'm sorry," Neza stuttered, frozen. "I think you're mistaken. It was the *vodz* I paid with."

She jabbed her baton at him. "Breathe me essence, selfish slut! Make me rich off Vashathke's reward." The crowd turned toward them. "He flashed talons, like that boy in the low market. It's him!"

"It was his coin!" I shouted. Anger sparked in my chest. "Leave him alone!"

No one heard me. A one-eyed shopkeeper yawned, "Let him go, Nojof," and the guard's grip faltered. But "Beat him!" cried another, and a chorus joined: "It might be him! Beat him! For the War District and the magistrate's gold!"

I clutched the bread like an enemy throat. Willing myself to disappear, though I wanted to will myself to grow talons and end them. *Too many. Too dangerous. I can only cower when the moment grows tight.*

"Enough, Nojof!" shouted a guard captain. "Let the boy go."

"I'll share Vashathke's bounty with you," Nojof promised.

"What bounty? That's the wrong boy. And I wouldn't put Vashathke on the throne for ten billion *thera*. What if he orgasmed on it?"

Neza slid free and slunk back to my side. I led him back through the crowd, ducked behind the loaves, squeezing his hand so the crowd couldn't drag him in.

"The dragon can't be a courtesan," said a *reja* driver as we passed. "If Dzkegé wanted a boy, she'd choose a virtuous one."

"She'd chose a stud," said a florist, "to quickly sire a new bloodline of dragons."

A stud. The explanation fit, much as I hated it. Dzkegé had chosen me as a walking set of balls, caring not if she tattooed a target on my soul. Even if Zega didn't send more guards after me, even if more undead didn't rip through the High Kiss, I still faced more danger than in all my living days.

"The dragon should have revealed herself—himself—to Rarafashi weeks ago," called a voice. "It's his duty."

"He might be afraid," said a grocer.

"What if the dragon's made a deal with Engineering?" asked an old man. "That'd explain why he hasn't revealed himself, and also why *dzaxa* Geshge didn't transmute."

I shivered. *Dragons don't affect transmutation!* But desperation clouded the air. Ten thousand years of drought-fueled starvation knew no reason.

"Fucking Engineers! They take everything!"

As that shout broke through Mouthmarket, an Engineer flung a brass ball high. The metal split into a dozen robotic bees, stingers tipped with sparking *shikia*. They set on the crowd. Electricity crackled. Pained gasps rang through the statue's lips.

"Blame your judges for your poverty." Her bright voice rang clarion. "Not their old victims. If you love War more than truth, know this: we Engineers won't let history repeat. If we fall, you'll fall with us."

BACK AT THE High Kiss, I gave the rolls to my employees—bread had no taste for me now—and readied for Akizeké's campaign meeting. Spurning mourning black, I donned a mauve skirt with a living brocade of fluttering eyelids, matching sash of iridescent green feathers, and elbow-length steel bracers inlaid with coral roses. While waiting for my co-conspirators, I updated our employee handbook to emphasize reporting sexual violence and threats to me. *I wish I could do more than blacklist clients.* Then, switching to something more light-hearted, I drafted a memo on powders and creams to sensitize assholes. *For internal eyes only.*

Finally, I ripped up Ria's unopened letters and flung them off my balcony as the starlings swirled.

Magistrate Kirakaneri of Shadowcoin Street arrived at the fifth bell, pale and deadly as a bad debt. Akizeké entered on her heels, and I draped myself across her lap. Dzaro and her fellow ladies arrived as a group, bunched tight in eager, friendly conversation, squeezing my aunt's hands and murmuring comforts. Faziz raised an eyebrow at me when he walked in and saw my arrangement. I pulled Akizeké closer, inhaling her scent of sweat and fresh tea, letting her fingers tangle in my hair. Refusing to duck his gaze. *Hello, punk rebel with your tattoos and sword.* He'd fastened the stolen ruby into a leather wristband. *Come see my power surprise you.*

"How much longer does Rarafashi have to live?" Akizeké said.

Estimates flew, all revised downward. Two months, came the consensus, though my heart feared for less. Geshge's death would shock the strongest hearts, and while Vashathke couldn't arrange a building collapse to finish her off—he'd need to attend her deathbed to receive her essence store—her decline could be sped through potions and drugs. Endorsements would fly more rapidly and rashly the sicker she grew.

We had to establish Akizeké as a serious candidate, or the whole city-planet would line up behind my father.

Wine flowed as we discussed Akizeké's policy platform, which came together with rapid speed. She knew where she stood, and though her ideas weren't fully developed, her air of command convinced me she'd figure it all out.

"If you'll forgive me for stating the obvious, these positions don't substantially contrast with Vashathke's," said Rezadzeré, lord of Towergarden, whose only contribution to the meeting so far had been glaring daggers at Faziz. "He captured the spotlight today, for good or ill. Those who loathe our neighbors' power will flock to join him, and those ambivalent about the ancient treaties have no reason to choose us when we offer nothing new."

"Everything will be new when I'm enthroned," Akizeké said. "Anyone who can't see so is blind."

"Then Lady Jedznigé and Lady Nakethera are blind," Kirakaneri said. "Both sent heralds to every upper-level commons on Victory Street, to read their public statements endorsing Vashathke. If he breaks the treaty, they can cease paying into the blightburn reparations fund."

"Their ancestors unleashed a plague that's still killing people," I said. "They'd risk planetary peace to save ten thousand *thera* a year on medical bills? They make five times as much selling medicines from their cursed laboratories!"

Too loud. Too much emotion. Quizzical looks darted onto me. I quailed.

"Well," Akizeké said. "It's not like they mixed up the plague themselves. Hardly fair, punishing them for someone else's mistake."

I bit my lip. *She's* dzaxa, I reminded myself. *She sees the world differently. It's not her fault she was born with her head in the clouds.* But I couldn't muster the spirit to let that slide. *Just ignore it. I don't need her to be my friend. I just need to put her on a throne.*

"Sorry, but what about Vashathke's funeral speech?" Rezadzeré said, more tactfully than I. "Inappropriately political over his child's body. Maybe there's something we can use..."

"He doesn't like the Engineers," Dzaro said. "He thinks our adherence to our agreements with them is weakness."

"Which it is," Akizeké said. "But the way he spoke of it—stupid. Undiplomatic. Like he held his balls over a brazier too long."

"We can turn those words against him," Faziz said. "He publicly called for violence. Nail 'warmonger' to his reputation and he'll lose key international endorsements. It doesn't matter how many ladies of War come to his call. To win, he needs support inside and outside our district."

"We can push that further," I said. "Look at the mass evictions he's caused. He has children's blood on his hands. If we amplify how his policies create poverty—"

"People get evicted every day." Kirakaneri shook her head. "That part's not interesting enough to get attention. But 'irrational warmonger Vashathke...' we might not even need to worry about domestic endorsements if we make that stick.

One or two hotheads might fall in line behind Vashathke, but most *dzaxa* know violence is a bad business strategy. Who would break the peace and endanger the world's essence store over a conspiracy theory?"

I gave a polite, quiet chuckle and told my uneasy soul to believe her. *The age of war's forever ended. The Treaty of Inversions keeps the peace.* But I remembered the Reclaimer humming and a dead woman tithing essence. How Zega had shown my father's strength by sending guards to destroy Faziz's apartments—and then how he'd sent guards to jump me in an alley. Violence lingered on Victory Street long after the conquests had ended. *Violence sown by Zega and my father.*

Time to play dirty. Do what it took to win and stop them. If my stomach churned, I'd mask it with a smile of icicles.

"I'm not sure—" Dzaro began, but Akizeké interrupted.

"I was about to propose the same tactic, Faziz. Don't pre-empt me in the future."

"My apologies, Akizeké," Faziz answered. "I only meant, it's such obvious genius even a dull like me can see it."

"Dull by choice," she groused. "You tithed away the essence I gave you."

When and why had she given him essence? Curiosity broke my silence. "You two know each other that well?"

"Yes," Akizeké said, and brushed me off. "I'll accuse Vashathke at Geshge's funeral banquet. He'll be a poor excuse for a mourning father if he argues with me there."

Kge opened the door. "*Dzaxa,* my apologies. Boss, we need you downstairs."

I apologized to my guests and slipped away. "Is it an emergency?" I murmured to Kge.

"Depends on how you feel about redecorating."

Before my holdlight-embroidered entry curtains—an irreplaceable fortune in custom work—Ria held a threatening globe of fire. "Koré. We need to talk. I heard what your dad said about Engineering at the funeral. Is he plotting against my district? Are you working with him? Is that why you won't give me what I asked for?"

Dzkegé's tits. "My father's a monster." *So am I.* "I don't support his stupid cruelties."

"So why can't you answer me cleanly?"

The joy in sex work, I reflected, was people compensated me for my attentions. "Please. I can't have this conversation here."

"Okay. Come for a walk?"

My heart sank. *Dzkegé's mercy. She wants me alone?* But Akizeké sat just upstairs, relying on me to secure the Engineering District's support. If she heard I'd turned Ria away, she'd know I'd failed her. And the fire Ria held spelled its own shimmering command.

Unable to refuse, I followed Ria out into the corridor. She passed bars and a florist's shop before stopping by a control panel, its glyphs worn by centuries, and typing in a code. I'd never seen anyone use a panel.

The sandstone swung open, revealing a shaft lined with shimmering rods of holdwater and holdair. A worn ladder had been cut down the center.

"Boys first," Ria said, and bowed to me. I climbed.

The shaft was dusty, the air thin. It opened on a chamber lined with holdlight screens, broken waves of Old Jiké glyphs flashing across their surfaces. Dials and levers lay rusted and cracked. A sleeping pallet had a stack of notebooks and a lizard's nest for a pillow.

"What is this place?"

"The environmental controls for this block of suites." She flicked a dial. "Five thousand years ago, that would have depressurized the High Kiss. Now it's busted."

So much power. Ria's people surpassed us in wealth, technology and ancient knowledge. Päreshi had even hinted they knew how the gods fell. I straightened my spine and willed myself cool. My skin crawled, being at her total mercy.

At being surrounded by forces I didn't understand and held not even meager power to control.

"No one can hear us," she said. "No one knows this place exists anymore. You can talk freely about your power here. You don't have to be afraid."

Whatever I'd expected her to say, it wasn't that. "You mean, you...you're not kidnapping me?"

"*Resishia Vorona,* no!" Concern swelled in her rich brown eyes. "You didn't feel comfortable talking in the High Kiss. I'm trying to make you feel safe. If this isn't enough, I can book us passage to Engineering and get you legal asylum. The judge and her heir will help me out. Every Fire Weaver will unite to protect you."

"Ria." A laugh built low in my throat. Small, twisted and bitter—yet still dissolving the tight knot of fear in my chest. *She's trying to show she cares.* "Nothing can protect a dragon. The world won't be satisfied selling my breath. Whatever *dzaxa* captures me will exploit my body, seed and children. War's law will let them, because essence matters more than people here, and certainly more than men. You heard Rarafashi at the state banquet. The crown of War. The treaty and our trade relationships with our neighbors. That's what she'll sacrifice. That's how highly she weighs my value in coin."

"The *dzaxa,*" Ria breathed. "I didn't think... of course you'd fear that. They're monsters. Do you think... if they had a dragon, would they go so far as to restart the conquests?"

A dragon to breathe new essence. A Reclaimer to steal back poisoned energy from the dead. "I want to believe we're better than that." Some *dzaxa* were monsters, like she'd said. Some were simply people. And some of us monsters of war had no *dzaxa* in our names. "But if this secret slips to the wrong person, I lose everything. I know you want your second bracer. I know you want to save the world! But this is my secret and my life. It's my choice what I do with it and you're taking that choice away from me."

"No." She stepped back from me. "Oh, Voro. No. I didn't mean to scare you... but I have. I'm so sorry. I could see your fear, but I didn't realize how real it was. I promise, whether you keep it quiet inside you or share it with the world, your secret is yours. You have my protection, no matter what you choose." Thoughtful softness tuned her words. Her topaz eyes widened. She reached for my hand, then paused. "I won't touch you if you don't want me to."

In what world is that my choice? Was this some new game, some manipulation I'd never encountered? *What does she gain from kindness? Perhaps she seeks my trust for some venture—but what does she gain by being inept at kindness?* All I knew about the Fire Weavers, about Ria, was their devotion to uncovering the world's history, preventing dangerous accidents, and healing the conquests' devastation. Good people. *How does this line up?*

It didn't—unless I let myself consider Ria was exactly who she said. A decent, honest, heroic soul who wanted to protect me and didn't quite understand how.

My laugh came real, heated. Rolling up through my cheekbones and ears like soapbubbles. "It's not you, Ria. It's me. All me! I couldn't consider your intentions were kind." I thought myself an expert on divining intent, but I always sought for wrongness first and imagined non-existent threats. Ria shone with soul-deep integrity, honest as the truth of the gods' fall. She'd only misunderstood my fear. "So many people have treated me vilely. My very bones grow suspicious when others draw close."

"I've never been friends with a boy before," she mused. "There's my dad, some of my exes, and we do let them into the Fire Weavers, but I've never considered how your... vulnerability... shapes your worldview."

"It's no fun having your fragile bits outside your body." And sexism was only the beginning. I attracted ten times the trouble of an average boy, even when I tried to dodge it.

Color rose in my face. "I'm not sure you can entirely see things how I do. But thank you for trying. I've never met a woman who's done that for me."

"Don't be impressed," Ria muttered, ducking my gaze. A curl slipped from the working scarf sheltering her curly hair. Reflexively, I pushed it back in place, and felt the sun's heat in the soft flesh of her cheek. "I think most women you've met have been assholes. Empathy is the bare minimum I should offer. Don't praise me for it."

"You're not the boss of me," I whispered. My fingertips tingled from the softness of her skin. "I think you're extraordinary, and I'll say it as often as I please."

"I'll keep that in mind next time I'm vomiting in a gutter."

"Don't talk yourself down," I said. Maybe I should still push her away. Anything to protect myself from the vulnerability she asked me to be open to. But I craved Ria's light, and I couldn't forget what Faziz had told me in the bathhouse. *Happiness starts with opening up to people.* If there was anyone on the city-planet I'd be happier for being open with, it was Ria. "You've worked for that second bracer your whole life, and people you care about give you shit because you haven't earned it yet. Putting that off to respect my secret—it's heroic, even if there's no fires to put out and swooning virgins to save. It means everything to me."

"*Rodi Vorona,* you've got terribly low standards." Ria shook her head. "You can trust me. And I'll prove it." She unhooked her golden *opesero* bracer and placed it in my hands.

I stared at the hot, heavy gold. "But... you need this."

"If I need a bracer to be a Fire Weaver—if I can't earn the trust of the people who need us—I don't deserve the title." She grinned. "I'll find another way to prove myself. Päreshi told me not to investigate Tamadza—now she's revealed as a necromancer, Päreshi wants more qualified Fire Weavers to handle her. But if I learn what Tamadza's after, it'll be almost as good as finding Dzkegé's shade."

"You're going to poke around Tamadza again?" My voice spiked. "She's dangerous."

"Maybe I'll use your tactic, and fall into her bed. But that's for later. Can I crash at the High Kiss again? It's dusty in here."

She wants to come into my sanctuary. My heart leapt at thought of her near, power, danger and all. My instincts screamed *guard yourself!* but this time, I said, "yes."

Everyone smiled to see her at dinner. Opal played the harp, Ruby sang, and Ria walked down the table on her hands, nearly knocking over Bero's crab stew. Her *opesero* pressed against my hip as I watched, safely knotted into my sash. I didn't know what to do with it. The last thing I had expected was for her to put it in my hands.

Riapáná Żutruro. Boldness, kisses and wit, and, beneath all that, good in her soul. A smile crept over my lips as Ria dared Kge to stuff twenty fried lizard eggs in her mouth. I'd sleep easy tonight, knowing a Fire Weaver guarded me and my people. Ria would return to her order once she had concrete findings on Tamadza, but while she lingered on Victory Street, I'd enjoy her company.

I'd also enjoy her power and connections. *The judge and her heir will help me out.* The endorsements she could bring Akizeké included two of the most powerful people in the world. I could deal with dead men and dragons for that. I could even face my own fears of friendship.

I prided myself on strategic cunning. But I hated thinking through the ins and outs before accepting Ria by my side.

CHAPTER TEN
The Slatepile Ruin

17th *Dzeri*, Year 92 Rarafashi

"After losing their dragons in the Fall, the Dzaxashigé could no longer afford their essence-costly wars and sued for peace. They chose the baton as their weapon for the new era: alike to their treasured swords, mostly nonlethal, adapted from police tools in Engineering."—textbook of the Old Dread Guard Academy

"In recognition of his devotion to enforcing the laws and ancient customs of War, I pledge my endorsement to Magistrate Vashathke."—statement issued by the press office of Lady Xezkavodz of the Archive

"Such a handsome weapon." Faziz inspected my mother's baton. "Short of a blade, you won't find anything better to defend yourself with."

"A good lawyer will do," I said, "especially if news gets out I'm sparring with the most wanted man on Victory

Street." The maze of old catwalks and speakers hung high enough up his cavern domain to hide me from dulls, but his guards saw me as I arrived each morning. "Have your people been gossiping? If the *dzaxa* hear I'm doing something this unseemly, they might shun the High Kiss."

"We don't give a damn, Red Eyes. You worry too much about how other people see you. Most people focus on their own lives and problems." He passed my baton back to me, then drew a paper helicopter from his sash and dropped it over the rail. Children laughed below, pushing and shoving for the privilege of catching it.

"You're not," I said. "You're focused on them."

"They're under my protection. It's my responsibility to ensure their happiness. Some of these people have worked for me ten years. The street pickpockets I took in as teenagers now have families of their own, kids who've lived their whole lives without their parents arguing or drinking because they can't make rent. It's a small miracle, watching them smile."

Strings of broken neon holdlight flashed around me as I stretched, warming up with the twists and lunges I'd learned as a guard cadet. Faziz's black eyes traced the lines of my body. He must have seen a thousand mistakes, but I wouldn't beg for feedback.

"Do you want children of your own?" I asked. "A partner, maybe?"

"Might as well ask for another dozen hours in the day. I'm too busy for that."

"Too busy to have your own life?"

"A bold question from a man obsessed with making his father sweat." He laughed. "I'm having a life right now. Here. With you."

My cheeks flushed. I didn't know what to say. Faziz shrugged and dropped into a Scholar swordfighter's stance—legs spread and bent, facing me head-on, blade held below his groin. His eyebrow arched. The scar through it flashed white.

An invitation. *Reach out, Red Eyes, and meet me halfway.* In his sanctuary, I had nothing to hide. A smile crept over my lips. I wanted to do this, and do this right.

Happiness starts with opening up to people.

Scales flashed down my arms as I leapt to meet him.

His sword traced silver against green slate walls, arcs of slow and practiced grace. Each step of his pushed me backwards. I blocked blows with the scalloped edges of my mother's baton, but I'd forgotten the footwork to advance. *Mother would hate me for that.* My heel touched a catwalk's edge. Spotting an opening, I hooked my tail around Faziz's leg and pulled it from underneath him.

My heart dropped at how slowly he stood. "Are you hurt? I'm sorry. I'm brighter. It's not fair."

"Fighting's not fair." Faziz smiled and spread his arms. For a moment, I thought he'd embrace me. Then he kicked my tail up into his hands and pulled. Nerves clenched at the spur of my spine. I stumbled back into him.

His blade touched my throat in a cold kiss. My bare ass pressed against the rough leather of his skirt. "You asked me to teach you, Red Eyes. Let me."

Tangled arousal and embarrassment bound me to him. His lips fluttered inches from my ear; his hot breath washed my cheek. My body wanted him, all sweat and steel, a need heavier than logic. *The need that blinded me to Zega.*

"Maybe I'm wrong, coming here," I said. "This— association. With a common, dull criminal." The tail vanished. I slid from his grasp and turned away, picturing my father's cold eyes until my arousal ebbed. Only when I held control did I face him. "You're awful for my brand."

"Save that boldness for your enemies, Red Eyes," he said, brusquely. "Your attacks are too timid. Strike hard. Use your full height. You'll never fit in three blows a second. Try for one, and make it shattering. Want it."

"Wanting things makes me break out in scales."

Faziz scratched a pimple. "We've all got unfortunate little skin conditions. You're safe here. Try to disarm me."

He held his blade low, parallel to the floor. I mustered speed and pressed him. Back his sword flicked at sharp, gleaming angles, holding me off with the flat. My baton cracked across his wrists. He cursed and dropped the blade.

"Dzkegé's mercy! Are you hurt?" His wrists were already purpling.

"A bruise. I'll be fine." He reached for his sword and winced. "In a few days."

I'm so sorry. Guiltily, I scooped up his blade and cradled it like another man's child. *Light and perfectly balanced.* Gold-foil hunting cats stamped the red leather of the hilt. *A true masterpiece.* Only the dragons' sword, War's closest possession to a holy relic, could match it for living, deadly potential. "Did you steal this from a museum?"

"Probably."

"How long ago did you come to Victory Street? You speak Modern Jiké with the local accent."

"Took a ship from the Street of Virtues nine years ago, after the blue plague ran its course. Wanted a fresh start."

The blue plague. Five million dulls in the Scholarly District had fallen to that sweeping sickness. The survivors awoke disabled from brain-swelling comas, their bodies covered with blue pox scars—like the three dark rosettes below Faziz's left nipple.

A fresh start. Faziz might have lost everything and everyone he loved. *Dzkegé's mercy, and I thought my life was hard.* He spoke of his own loneliness like a career choice, a practical necessity. But to witness such an apocalypse would challenge anyone's ability to build intimate bonds. "That must have been crushing. Coming alone to a new district, after suffering so…"

"It wasn't fun." He eyed me sideways. "But I'm used to getting my ass beat."

The strange mix of anger and envy I'd felt the day we met washed back over me. "Are you trying to hint you're attracted to other men? Because half the time you're the queerest tough on Victory Street, and half the time you're sweeter than spun wine."

Faziz shrugged. Muscle rolled through his back. I bit my lip, frozen. *I'm wrong.* I'd never asked if a man liked other men—if it mattered, they'd made it clear within seconds of meeting me. Faziz didn't act straight, but that meant nothing. I played straight for my work and mission, and I was as bisexual as birth could shape me. *I'm wrong. He hates me—*

"The armpit hair may be signaling overkill." Faziz grinned. "You're staring at me like I've grown a second head. We do have queers among the Scholars, though they try to keep us out of sight. Yes. I mostly entertain men."

"Mostly?" I raised an eyebrow. "Who's the mostly?"

"I don't like labels. I'm not even sure I like the label 'man' for myself, though I don't have one I like better. It's only something other people push on me."

That was new information. "Did you sleep with Akizeké?" He jumped at the name. "She gave you essence once. That's how you know she's possessive."

"Only *once*." He leant hard into the word. "Our candidate collects ancient relics. She paid my gang to smuggle goods for her private museum. Once we discovered we both wanted Vashathke off the throne, we made a deal. And a brief... partnership. When she's crowned judge, she'll have the Slatepile reincorporated as a legal building and name me its lord."

Only once. I chuckled. I could see it—and see both regretting it. "You, a lord? Nothing against ambition, but you're the one who teases me for seeking *dzaxa* favors. And you wish to join them?"

He pointed down into the cavern, where a team of harness-strung workers scuttled over a tall support column. They packed bags of holdweight chips against its cracks and sprayed liquid concrete into the bigger gaps with rattling hoses. Below, children wove nets and sorted salvaged metal by alloy. A trio of elderly overseers talked the children through their work.

"Once the pillar is reinforced," Faziz said, "we'll build modular apartments off its base. Like the ones they have in Engineering, growing and shrinking to fit the number of people in a unit. Thanks to your father's evictions, I've never had more people begging me for shelter. I'm robbing substance shipments twice a month to keep us supplied with holdwater and holdair. I kidnapped an artisan to get a holdfast lock made for the main gate. I still can't keep up with the demand. We need legal status and aid. Victory Street must support us."

"Even your ambition is noble," I said. "Let me guess: you gave Akizeké's essence to a starving family?"

"Yes," he said. "But I'm not noble. Too much essence makes me feel sick. Gives me nightmares, makes me feel like a different person. I'd rather be limited in ability than feel so... off. It's a foolish choice, I know, but—"

"I don't think it's foolish, not to want essence inside you," I said. "I was born too bright. It made me a target. I'm all scarred up from people who said they loved me and tried to drain me dry. But you and my friend Ria, you saved my life and kept my secret. Maybe I can trust—"

"Don't." His dark eyes cut into me like obsidian blades. An unfamiliar anger filled his voice. "We're allies, Red Eyes. Nothing more. You're too smart to get attached to me. Listen to your instincts. Not your heart."

"What are you talking about? You invited me here. To spend time with you."

His brow furrowed. Like his cunning mind had somehow outwitted itself. "I just needed to get you somewhere private to talk." A silver vial flickered into his nimble fingers. "Poison from Shadowcoin Street. Made to kill a bright. Painless and swift." He tucked it into my sash. "By the funeral banquet, a month will have passed since I warned Zega. He won't listen. He won't step down. I have no other choice."

Understanding dawned. My eyes widened. "No. I won't assassinate him."

"You slew those guards in the market. I heard what you said in the bathhouse—there's already blood on your hands. One of my guards had a daughter, Gei-dzeo. She's often cursed the red-eyed young *dzaxa* who slew her. My spies helped me put the picture together. Only fifteen—"

Gei-dzeo. A name from my past, as heavy as Old Dread's anchor. "I never wanted to kill—" I began, then clapped my hands over my mouth. My scales snapped back into human flesh, my heart slamming shut to him. *Listen to your instincts, indeed.* Years of training and evasion took me over. Even spinning with shock, my mind knit the pieces together. "You're blackmailing me?"

"I am."

I almost vomited off the catwalk. He wouldn't reveal the truth of my power, but a murder charge would follow me long after I'd paid the essence-fine to Gei-dzeo's next of kin. I'd lose my reputation, my business, my chance at revenge. No one would hire a murderer to warm their bed.

Faziz said nothing to fill the silence. Another would have offered excuses, but he owned his deeds. He believed Zega had to die for the good of his people, and he'd always put his people first. I'd so foolishly underestimated him. My heart had ached and pled to spill its secrets, to gleam one honest moment with another soul, and I'd trusted a man who promised to stab me in the back.

Please him. Protect yourself. "I'll do it," I said. The vial grew heavy on my hip. "From there, we're done."

"I'm part of this campaign until Akizeké tells me I'm done," he said, "but if your regard is the price I pay for Zega's life, I'll miss you."

Acceptance weighed heavy in his words. I couldn't protest. I couldn't push him away harder than he'd pushed me, though my seething, angry soul wanted to shove him off Skygarden.

I leapt from the catwalk to the entry tunnel, leaving my dull teacher behind, and fought tears all the way home.

DUSKLILY MET ME in the High Kiss entry arch. My aunt's concubine was sweat-streaked, dark curls tumbling from the band he pinned them with, gold-brown chest rising and falling with each gasped breath. *Dzkegé's mercy, he ran from the Surrender's other statue.* He'd brightened with Dzaro, but shone nowhere near as much as me, since he cared for her enough to reciprocate bedroom tithes. I'd normally scorn a sex worker who developed feelings for a client, but some foolish part of me hoped they'd work out.

"Dzaro's locked herself in her office," he gasped. "Won't take visitors…"

Lightning shot through my veins. "Is something wrong?"

"Something's different with her. She made me give a letter for the visa council to her herald." He swallowed. "She confessed to sneaking bombs on the hovership. Testified the ship is functional. The council rescinded their flight ban. The hovership is pivoting inland."

I couldn't believe my ears. *Pivoting inland. Carrying Tamadza, her Reclaimer, and her secret deal with my father to the Engineering border.* All small details besides the knife, the one Dzaro had rammed in my chest beside Faziz's. *She never loved me. She was waiting to betray me.* It almost came as a relief. I'd been anticipating this gut-punch for as long as I'd known her. Now I could lash out without fearing she'd push me away.

"I think Dzaro needs our help," Dusklily said, "She's not herself—"

"This is exactly like a *dzaxa*," I spat. But I had *dzaxa*

blood too, and a dark streak deeper than any Dzaro or even Faziz could hope to match. Someone else would suffer for my pains this time.

I'd find what Tamadza and my father plotted, and bring both of them down. If Dzaro stood in my way, she'd fall with them.

INTERLUDE: AGE TEN
The Prizeheron

9th *Dzk*, Year 76 Rarafashi

"Koreshiza is a joy to teach. Quiet, demure, never makes trouble in class. Naturally talented in all subjects, save history. All his achievements are due to the essence you so wisely invested in him. The credit is yours as a parent."—report card addressed to Captain Briza Steelstair

"…ONE BILLION *THERA* in profits." I scrawled the last glyph on the holdlight tablet screen. "Over seven years with cumulative interest."

The tutor clapped her hands. Iradz remained silent, and the other children followed her lead. I froze. Sweat ran down my neck. *Dzkegé's mercy, let them all be happy with me!*

"The function is exponential," finished our tutor. "Now do you see your mistake on the test, *dzaxa* Iradz? Koré had the right answer."

"He's brighter than us," Iradz complained. "He didn't *earn* his marks."

"You haven't earned a mark in years," said one of her

191

friends. "You've made Koré do your homework since you were betrothed."

"Not true," I lied placatingly. "*Dzaxa*, please don't argue over me. I'm not worth it."

The tutor ruffled my hair. "Wise beyond your years, boy."

The lesson turned to history: how the dragons had given us their sword so we could discern truth on the rare occasion a *dzaxa* had to testify at trial. The girls were dismissed to the training yards, and the boys set to embroidering the poem 'Truthful Harmony' in the shape of our favorite flowers. When the fourth bell rang, announcing the end of arms training, I flung down my needle and fled to the safety of the kitchens.

As I entered, the cook Keshi passed me a spoon of tomato sauce. "Fresh vegetables from the down-neck gardens. Feast your bright senses. Needs more salt?"

The sauce ran thick with pulpy texture and the flavor of sunshine. "Basil."

Keshi plucked leaves from a plant in a small holdlife block. An earthy, crisp scent filled the room. "Why didn't you let Iradz cheat off your test this time?"

I bit my lip. "I dreamed I was drowning last night... and screaming, in Modern Jiké. When I woke, I realized I was thinking in Modern, too."

"You're a gifted linguist. How many do you have now? Four?"

Five. Besides Modern, I'd learned Old Jiké and common Engineering, and begun Shallow Street's Warmwater *Jidzoi*. A lady's husband needed to talk trade in many tongues. But the creole of Lower, though common in Lady Fidzjakovik's household, wasn't proper for me. After I'd been caught talking with stableboys, and the whispers of an improper friendship had spread, the household had been ordered to address me in Modern or not at all. Now only *dzaxa* and Keshi spoke to me.

"But I didn't choose that. I'm angry," I confessed. "It feels like something was taken from me." That sounded silly. Modern was shaping me into the man I needed to become. I should be grateful for the gift, not angry about how it had been given. "I wanted to punish someone."

"War loves remaking its victims' souls." She held two bottles out beneath my nose. "Which one's fresher?"

We were roasting onions when Iradz burst into the room. Keshi stepped between us, but the *dzaxa* had already spotted me.

Even at fourteen, Iradz had grown into her mother's compact, lean muscle. She shoved past the cook and grabbed my arm. "Koré. My mother banned me from Judge Rarafashi's welcome banquet because I broke my sparring partner's arm. Should I submit to her, or prove myself a true daughter of War?"

"Don't answer, Koré," Keshi commanded. "Be smart. She wants your help defying our lady. Tell her to follow the rules."

Iradz's grip tightened. *My wife-to-be.* Her pointed glare said I'd done something wrong. Her nails would draw blood if I didn't fix it. "I'm sorry, *dzaxa* Iradz. I don't…"

"Boys. Always mumbling." She shook my arm. "Speak straight!"

"You should do what you want," I said. She would, with or without my blessing.

"Was that so hard?" she said, and dragged me out.

Intent on at least seeing the ruler of the War District arrive, Iradz led me into an abandoned maintenance shaft above the apartment's entrance. Together, we scaled its sides and peered down through wavy glass. Hairline cracks let the sound up to meet us.

Six dozen heralds trumpeted a judicial salute. Guards arched their batons as pages rolled out a red carpet beneath them. Rarafashi swept through their ranks and greeted Lady

Fidzjakovik with a bawdy joke. Booming laughter swept the hall.

"That's hilarious!" Iradz declared. "Look how bright she is!"

The judge shone brighter than the noonday sun. But my eyes went to the man behind her. Tall, slender and pale, upturned nose and aloof cheekbones. Blush silk wrapped his hips. Titanium and diamond crowned his golden hair. The picture of a demure husband, save for the wicked scarlet fire of his eyes.

My eyes, I thought. Would I ever look so perfectly at ease on Iradz's arm?

"Vashathke," Iradz said. "The judge's third husband. He's, what, twenty-seven? He'd look younger if he smiled. I'd do him. What do you think, Koré?"

I blushed. "You mean... would I... "

"No! How would two boys even work? Just tell me what you think!"

Vashathke bowed to Lady Fidzjakovik. His thin smile didn't touch his eyes. "I like him well, *dzaxa* Iradz. I want to be that for you when we're wed. If it please you."

She studied me. "Smile."

I smiled.

"You'll do. Though you are as dumb as a lizard." She giggled. My spine ran cold. I hugged my needlework to my chest like a shield. "Can't you see? I figured it out years ago. Vashathke—he's your father."

For a moment, delight filled me. I'd thought my father dead. This graceful, beautiful *dzaxa* was everything a man should be. A picture-perfect sire.

But I saw past my initial joy. Vashathke and his essence belonged to the judge, not my mother. He was forbidden. I was forbidden. My skin, bones and soul were all evidence of a theft.

"You think you're too good to do my homework? You're

a bastard. Only your essence matters. Be grateful you have me to take care of you."

"What?" Tears blinded me hazy. "What do you mean?"

Iradz smashed her lips down on mine. I froze. Let her finish. She was right. My value lay in the essence I could give her when we wed. I had to prove I'd give everything she wanted.

"Did you like that?" Her grip tightened. I nodded, lying. "Good. You're mine, like Vashathke belongs to the judge. Use your tongue next time."

She left. I fled to my bedchamber, willing my soul to curl up and die so I'd feel as peaceful as Vashathke looked beside his wife. What was wrong with me? I tried to be good, do right. Yet I couldn't please my future wife, I hadn't enjoyed her kiss, and... I was a bastard. A rare creature, born of adultery and spite. For all his beauty, Vashathke was a slut and a seducer. Had I inherited his wickedness with his flashing eyes? How would Iradz punish me if that wickedness sprang out?

When my mother found me, I was ruining my math homework with tears.

"Oh, my boy." She pulled me onto her lap, cradling my head against the steel cup of her *fajix*. "I'm sorry."

"Why didn't you tell me my father was alive?"

"I planned to tell you when you turned sixteen. I should have realized it would come out sooner. You look shockingly alike." Her grip tightened on my hair. Her voice thickened. "Your father ruined my life, but he gave me your essence. I lied because the past doesn't matter. Only marrying you well to build myself a new life."

How did he ruin your life? The pain in her words warned me not to ask. *Of course.* Like in a story, my father's marriage to Rarafashi must have been arranged without his consent. He'd loved a humble guard instead, and passed her my essence as a parting gift. He'd broken my mother's heart when he'd wed the judge instead of running away with her, and she'd conceived me as a last living token of her lost love.

I liked thinking of myself that way. As I sobbed into my mother's shoulder, I vowed to reunite them.

My first attempt to enter the judge's rooms, by sauntering past the guards, got me dragged out in disgrace. The second, where I ducked in with the kitchen servants, got me to the parlor before my discovery. For the third, I eavesdropped on Vashathke's bragging manservant and learned my father's bedroom lay to the outside of the guest apartment, protected by a thin wall of tin.

I also learned my bright legs could kick through metal.

Vashathke returned from dinner, nose buried in a much-loved copy of *Nineteen Commercial Conquests*, and found me sitting on his bed.

The book fell. His jaw dropped. "Dzkegé's tits. You're Briza's spawn."

Spawn? I'd expected warmth and welcome, even love. Nervously, I hopped down and smoothed my skirt. "I'm Koreshiza. Briza's son... and yours. Do you remember my mother?"

"The one who escaped," he hissed. "How could I forget her? Shit, I'm fucking dead!"

His crudeness struck me. I took his hand. He tried to jerk away, but my bright strength held fast. "Please don't say that. You're my father. My—"

I stopped. A sob weighed down my throat. Ugly, terrible tears threatened to spill free. Why couldn't I be as cool as he was? What if my inconvenient neediness spurred him to push me aside—or worse, hurt me?

Vashathke hesitated, then ruffled my hair. "I'm sorry, Koreshiza. A father shouldn't be so selfish. What do you want, sweetheart?"

"I want you to apologize to my mother for what you did." I wanted to live in his household. Meet my little brother. Learn from a loving father how to fit the role I'd been given. But I'd start with an apology, to help my mother most.

"Dzkegé's tits." Vashathke eyed me like an unchained raptor. "How much do you know?"

"Vasha, pet?" Rarafashi sauntered in. "Service me before——"

She saw me and tensed like a piston. In a bright blow of motion, she crossed the room and punched Vashathke in the jaw. Bone cracked. My father sprawled across the bed and coughed a bloody tooth into his palm.

"You stupid slut!" Rarafashi bellowed. "I knew your little mistake would haunt us. And you're talking to it instead of wringing its neck!"

She reached for me. I twisted through my child-sized hole in the wall and fled.

By the time sunrise filled the Prizeheron's glass with rainbows, I'd dismissed the encounter as a bad dream. In class, I raced through an Old Jiké exam, and daydreamed through a lecture on the conquering dragons. As I began my usual afternoon flight to the kitchens, a whip cracked. A familiar voice cried pain.

I ran.

They'd strung my mother's wrists across the grand entrance arch, looping leather ties around the necks of the jade birds. Her *fajix* was gone; blood stained her skirt. The judge stood behind her, flanked by her guards, lifting a gold-handled whip. "Confess, essence thief!"

"Mama!" I screamed.

"Koré, don't——" The next blow silenced her. I raced forward. Guards darted between us, but I was brighter. Stronger. I pushed through their ranks, crying, reaching——

Lightning caught my chest. I fell. Air flew from my lungs.

"How stupid." Iradz's hazy face appeared over mine. She grabbed my sides and hauled me backwards. My legs weren't moving. My body couldn't answer my pleas. "The judge is bright enough to crack you like an egg. You won't delay justice."

Justice. A word for bloody floors and lifted whips.

"Confess!" Rarafashi continued. "You seduced my husband. You despoiled his innocence and robbed me of his essence. That child is proof!"

"You know what he proves," my mother gasped. "You wanted a husband who could—ah!"

The whip sliced across an already-open cut. I glimpsed torn muscle moving and vomited over the glass floor.

This is my fault. Stories warned that bright men hid the falsest hearts, but I'd gone to my father all the same. *I broke into his rooms. A good boy would have sought a polite introduction.* Something was wrong inside me. I wanted everyone's happiness. I spread misery instead.

"How disgusting." Iradz wrinkled her nose at the smell of my vomit. "Leave, Koré. Let Briza take her punishment."

"Please," I gasped, not knowing or caring if I was right to ask. "*Dzaxa* Iradz, if you love me, tell Rarafashi to stop!"

"I can't. She's the judge. Let's go." Iradz pulled my arm.

But I was brighter than her. I wasn't moving.

"Apologize to me and my husband," said Rarafashi, "and I'll let you keep half your store. He must have tempted you with his wicked eyes."

"I apologize for insulting you, *dzaxa*," said my mother. "But I'll die before apologizing to your whore husband."

Rarafashi cut the leather ties. For a moment, I relaxed. Then two guards lifted a holdfast brand.

"No," I said. "Please! No!"

"Captain Briza," said the judge. "I name you Unrepentant."

My mother screamed as they pressed the white-hot circle to her cheek.

My world went dark. When my eyes fluttered open, I lay in Iradz's lap. My mother was struggling toward the door, hands clamped to her face. Guards slid wordlessly away from her.

"That was cool," Iradz said. "I've never seen a branding before. Sorry about losing your mother."

"Lost?" A wild strength filled my voice. "She's right there!"

"Koreshiza," my mother commanded. Her voice cracked. "Come with me, boy."

Iradz grabbed my hair as I struggled to rise. I yelped. "Let go! I need to talk to her—"

"You can't acknowledge the Unrepentant! Our laws would be worthless if we did."

Our laws are worthless already. A dark thought, born of bastard wrongness within me. *Be pretty. Be obedient. Be smart. Be a good boy. Please them.*

"Koreshiza!" my mother said. "Now."

No story or teaching had prepared me to choose when my mother bid one thing and my betrothed another. *A good boy would know how to decide.* But I had no answers.

I let Iradz pull me from the hall as laughing guards kicked my mother away.

Then, when the corridor lights dimmed for sleep, I snuck out and followed my mother's broken-rib breathing to where she crouched in a chip of the green glass.

"You could have obeyed eight hours ago," she muttered as I pressed a holdice pad to her cracked and bleeding cheek.

"I'm sorry, Mama. I worried they'd beat me too."

"I suppose you at least love me enough to come now. That's something." The grumble in her throat said it wasn't much at all. She pushed a pile of rags my way. "Cover yourself. We've got a long walk downstreet and I don't need anyone spotting your bright eyes."

We're leaving? I knew nothing but a world of green. I'd never stepped beneath the open city sky. Never dreamed of life beyond the clutch of my ancestors' massive glass trophy.

But disobedience frightened me more than death. My own choices were dangerous, my own yearnings wrong. I did as my mother bade, and she smiled as we snuck from the halls—a smile that would dissolve forever as Victory Street claimed us for its own.

CHAPTER ELEVEN
The skies above Victory Street

17th *Dzeri,* Year 92 Rarafashi

*"Not intended for multiple users."—disclaimer
attached to Fire Weaver grappling hooks*

I SPRINTED THROUGH the High Kiss's halls. Sweat and slate dust lined my hem, my baton hung naked at my waist, and wild anger filled my eyes—but I didn't care how I looked. Everyone's else's monstrosity was now on full display. I'd show mine.

"Seven!" Ria straightened her leg as I entered the gym. Seven weight disks wobbled atop her foot. Kge laughed and dropped one more on the stack. "Eight!" The watching boys applauded. "Koré, sit on my leg! It'll be funny!"

"Emergency," I told her. "Can I trust you with breaking and entering?" *Can I trust you with anything?* But I still held her bracer. We both needed to know what Tamadza was planning. This would be our last chance.

I needed someone to rely on. An acquaintance, a business partner, if nothing more. Ria, with the innocent swagger of one who'd never been hurt and never needed to hurt someone back, had offered me that.

She kicked the disks up and caught four on her outstretched wrist. The other three hit her shoulder, neck and ass. "Keep my dinner warm, boys. I've got a mission."

We piled into the *reja*. Whip in one hand, bag of raw meat in the other, and a racer's regard for Victory Street's traffic customs, Ria brought us to full speed. Raptors pelted down an access ramp, rounded a traffic circle, and ducked into a crumbling crossway tunnel. Shouting curses in her own tongue, she urged them over a two-meter gap.

"Don't let Tamadza hit you with shadow essence," I told Ria, squeezing the hoverplatform's edge for dear life. When I closed my eyes, I saw Tamadza spinning her staff, drawing shadow from her Reclaimer to taint Geshge and me. *Splintering my family even further.* "The shadow offers a reward if you let it possess you. You can fight it off, but it costs essence, and if you give in, you brighten. Once it has you, you're hers. If you die, she brings you back to serve her."

"Päreshi told me as much," Ria said. "She studied our secret files on necromancers before traveling to the Lost District. You must be strong, since you fought off the shadow, Koré."

"Strength doesn't matter when you battle in your mind." Bones fractured differently than souls. I had nothing innate Geshge lacked. "I simply understand how manipulation feels."

"That's useful. How come?"

Happiness starts with opening up to people. Faziz's words swam through my head, tainted with my anger, impossible to ignore. How much could I tell her? "I attract disappointing acquaintances like a carcass summons flies. An associate is using my past to make me hurt an old... friend. A relative took my father's side in an argument when she promised she'd take mine. That's just today." Merciful dead gods, even such vague language weighed like concrete on my tongue.

"I hate unreliable people. My mom's like that." She swerved

to avoid a passing beggar. The hoverplatform nearly spun out from underneath us. I fell on top of her, locking white knuckles on the platform's edge as we flew up the entrance ramp of the Archive.

"Who taught you to drive?" I gasped.

"I used to race *reja* in the tournament ring!"

"I bet you were a champion."

"Of the afterparties." She craned her neck skyward. The hovership was already moving. "Are you sure you want to come? Confronting Tamadza will be dangerous. I don't want you getting hurt so I can prove myself."

Dzkegé's mercy, she thinks I'm doing this for her. "Tamadza's arrival sent Dzkegé's shade to me. I'm meant to be here." *Perfectly good reasons to join. Nothing to do with a malevolent vendetta against my father. Or my desire to draw out Tamadza's answers with a* shiki.

"Okay. We'll start looking near her Reclaimer. It's the source of her shadows." Ria drew a long brass cylinder from her sash and pointed it skyward. A holdfast grappling hook flew from its lip, trailing fine cable, and stuck on the hovership's side. "Hold on." She hooked an arm about my waist. I grabbed her with one arm and the cylinder with another. The cable went taut.

Together, we shot into the sky.

My chest burned with effort. Ria cursed gleefully as Victory Street fell away beneath us. Blue sky flashed. The open port rose up. We tumbled across the metal floor of the entry shaft.

Ria rolled onto her back, panting as she reset her grapple. "When I said I wanted to earn your trust, I meant so we could go to a *reja* race or a movie. Like a date. For normal people."

"I'd expect a date with a Fire Weaver to be anything but normal." Too late, I realized I'd made her grin. "This isn't a date. It's a mission."

"It's a date."

My cheeks reddened. Zega had never even taken me to a movie. I stood, baton in one hand and a holdlight in the other, hiding my smile. "Careful. The ambassador's servants will be waiting for us."

"Good." A note of uncertainty wavered behind her smile. "I haven't had a decent brawl in ages."

You mean you've never fought with your life on the line. Anyone could prove a coward when true fear hit. Anyone could be Iradz. Anyone could be my mother.

A quiet clicking, like lizard footsteps, echoed off the walls. Blue flames flickered along dark iron corridors. Chemical scent hung in my nose, thick and heavy. Even Ria lowered her voice as the soul-deep chill crept over us.

"Control panel." She tapped a seam beside a brazier. "Here. There should be a common passcode."

"Like this?" My fingers traced the glyph phrase I'd seen in Faziz's stolen papers. *Thank you, asshole, for your help.* A pattern of silver flowers and snowflakes spiraled through the metal. When it dissolved, the panel vanished with it. A long tube lay in a shaft opening on sky, its sides streaked with orange holdfire and green holdspark.

"A cannon." Ria opened a second panel and whistled. "Many cannons. Fascinating! I've only seen weapons like this in museums."

My stomach sank. "How many cannons could a ship this size carry?"

"A few hundred. They're in excellent shape!"

This ship is an executioner's axe hanging over Jadzia's throat. Wind howled outside the cannon shafts. The hovership was gaining speed. "We need to hurry. Someone will hear—"

As I spoke, a wall panel dissolved. Bone clicked on metal.

"Weapons!" I screamed, and lifted my mother's baton.

The attacking soldier raised a dull bronze blade. Though her hands and feet were bare bone, flesh covered her figure, her cheeks sunken and green. Violet coals glowed in her eye sockets. She jerked forward like a puppet, her smile full and kind. A parody of life with its own artful beauty.

Let this work, I hoped, and fired a *njiji* dart into her neck. She lowered her sword at my gut and lunged.

"Get away from him!" Ria shouted, leaping between us. Her grappling hook fired. A bone hand shattered into dust. The soldier caught the falling blade in her free hand and swept at Ria's stomach.

Blood flew. A pink line laced across her skin.

"Ria!" I shouted, driving my *shiki* into the soldier's back. Electricity sparked against her rotting fur cloak. The dead woman didn't flinch. Furiously recalling Faziz's lesson, I pivoted. The full length of my arms slammed steel down on her head.

Bone crunched. The soldier's head lolled sideways. Still smiling, she turned and advanced on me. I scrambled back, swinging at her sword with my baton. Vibrations swam up my wrist. My racing heartbeat drowned out the world.

"Oh no you don't, fucker!" Cables lashed around the soldier's bent neck. Ria stepped on the cords and yanked, dropping the corpse on her back. "No you fucking don't!" She grabbed her second grapple and fired. The small holdfast hook punctured neatly through the soldier's brain. Thrashing limbs went limp. The sword fell.

Ria whistled. "Wow! Batons are shit against these! Are you okay?"

"Me?" My heart kissed the bottom of my throat. My palms dripped sweat as I wrapped my sash around her stomach wound. Sluggish blood tinted silk. I held my breath and waited for it to cease. *Dzkegé's mercy, let it not be bad.* "You got stabbed!"

"Oh?" She looked down. Her voice wavered.

"That's... new."

"Do you feel sloshing inside you? Is your head light?"

Essence sped healing, but some wounds went too deep for its potency. "Sit down. I mean it. Want a tithe?" My instincts screamed I needed all my store. But I couldn't stand by while her brilliant soul slipped away.

"I'm fine. I'll power through. I do that always, and I'm fine."

"Bullshit. You're wonderful, not immortal. No one's fine all the time." I took a deep breath, comforted by the heat and shift of her skin knitting together under the silk. "That's normal. That's okay."

She sighed. "My friends back home... they only want to hang out with me when I'm fine. When I'm bubbly and fun. I'm normally happy... but not all the time. It's nice to hear you say I don't always have to be fine."

Her throat's pulse evened. The blood flow slowed to a trickle. To keep her mind from the wound, I said, "You said making friends was your biggest talent. But it sounds like you've just attracted a flock of shallow assholes."

"When you word it that way, I sound like a completely talentless fuckup." She laughed. "Ten thousand years of Fire Weaver tradition, culminating in me, who contributes nothing but suspicious stains on the entry rug."

"I bet it was an ugly rug before," I said, affectionately, pulling the sash away. Seamless brown skin covered the site of the wound. "How do you feel?"

"Like ruining my enemies' furniture for once." She cracked her knuckles. "Come on. We're almost to the Reclaimer chamber."

Cautious, I peered through the door the soldier had emerged from. On the far side lay a vast and empty hangar where half a million people could have comfortably stood.

"What's in there?"

"Nothing. Yet." My spine tingled. I wiped my bloody fingers in the sash and tossed it away.

Beyond another twist in the hall lay the audience chamber,

exactly as I remembered. Round, blue-lit, and perfectly clean—absent the Reclaimer.

"It's not here." My cheeks flared. Of course Tamadza would move the machine. It held the key to her power. *You fool. You get everything wrong.* "I'm sorry. Shit, I wasted your time and endangered us both—"

"Don't beat yourself up."

I arched an eyebrow. "What qualifies you to give that advice?"

"I'm an expert."

"In self-deprecation, or ancient technology?"

"Both. So I know they couldn't have moved the Reclaimer that far." Ria pressed her cheek to the floor, inspecting the grain. "There must be more panels. What's this—oh, shit!" The center of the floor dissolved as she drew the passcode. She leapt backward as a deep well opened before us.

Voices rose from the chamber below, the only furnished room I'd seen in the hovership. Tamadza sat at a pilot's controls, her white wooden staff propped against her chair. From this angle, I saw a rose of the strange purple substance set in its curling knob. Ambassador Sadza stood before her, head bowed, eyes downcast. The heavy Reclaimer hung chained to the wall. Tamadza's fingers absentmindedly spun a silver ring. *The trigger from Dzaro's detonator.*

The envoy had pickpocketed Dzaro—but when?—and, as I'd so briefly drawn close to Geshge, set off our bombs herself. *Why? She nearly lost her chance to cross War. What did she gain? What am I missing?* What had my father bought from them more valuable than Sadza's public endorsement?

Threads of suspicion crept together, unwilling and awful in the message they spelled. Vashathke wouldn't need the endorsements if he too meant to break the Treaty of Inversions. If he'd always planned to break the rules and crown himself by trickery, by force.

Tamadza addressed the ambassador in a tongue I'd never

heard: like Old Jiké, in its harsh peaks, but with an underlying whisper. Command saturated each phrase.

I lowered my voice. "Ria, do you know that language?"

"Old Jana. I took three semesters of dead languages. I could probably translate writing. Spoken... oh, *rodi Vorona*, I'll give it a shot. Sadza... Sadza says the magistrate is upset about Geshge's death. He was... fashionable? *Dzapimyn?* No. He was useful. Envoy Tamadza says... they all agreed the plan required control of Vashathke's sons. Geshge's anger let him partially resist her shadow. Tamadza doesn't know what's up with you, but she doesn't like you fighting free without losing essence."

My guts knotted. "Do they suspect...?"

"No," Ria said. "If I heard them mention dragons, I'd jump down and throttle them both. No one touches you."

Fire rushed to my cheeks. She'd spoken like I was worth protecting. "While I appreciate the offer, monitoring everyone who touches me will be a full-time job." *Please don't get too close. I drive away everyone who does.*

Tamadza made a cutting gesture with her staff. Sadza's knees buckled. She clawed at her throat. Dark rings glittered below her eyes. *Plots within plots. The ambassador is Tamadza's puppet.* As my brother had been. How many souls could she enthrall?

"Threats, I think. Colloquialisms. Testicles. Tamadza says the magistrate isn't her boss. Tamadza won't act until she has a... *rudzav dusa*? Literally, that means 'a chemist' but I think it's a metaphor. Um. That term was on my final exam. I went speed skating instead of studying. I'm blank."

I bit back an absurd, inappropriate giggle. "What will Tamadza and Vashathke do when they've brought the Reclaimer to Engineering and acquired this *rudzav dusa*? Will they make their endorsement public then?" My words felt desperate. Feeble. Still grasping at the hope this was something small.

"They'll take the *rudzav dusa* and… earn all the money in the world?" Ria screwed up her brow, concentrating. "No. The archaic usage. Conquer. They'll conquer everything. I read that form in a poem once. Dad always yelled at me for skipping the assigned reading, but… Oh. *Sakriu su riu.*"

The cold of the metal floor seeped into my bones. Blood drained from my cheeks. This was how the world broke. How millions fell to the hungering tide, how billions saw their loves and dreams burned on ambition's altar. *Vashathke. Evil words to evil deeds.* "Holy shit. My father's trying to conquer the world."

Ria gasped. Too loud.

Tamadza rose, barking a question in her native tongue. When neither of us answered, she shouted, "Who's there?" in Modern.

Ria set her jaw. A decision flashed in her eyes. "Don't move," she said. Then she snatched my mother's baton from my sash and rolled into the pit.

"No!" I grabbed for her arm, but she was already out of reach.

"What the fuck are you doing?" Ria shouted as she landed.

Tamadza lifted her staff. "Why the fuck are you on my ship?"

"I am Riapáná Żutruro *reru* Päreshi of the Fire Weavers." Essence filled her voice, shaping brass from sheer determination. "It's my sworn duty to guard this planet from you."

Dzkegé's mercy. She meant every word. Foolish, self-destructive, short-sighted… and utterly heroic. Good to her core.

I was the monster who'd let her die for me.

"A Fire Weaver?" Tamadza laughed. "I don't see your bracer. Only an untrained child who fears she's in trouble."

"Fear for yourself." Ria fired a *njiji* dart into Tamadza's chest.

"You have courage." Tamadza plucked the dart free. She showed no signs of the sedative having an effect. "I'll enjoy breaking you."

A shadow miasma leapt from the Reclaimer. Tamadza spun her staff and sent it rippling forward in a wave. Ria tumbled free.

"You'll have to do better than that!" Ria called.

Tamadza bowled a shadow down the floor. Ria leapt over it, landing atop Tamadza's control panel with a satisfied grin. Baton met staff with an echoing crash.

I couldn't let her do this. Couldn't risk losing her. Couldn't live with it being my fault. Looking from the fight took nearly all my will. As blows echoed, my bright eyes searched frantically for panel seams, for controls, for an escape route. *There must be another way out!* There—neat scratching in the iron. Words in a script I didn't know.

A shout cut off—strangled—below. Flesh slammed into iron. Tamadza laughed.

"Please!" Ria shouted. "Please don't—"

Tamadza's staff whistled down. Ria's plea ended. Metal rang as she convulsed, slamming her feet and head against the floor.

The shadow. It's inside her. My fingers flew over the panels, tapping Faziz's stolen passcode over and over. *Please. Please. Please!* Gears and engines spun overhead. Lockers opened, spilling ancient guns and ammunition. But no escape appeared.

"The shadow grants the fondest wish of your soul," Tamadza hissed. "Serve me and be rewarded."

"No!" Ria shouted. Something dulled in her voice. "I've got everything I want. It takes more than whispers to break a Fire Weaver."

"Tell me the same after your next drink of shadow. Ten thousand years your order preserved that barrier. I'll spare a few hours for you."

Do something! I stared at the panels, scratched with unreadable glyphs. Why couldn't they be in a tongue I knew? It might not even be useful translated—might just be a warning about the dangers of opening airlocks, as commonly written below...

Below.

I scrawled the passcode on the blank metal atop the panels.

The wall of Tamadza's office flickered silver and dissolved. A screaming rush of air blasted into open sky. Sadza pulled her master into a sheltered hallway. For a heartbeat, victory thrilled me. I'd done it. I'd helped. The monster in me would strike my enemy, not my dear—

Silver holdweight pulsed gravity down the breach—the ship, correcting its stumble. The wave of force caught Ria's skirt. "Run!" she called as I reached for her. Her foot slipped. She tumbled into empty space, punched out and falling faster than a bullet.

I wasn't running. Not after what she'd done for me.

I dove through the gap. Blue sky and busy planet flashed above and below. Beneath me, Ria plummeted, shouting and flailing at the air.

All my fears and worries ceased to matter. Nothing remained but a brown speck against blue. *I may be a monster. But even if it destroys me, I'll catch you.*

My desire seized me. Washed through me. Made me whole. Wings unfolded from my back, whistling as they caught air. The bones of my skull shifted forward, settling angular and lithe. Silver and ruby scales sheathed my skin. Sweeping lightness filled my bones and gut. Alien instincts and knowledge buzzed across my brain. A wild cry split my lips as the hot wind currents claimed me.

For the first time in ten thousand years, a dragon streaked through the skies of War.

CHAPTER TWELVE
The skies above Victory Street

17th *Dzeri*, Year 92 Rarafashi

"Surrendering to shadow comes easier to some souls, but surrender is ever a choice. It tempts with the promise of peerless reward, but under its thrall, one loses the chance to better the world. Where free will remains, so does a chance to choose good."—letter from High Master Sonuafi reru Nori of the Fire Weavers to her heir Eprue Zucho

"Not a soul in War will deny that the Treaty of Inversions asks too much of us. But screaming conspiracy theories in the street does nothing to uphold the pure and ancient dignity of War"—statement published by Magistrate Kirakaneri of Shadowcoin Street, formalizing her endorsement of Magistrate Akizeké

RIA'S EYES WIDENED—and then we collided. Her knee slammed into my chest. Her fist locked around my neck tendrils, wrenching my head painfully backwards. Then she was on my shoulders, legs tight against my hips, arms locked around my neck. My wings opened wide. Delicate bone and translucent skin bit the air. We rose, soaring, through cloudless sky.

"Holy shit!" Ria shouted as we crested Skygarden. Golden spines flickered beneath us. Guards stared up in awe. With a graceful whip of my tail, I banked into a turn, and we shot past the stacked glass cubes of the Towergarden building. Thousands of gardeners ran to the glass, screaming and cheering in awe. "This is awesome!"

I shrieked agreement. Silver fire fell from my lips instead of words. Joyful shouts rose from the Victory Street as essence filled the crowds.

"For Vashathke!" came a high, distant shout. Air whispered above me.

Dzkegé's instinct guided me—I'd already started rolling at my father's name. "Watch out!" Ria shouted, yanking my neck tendrils. My tail traced a daring corkscrew across the sky. The net spun harmlessly past. Frustrated shouts rang from Towergarden's terraces. "Another—" but I darted forward, and it struck the hovering third bell with a melancholy tong.

They can't touch me, I realized, with dawning, consummate glee. *My father can't hurt me in the sky.*

My wings stroked sunlight, pushing us higher and higher. Ria's grip tightened as we arched across Victory Street, her laugh rich with glee and terror. My silver skin threw sparks as I whistled through the air.

Freedom. At last. All eyes would marvel at my beauty. No soaring arrow would bring me down. *Safe. Lovely. Burning.* My heart beat triple-time to fill my wings, pushing me on into this new discovery. *Joy. Glory. Myself.*

Bigger than politics. Brighter than the fires of War.

The Surrender dropped beneath me, the tall soldier statue glittering with quartz fire. *There!* I flung my wings open to catch myself. The twist of my torso flung Ria backwards. Her hands slid up my throat, throttling me, and her weight flipped our momentum backwards. Blue sky flashed. The next thing I knew, I lay atop her, her hands still tight on my neck.

"Sorry about that," I muttered. Silver light rolled through my throat and face, shaping them human. "Stop choking me or I'll invoice you."

She released me. I rolled over atop her, my back and chest aching. Our hips pressed together. Our eyes met. The edges of hers crinkled with delight. Winds whipped across the empty sandstone of the tall soldier's head, clouds cupping us in secret, reminding me we were safely alone together.

I should move. This isn't proper. But I didn't want proper. I wanted to kiss her smiling lips, draw out our happiness until I could forget the ground's claim on my flesh. Forget everything but her.

Choosing a half-measure, I breathed a stream of essence onto her neck. Silver clouds flickered and settled into her skin. "I'm so sorry. She hit you with the shadow essence, didn't she?"

"Yeah. Felt icky. It offered me the Fire Weavers' respect. My second bracer, my father's approval. I'm sure that doesn't surprise you. But just like with Päreshi, I don't want to cheat or take shortcuts. I want to do this my way. So I said no." She hesitated. "If it's okay to ask... what did it offer you?"

All my dark desires. "A meter-long cock. But what's such a sacrifice for a few more inches?"

"I'm sure you could make that, with your magic." My nerves hummed as she stroked my scaled wrist. "In old photographs, some dragons rivaled buildings in size. Morph big next time! And give me a rope to hold."

"Next time?" I'd exposed myself a hundred ways, each more likely than the next to ruin my life. I wanted to do it again. Feel her straddle me and carry her laugh into the sky, both of us safe, sure, and trusting. "Yes. Next time.

Something softer than rope. It chafes."

"I'll respect your expertise." She giggled. "For a courtesan, you're as adventurous as a Fire Weaver! I like that you do stuff like this."

Like minor felonies? To Ria's bold heart, a wicked streak might be attractive. Not too wicked, though. Not the truth. "Thank you," I whispered. "For everything."

"For me dragging you onto a hovership full of undead so I could win my second bracer?"

Right. She still thought I'd done it for her. "Thank you for… being in that moment with me. I loved it. I'm glad it was you." I stood, my feet and legs returning human, burningly conscious I'd lost my skirt in flight.

"Here." Ria unfolded her sash and offered it to me, along with the scalloped steel of my mother's baton. I knotted the garish red fabric about my groin. Not a proper skirt, but enough to serve.

"I've got extras in my aunt's apartment," I said, remembering. "It's beneath us."

I needed a fresh outfit. And I needed to confront Dzaro about her treachery.

The landlady's apartments, in the tall soldier's brain, rang with chaos. Half the guard was driving trembling servants out the entry arches; the other half fought to bar the nervous tenants gathered at the entryway. I swallowed and pushed forward, conscious of my exposed thighs, my naked baton. *Will they see Koreshiza the sweet courtesan? Or an abnormal deviant who threatens all society?*

I bowed respectfully before the guards. Playing stupid might win me through. "Please. I need to see my aunt."

"No one gets in," a captain said. "She's already smuggled out too many of those damn letters. Thank Dzkegé we intercepted the last herald. She was about to read a public statement announcing the transfer of the Surrender's ownership to Vashathke."

"What?" My jaw dropped. Had my aunt changed loyalties that completely?

"It's like she's gone mad," whispered another guard, young eyes wide with fear. "Envoy Tamadza did something foul when she visited."

It can't be.

Anger slipped me careless. I brandished my baton. "Let me in, or I go through you."

"Boy—" A guard raised her *shiki*. Ria slid between us.

"Go, Koré," she said, and twisted the guard's wrist backwards.

As the women cursed and yelled, I pushed through the curtains and ran to Dzaro's study.

My aunt sat shrunken in her high-backed wooden desk chair, the room's light guttering dim. Purple shadows glimmered under her eyes. At her heels, Slayer yipped and three collie puppies tugged at her skirt. She ignored her dogs, penning letters in a hand that burst from frantic to slow. Uncertain. Aching.

She hadn't turned on me. Not willingly. This was Tamadza's shadow and my father's clumsy hand. *It isn't just his sons he wants controlled.*

"Dzaro?" I whispered. "Can you hear me?"

She turned. "Vasha? How are you?"

The warmth in her voice broke my heart. "It's me. Koreshiza. Vashathke's oldest son. Can you see me?"

"Koreshiza? I—Vasha, sweet, what do you mean?"

She thinks I'm my father. The shadow spun her a dream where they never feuded. Dzaro fought twice as hard as other women to stand strong, to tuck away weakness and unwanted parts of herself. I knew she missed Rarafashi's friendship, her brother's love—but their rejection had wounded her deeper than she'd ever let me see. To feel in your skin, bones, and soul you belonged—the shadow could offer that illusion. But I'd never imagined all my aunt wanted was a family.

"It's okay," I said. "I'm here for you. I may not be all your family, but I'll never cast you out." I brushed her temple, letting my essence slip. It tugged on my gut as it filled her, nervous heartbeats pumping it free. *Take this. I love you. Even if I can't trust Faziz, I love and trust you.*

The shadows cracked. Purple rings faded from her eyes, cheeks soft and elegant beauty, her brightness blooming free. I wasn't sure who reached out first, but suddenly we were holding each other tight while Slayer ate my hem.

"Koré?" She blinked. "What's going on? You... your essence store. I'm sorry—"

"Please don't worry about it." I slid a puppy into her hand. "When did Tamadza attack you?"

"The third bell." Dzaro cradled the shivering pup. "She knew we'd planted the bombs. Made me write a confession."

"I know." We'd felt so clever sabotaging Geshge on the hovership. But Tamadza had held the detonator. And the power. *Something's wrong.* Other worries shrank beside the broken pipe of my aunt's voice. I had to help her first.

"I tried fighting," Dzaro said. Tears flooded her eyes. The puppy licked her cheek. "It offered me family. Like before Vashathke turned against me. I know my brother's people are hurting Victory Street. I shouldn't want to be part of his family. But we were all each other had as children. I hate how our choices have split us."

"I'm proud of your choices," I said. "And I'm here for you. I'm sorry. I should have come sooner."

"It took you quite a while," she grumbled. I might have flinched—but she wasn't truly rebuking me. She was covering something painful she wished to hide. I did the same thing, in my own way. But Dzaro and I could only hurt each other by holding our tongues.

"I... I thought you'd betrayed me. Truly."

"What? Don't be daft, boy. Why would I do something like that?"

"I don't know. I never quite know where we stand. I'm the bastard of a *dzaxa*. I never know if I stand within or without the circle of power. If you see me as a nephew or a servant. If I can speak freely when you hold the High Kiss over my head."

"Look in the drawer." She waved at her desk. "Humor me, boy. Go on."

I did. Dzaro's papers lay in their typical mess, receipts, letters and accounts tossed in a jumble. But one bore my name: a signed and notarized deed, placing the High Kiss in an independent trust, with me as the sole stakeholder.

My heart caught in my throat. The suite wasn't just rent-free. Dzaro had carved it out from her holdings. Nothing short of a magisterial decree could pry it from me.

"I was saving it for a surprise," Dzaro said. "A gift once we enthroned Akizeké. But I should have shared it with you long ago. This fight is yours and mine in equal measure. You've more than earned my trust."

I clapped a hand over my mouth, tears welling. "I don't know what to say."

"Say that you'll keep being a great kid."

I winced. *I'm not, Dzaro. I never was.* But that didn't matter, not with her suffering. Not with the hovership gone and my father's plot in motion. "Stay here. I'll go get Dusklily. You're not alone."

But she had been. When Dusklily came, I'd been convinced my unlovable wretchedness drove her to betray me. I'd missed her desperate need. *My father. Zega. My mother.* The list of my betrayers ran longer than Victory Street. But Dzaro wasn't on it. Neither was Ria. Convincing myself honest souls held secret evil only excused me to push people away. To defend my broken soul and the dragon inside it. To protect others from cutting themselves on the shattered shards of me.

People can be good. Even Faziz, with his dark eyes and

daring smile, hadn't acted purposefully to hurt me. He'd been honest about his aims and the means he'd take to win them.

Maybe the world wasn't all evil. Maybe I only needed courage to take it as it was.

BY THE TIME I arrived at Skygarden for Geshge's funeral banquet, the cuts, bruises and calluses of my mad hovership adventure had faded to nothing. I'd breathed fresh essence into Ria, and she'd tithed back it into me, matching the gift I'd given Dzaro. None who looked at me would see an amateur burglar who'd nearly gone dull or died.

I was attending as Akizeké's date, not a family member, and I'd mocked morning with the flashiest outfit Akizeké's purse could buy. A mesh of stars draped my pale blue skirt and fell from my bare shoulder as a *thevé*. Plain gold bracers wrapped my wrists; my matching tiara held a fist-sized star sapphire on my brow. Rings tipped my fingers with filigree talons. The long one on my middle finger neatly hid Faziz's poison vial.

"I could have hired twenty guards for the cost of that outfit," Akizeké grunted as she threaded her arm through mine.

"Twenty guards won't bother Vashathke."

She laughed. "Men! Pricking each other open over the smallest things. Tell me, did your spat with your father start because you stole one of his suitors?"

You didn't bother sending spies to investigate our history?
"A woman shared us once."

She laughed. "Lucky her. Speaking of Vashathke, did you see those idiots he hired to shoot the dragon? They couldn't hit Skygarden!" Trumpets blasted our fanfare. "I'm putting my own people on dragon watch. Well trained in siegecraft. Never miss a shot."

My own allies might bring me down. But Akizeké was a magistrate of War. Of course she'd jump at a shortcut to the throne, even if it meant accepting Rarafashi's invitation to break the treaty. *Every* dzaxa *would shoot a stranger for power. Only my father sacrifices his own children.*

Down the gravel garden path we strode, under a canopy of ivy and baby's breath. Silent men lifted white ostrich feather fans above us as we approached the small table. *An intimate setting.* After Rarafashi's fall, the banquet in Geshge's honor had been hastily downsized: family, magistrates, ladies, counselors and servants. Barely three hundred breathed in the quiet garden. All eyes watched the judge, enthroned at the table's head. Sprays of lilies and rising night clouds fanned out at her back.

I bowed before her, trying to hold down a poisoner's guilt. "*Dzaxa* Rarafashi, you look strong. I was so worried when you fell."

"I turned my ankle in baton practice," she snapped.

Her hands hadn't touched a baton in decades. The fingers of her left lay slack as the right curled into a fist. *She's suffered at least one stroke. But she's still lucid enough to brag. We might have two months.*

Akizeké led me toward our seats. Fear pressed my throat as we passed Zega, deep in conversation with a councilor. The vial slipped into my palm. *Do it, cold monster. It's him or the High Kiss, your reputation, eight years of building.*

"Don't dawdle!" Akizeké yanked on my wrist. The moment ended.

Later, I resolved. When the servants refilled the wine glasses, I'd slip to the bathroom and dose him as I passed. *They'll be blamed and punished in my place.* But I'd come for dark deeds. My plans always came at a price.

My father, still dressed in black, shot me a hateful glare as I sat. The ghosts of tears streaked his peerless face. I refused to believe he mourned Geshge, that he'd truly loved him. *Your need for control killed Geshge and nearly me. You devour your children to rise.*

"The Lost District envoys have fled our skies," Vashathke said as servers poured lime-and-pomegranate soup, gas hissing from the dry-ice beads that cooled it. "They've flown to the Engineering border, where Armory Street intersects with the Street of Inversions. When you received them, Rarafashi, they offered us friendship. Now they meet our son's killers and conspire against us."

There breathes a magnificent liar. If I hadn't overheard his message to Tamadza, his teary anger might have fooled me. I bit my lip before my sick grin could creep free. *I'm right. He feels no love.* He'd forge his feigned sorrow into a weapon against the Engineers. He'd rise to his throne on a violent tide.

I'd protect my secrets with Zega's death. The same cruel bloodlust tainted us both.

"Are you calling for war?" I said.

"Any magistrate has the right to demand martial intervention," Zega said. "That's ever been our custom, before the Treaty of Inversions strangled us. Do you think a man isn't strong enough to fight for our district?"

I rolled my eyes.

"Don't think your gender exempts you from hard questions, Vashathke," Akizeké said. "Are you calling for war?"

"I'm exploring our options," he said. "War has more power than the world knows. Even the deficit doesn't matter if—"

"Grow some tits and give a straight answer. Yes or no?"

"Yes," he snapped. "They killed my son. They should pay a thousandfold in their children's blood."

Akizeké stood, flourishing a wave down the table at the gathered magistrates and ladies. "You see, friends? The time draws near for a new judge to rise. One of strong temperament and wisdom. Dear, sweet Vasha here risks destroying half the world's essence store if he rises. I ask you grant me your endorsements in his stead."

My father clenched his soup spoon so tight the metal warped. "Judge Neguruyaza che Yetzev thinks my temperament sufficient for War. She wrote to offer me her support after my funeral speech."

I froze. *The Judge of Scholars.* I should have anticipated as much. The government of the Scholarly District had competed against Engineering for years to secure lucrative infrastructure contracts in War. They'd support a candidate promising to reshape the alliances—but nearly as many Scholars as Engineers had fallen in the old wars, and I hadn't imagined they'd agree to something as risky as supporting my father.

That put Vashathke over halfway in international endorsements and climbing fast in domestic. How many more powerful voices would decide his violent stirrings were worth saving a few silver on import taxes and a contract for a crossway arch?

"Peace," Rarafashi grumbled as murmurs rolled through the guests. "I value peace, of course I do. Anyone who's fought the battle of the bloody stool should understand the true cost of feckless warmongering. The hand that passes the throne is mine, no matter who endorses whom, and I'm not dead yet. If the ladies of War back Akizeké—"

"I don't believe you," Vashathke said, pushing his stool back from her. "You think I don't understand consequences because I've never given birth?"

"This is my legacy at stake," Rarafashi said, not looking at him. "I loved Geshge, but I won't taint my final pages in the history books by shedding blood over one boy."

"But you'll consider Akizeké for my rightful place? A sexist—"

"If I'm sexist," Akizeké said, "why is Koreshiza on my advisory committee?"

"I thought he was your whore!"

The word cut like a whip to the face. I balled my fists. *I built my life from nothing, Father, with nothing to trade but my service in bed. We've paid prices Rarafashi and Akizeké can't imagine to make it to this room. With all we have in common, the beauty, the monstrosity, you'd cut me down with a word?*

"How crude," Akizeké said. "The boy has grit. I've promoted him."

Akizeké hadn't told me she planned to promote me—but Vashathke turned scarlet, and I didn't care. I knew I shouldn't, but I flashed him the tiniest smile. *You're not the only man who can rise high.*

"You've done well, Koré," Zega said. "Magistrate Akizeké is quite seduced. Have you told her the secrets you hold behind your smile? It would be a rare coincidence indeed for you to find another person who could love the real you."

I flinched. The elemental fear at the heart of me fell smoothly from his tongue, eating like acid the joy I'd felt when my aunt had embraced me. *Dzaro loves me.* But she only knew the perfect nephew I'd played. *Ria would hate me if she knew.* Even Faziz, who'd offered understanding like balm beneath the Slatepile, kept me as a piece in his game and handled me more carefully than explosives.

"Don't dirty my name with your painted lips," Akizeké said. "You, Zegakadze Kzagé, were born with a leash between your legs. Anyone can lead you around by it. Mine is the wisdom and empathy of the ancient Dzaxashigé line. Koreshiza will go to Engineering as my herald. He'll bring me Judge Žeposháru Rena's endorsement. When I take the throne, I'll heal the rifts Vashathke has opened between our districts."

With all my steel, I kept my spine straight. I'd promised Akizeké a district. It was time to pay her price. But already, my selfishness had left Dzaro burned by a necromancer. Now I'd expose kind, unwitting Ria to the bitter power struggle at War's heart. I'd play with the faith of the one person I trusted as a friend.

"I'd be honored to tell Engineering how Magistrate Akizeké supports peace." I bit down my fearful self-loathing and smiled. "The last thing I want is a violent man on the throne of War."

"But you'll take a violent woman." Zega smirked like he'd made a cutting point. *Empty air and flashing powder.* In the small curve of his lip, I glimpsed what Faziz hated in him. A boy who claimed to care for other men, but drove the poor from cheap apartments to make them rent from deeded *dzaxa* landladies. A child whose sense of fairness stopped with securing his own.

Am I any different? I opposed Vashathke, and therefore Zega—but foremost because of the scars in my heart. *If Akizeké had done worse than them, would I still support her?* The thought chilled me—but no one could do worse than conspiring with necromancers to conquer the world. I'd been spared the choice.

Zega, frowning as no one laughed at his quip, held out his wine goblet for a passing servant to fill.

A chance. My heart sped. "Might I wash up?" I asked Akizeké, only rising at her nod.

Step. Step. The vial popped open in my palm. Zega was arguing statistics about the history of Dzaxashigé male military commanders with an imperial councilor. He wasn't looking at his cup. *Bright, quick and smooth, Koreshiza. What's one more body? You ruin everyone you love. Everyone who loves you.*

What if Zega was right? If only another monster could love the real me, was he my chance at happiness?

My fingers glided over the cup. I didn't look at my hand.

Then, as soon as the bathroom curtains hid me, I poured the still-full vial down the sink.

Dzkegé preserve me. I grabbed the pedestal's edge with shaking hands, panting like I'd run halfway down Victory Street. *I've ruined all. The High Kiss, my reputation, my life…* Faziz would make me pay. Though kind and honest, he'd punish me ruthlessly. He had to, to hold power in a world bent against him. *If he drags me down, my employees will fall with me.*

I'd become a magnet for danger. Leaving Victory Street for a while was the least I could do to spare them.

WHEN I RETURNED to the High Kiss the next morning, sore but brightened from Akizeké's affections, I summoned Ria to my room.

"You need to know what my father said at the banquet last night," I said. "And brace yourself. It's unpleasant."

"Tell me." Ria grabbed the jar of birdseed off my desk, dislodging an errant feather boa. "I want to feed the birds."

We stepped out onto my balcony. Ria pulled out a fistful of seed and flung it; starlings leapt back in alarm, then quickly gathered pecking at her feet. Before I could suggest doling it out slowly, she upended the jar at her feet and the whole flock descended. The chorus of cooing and feathered wingbeats did little to blunt the harsh truth of Vashathke's words: *they should pay a thousandfold in their children's blood.*

"Fuck." Ria shook her head, loose curls lifting on the morning breeze. "This is my fault. I killed Geshge—"

"Vashathke killed him. He sent Geshge as his messenger to Tamadza." Quickly, I detailed what I'd overheard at the state banquet, making it sound like I'd just happened to lean against the right wall to eavesdrop. "We also spoke at the visa council demonstration. It was… strange. I think Geshge nearly gave away their plot to me, and so Vashathke and Tamadza shut him up with shadow essence. Now Vashathke uses his death to drum up xenophobic sentiments and bolster his campaign. It's no coincidence."

"Well," Ria said, "some of it's a coincidence. There's no way Vashathke could have predicted I'd save you from

Geshge. The *opesero* burns on the corpse bolster Vashathke's rhetoric, but he couldn't have arranged for me to kill his son, even if he had the temperament for filicide."

His temperament is toxic radiation. Still. "I overreached my logic," I acknowledged. "But I'm concerned. My father's power is growing. He's made threats against your district. Shouldn't you do something about that?"

"Do what? I'm not the High Master. International politics aren't my responsibility. Don't get me wrong. Your dad's an asshole, and if I had him alone in a quiet apartment I'd shove his head down a toilet and make him taste his words. But I'm not senior enough to intervene in the succession, not unless I have proof he's an immediate threat."

"He said—"

"A lot of *dzaxa* make violent threats against my district." She ground her heel. Starlings hopped and leapt clear of the trembling sandstone. "I'm a Fire Weaver. I've studied history. I hate how this bullshit is still happening, and I want it stopped. But I also know that facts matter. Truth matters."

"I could tell you truths about him that would flood your throat with bile."

"Can you put solid evidence of his guilt in my hands?" When I shook my head, Ria began marking points on her fingers. Sun glinted off the gold-trimmed straps of her *fajix*, warm and welcoming as the brown of her eyes. "Vashathke threw the envoys a parade to win their friendship. We can assume they weren't allied at that point—after all, for the afterparty, they went straight to the High Kiss. Tamadza spent the next few days evading branding for Stonefire's murder. But Geshge signed that contract at the state banquet. So when, in that time, did Vashathke first connect with the envoys?"

"It could have happened any moment, out of sight. My father employs hundreds of personal heralds. No one could monitor each communication he makes."

"Okay," Ria allowed. "But remember what happened at the state banquet? Not only did he trash the Fire Weavers, he insulted the envoys for befriending Päreshi. Why rock the hovercraft if you've agreed on this master plan together?"

"So that no one will suspect my father of signing a secret deal. He's a practiced liar." Dimly, I recalled Vashathke's argument with the judge after the banquet. How frustrated he'd been by the envoys' indifference towards him. But my father had mastered pretence long before my conception. We couldn't trust his words, only his intentions: he would burn down buildings just to light his cigarette.

"All we know for sure is a magistrate—okay, probably your father—wrote them a whiny letter complaining that Geshge is dead and they're not doing enough to support him. Vashathke could have sent that same note to every *dzaxa* on Victory Street. Yes, Tamadza said their plan ends in conquest, but I couldn't translate well enough to judge culpability; if the magistrate is their willing partner or just a useful idiot. So Tamadza's the one we need to capture and question. This is bigger than politics."

Vashathke is just as dangerous as a necromancer. She saw only an irrational man and a boy scared to confront him. Our lovely masks hid our truths. Vashathke was as cruel and bitter as all our murderous ancestors combined. And the fire of revenge flamed my heart, urging me to scheme, lie, and fuck over whoever it took to undo him.

If Ria knew of my twisted past, of my unmanly desire, she'd hate me. And I needed her too much. But she didn't need to agree with me to aid my goals.

"I'm going home," Ria continued, "to report Tamadza's plot to the Fire Weavers and our judge. We're responsible for stopping her and preventing this war. She's brought her Reclaimer to the border. When she gets this *rudzav dusa,* whatever that is, she'll unleash something terrible."

On my father's behalf. If he took the crown, he'd find a way to start the war he wanted, even without Tamadza. Stopping him mattered just as much as stopping the envoy. That meant promoting Akizeké, at any cost. This plot mattered far beyond politics—but politics was the road down which it rode. The politics mattered.

We could achieve two goals at once.

"I'll come with you to Engineering," I said, fighting to sound like this was a recent idea and not the reason I'd befriended her to begin with, "and I'll vouch for everything you've witnessed. We'll gather support to stop the necromancers for good. Together."

I opened my holdfast safe. With trembling fingers, I drew out the *opesero*, and offered it to her. She hadn't asked for it back; she'd trusted me enough to leave it in my hands. *She has feelings for me. I can play those. I can play everything and everyone.*

"Perfect!" Ria flung her arms around me. "And I'll get to show you a decent party!"

I hugged her back. My heart sank under a prickling weight of guilt.

CHAPTER THIRTEEN
The Street of Inversions

22nd *Dzeri*, Year 92 Rarafashi

"As one, we rise."—motto of the Engineering District

"You owe your clients nothing beyond what you're willing to sell. No acts, no comfort, no honesty. The first priority is your health and wellbeing, the second is their enjoyment. Creatively wielded, a lying tongue pleases body and mind"—High Kiss employee handbook

DZARO EXPERTLY STEERED the helicopter between two broken pillars. The snow-capped pyramids of Armory Street fell away beneath churning rotors. The helicopter, with the sail-like fans protruding back from its nose, and the blocky patterns engraved on its steel shell, resembled an unwieldy beetle in the cloudless sky.

"Nice to see my nephew has a... friend?" Dzaro cast a puzzling eye on Ria.

"He's a sweet man," Ria said.

No, I'm not. I buried my face in my book, wishing I could fall between the bench's cushions and disappear.

While Dzaro gave Ria flying lessons in the cockpit, I reviewed the history of the Engineering District: struggles between magistrates, major plagues and building collapses, the history of the Fire Weavers as scholars and adventurers worked to repair the damage of the ancient wars. 'Nothing lies beyond us,' was their motto, 'not healing nor Jadzia's heart.' *A fit order for Ria. People who don't understand some things are broken beyond fixing.*

My target was Judge Żeposháru Rena, age one hundred and thirty-two, mastermind of inter-district infrastructure construction. Like all the judges of Engineering, she'd earned her crown through business merit, and she'd recently selected her own heir: Tożätupé, who'd built her fortune in the *reja* racing industry. Akizeké was shipping me twelve tons of holdspark to use as a bribe, but Żeposháru Rena had substance to spare herself. I'd have to convince her with words, not money, to back my candidate.

Holdspark engines thrummed under my feet. Holdweight strips on the undercarriage pulsed as they devoured gravity's light pull. Ria pulled me into the cockpit as we accelerated. "The Street of Inversions. My home."

A vertical loop of road rose from the city-planet's surface, supporting a domed lattice of iron, bone and copper scaffold, woven in a billion messy stitches. Abstract mosaics of holdweight ran in waves along the street and its crossways, holding *reja* and runners at impossible angles. Steam, sparks and fire leapt from whirling bronze machines that ran along the dome's outer surface.

Another world. Brimming with possibility and motion. The sky quivered where massive holdair arches locked in atmosphere. Flocks of archaeopteryx, feathers flashing white and black, watched us from craggy nests in concrete. *Built for change and motion. For fitting life, not towering over it.*

The clockwork brass cubes of apartments in their millions crawled across a spiral steel lattice. *A street changing shape as needed. Not like Victory Street, where monuments to past atrocities cast human lives in shade. The fruit of conquest and genocide. A world where nothing grows.*

A thousand miniature robots swarmed into an arrow, guiding Dzaro to a crack in the dome's side. As we entered, I glimpsed the Lost District hovership floating above the eastern border ruins. *Waiting*, I thought, *but not patiently. And certainly not ready to hear the word no.*

"Here's where I leave you," Dzaro said once she'd landed. "Any further and the gravities will wreck the internal gyroscope."

"I'll hire a *reja*," Ria said. Bug-eyed machines clacked and hummed as she leapt down to the platform, dragging my chests one-handed over to the waiting traders.

"Is it her or Faziz?" Dzaro wrapped an arm around my shoulders. The green light of the helipad entrance gave her face a knowing pallor.

"What?"

She elbowed me. "I saw how you looked at Faziz on the hovership. Are you falling for him or Ria?"

I coughed and stammered before words came out. "Neither. They're just part of our plan to stop Vashathke." I didn't trust Dzaro with the truth of my hatred for my father. I couldn't trust anyone with my heart.

"Do they know that?"

This question had no good answer. "I... I..."

"Slayer! Stop!" My aunt's terrier had tackled a small robot. The brass bug hissed, its gears grinding in the little monster's teeth. Dzaro pried them apart. "Good luck, Koré. Get the endorsements. Embarrass Vashathke. Enjoy your life."

Enjoy your life, I thought scornfully as I climbed in the rented *reja*. I hadn't enjoyed life since I'd hit Bodzi with a ripe plum at age six.

Treacherous nerves tingled where Ria had touched me as we'd flown over Victory Street. *Joy like sunlight flashing on quartz, made to dim and die at sunset. Though being happy with her feels natural and right.*

The judge's palace hung like a pendant from the street's center. Three hundred stories cascaded in teardrop tiers, its towers crowned in holdlight like falling suns. Clocks and gauges on the walls traced the paths of stars and planets, bells chiming with each click of gears. Steam slunk from the throats of massive pipes, warped in its course by intersecting gravities. Blue-feathered birds flocked between windows, message scrolls clipped to their talons. *Marvel upon living marvel.*

My stomach churned as the main access crossway flipped upside-down.

"You'll get used to it." Ria patted my green cheek. "Look down there."

An enormous bronze globe lay near the bottom of the Street of Inversions, crawling with *njiji*-armed robots and giant dragonflies. Pipe-like tunnels snaked from its heart, threading their way past the street's boundaries. A map of the city-planet lay chiseled into its surface.

"That's the Hive. The headquarters of the Fire Weavers, where I grew up." She sighed. "If we'd gone there first, we'd be drinking with my friends now."

And you'd lose days in a hangover. Which was why I'd insisted we visit the palace first, though I hadn't said as much to her face. I needed her standing to get me the endorsements I'd come for.

A strange shadow flickered at the building's base, then vanished. I rubbed my eyes and shivered. *Just the shadow of my guilt.*

The entry court of the judge's palace lay in a yellow glass globe. Ria flashed the gold foil of our official invitation as we dismounted. The guards took my luggage and escorted us to a brass-walled elevator big enough to hold a bronto. Holdweight shimmered in its sides as it lifted us. The guest apartment they led us to boasted a luxurious sitting area, a balcony opening onto the street, and—mercifully—two separate beds.

"We're on floor three hundred and seventy-two," I muttered when I emerged from the bath, switching to the common Engineering tongue. "Does that symbolize anything?"

"It means they had an open room. Stop overanalyzing." Ria wore a silver jumpsuit embroidered with piping teapots, cinched at her ankles and left wrist with white leather cuffs. She fastened her *opesero* on her right. "Relax. This will be fun."

Stop overanalyzing. I huffed. Blood and the fate of districts hung on the line. "I don't like fun."

"Really? Why bother waking up in the morning?"

To send the tears of my father washing down Victory Street to the sea. "I provide the pleasures others dream of for a fee. Fun is a commodity."

"There's other fun things besides fucking." She flicked one bronze-painted fingernail against my navel. "After you talk to the judge, let's get drunk, rent a private theater, and watch bad movies."

"I'm not practiced enough in your language to appreciate terrible dialogue."

"Don't worry." She grinned, pulling me to smile along. My whole being ached to be what she saw: a normal man, if a bit of a slut, who could turn off his worries for an evening and just *be*. "I'll sit on your lap and explain every stupid joke and plot hole. If your *thevé* chains don't get stuck in my hair."

I'd dressed in stylized armor. Triangles of ruby-edged scale mail draped the front of my skirt. A full-pauldron *thevé* sat on my left shoulder, steel plate linked by electrum chains to my bracer. Red paint bordered my eyes. "I don't look too much like my father in this, do I?"

"Why would that bother you? Isn't he, like, famously beautiful?"

"Never mind." Home filled her with a relaxed glow, a calm certainty in her place and future. I wouldn't snatch that from her with my pain.

Ria frowned, but didn't push me. "Right. Time to be cool."

MY HEAD SPUN as we entered the banquet hall. The chamber was a cylinder, faces lined with brass mirrors, sides tiled in holdweight mosaics. Chefs and servants ran across the top and bottom. Smoke billowed from grills and ovens, cascading over the table that wrapped along the shaft. I caught the complex notes of a curry: sharp cumin, thick turmeric, heady paprika, and chicken crisped to perfection.

A herald announced our names. The judge's eyes fell on us like lightning. Tall, thin and narrow-shouldered, Żeposháru Rena and her three-tiered bronze crown imposed over the table. Her eyes were liquid leather; her long fingers tapped a tablet's screen. Though not as forcefully bright as Rarafashi, her gaze still set my knees trembling. A thousand calculations flashed behind her eyes, weighting our value.

I snatched a mango juice from a walking tray, downing it to settle my nerves. Cool, creamy, and utterly non-alcoholic. *Shit*.

"We've missed you at court, Riapáná Żutruro." She spoke in a voice smoother than a polished gem. "Just because your father keeps his distance from politics doesn't mean it's wise to follow his example."

"Not to worry. I'm pretty obviously not my dad."

"Speak formally. We're at court."

Ria's slippers shuffled on the holdweight-imbued mosaic, tiny copper petals gleaming under her toes. "My apologies, Honored Teacher. My errand tonight is quite urgent. I need your guards to detain the Lost District hovership and arrest its pilot."

"You ask me to detain a foreign dignitary?"

As smoothly as she could—and I assumed the urge to rush or swear rose several times on her tongue—Ria laid out what she'd witnessed of Tamadza, from Stonefire's murder to the fight on the hovership. "You must act immediately," she concluded. "The Fire Weavers take no evil as seriously as necromancy."

"And yet, you, a mere novice, with a known… habit… of overindulgence, are the one to bring such important charges before me?"

Ria winced. I stepped forward, lowering my eyes. "Honored Teacher, I too witnessed the diplomats practice necromancy. I swear by my own business investments."

"You see?" The judge gave me a brief glance, then turned back to Ria. "You bring a prostitute before me as a witness. I speak with your best interests in mind when I tell you—"

"He's not just a prostitute," Ria said, balling her fists. I would have kissed her, would it not critically undermine her point. The judge needed to hear what I'd come this far to say.

"I… I am Koreshiza Brightstar, son of Vashathke Faraakshgé Dzaxashigé, proprietor of the High Kiss, and herald of Akizeké Shikishashir Dzaxashigé. I came to testify to Tamadza's perfidy, and to seek your aid to soothe a rising tide of violence on Victory Street. My father swore violence against Engineering if he ascends, but Magistrate Akizeké understands peace is prosperity. For your people, and for the sake of the Treaty of Inversion, I humbly plead you endorse Akizeké's campaign!"

"Endorse her?" Żeposháru Rena's voice cut like a sword. "Akizeké hasn't paid interest on her loans from me in six years! I'm tempted to hold you hostage for repayment. Don't speak of treaties when your own people break sacred contracts."

I flinched as my rhetoric crumbled. Why hadn't Akizeké paid off her loans? Even the holdspark bribe she was sending couldn't cover that debt. How had she expected me to secure the alliance when she'd already handicapped me?

But I couldn't make excuses. Akizeké could have done it. Any woman on the judge's council could have done it. Vashathke could have done it. I simply wasn't worth trusting.

"Sit down," Źeposháru Rena commanded me. "Tell Akizeké we can discuss endorsements when I'm paid. And Ria—you're no longer a child. If you want me to take you seriously, realize not every pretty boy who smiles at you is your friend."

I bowed and backed down the table, head ringing with self-shame. Ria pulled me into a seat and passed me a tray of samosas. Some experimental chef had supplemented chickpea stuffing with orange zest. Flavors clashed.

"Well, that sucked," Ria murmured, shaking her head. "And since when are you working for Magistrate Akizeké?"

"It's just some light volunteering." I bit my lip before I could spill the truth of how I'd used her. "Is all well with your father? The judge seems displeased with him."

"Yeah, sometimes she'll ask Dad to dig up historic documents that justify some controversial policy." She shrugged. A chickpea nearly tumbled from her stuffed cheek. "So he just pretends he didn't get her message. It gets awkward. Glad it's his job and not mine."

"Ria!" A woman in a high-necked blue jumpsuit bent to kiss Ria's forehead. She was in her mid-thirties, with thin features and silver tattoos ringing her pale arms. I could have kissed her in gratitude for the distraction. "Welcome home!"

"Koré, this is my old girlfriend, Tožätupé *reru* Źeposháru Rena." Ria smiled. "Voro's tits, that name feels strange on my tongue. Congratulations on your appointment!"

Tožätupé laughed. "Źeposháru Rena interviewed fifty candidates before choosing me. All fine women—and a few men!"

Źeposháru Rena considered men. Engineering looked to the future, instead of yearning for a bloody past. They'd never fall into petty squabbles because a judge had only young sons. War could have an heir with Toźätupé's intelligence and spark, not discord threatening to tip into violence.

As Toźätupé sat to Ria's other side, scarlet flashed in her eyes. "You're Dzaxashigé?" I said. Only my bloodline had that mark.

"I'm an Engineer. My grandfather is a *dzaxa* of War." The title dropped shockingly casual from her tongue. She smiled a politician's grin and shook my hand. "What industry are you in, Koré?"

"Adult entertainment," I demurred.

"He's the most famous courtesan in War," Ria said. "And he's taught me some tricks. Did you know there's a pleasure spot at the base of your tailbone?"

Toźätupé's golden eyebrow arched. "How'd you figure that out?"

Accidentally. I turned scarlet. *It requires a tail to stimulate.* "Honored Teacher, why has my patron Akizeké stopped repaying her debts?"

"Because she can. She's as proud as Źeposháru Rena, though not nearly as wealthy. We're suing her. She's a fool to think your sweet words can mend the breach between us."

Us. Toźätupé also had an endorsement to give, as the judge's heir.

"Politics," Ria sighed. "Give me mysterious necromancers every day."

"Are you staying long?" Toźätupé asked her.

"I'm going back to the Hive tomorrow. If the judge won't act, we'll have to stop Tamadza ourselves."

"Always running off on some mission. You truly are the Muruná Davé to my Trochänä Efuä."

I bit into a frozen globe of yogurt and mint-leaves. *We're leaving tomorrow.* My thoughts spun in tangled knots. Akizeké stood below my father in Rarafashi's favor. I couldn't go to the Fire Weavers until I had secured Źeposháru Rena's support. I couldn't sway the judge nor coax Akizeké to pay the debt, but Tożätupé could serve me. I could slip past the electric walls guarding her trust and nudge her thoughts to wicked tracks. *Despise Vashathke, the perfect and polished, on the word of a foreign whore.* A daunting task, fit for a master courtesan. *Make her feel comfortable. Happy. Safe and adored. Open her ear to suggestion.*

My feigned pleasantness could crack open the heart of this district and leave it bleeding in my fists.

I donned an innocent smile. "Honored Teacher Tożätupé, how did you and Riapáná Żutruro start dating?"

In a tale that shouldn't have surprised me much as it did, Tożätupé recounted how Ria had entered a *reja* race at a track the heir owned. She'd convinced her friends to bet fortunes on her victory, but crashed off her hoverplatform as the first javelin struck. Tożätupé, who arrested her, found an injured, embarrassed girl instead of a race-fixer. She'd tended Ria's broken arm. Things had proceeded from there.

"I taught her everything she knows," slurred Tożätupé. One walking tray carried biscuits that looked like tar and smelled of raisins. They'd each eaten three; Ria had cautioned me against them. "She used to think everyone enjoyed being bitten in bed!"

"I enjoy it," Ria huffed.

I jabbed a bird-shaped frozen mango her way. "You're a minority. Take lovers with balls, Tożätupé. We understand the importance of a gentle tongue."

"I prefer practicing my skills on the clitoris. It requires so many different stimulations. I like the challenge."

I'd already failed the first challenge I'd set myself in Engineering. I couldn't fail this one. "If you wish to reach new heights of pleasure, I'd be happy to assist. Between you and Ria, it would only cost five hundred *thera*."

Tożätupé sighed, ruffling Ria's silver hairbands. "I have to pay for your admission?"

Ria nodded. "Sorry, babe. I'm pretty but broke."

Tožätupé kept a salon for these purposes: a room tiled in multicolored mosaics, walls embossed with mated birds, the only furniture a short futon. I hung, pieced and screwed my instruments together, unpacking each with care. *A true professional is always ready to practice their trade.* One case held a green slate anal plug. My cheeks reddened as the stone recalled Faziz.

As the seventh bell struck, I changed my evening dress for a black leather thong and an ebony mask shaped like a snarling dragon's head. Ria and Tožätupé entered clad in loose blue robes, their hands bound by silk ties. At my command, they knelt.

"Simple rules." My fingers rested on the roulette wheel's silver pins. "The first safe word is *vthasha*." Silver, in Old Jiké. "That means I should slow or ease. The second safe word is *thijo*. That's—"

"Dragon," Ria choked past pent laughter. "Seriously?"

I cracked my whip at her buttocks. Her lips shut. *You're a piece on my board, darling. I'll play you both like fine horns, and leave you aching while I glory in victory.* "Say *thijo*, and everything stops. Don't be afraid to use either word. This is for pleasure, not pride."

Tožätupé's thick wrists casually tested her bonds. From the taut arch of her spine, I could see she was fighting to stay quiet. Pride and pleasure were one for a self-made plutocrat. She would revel in contests of the mind and body, satisfied by nothing less than complete victory. *The blood of War courses in her veins.*

The trick wasn't to break her. The trick would be breaking Ria in such a way Tožätupé believed she'd won fairly. To conjure the perfect blend of triumph and delight to render her open-eared before me.

"I spin the act," I said, "and give points. Should you refuse, you'll be punished and earn no points for your turn.

The game ends when I peak. She with the most points wins."

My fingers slid over the sliver pins. The wheel vanished into a blur.

"Riapáná Żutruro," I called as it clicked to a stop. "Pleasure yourself."

The wand hummed as I lifted it off the table. It resembled an artfully curved small baton, down to the pulsing green button of holdspark. A common instrument. Still, manipulating it with bound hands provided a unique challenge.

Ria hiked up her robe and slid the wand around the lip of her anus, hissing as it brushed tender flesh. Her wrists strained. Her spine stiffened as she reached her slit, breath speeding with each electric pulse, sides heaving as she slid into her peak.

"How many points?"

"Ten." I rested a threatening hand on her ass. *Keep her score low.* "Minus one for speaking out of turn."

Tożätupé's spin landed on a minor humiliation. *Good.* "Beg for a kiss," I called. "Until one of us relents."

"Should I beg my little Ria?" she mused. "She's all grown up. A sworn Fire Weaver."

"I'm still only an initiate," Ria muttered.

"I can't beg her to love me. Her soul was shaped for adventure and discovery, not racetracks and banks." Tożätupé crawled forward. Her lips brushed my feet. "You, Koré, could be everything I needed."

If you paid enough. "Say it again. Say you need me."

"I need you!" she ordered. The power of her voice struck like a blow to the chest. I caught her shoulders and brought our lips together. Her tongue tested mine as she leant into the kiss. Her essence twined around my temples like creeping vines. *Strong, powerful and bold.* A less trained boy might have let himself enjoy that. I drank her essence and tallied scores.

"Ten points. Five bonus for excellent use of tongue."

Ria's next spin came up as *kaki*. She refused; it took a certain type to enjoy defecation challenges. I spanked her five times with the flat of my hand. Tożátupé's next challenge was to fit the largest possible dildo inside herself. For this, I untied her hands and laid her back on the futon. Her squeals of effort came to naught as the rim of her wetness failed to enclose the thick ivory instrument she'd chosen.

"Another failure!" I turned Tożátupé over on my lap, cupping my fingers to soften my blows. "Will I have to push you both until morning?"

"I'm down for that if you are." Ria grinned at me. Something tugged at my soul, stronger than arousal. I wanted to kiss every inch of that smile.

That way lies failure. Tożátupé wouldn't like it if I showed preference for Ria, and impressing the judge's heir was my chance to prove my worth to Akizeké and cut my father down. *Think of your dead siblings,* I told myself. *Not Ria's laughter catching low in her throat. Not how part of you wishes you'd watched bad movies with her and fucked together in the dark. That way lies love. That way lies pain.*

Ria spun *dzeza*—the adoration of the foot. "Well," she chuckled. "I'm glad I washed them before we started."

I swept her up, set her on the futon, and bound her ankles with silk. "It's your dear Tożátupé who'll be glad." I waved the plutocrat forward. "Make love to them."

"You can't make love to feet," she groused, mounting Ria's ankles.

"Hardly the spirit I'd expect from a future judge." I guided her bound hands to Ria's mound, closing them around black curls. "There. Everything you need."

"There's no one on my top!" Ria gasped as Tożátupé's sex brushed her foot. "I need—I need—"

The yearning in her voice compelled me. This need, at least, I could provide for her. I knelt and circled her nipple with my tongue. She pressed up against me, and I cradled her head like a priceless treasure, holding her as Tożätupé thrust against her feet and clitoris. The judge's heir moaned in pleasure. Ria stiffened, brightening under my lips. For a heartbeat, we lay connected in one gasping, shuddering chain.

"I need you." Ria's essence slipped, fluttering gently into me. "Koré, I need you."

I almost forgotten to give her the points, and the number I called was impulsively high. *Shit.* I'd put them too close together to ensure Tożätupé's victory. The next spin had to land in my favor.

Nixkia. Whips. Heat shuddered down my spine and gathered in my loins.

"Come here." I tapped the silver frame of my cross. "I sentence you to ten lashes."

Tożätupé rose, blindfolded, and stalked over to the frame. I cuffed her wrists and ankles, then grabbed a raptor-headed whip. Her ass flexed as I teased it down her spine.

"Push me, boy," she said. "We'll see who breaks first."

I don't want to break anyone. The thought arose unbidden. My skills were tools of my trade. I'd never considered what sort of sex I liked as a person. *Focus. You're not free to choose, no matter how Ria's smile makes you feel. Be pleasing. Be cruel. Be what they want and expect, not the monster and dragon you are.*

The whip's crack echoed off the walls. Crimson leather tips grazed Tożätupé's cheeks. "Don't be cocky," I said. "You're in my power now."

My wrist snapped. Leather vanished in a blur. Tożätupé grunted. "Such a light touch. Do you think I'm some fragile virgin? Push me, or I'll rip that sack between your legs and leave your future wife cursing."

"You want to be pushed?" I rotated the cross into its horizontal position and shoved the lower bar apart. It locked, pinning her legs in a split. She bit back a cry of pain. "Careful what you wish for, beautiful." The words curled from me, low and wanton, like some seducer in a film. I settled my fist on the pucker of her anus and donned my most wicked grin. "For every sound you make, I force a finger inside you. Is that pushing hard enough?"

Without waiting for an answer, I brought the whip down. Her shoulder jerked. Her gold tattoos flexed. "Again!" she called.

I buried a finger inside her, seizing control. The whip flashed down. The cross trembled as her bright strength pulled against it. *Again. More of this.* Air hissed at the cut of leather. She clenched against my finger. *Again. This is my life, my skill, my only power. All I have.* "Mercy!" she called. I tucked another finger inside her and tugged.

"Ten!" she shouted as the final blow fell. "I did it!"

I was hard, panting, exhausted, half-shattered. Crimson lines marred her fine tattoos. *I did that?* Her bright flesh shimmered with healing heat. No permanent harm done— yet the marks still looked like the work of a stranger. My head and stomach swam. How could I consent to this? *I'd consent to anything for my vengeance. It's the only safe thing I can want. I will break myself, body and soul, to rip out Vashathke's heart.*

I held my breath and spun for Ria. *Shikikazevzi.* My stomach sank. "The Torment of Humiliations. Remember, you can refuse if you choose." *Please refuse.* I couldn't let her pass Tożätupé's score. I couldn't hurt her deeper than kissing whips.

Ria laughed. "I'm a Fire Weaver. How bad can humiliation hurt me?"

With the room spinning around me, I rubbed the cross with alcohol and helped her into the straps. Her flexible frame slid easily spread-eagled. Like a fool, she smiled.

Be as cold as Vashathke, I told myself. *Play like him. Manipulate like him. Bring him down.*

"This will be... disconcerting," I said, and flipped her upside-down.

Her plume of hair flew in a perfect arc. Steel clanged as the cross's joints locked. Her robe dropped open. She shivered as cool air brushed her inner thighs. I kissed her sweet center and felt her whole body tremble.

"Careful," I teased. "Take too long to please me, and all the blood will rush from these parts and leave them useless."

"I've waited too long for this." Her teeth plucked open the front of my thong. Her tongue curled my tip down her throat. I pressed tight against her, her every sweat-streaked breath brushing me, every gasp shuddering down the back of her throat. *My Ria.* I wanted to throw back my head and give myself over; I wanted to push my tongue inside her and make us melt together.

But that wasn't the game. Wasn't my goal.

"Confess," I whispered. "What's your deepest shame?"

With a last press of teeth—electrifying my spine—she released me and spoke. "I stole another girl's hairpin and gave it to Tożätupé as a birthday present because I'd forgotten to buy her one."

"That was stolen?" Tożätupé said.

I clucked my tongue against the inside of her thigh. "I'm not joking, Ria. The game demands a confession." I lifted a honeycomb-shaped pot off my table. Wax, golden and hot, swirled in its depths. "This will teach you honesty."

She cursed as I upended it. Gold washed through the dark hairs of her mound, down the curved bronze of her rotund belly, filling the room with the scent of lavender and wildflower. Her back arched, wrists straining against cuffs as her moan of pleasure split her lips in an exquisite arch. "Punish me again." Drops rolled off her shoulders and onto my feet. Her breath slid down my exposed shaft. I wanted to drown in her, play her body like an instrument, both of us singing together. *If it was only you and me, I'd bury us in wax and honey until our lips swallowed all the world's darkness. I'd hold you forever.*

"If I keep punishing you," I threatened, "you'll pass out. Tell me. What's your deepest shame?"

"You already know it." Her teeth, impatient, plucked at the fine down of my groin. "I'm embarrassed I don't have my second bracer. I'm not a full Fire Weaver when everyone else my age is."

"Is that all? I want more blood rushing to those pretty cheeks. Expose yourself. Place your whole soul and secrets into my hands and give yourself over. You can trust me."

"Tell me yours," she pled.

"Don't you know?" I chuckled deep in my throat. "I'm broken. In my skin, bones, and soul. I'm in every way shattered, and I deserve it." With that, I slid her clitoris between my lips and pressed down firmly.

Once more, her back arched against her bonds. Then she sagged, limp, languid and warm against me. "I drink too much," she muttered. "I missed tests and failed missions because I was drunk or high in a stranger's bedroom. I started because it made me feel good fast, when everyone wanted to tell me I was doing something wrong, and now I'm scared I'll never feel good without it." She pressed her face to my abdomen, whispering so low my bright ears barely caught it. "Except for when I'm with you. You make me so effortlessly happy. Jumping off the hovership with you was the best moment of my life."

Mine too, my sweet disaster. Tenderness, lovely and unexpected, bubbled in my stomach where her small, sharp chin brushed me. I wanted to sweep her into the dark privacy of bedcovers. I wanted to fly her into a world's worth of sunrises.

I twisted the cross and spun her flat on her back. Metal clattered. Cuffs bit into the soft meat of her wrists and ankles. Her eyes widened, shocked to remember how trapped she was. Pliable. Beautiful. Easy to warp.

"You worthless drunk fool," I hissed, bracing my hands on her hips. "Why would anyone ever respect you?"

She gasped, all tears and no pleasure, shuddering as I entered her, spearing through wet, aching flesh. Her legs quivered. Tears rolled down her cheeks. I could almost hear the safe word bubbling on her lips. *Break for me. End this. Please. I hate this.* "You're useless. Weak. Your cravings control you."

She whimpered, clenching against me, the shudder of another orgasm rolling up her spine. *Shame and deprivation, pushing her over the edge.* This time, her essence stayed locked inside her. *Like I taught her. Resist feelings. Resist me. Resist all love and warmth.*

My soul seemed to slip from my skin. I couldn't let our connection grow cold. I didn't want to hurt her and I didn't want to see her hurt, not after everything we'd been through. *Holding each other against the weight of shadows. Whispered secrets at the heart of skyscrapers.*

I do not consent to having this be what we are and what we do.

"*Thijo,*" I gasped, and sobbed into her collarbone. "I'm sorry. I'm so, so sorry. I didn't mean it at all." I slid out of her, shivering, hating my own skin as I spilled myself on the floor. "I didn't mean it. I didn't mean it." My father's monstrous mark stamped every cell of my body. His legacy weighed my shoulders like a *thevé,* covering all I did.

But I hadn't committed to the game. I couldn't break her.

Who was I if not Vashathke's punishing mirror?

"Ha!" Toźätupé shouted. "Game's over! I win!"

She unstrapped Ria and, together, the two women helped me to the futon. I rested my head on Toźätupé's shoulder, panting as the world shook around me. Bondage could have strange effects on people, but I'd never felt such a crash in me. Like I was the one, instead of Ria, who'd lain down to be broken. *I broke myself. I'm always breaking myself.*

"It's okay," Ria whispered, stroking my hair. "We've got you."

"*Dzajeoz-dzi,*" I gasped, slipping back into my native Lower. My other languages had fled me.

Tożätupé clucked her tongue. "You shouldn't push yourself through such acts if you've no taste for them, poor boy. How does someone like you end up selling his body for coin?"

Oh. I thought I'd broken my connection with Tożätupé when I'd ended the game. But in showing my vulnerability—a real weakness, unlike the simple fears and worries I pretended to before the watching world—I'd won her concern. Her care.

I still had a chance at my prize.

I cast my eyes down, as if ashamed. "My father, Vashathke, has hated me from the moment I was born, prettier than he. My mother raised me downstreet. For ten years, she hid me from his jealousy. But he found us and had her branded Unrepentant."

"Voro's tits," Ria said. "That's awful."

My cheeks flushed. I wished Ria didn't have to hear these lies. "My father offered me a place in his household. I thought it meant he loved me. But he banished me to the kitchens. Dressed me in rags and made me sleep in ashes. He still couldn't hide my beauty as I grew."

"He sought to punish you," Tożätupé said. "Out of mere jealousy."

Yes, that's how the story goes. "A bright young Dzaxashigé woman fell in love with me. She wanted to marry me, bastard or no. But my father envied and hated our love. He sold me to a brothel and told her I'd been murdered. She killed herself in grief." I bit back a sob.

"Oh, Koré!" Ria squeezed my arm.

Focus. Sell it. "Vashathke is cruel, vindictive, and evil in his desires. I beg you, Tożätupé, don't let him take the judge's throne. Magistrate Akizeké may not pay her debts. But my father will ruin lives for his ego."

"Disgusting," Toźätupé said. "You should have told Źeposháru Rena this. She would have endorsed Akizeké right away. For War to enthrone a man who sold his own son into debasement…"

A debasement you've thoroughly enjoyed. I probably should have just seduced the judge. I'd tried to win with words alone, to justify Akizeké's faith in me. But I couldn't change what I was. Could I?

If my blood forever tainted me, why did I care enough for Ria to stop my own game?

Loneliness screamed in the back of my mind, shaking the cage bars locked by turning backs. *My mother. My father. Zega.* Everyone meant to love me had turned on me when I needed them most. *Iradz. Gei-dzeo. A hundred judging eyes calling me an abomination.* If they were wrong about me, a whole district was wrong. I couldn't gainsay the weight of a world.

"Judges don't trust courtesans, Honored Teacher." I took Toźätupé's hand. "But they trust their heirs. If you… not for me, but for the world…"

"You'll have both our endorsements if I need to rip Źeposháru Rena's seal from her fists! And my sanctuary, if you need it. From that filthy stud Vashathke."

So earnest and fiery. So easy to provoke. Whatever I was, I'd won. I would have laughed all the way back to our apartment—but Ria's terrible silence weighted heavy on my soul.

CHAPTER FOURTEEN
The Hive, the Street of Inversions

23rd *Dzeri*, Year 92 Rarafashi

"In the Hive, like bees, we serve the common good and plate out the honey of knowledge. Alone we sting; together we soar."—Reve Raźa reru Mokli, third High Master of the Fire Weavers.

"The children of War shouldn't hear their district slandered. There were two sides to the Brass War, though the Engineers deny it. Such offensive distortions must never be taught in schools." Judge Tharithara II, Year 3 Tharithara

"I'M SO SORRY," Ria whispered once we were alone. "I didn't understand. In my worst dreams, I never imagined your father had hurt you so deeply."

Then you'll never accept the truth. I squirmed from her gaze, my nerves still fizzing with restless energy. "Where can I hire a herald? Akizeké should know what happened. I can contact her quickest through the warehouses she rents

251

beneath the Hive." She'd ordered me to go there tomorrow to pick up her holdspark bribe. She'd be pleased to learn she could keep the goods.

Thank Dzkegé's mercy, Ria let my story drop. "Use the power-mind and talk remotely."

"The what?" She'd used the phrase *riryu-popá,* which meant nothing to me.

"Right, you don't have those in War any longer." She tapped an owl-shaped panel on the wall. Its round face unfurled in a spray of metal feathers, revealing a holdlight screen. "Mass communications technology was invented in the War District, on Shadowcoin Street, but your judges banned it after ancient generals used it to incite atrocities. We allow it, though it's regulated where and how we send data. We can certainly make direct calls to business addresses."

"I never learned any of this in my history lessons." And I suspected the omission was purposeful. "Tożätupé made a reference at dinner I didn't quite understand—*you truly are the Muruná Davé to my Trochäná Efuä.* Who were they?"

"A famous pair of lovers. The founders of the Fire Weavers, sort of. Trochäná Efuä was a landlady who hid millions of historical relics from the invading *dzaxa.* Among her collection were weapons, which her girlfriend, the insurgent Muruná Davé, smuggled into occupied buildings to liberate the slaughter camps. There's like fifty movies about them."

"Those movies are probably banned in my district. But they sound incredible."

Ria winced, her fingers still flying over the screen. "They mostly leave out the ending. Trochäná Efuä's building was besieged. Muruná Davé went to Voro, the God of Engineering and begged for aid. The god gave her a powerful amulet, one the High Masters carry to this day. When Muruná Davé returned, she discovered Trochäná Efuä had surrendered, on the condition she, her lover and her archives would go unharmed. Muruná Davé marched in as she hosted the *dzaxa* at dinner, and unleashed Voro's power, killing herself and everyone at the table."

"Oh. Then… it's a bit odd for Tożätupé to compare you?"

"It's a common saying. Just means two people who love each other with a big fucking disagreement between them. She wants to be judge. I don't know what I want, but I'm sure I don't want to be a judge's partner." The screen sparked, resolving into the image of an empty warehouse. "It sounds so isolating."

There's a million ways to be isolated. I stared at the screen. "Where's the steward? She should be working—an overnight shipment is coming—"

A panel opened in the warehouse floor. Pale, lean women, dressed in simple linen skirts and *fajixa*, winched up holdfast-locked crates in nets of heavy cable. Each had a black tattoo on their shoulder. My stomach sank.

Of course Akizeké would smuggle in her bribe.

"Red Eyes." A disheveled Faziz dropped down in front of the screen. "Leaving Victory Street with your work unfinished?"

Zega's assassination. I swallowed. "I'm the wrong choice for the job."

"You're not the one I would have chosen." He sighed. "But it has to be done, and you're the tool I have."

"You have spies in Skygarden and the Surrender. Don't play pitiable with me." Even as I pressed him, I knew the regret in his voice was real. He hadn't wanted to force this on me.

"Getting just anyone in Zega's bedchamber is easy," Faziz said. "But I need a killer. A woman—or man—with the will to destroy Zega and his bright essence."

Woman or man. The gendered slant reminded me I spoke the same fluent Engineering I'd used since my arrival. Faziz, a dull, had switched to match me. *Odd.* I knew the languages of Victory Street and common Engineering. I could read

Shallow Street's *Jidzoi* and the Scholars' Tongue of Poems. But dull brains took years of practice to gain fluency.

"You think Koré's a killer?" Ria side-eyed the screen. "Just because he's a sex worker—an overdramatic sex worker at that—doesn't mean he's a criminal."

My heart skipped. Would Faziz reveal me?

He laughed. "Speaking as an expert, Fire Weaver, you're right. Koré would make a shit criminal. He's never tasted a secret he doesn't long to spill."

"You do know Koré!" Ria chuckled. "Have you noticed he chews his lip when he's hiding his feelings?"

"And he turns pink the moment you see through him."

They laughed. I folded my arms, pouted, and tried to peer around Faziz to glimpse his crew's work. "Let me guess," I said. "You moved those crates underground to avoid the sun's heat. I'm sure the customs officials lauded your sensibility when you winched up those crates for inspection."

"Our whole planet is built on ruins. Magistrate Akizeké pays well for my knowledge of the undercroft tunnels." Faziz shrugged. "Borders can't stretch to the planet's core."

"They don't need to," Ria said. "My people have thoroughly explored Engineering's undercrofts. There's weird, dangerous shit down there—including monsters who eat mouthy smugglers."

Faziz laughed, glancing backwards as an enforcer waved her arms. "The last crate. Nice to meet you, Fire Weaver, and nice to see you too, Red Eyes. Once I've spilled your secret to Victory Street, and you've lost all your clients, you'll have the time to join me for another sparring lesson."

He blew me a kiss and stood.

Faziz was flirting with me. I wanted to hate him. But, unfairly, my heart leapt when I remembered what we'd shared in the high catwalks of his domain. How even when he played me, it felt honest. How he peered into my shadows and didn't loathe what he saw.

A bright shadow blazed across the screen.

Faziz screamed. Blood arched from a deep cut in his shoulder. He pivoted, drawing his sword. His crew pressed back against their cargo, batons lifted. He ran toward them without a word to us.

They're not bright enough, I realized, heart sinking. The shadow blurred in a poorly resolved whirlwind of death, her knife catching throats with every frame. *An image from War's conquests. My Dzaxashigé ancestors slaughtered hundreds at a blink.* Like loose puppets, the smugglers fell, batons shattered by bright strength. Faziz leapt to block the bright woman's dagger.

Dzkegé's mercy—his sword blade held strong.

"I have to fly!" I told Ria, sprinting to the apartment's balcony, scales sheathing my arms. "He needs help."

"Then he needs us." She squeezed my shoulder. "Let's go."

My hope for Faziz enveloped me. Lightness settled through my bones, twined with pulsing strength. Iron creaked under my bulk. My talons flexed open, large enough to crush heads. This time, I was shaped like no nimble kite, but compact, spike-armored, and ready to fight.

"Watch out for the gravities!" Ria shouted, crouching low over my back.

Together, we leapt into the whirlwind of forces.

A thousand different paths tugged my wings. With one strong stroke, I pushed myself towards a hexagon holdweight on an open plaza. My momentum built. The street rose. I whipped myself sideways and let the next field drag me on.

Ria squeezed my shoulders in a death grip as I shot down a crossway. My wings whistled as they sliced over pedestrians' heads, decapitating a statue with a cracking blow. Pain rolled through my shoulder as I shot into the center of the street's looped arch.

At the heart of the Street of Inversions, I hovered. Dark

bronze and golden holdlight wove around me in a humming cocoon. Dragonflies and gold-feathered finches scattered from my downdraft. Voices rose in a dozen dialects from windows and ramps. *Hope,* they called. Not one asked to cage me. Not one net flew my way.

"That angle!" Ria shouted. "Bank off that field into the cleft beneath the Hive!"

I banked. The brass globe of the Hive flashed past. The bottom of a cleft sucked me into a dark alley.

A warehouse door lay crushed open, metal sundered by bright fists. Dead smugglers lay in broken heaps. The shipment crates rose tall, locked with holdfast. Faziz sprawled across broken machine parts, bleeding from a dozen wounds, still holding his sword.

Silver light shaped me human. *No. Oh no.* I cradled his head to my chest. My fingers twined through his bloody, uneven mane. *Please. Please.* "Can you hear me?"

His response was a feeble breath on my bare skin.

"Someone tried to steal the shipment." Ria plucked a severed hand from the pile of parts. It still clutched a bloody dagger. "Faziz wounded her. She ran, but she might come back with friends. We should go. Koré, tithe to him until his wounds close."

"No!"

"Fine, I'll tithe. Whatever—"

"No. He doesn't want essence. I won't tithe to him without his consent." Even if it meant holding him while he bled out.

"Then let's get him to the Hive. Our tech can heal dulls. Five hundred meters straight up."

I slung Faziz over my shoulders and whispered, "Hold on."

Raw stone and rubble crunched under my feet as we climbed the ruined slope to the Hive. Glass cut my soles. Blood ran down twisted iron artwork. Scree slipped loose. My spine prickled at every darting shadow.

"I feel like we're being watched," I said.

"It's okay." Ria's voice strengthened every meter closer to the Hive. "You'll be safe with my people."

My people. Such naked trust in her voice. Such open confidence. *Everything will be okay. I've got people at my back. A sword in my hand.* Faziz had charged his attacker with the same wild light in his eyes. Didn't they know the world was terrifying? Ria's courage, at least, came from power. Faziz crossed the fire of all fears with an intact heart.

I had to save him. Even if he turned all my secrets against me. Anything else was blasphemy against his glorious soul.

"Help!" Ria shouted, leaping over the final crumbling ledge. Guard robots flicked up *njiji* arms. Settled birds burst up from her feet. "I need a medic!"

The round bronze door, only as tall as a woman grown, spun halfway in its socket. "Password?"

"Bronto and onions? Applesauce? Ugh. Tell Dad I forgot, and I'm sorry, but we need to get in!" She lifted her *opesero.* "Don't make me blast through!"

The door unfurled open like an eye. Two bright Fire Weavers ran out and lifted Faziz from my shoulders. Ria followed them inside.

A bright young man, one bracer wrapped around his prosthetic right arm, stepped into my path. "You can't enter without clothes. Let me bring you some."

Right. I'd lost those when I'd shapeshifted. "Thank you," I said, and tried not to blush as the watching Fire Weavers giggled.

They brought me a *lufoa,* a tight sheath skirt with wide straps that hooked over my shoulders, made of crimson linen embroidered with swirling gold starlings. The weight fell awkward—I wasn't used to how the straps covered my nipples—but the swoop of my favorite birds caught in thread calmed me. Made me feel at home.

"Drink this." The man passed me an enormous ceramic

mug. Notes of pear, cinnamon, and stranger spices wafted up from the tea. "It'll keep you standing."

They're being too nice. I drank, and kept a skeptic eye open as they escorted me in.

The Hive's atrium hummed with darting hoverplatforms. Unharnessed to raptors, they raced down holdweight tracks like buzzing bees. High above, glass bubbles enclosed libraries and laboratories. Hundreds of young women and men dangled off brass rings, reading, eating, lounging, each as bright as any minor *dzaxa* of War. A behemoth skeleton, ten times larger than a bronto, hung from the apex of the dome.

"How are you feeling?" said the young man, passing me a cloth.

"I'm fine," I snapped, wiping Faziz's blood from my hands.

"It's okay not to be fine." He took the cloth back with the jerking gears of his right hand. Flames from his bracer incinerated the cloth. "You've had a big shock."

I didn't answer. The young Fire Weaver kept smiling at me. Like a blood-spattered courtesan was welcome in their Hive. *No one welcomes me.*

"They're in Artifact Vault S," he said, and waved me onto a hoverplatform.

It swept me off to a high-vaulted hall. Strange creations lined the walls and ceilings, but I only saw Faziz, lying in a glass tank inlaid with twisted holdair spirals. Finger-length robots, carved from granite and silver wire, crawled across his prone form. His animating, infuriating grin had relaxed. He looked young. Vulnerable.

The rise and flutter of his eyelashes drew me like a magnet. *Long, full and delicate.* I didn't dare watch him like this in our waking hours. Now I couldn't turn away. My scattering heart whispered *mistake. Trouble. Danger in a dull heart.*

I didn't realize I'd pressed my hands to the glass until Ria walked in.

"He'll be okay," said the man behind her. "My ancestors pulled that tank from a Warmwater ruin. Shaper-made. Never fails. We offered to return it, but their judge gifted it to us. They have peace, but we still have our battles."

A beaming Ria squeezed the man's arm. "Dad, meet Koreshiza Brightstar. Koré, this is Eprue Zucho *reru* Sonuafi. The High Master of the Fire Weavers."

I bowed. "Honored Teacher. Thank you for your help."

Eprue Zucho, who Ria loved and her mentor Päreshi loathed, was short of frame, dwarfed by the surrounding bookshelves, dusk-brown to his daughter's rich teak. Somber grey clouds covered his *lufoa*, the skirt sides split to reveal matching leggings. An *opesero* and a holdice *riasero* shone on his wrists. A heavy medallion lay centered in his golden torc: holdspark, shaped into the triceratops horns of Voro's giants. "Ria told me you witnessed necromancy from the Lost District ambassadors."

I nod. "They've partnered with my father—from whom I'm estranged—to conquer the world and turn districts into undead essence mills."

"That's Koré's theory," Ria added. "I'm not sure Vashathke is nearly as important to this as he says."

Eprue Zucho tapped a nearby robot. "Bring tea. We'll be talking a while."

Spiny-limbed brass insects clambered off the ceiling. Their bodies rippled and folded, morphing into a low table and three high-backed chairs. One produced a steaming teapot and three cups from its innards. Another plated flaky honey cakes. I sucked them apart, eyes watering from hot pepper filling, as Ria told her father everything, only changing how we'd flown together. "A gravity pulse knocked us both off the hovership, fast and hard enough to do real damage. Thankfully, we hit a soft landing—a mushroom building on Shadowcoin Street."

When she finished, Eprue Zucho grabbed a small, cylindrical

robot, and spoke to the ball at its base. "Commission a *riasero* to fit Riapáná Żutruro's measurements."

She jumped, smiling wide. "You're naming me a full Fire Weaver?"

"You infiltrated a Lost District hovership. You uncovered a great evil. You faced a necromancer, with only a baton, to save an innocent boy. You've earned that bracer a hundred times over. I'm so proud of you."

Pride also blossomed in my chest, but I bit it down and stared into my teacup as they embraced. Were all fathers meant to offer love and welcoming pride? Or did only good people like Ria deserve it?

"I made mistakes in War," Ria said. "I'm not as ready for full Fire Weaver duties as I thought. But I'm ready to learn."

"You'll be amazing." He kissed her forehead and turned to face me. "Koré, I think you're owed an explanation. Do you know the rule of entropy?"

I searched memories from my childhood schooldays. "Organized systems slowly fall into disorder. Like... Jadzia itself."

"That's the simple version. Our city-planet isn't a closed system. It exists within the wider universe, drawing energy from elsewhere to build and grow. When the gods and their Shapers began, such energy flowed free through heralds like dragons and giants. Construction reigned over destruction. For countless eras, we built marvels."

"And shattered those marvels through war," I said.

"Your ancestors' wars. Have you heard the true tale of how the gods fell?"

I shook my head. "I was taught the truth was long forgotten."

"Forgotten by choice, by some. Holdshadow, the twelfth substance, grows up from the planet's core whenever blood is shed. As the Dzaxashigé conquered districts, holdshadow conquered the Temple District priests. Their essence became shadow. They tithed, loved, and enthralled whole cults.

Bright Dzkegé, god of soldiers and sacrifice, had charged her followers to fight destruction, death and necromancy. But the ancient Dzaxashigé grew arrogant. They turned to thievery and genocide and forgot their sacred calling." He took my hand. "This may be hard to hear. But your ancestors committed terrible crimes, and you need to listen to the truth, not defend them."

"I understand," I said. "I know I've the blood of monsters."

He gave me a strange look, but continued. "The dragons tried to warn the Dzaxashigé from their bloody course. Aided by giants, they crafted a blade of titanium and holdfast, filling it with the power of their souls. It would offer a Dzaxashigé champion countless victories against the forces of destruction. In return, it would compel its wielder to speak absolute truth and denounce the conquests as evil. No Dzaxashigé lifted the sword. The dragons left the War District and returned to Dzkegé's side."

The dragon's sword. The artifact used to compel truth from Dzaxashigé on trial. As a child, I'd been told it was a gift. I should have known a dragon's gift would be more burden than boon.

"The Dzaxashigé were displeased." Eprue Zucho sipped his tea. "They felt entitled to limitless essence."

It came together. *How like the War District. How like the dzaxa, the people who created me, bounding unchecked toward bloodshed and death.* "We killed the gods."

"The Dzaxashigé turned Skygarden against the Temple District. Every day the dragons remained defiant, they blew up another building. The necromancers had hidden Reclaimers across the district. They spread shadows, and the dead, unlike the living, couldn't resist the thrall. They rose in the millions. Demolished what remained of the Temple District and tore the gods from their thrones. As their dying act, the gods created a barrier to seal off the undead from the world."

"The barrier fell." *A hundred Reclaimers spewing shadow.*

Thousands, millions, dead and broken. "How?"

"I don't know," Eprue Zucho said. "The Fire Weavers have watched it for millennia. The necromancers' shadows have dimmed with time. My predecessors hoped them gone forever. They've likely been gathering power to break through."

"Have you spoken to Päreshi?" Ria said. "She was in the Lost District when the wall fell. She traveled with Tamadza. She might know what happened."

"She's returned to the Hive, but hasn't reported to me." Eprue Zucho sighed. "I could command her presence, but I don't want to anger her."

"I'll talk to her," Ria said. "By the way, Dad, what's a *rudzav dusa*? The necromancers wanted one, but I couldn't translate it."

Eprue Zucho spit out his tea. "A shadow-Shaper. An avatar of destruction. Buildings fall in their wake—but none have existed since the gods fell. Where could this necromancer get enough shadow essence to become one?"

"Maybe they're super patient?" Ria suggested. "The Scholars have been trying—and failing—to recreate their lost Shaper for years. This could be good. Tamadza won't help the magistrate until she's a shadow-Shaper. If she spends decades on this quest, we don't have to worry about Vashathke."

"You always need to worry about Vashathke," I snapped. "Everything he makes overflows with vile poison. The dead rage with the evil that rose them. My family breathes evil free and living."

Eprue Zucho gave me a sad look. I flinched. My father's anger had crept through me.

"I'm sorry," I said, surprising myself by how much I meant it. I felt smaller, somehow, remembering how thoroughly I'd schemed to sneak into this man's trust. Petty effort for what this moment demanded. "It's just—he already plans to break the treaty to seize power. I'm worried what else he may do."

"Whatever happens, we'll take care of it," Ria said.

I didn't know if her *we* included me. But I also wanted to help. "My district started this. I'll help make it right."

Eprue Zucho smiled. "That's very kind of you, Koré. Ria, could you take your friend to a bed? He looks exhausted. I'll keep an eye on Faziz and send him up once he's healed."

Ria tugged me standing. "Come on. It's almost the second bell. You need rest."

With a last look at Faziz, I let her pull me from the room.

CHAPTER FIFTEEN
The Hive, the Street of Inversions

23rd *Dzeri*, Year 92 Rarafashi

"Can you hear me, Eprue Zucho? It's cold. The winds howl through the hull breach. There's footsteps. There shouldn't be footsteps. This is your fault, Epe, but I don't blame you. I loved you once. We were both too stubborn for our own good."—radio transmission, unreceived

WHY DID *I offer to help them?* I thought as our hoverplatform glided through another tunnel. The Fire Weavers uncovered legends from our city-planet's heart. What could I do to aid them? Seduce destruction itself? I was good for nothing else.

The hoverplatform carried us to Ria's personal room, a small chamber littered with trophies from *reja* races, gymnastics competitions, and *jikir* sparring tournaments. Jumpsuits, skirts and sashes spilled from bronze chests. Textbooks and maps covered every open surface. Her rumpled quilt smelled like her, through dust: vanilla oil and pen ink.

She didn't bother cleaning before she left. I hid my sudden smile behind my hand.

"It's nice to be home." She sat on the bed. I sprawled flat beside her. Fog rose in my mind. Essence could extend my waking hours, if I pushed, but the mattress lured sleep. "Are you comfortable in my bed?"

I nodded, touched she'd asked.

"Okay. Since you stopped our game at the palace, I wanted to make sure you felt comfortable around me."

"I felt wrong in the game, but not in a bad way." Truth slipped free, lured by her sweetness, unleashed by fatigue. "I'm not comfortable being with you as a client."

"How do you want to be with me?"

"I'm not sure. I've never had the luxury to want things for myself. Not without fearing everything would be snatched away. You probably can't understand that."

She sighed. "When I was twelve, my mom moved to another street. Me and Dad never talked about it. I still don't know why she left. So yeah, I understand fearing that someone you love can't be relied on. Because sometimes they can't, and sometimes it's easier to only build shallow connections. Make friends who don't care enough to take the bottle away."

Was I a better friend? I cared for her, certainly. But I'd used her for my own gain. More active and purposeful unkindness was mine.

Ria continued. "But there's consequences, to living only in the shallow moment. I used to think the worst-case scenario was disappointing Dad or Päreshi. Now all I can think is, if I hadn't been drunk during the welcome parade, I'd have reached Dzkegé's shade before you. You'd be safe."

"Ria, you can't blame yourself." Her full lower lip pursed with nerves. Did she honestly fear I'd leave her over such a slight imperfection? "Even with two bracers, some things are beyond your control. I'm handling the magic well enough. I'm used to being vulnerable."

"The story you told Tožätupé." She swallowed. "So awful. Sold by your own father?"

I couldn't stand the pain in her voice. *She's suffering because I lied.* "No. I entered sex work of my own free will."

"You... lied? Why?"

"It's... a reflex of mine." I fumbled to set myself in words. "People like thinking I'm not a 'real' courtesan. They're uncomfortable knowing I exploit their desires for profit. Men should be sexy, devoted, smart... but for others, not for ourselves. We're not supposed to be anything for ourselves. I pleased Tożätupé so she wouldn't get angry and hurt me."

"Tożätupé would never hurt a sex worker. You manipulated her to get the endorsement, when you could have just asked."

"Vashathke's evil. I framed his evil so she'd understand. The truth is messy." Tears twisted knots in my throat. "You heard my confession. A normal man might have asked for it, but I'm broken. There's something dark and wrong in me. This is how I work."

"What do you mean?" She lowered her voice. "Does this have something to do with you serving as Akizeké's herald? Why didn't you tell me before our audience with the judge that you'd be asking for her endorsement?"

"Because I didn't want you to stop me!" The words burst out as all possible lies died on my tongue. *Stupid. So stupid.* I should have prepared for this. It was only a matter of time before Ria realized how I'd leant on her to make my case. "Because you think politics don't matter!"

"Politics makes decent people play stupid games for no reason. Like you! I can tell you anything, and you listen and make it all okay—but whenever I try to get inside your head, to understand why you do stuff like this, you slam a door in my face. Do you think that's funny?"

"Do you see me laughing?"

She stomped her foot. *My ever-honest Ria. Ready for anything except, well, everything.* "I'm going to Päreshi's apartment. I'll be responsible and convince her to report in to my dad. And you, useless pretty liar, can go fuck yourself."

She marched through the door—nearly slamming into Faziz, who stood with one fist ready to knock. He stared bewildered as she stormed away.

"Is this a bad time?" he said.

I sighed. "It's always a bad time when you show up. That never stops you. How are you feeling?"

"Shitty. Twenty of my crew died." Faziz winced as he sat beside me. He wore a white robe covered in leaping snow leopards, and he looked softer and a little lost. "I thought working for Akizeké would protect us. People trusted me with their lives, and I failed them. Every time I fail, it—"

He broke off, rolling over the inside of his wrist. Hundreds of small poked dots tattooed a billowing abstract plume of smoke. Some were fresher than others—one, sore and new. Faziz wrote death on his skin.

"It wasn't your fault," I said, thinking of the new support pillar under construction in the Slatepile: he too held the weight of Jadzia on his shoulders. "Don't let it crush you."

"I'm the one who couldn't save them."

"You didn't send the blade. Vashathke must have hired the robber to steal Akizeké's bribe. He killed fifty in an apartment collapse to make himself magistrate. Why not twenty to sabotage Akizeké's diplomacy?"

"I know who sent her." Faziz's high-arched, gold cheekbones turned green. "I should go. The Fire Weavers sent me here because they thought I was with you and your girlfriend, but I'm clearly the last person you want around—"

"I'm the last person I want around myself." Seeing him alive made blackmail feel small. "Lie down. You need rest."

He hesitated—then stretched back beside me, uncurling like a cat. I grabbed a brass-backed hairbrush and ran it through his tangles. His breath caught as I hit a stubborn knot, but he didn't pull away.

"You're a fucking hypocrite," he groused. "Loathing

yourself while worrying I'll catch survivor's guilt. Like it isn't already four-fifths of my brain."

"At least your trauma makes sense. You put your people above everything, because someone must, and you draw zero boundaries to keep yourself sane. You can't save everyone, but please don't let that break you. The lives you can save are enough." I began to braid. "I'm the fucked-up asshole. Even your dull ears should have caught my argument with Ria. I lie like breathing."

"Trauma isn't logical. Neither is how we react. You're protecting yourself. But the habits we build to ward off cruelty can also keep out kindness. You saved me. You could have let me die to protect your secrets. You're a good person."

"On Victory Street, they'd call me a monster for saving a criminal."

"They call me a monster for renting cheap apartments. I cut into *dzaxa* profits. You sneak essence from their stores. They call anyone a monster who doesn't make them rich."

"It's more complicated than that."

"No, it isn't." He laughed. "Essence lives in souls, not bank vaults. The *dzaxa* build cages of customs and cruelty to keep souls like yours docile. They want to trade you like a chest of treasures."

A chest of treasures. Almost everyone saw me as such. A gem for my mother to sell at the best price. A trove for Zega to plunder empty. A poison investment my father sought to divest. I'd always known some unfixable monstrosity inside me had provoked their hatred. But Victory Street defined monsters as lines on a balance sheet who dared act like people.

"It's the *dzaxa* who are wrong," Faziz said. "Not you."

No. My fingers trembled as I locked off his braid. If my world flipped over, like he wanted it to, I might tip off the edge of time and space entire. "I've done terrible things."

"So have I. So has everyone in War. It's a terrible world."

"Nothing makes sense anymore." I slipped a wooden pin, topped with a knob carved like a cat's head, into the twist of his hair. "I've lived for years off my hatred—for myself, my father, everything. You and Ria make me wonder if there's a better way to live. If you want me around, maybe I'm not a monster." Sleep called to me. I knew I should take my hand from his shoulder, but my muscles weren't listening. My silver talons flickered free. Faziz trembled where they brushed him. "You blackmailed me and I'm still happy I sparred with you. I want to trust you. That terrifies me."

"I'm sorry." Faziz ran a finger along my talons. Sank down on the bed, and I closed my eyes beside him. "I'd do it again, and I'm sorry."

The heat of his body held me like a quilt. I dreamed the scent of him, the texture of his hair as his head curled against my chest, the dry calluses of his fingers on my shoulders and spine. *Rougher than Zega. Carved from slate and ashes. But better an honest cutthroat than a pretty boy who rips out your soul.*

I wanted him, and Ria. Wanted them deeply, even though they threatened to change everything about how I lived my life.

When I woke, he lay pressed against me. I would have held him for hours, were it not for the robot at the foot of the bed, holding a note and a deep violet skirt.

Please join me in the conservatory for breakfast. E. Z."

THE CONSERVATORY WAS a riot of green leaves and rich, earthy holdlife. A guitar played a gentle measure on its own strings. Jewel-winged beetles hummed through humid air. Pecking peacocks surrounded Eprue Zucho's table.

When I sat, he offered me a platter of flatbreads, candied yams and yogurt sauce. "You upset my daughter last night."

"I'm sorry."

"Once Ria lets someone into her heart, she needs them to be dependable. The fault is her mother's and mine—when Järecho left, I threw myself into my work. I didn't give my daughter any way to connect with me, outside becoming the best Fire Weaver she could, and I certainly didn't teach her how to build relationships on strong foundations. She dumped Toźätupé for breaking her favorite sandal strap once." He laughed. "But last night, she ran to me to ask for 'boy advice.'"

She said she would convince Päreshi to report in. "What did she say?" I asked, morbidly curious. "If you don't mind me asking."

"She felt betrayed, to realize you'd had other reasons to accompany her beyond just testifying about the necromancers. I told her that yes, you should have been honest about what you planned to say to the judge. But secrets aren't always kept out of malice. When Fire Weavers interview survivors of catastrophes, often their memories lie cloudy, shame-drenched. The mind builds a prison for what can teach nothing but weeping." He sipped his tea. "Ria told me you've witnessed terrible sights recently. And I think you've faced more horrors than she knows."

I froze. Part of me wanted to weep, to embrace him. *I carry so many small cages within me.* I'd grown used to them, until he'd pointed out the weight. But I hadn't been an innocent bystander in my own disasters. "I... thank you for your wisdom, Honored Teacher."

"Don't just thank me. Make things right with my daughter. *Communicate.* Both of you. Ria can't only date the parts of you that please her, but she also can't navigate your relationship if you keep giving her bad information."

"We're not a couple," I muttered. My cheeks flared.

"How do you feel about her?"

Engineers didn't practice marriage. I was beginning nevertheless to feel matchmade. "I want to be the sort of man who makes her happy. Even though I don't think I can. I... I'm a sex worker."

"What you do for a living is your business. You're allowed a personal life, and you're clearly quite good for my daughter. She fought a necromancer for you. She's becoming the leader I always knew she could be."

"Well, how nice for Ria," I snapped, working my pain into a shield. "I'm proud to be the sexy prop helping an immature woman reach her full potential."

"That's not at all what I said. Ria needs to grow up herself. I'm happy she has someone to grow for. And I'm humbled to realize she's come this far by stepping outside my reach." He sipped his tea. "You don't distinguish between being loved and being used."

Occupational hazard. I sighed. "No, I don't. It's something I need to work on."

"How fascinating. Mistrust keeps people from seeing your true self." He peered into me, his eyes the clear brown of holdlife, rolling back curtains and uncovering secrets. "The heralds of the gods are natural shapeshifters. Their true forms are living beacons of their patron's glory. It takes an especially guarded soul to hide that magic."

The teacup rattled in my hands. "Ria told?" I whispered, voice breaking.

"No. She never would. But the whole hemisphere has heard of the boy dragon spotted in the Surrender, and a hundred witnesses saw my daughter on a dragon's back. When she showed up with you..." He took my hand. "You have the Fire Weavers' protection. And, though I won't force it on you, a place in our order and an *opesero* of your own."

I almost choked on a yam. "You're joking. You want me to join the Fire Weavers? Me, with Dzaxashigé blood?"

"Many of your family have spurned the *dzaxa* and come to enrich our district. Some Fire Weavers won't trust your eyes, but you can prove yourself. You're qualified, all your magic besides. You founded your own business. You confronted a necromancer. With a few years' training, you could catch up to Ria. No one would be able to claim you without your consent. Interested?"

I'd never expected this. *Koreshiza Brightstar of the Fire Weavers*. What would it be like to live in the Hive? My face wouldn't recall Vashathke. My bisexuality wouldn't raise eyebrows. My brightness wouldn't mark me a slut. When I'd flown through the Street of Inversions, Engineers had watched and marveled. Not one had shot at a stranger. *Of course not. War can't overshadow all the city-planet.*

I could be safe here. I could be respected as myself. I could fly free.

"Maybe," I whispered, a word with all the promise of sunrise. Anger cried inside me—*what about Akizeké, Vashathke, revenge?*—but its voice felt small beside my blooming joy. *Eprue Zucho speaks like welcoming me is easy. Maybe it is. I'm wanted here.* Light splashed across the conservatory as wings burst free of my shoulders.

Eprue Zucho gasped.

"Get used to that," I said. "What are Fire Weavers paid?"

The alarm went off.

First came a rattle in the walls; robot arms knocking at the concealing panels. A hissing scream rose from holdair vents. Eprue Zucho rose.

"We're under attack," he murmured.

We dashed down the hall to the thick globe of a control room, my heart pounding fast in my ears. Inside, a hundred high screens flashed red. Delicate Engineering script flowed across them in unbroken lines, a single word repeated: Żemchuä. Danger.

"We're pinpointing it, High Master," said a Fire Weaver, her fingers flying over screens. "In the west tunnel—holy shit."

She'd noticed my wings. I waved. "Hi. Ria invited me."

"Someone say my name?" Ria burst into the room. Päreshi followed, still weaving her furs and heavy goggles, along with a group of young Fire Weavers. Faziz entered on their heels, sword swinging at his hip.

"I see you're back to wearing just a skirt, Red Eyes," he said, thumbing the straps of his midnight-black *lufoa*. The garment wove crossing chevrons down his chest. "Are you allergic to covering your nipples?"

"Can't have the Fire Weavers think me a prude. What have you and Ria been up to?"

"We went to Akizeké's warehouse and transmuted my people." He sighed. "Ria's letting me keep the holdlife we got from them. We'll start a memorial garden plot in the Slatepile."

"It's the least I could do," Ria said. "And I'll help install it—can't wait to see that pulley system Faziz told me about building. I wish we could have recovered the cargo, but the crates are gone. Whoever killed his crew must have come back to finish the robbery."

"Akizeké can take the loss." Bile lurked in Faziz's words. I winced. The last thing I needed was mediating a conflict between him and the magistrate. Though would I continue on Akizeké's campaign if I joined the Fire Weavers? "But thanks, Ria. You've helped more than I can say."

"You two can't become friends," I told them. "You both smile too much."

"Hardly," Faziz said. "I only smile around you."

"Concentrate, boys!" demanded Päreshi. "The Hive's under attack. Don't blather on like our High Master."

Ria squeezed Päreshi's shoulder. "Not cool. You said you'd be respectful when I brought you to report in."

"Eprue Zucho doesn't respect me." Päreshi brushed Ria off with a stiff right hand. "Wasting my skills up north. I've come to finish my mission. That's all."

The screens cleared. Sepia footage wrapped the walls,

showing the exit of a Hive tunnel surrounded by ancient rubble. Skeletons in tattered furs clawed at its gate, Tamadza watching with a cruel smile. By her side, the Reclaimer beat like an exposed heart.

"Stupid," Eprue Zucho murmured. "We can blow up those tunnels remotely. She'll never invade the Hive."

"You'll collapse a whole tunnel to avoid a fight?" Päreshi poked his holdspark medallion. "Sonuafi didn't choose you so you could cower from danger. A real High Master would face this. I'm going down that tunnel. Follow if you dare."

"I am a real High Master," Eprue Zucho said. "I'll lead us down."

Our group raced from the control room and packed onto the nearest hoverplatform. Eprue Zucho typed an override code to maximize its speed. Ria passed out batons. I raised my mother's weapon in a taloned hand.

Why do my scales linger? Strangers watch. I should hide. But I didn't want to, now Eprue Zucho had welcomed me. Though Päreshi gazed hungrily at me, the other Fire Weavers didn't stare. I trusted these people, this building, this district. *A true form isn't easy to hide. Not when it shines like a beacon of glory.*

"Pre-battle essence, anyone?" I offered.

Päreshi sniffed and declined; I didn't bother offering Faziz. But the rest took it freely. Bright fists tightened. Bracers gleamed golden. Ria hummed a jaunty tune as we reached the tunnel's end.

The beat of rotting fists on metal drowned out her voice. One lower gate panel already bore a dent in three-inch-thick bronze. Dead hands probed the gaps between panels.

"Reinforce the gate!" Ria shouted, wedging her shoulder beneath the hoverplatform. I and the others fell in beside her, grunting with effort. The platform popped free of its track and grew achingly heavy. Bone fingers cracked as we rolled it against the dented panel. Through the hole in the gate,

I glimpsed the border ruins—what had been east Armory Street until a massive quake shattered its foundations.

Tamadza lifted her staff. A wave of shadows leapt at us from her Reclaimer. I shoved Faziz flat against the tunnel wall as it passed us.

"Thanks, Red Eyes," he gasped. "What's Tamadza doing here?"

"Whatever she came to the Engineering border for." *The power of a shadow-Shaper.* Fear too dark to speak. *What in this ruin can give her the essence she seeks?*

"Resist. Resist. Good." Eprue Zucho helped a dulled Fire Weaver to stand. She'd been hit by the edge of the blast. "Don't let the shadow turn your essence. We can't let Tamadza possess one of us."

"Can't waste a good Fire Weaver," Päreshi grunted, glaring behind her heavy goggles. Her baton dangled awkwardly in her left hand, her right immobile and stiff. *Some arthritis of the joints?*

"Cut this passive-aggressive whining," Eprue Zucho said. "Monitoring the barrier was legitimate work, even if you disliked it. I didn't target you."

Metal crunched. A bone fist, reinforced with dark iron joints, punctured the panel near my leg. I slammed my baton down. The *shiki* sparked uselessly on dead flesh.

"Get back!" Ria shouted. Fire streamed from her *opesero*. Bone crisped to white ash. Simmering red iron fingers clawed the hole, tearing bronze with ear-splitting sound. I struck them until they shattered.

So many dead. "Eprue Zucho," I said, "this tunnel lies on War's doorstep. Your order must have fortified it against invasion."

"There's holdfire charges in the walls," he said. "All sections of the Hive can self-destruct to avoid capture. If things go badly, I'll send you all back and collapse the tunnel."

"Dad!" Ria gasped. "You can't—"

Three more iron hands tore through metal. Faziz shattered one with his sword. Flames devoured the others.

"I'll call reinforcements," Päreshi said, running back to a nearby control panel.

Something heavy struck the brass. Metal boomed and buckled. Locks shattered. Panels fell.

The first undead leapt through the gap.

A wave of *opesero* fire met it. Its still-lovely face smiled as its eyes melted. I cracked my baton against its skull. Bone shattered. My heart thrilled, battle sparking me to life.

"Barrier!" Eprue Zucho shouted. Shards of ice flew from his *riasero*, spearing undead as they clambered through the breach. The other Fire Weavers followed suit. Air crackled cold as the crystalline wall plugged the gap.

"That'll hold them?" I asked, turning back. Yearning for a yes.

Fear flashed in the High Master's eyes. "Ready your dragon's fire. Essence erases shadow. Makes the dead stay dead, helps the living resist."

That I'd learned freeing Dzaro and myself from Tamadza's thrall. I inhaled, reaching for the soul-cords that let essence flow—

"Watch out!" Faziz knocked me down as a shadow blasted past my head. My concentration slipped. Fire fell impotent from my lips.

"You shouldn't have done that," I muttered, rolling out from beneath him. "I'm bright. I can dodge."

"Does your store give you eyes in the back of your head?"

"No." I blushed. "Don't risk yourself for me. I'm not worth—"

"Get back!" Ria shouted, and we both leapt away as three more undead punched through the walls. Her *opesero* fire caught them in a crushing wave. Sweat rolled down her cheeks as the heat washed back over her. Bones crisped. Iron melted. Bodies still poured through the breach. "Die, fuckers, die!"

A Fire Weaver fell screaming as bone shards ripped through her stomach. Another dropped as a bronze blade fractured her neck. Faziz and I pressed close to Eprue Zucho, beating and slicing at the closest undead. The High Master's stream of ice raked heat from the air until at last the dead faltered on the second ice wall.

"Reinforcements aren't coming." Eprue Zucho's voice broke. "I'll charge the metal. Everyone, on the hoverplatform!"

Ria rolled the hoverplatform from the wall to its track. "Are you sure, Dad? I could—"

"This is my duty." He touched the holdspark medallion in his torc. "Up! Now!"

The rest of us packed tight atop the hoverplatform. Eprue Zucho punched through the ice barricade and raised his hands. The air whined and charged. I buried my face in Ria's shoulder.

Lightning struck.

Force exploded through the tunnel walls. A great hand flung the hoverplatform backwards. Metal tore. Undead screamed. I hit the ground hard and rolled, cursing, to my feet.

Half the hoverplatform lay against the wall, its lights dimming. The other half pinned Eprue Zucho to the ground.

Is this over? The gate's gaps lay exposed and open—but the blast had felled the dead. Hundreds of unmoving, blackened corpses lay strewn across the rubble. Tamadza had been knocked on her side.

"We did it," Ria said.

Tamadza stood. Smiled. Lifted her staff.

Another line of corpses walked over the hill, their ranks as ceaseless as waves on the shore.

Faziz squeezed my hand and lifted his sword. I pressed my shoulder to his and braced myself. Before us, Ria filled her hands with fire. *I don't face this alone.* Absurd gladness washed through me.

"Eprue Zucho!" Päreshi yelled. "We have no choice but the charges!"

"You're right," Eprue Zucho said. "Ria! Come here!"

She dropped her fire, ran back, and knelt by where he lay, pinned by the hoverplatform. He whispered something in her ear, then shouted, "Go! Press your bracer to the panel and enter the code! Be sure you only blow this tunnel—not the whole Hive!"

The twisted wreckage of the gate strained under the weight of the dead. I knocked two grinning corpses back with my baton, raking another with my talons. Armored scales spread across my bare chest.

"Hurry!" I shouted to Ria. When the tunnel collapsed, we'd be trapped between rubble and the horde. But I'd die happy, surrounded by those I cared for, wings and talons free. Welcomed at last, where my light could shine against the dead.

"Do it!" Faziz's sword sent a dead man's head flying in a spray of rot. "We can't keep them back much longer!"

The control panel bathed Ria's face in blue light, flashing a map of the Hive and its tunnels. Her fingers typed a passcode. She reached for the icon of the tunnel where we stood—then looked to me. Her deep brown eyes widened, fearful. Her finger trembled above the fatal button. Her lips shaped my name.

She's scared. And this burden is too heavy.

"Voro's tits." Päreshi ran back down the tunnel. "Girl! Out of my way!"

Ria stepped back to the wall, still trembling. Her mentor took her place, swiping her left hand clumsily over the panel. Her right hand hung limp, slashed by a blade—

No. Her glove had been slashed. Sand spilled from the inside.

Someone had cut off her right hand. The stump lay rotten and spongey as a month-old corpse.

Bodies heaped around holdfast-sealed crates. Blood dripping onto brass. A hand, severed by Faziz's blade, still curled around a knife.

"She's been dead all along," I whispered.

The goggles, the heavy furs. Outrage upon witnessing Tamadza's necromancy—a front. Tamadza had sent her brightest undead to slaughter Faziz's people and capture Akizeké's goods.

My father's long, soft fingers seemed to tighten round my throat.

"I should have led the Fire Weavers, Eprue Zucho." Päreshi typed a final code into the screen. The virtual map of the Hive and its tunnels all lit bright orange. Dark circles flashed beneath her sunken eyes as she pulled up her goggles. "But you took what was mine."

"You're one of them," Ria whispered. "Päreshi! You can't—"

"The shadow promised me," Päreshi hissed. "If I brought down the barrier and lit up the bombs, the Fire Weavers would always remember my name."

A noise like a thousand screaming engines rolled through the walls. Heat, white and dreadful, punched out. Metal and stone rained from above. I spread my wings in a shield and dove atop Faziz. Rubble slammed into my back.

Tamadza laughed. The dead crawled towards her, essence flooding from their bodies to hers. *Bright. So terribly bright.* She advanced like a devouring star.

A stone struck my head.

INTERLUDE: AGE FOURTEEN
Old Dread

17th *Shefi*, Year 80 Rarafashi

"A mother does what she must to feed and shelter her family. But a father provides his sons a moral model, the soul's example of what they should become."—The Essential Parent, book commonly gifted to fathers at weaning parties on upper Victory Street

"The suspect is young, pale, blond and bright. Approach with caution."—memo to guards serving the Lady of the Old Dread

HEADMASTER MOFEZO EYED the three boys lying breathless on the ground. One bore a melon-sized knot on his head. "Don't be so aggressive, Koreshiza. It's unseemly."

I'd done too well. My cheeks flushed. "I'm sorry. But see how I've mastered your lessons?"

"Because you're brighter." Mofezo shook her head. "It's not fair you stand out like this."

"Don't be hard on Koré." Gei-dzeo stepped back from her

own sparring partner, who she'd felled with a knee to the mound. "We've been meeting on Old Dread's top deck every night to practice."

"Every night?" called the fallen cadet. Both girls giggled. I lowered my eyes. Gei-dzeo was my girlfriend, but I hadn't given her my virginity yet. I wanted to be good, to save my essence store for my wedding night, so no one could laugh and whisper about me.

But laughs and whispers still came. I was leading all my classes and failing goodness.

After the physical exam, we had to recite the laws of Victory Street. Gei-dzeo stumbled in places, but my brightness let me answer seamlessly.

"Not bad," Mofezo said after I recited the protocols for approaching married Scholar men. "We'll make an archivist of you yet."

A guard archivist. Cataloging criminal records in an office, baton skills forever unused. A good job for someone bright.

It sounded like death. I wanted a life where I could fight for something that mattered.

"That sucked," Gei-dzeo muttered as we left, ruddy curls falling loose from her kerchief as she threaded her arm through mine. "Even after I stole Mofezo's answer key—"

"You stole the answer key?" My voice peaked.

"Not that it mattered. I could barely memorize half of it. You're lucky to be so bright. Once you're an archivist, you can work for your rich Dzaxashigé uncle. I could never concentrate if you chose something dangerous, like street duty."

"I want—" I bit my tongue. I couldn't risk her peace of mind for my silly desires.

"Let's get some fried kelp twists. My treat."

My stomach wrenched. I hated fried kelp. But Gei-dzeo loved it, and I wanted her happy, so I nodded a lie.

Mofezo caught my shoulder as we approached the door. "Koreshiza. My office. Now."

The headmaster's office sat inside an ancient shipping container. Like everywhere this low on Old Dread, it had no windows, only holdlight orbs caught in seaweed nets. Broken training batons, *shikia* sparking wildly, lay stacked in the corner. I gave them a wistful gaze as I sat. Boys couldn't practice with real *shikia*. We didn't have enough body fat to resist the sting.

"You're behind on your tuition," Mofezo said curtly, sliding a balance sheet across her desk. "You owe me ten *thera*."

"I said when I enrolled, my mother lost our fortune in a bad investment. My *dzaxa* uncle sends the payments. He's just forgetful." My invented uncle grew more forgetful whenever my mother found whiskey.

"Send a herald to remind him. Until the debt's cleared, you're barred from classes."

My foul mood had festered when I reached Old Dread's top deck. The ancient beached ship lay on the Warmwater border, all day drinking sunlight. The Shaper-made coating that kept its metal hide from absorbing heat had degraded, and the maze of bronto-sized boiling panels made it a death trap for the unwary, a haven for criminals.

"How was your exam?" asked my mother as I slid beneath the canvas concealing our handmade apartment. The smell of moonshine flushed me. I tried to ignore it.

"I gave someone a concussion." I sat on a crate and dug a wrinkled plum from our half-empty store. "But I got full marks."

"Showing off's rude. Worse, it draws attention. I can't intervene if you draw the wrong eyes."

Admitting her own helplessness cost her. Everything had cost her, these last four years. Grey hair limply covered her branded cheek. Skin sagged on her wide frame. She'd painted her breasts with silver swirls, but couldn't hide her wrinkles.

It didn't help she'd stashed most of her essence in me.

I chewed a strip of dried meat. Harsh, stringy, edged in rot.

283

Shame for complaining to her stung me. "I should drop out and get a job so you won't have to—"

"Does that Gei-dzeo still like you?"

"Yes."

"You're staying until she marries you." She hugged me. I tried to ignore the scent of stale perfume and liquor, to focus on her warmth and love. "Gei-dzeo's no *dzaxa*, but she'll make captain one day. Your marriage is our best chance at getting back a comfortable life."

I don't want to be comfortable if it means you'll destroy yourself. But she'd ended that conversation. "I'm on tuition debt probation," I said instead. "They won't let me back until I pay ten *thera*."

She swallowed. "Okay. There's a woman who'll let me earn the money off her. It'll take a month. See how long you can stall the headmaster."

An Unrepentant female sex worker earned three *vodz* per go. Old Dread dulls never had enough essence to worry about losing it; no one saved theirs up unless they wanted a baby. Less stigma about sex, more competition, low prices. "Why is this woman so desperate?"

"Don't worry." My mother kissed my forehead. "And take this—I don't need so much." Her essence washed into me, glutting my skin with sweet power.

But as I dozed in my tangle of blankets that night, I knew nothing but the fear my mother would get hurt for my tuition. I didn't deserve that much love. I'd gone to Vashathke four years ago. I'd brought her to Rarafashi's attention. Still, she supported me. She was a far better person than I.

The next morning, I returned to the headmaster's office.

"You lied to me?" Mofezo shouted as I finished confessing. "I let you in my school. I trained you myself!"

I'd told her almost everything. The rich uncle was a lie. The gold wouldn't come. I'd only withheld my mother's brand and my father's name. "I'm sorry. When we first came to Old

Dread, my mother made me lie to you. But you taught me to behave better." The last bit was empty flattery—Mofezo had taught me nothing I hadn't already read in textbooks, and no one knew virtue like my mother—but I used each tool I had. "I'll make this right. I can pay you in a month. Please, let me come back to training."

"You think I'll make an exception for you? Because of your brightness?" The careful attention she'd paid me yesterday had evaporated. "This is inconvenient for me."

Inconvenient? For you? This is my life! An unfamiliar sensation pulsed behind my breastbone. Pain with a bite like a *shiki*'s kiss. *My life doesn't matter. My wants and choices don't matter. They never have. Only what I offer her.*

"Lying to me. Sneaking around behind my back." Mofezo spat her wad of greengrass chew into a tin. "Was it you who robbed my office last week? Never trust a bright boy—"

"That wasn't me."

"I bet you know who it was, you little sneak." Her eyes sized me up like lobsters in a market tank. Seeking the most meat for her coin.

I could strike a deal. It was Gei-dzeo's name she sought. *My girlfriend. The one person on Old Dread who makes me smile.* But my mother was selling herself for my place here, and maybe Gei-dzeo wouldn't get in much trouble, and the headmaster's eyes wouldn't release me. *Please her,* my instincts whispered. *It's your best chance to not be hurt.*

I gave Mofezo her name. She gave me a month to pay.

I RETURNED TO the practice courts, avoiding Gei-dzeo's eyes. Moments later, Mofezo called her upstairs. My bright ears caught both women shouting. Then Gei-dzeo's tears. I bit my lip and carried on morning drills. The pit in my stomach sank deeper.

If I'd made a mistake, I couldn't right it with a smile.

Gei-dzeo didn't cross my path for eight days—not in class, not in our favorite restaurants. Then, in a burning foul mood, she caught me on my walk home.

It was my fault. I'd shown her the secret routes through the boiling panels. I'd brought her close to our hidden apartment.

And I'd gotten her expelled.

She jumped off a cool panel and drove a *shiki* into my back. Lightning squeezed my spine. I dropped to my knees, screaming, the world a red crush in my ears. My fumbling fingers barely lifted my training baton in time to block her second strike. My cheek rolled so near a boiling panel I felt my skin sizzle.

"I trusted you!" she shouted, face wet with tears.

"Mofezo would have thrown me out if I didn't! I had no other choice!"

"You could have dropped out! You would have, if you weren't so selfish!"

Had I been selfish? I'd chosen my career over hers. But I hadn't thought of my own advancement in that moment. Only the tangled web of people about me. How hurting one would please the rest. *My mistake.* "I'm sorry!" I said. "Let's talk—"

Her baton cracked against my hand. Bone burst. I screamed and dropped my weapon.

"Stay away from my son!" My mother slammed her shell-patterned baton against Gei-dzeo's back.

Gei-dzeo twisted and pinned her by the neck. My mother's sun-leather face purpled as Gei-dzeo choked her. Hair slid off the white circle of the brand.

"Unrepentant thief!" Gei-dzeo shouted.

I couldn't believe the sight. My mother had been a guard captain. She could withstand anything. But Gei-dzeo was brighter. Stronger.

No one could fight forever.

My mother curled forward. Gei-dzeo's feet came off the

ground. Sunlight wavered off a boiling panel as she slammed my girlfriend against it. Gei-dzeo screamed. Her back blistered.

"You don't touch my son," spat my mother, throwing her down. "I don't care if you've fucked him a hundred times. Come back and I'll force your *fajix* down your throat!"

Gei-dzeo trembled. "We're done, Koré. Unnatural slut. Talking to Unrepentants. No one will ever want you!" Coughing and cursing, she stumbled away.

My mother grabbed my hair. My healing hand burned as she dragged me back to our apartment. "Why'd she jump you?" she demanded when we were safe. "What'd you do?"

Sick self-loathing churned in my gut. "Have you ever made a mistake you couldn't fix?"

She looked at me like a stranger trying to steal our food. I flinched. "No, I haven't. I was a guard captain. But your father—"

She hadn't mentioned Vashathke in years. As if his memory triggered her, she clutched her stomach and coughed. Her bloody lip glimmered in the cast of our single holdlight.

"Your client gave you a disease," I whispered.

"And two *thera*. At least she gave me something in exchange for ruining my life. Not like Vashathke. Not like you."

The words sank deep as a thrown dagger. Crimson steel carving a forked path into my soul. *Not like you.* I didn't flinch.

I'd braced myself to hear those words for years.

"I shouldn't have said that out loud." She sipped from the moonshine she'd stashed behind our lobster shell bin. "Alcohol loosens my tongue. I love you."

Love. I tucked the word to my wound like a bandage. It couldn't staunch the bleeding of my vulnerabilities laid bare. Something strange and terrible grew in the gap she'd carved, red and seething with heat. *Anger.* More powerful than her empty love. A urge to please no one but me.

"What did my father do to you?" I demanded. I'd never

let my tone grow so hard with her. I knew her answer would sunder me, but if I didn't turn my anger toward Vashathke, I'd lash out at the only person who'd always cared for me.

"He said he loved me." Again, she drank. A slur crept into her dull voice. "He was sixteen when he was betrothed to a *dzaxa* he thought beneath him. I was the captain of his household guard. The ambitious little cock seduced me with his red eyes and innocent smiles. I see him when you look at me."

"I'm sorry—"

"Don't interrupt your mother!" She leant in close, breath hot as butter on my bare chest. "I should have known he played me. Vashathke had bed tricks no honest virgin knew. But he flooded me with money and essence, flattered me, and asked me to conceive a child. Said his mother would give him to me rather than risk the scandal of a bastard."

My father. A lying slut at his core. Wasteful with his essence. *Small wonder she hates my face.* I tried to please her. To stop her. "I'm sorry, Mama. He's evil—"

"When you were near full-term," she said, slapping her belly, "masked guards dragged me from my bed. Bound and gagged, they threw me down before Rarafashi's throne. Vashathke was there, my loving boyfriend, smiling as they stripped me bare. Rarafashi had no children from her first two husbands. She needed a fertile young stud. And you were proof of your father's prowess."

My skin crawled. My whole body itched. *Even in the womb, I belonged to something fetid.*

"Rarafashi said she'd marry him. She ordered her guards to kill me—probably because I'd had her husband first, the jealous soul!" She laughed. "I was the best baton on Victory Street. I fought free."

Her weapon still hung in her sash, the scallop pattern drawing my eyes. A guard's instrument, a tool of value. A symbol I yearned for but would never be worthy to wield.

"Look at me. Dull. Poor. Branded. I don't keep a coin or a drop of essence for myself, because I'm investing in your future." Her eyes bored into me, like she could expose my selfish soul. "The gods gave women the power to conceive because we best judge our family's needs. But even the gods couldn't have fathomed your father's wickedness."

"He's evil." My lips moved by rote. I yearned for privacy to think over what she'd told me. But I couldn't leave until I'd pacified her. "Sorry," I gasped, like words could erase me from time.

"Is that all you can say? You have your father's looks, but not his cunning. That could be good or bad, but it's certainly disappointing." She grabbed my chin. Essence burrowed from her fingertips deep into my skin. "Get smarter."

My mind raced. What did she want me to say? What had I done to set her off?

"Still quiet? How typical of you. I'm sick. I'm broken. I gave you everything and you give me spite. I can't look at you now. Go to your girlfriend's apartment; they'll welcome you. Who wouldn't welcome your pretty face?"

I fled.

But I couldn't drag my problems to Gei-dzeo's door. I had to face my curse alone.

A wave had doused the lower smokestacks, and night air kept those boiling panels cool. I climbed a listing spire, stars and planets swirling above me, and stared out at the glass and copper domes of Warmwater. Megalobster and warsquid slid through turquoise shallows, massive keratin shells casting ripples through my reflection. *A monster's reflection. Proof of an unnatural plot.*

A father's duty to his children came as close to sacred as anything Victory Street had left. Conceiving a bastard as a game piece, delivering your girlfriend and child to the judge... *Small wonder everything I do goes wrong. I was created wrong.*

An aberration of flesh and blood. A flaw to mar the judge's own family.

Stamped in every way a monster.

When I returned to the apartment, my mother wasn't there. Like a coward, I was glad of that. At some hour of the night, I heard her re-enter. Her thumb brushed my cheek. *I'm sorry, Mama. I am what I am.* Then she was gone.

I woke in all euphoria. Sunlight rippled through slits in our canvas roof. Gull calls rang with extra music. Even the odor of floating trash stung sharper.

My reflection winked at me from the bottom of a plate. *Oh.* Some magnificence had come over me at my mother's last tithe. Full fire burned in my scarlet eyes. The cool, even curve of my lower lip promised something I didn't yet understand. The childhood fat of my abdomen had begun smoothing to sleekness. My body needed to be carefully explored. One day, I'd reach Vashathke's beauty—

My father. My mother. Truth washed back. My stomach dropped. I looked about me and found a purse of golden *thera* lying on the floor. Beside it, a note in my mother's hand.

Keep the essence and the money. Be strong. I love you.

She'd drained herself of essence. Invested in me the last drops of power that held back her illness. She'd gone to her fate and left me a suicide note.

No.

For hours, I searched the top deck alone, darting away from boiling panels and gang guards, keeping my head low. The sun rose noon-high. Sweat glistened on my arms and neck. Part of me yearned to slink back to our apartment, to hide, cry, and never know.

The dark shape I found below a boiling panel didn't look like my mother. Limp and lifeless. Dark, fist-shaped bruises on her chest. Her baton missing.

A strange calm swept me, like I'd slipped into dreams. As guard training taught, I brushed her throat and found her pulse lifeless. *I should file a report. Send transmutationists to turn her into holdstone.* My head spun as a door slammed on part of my life. My tears felt stuck in traffic streets away.

I'm in shock, I decided. *I'll cry once I've eaten.*

I wandered to the kelp-knot shop beneath the top deck. Customers stared as I ordered wasabi-ginger knots and a cup of black coffee. My skin crawled as I slunk to my usual table. *They can tack my bright hide to a wall if they choose.* Who would protect me, if not my mother?

When a smiling Gei-dzeo joined me at the table, I almost wept in relief.

"I haven't seen you in a while," she said. "Are you okay?"

"No," I whispered. But her presence softened my fear. "I have to confess. I lied when I joined the academy." Everything began spilling loose. I needed her to know the real, darker me. To accept me, somehow, as I was.

"There's no rich uncle?" she said, interrupting me halfway through. "You're homeless? Your mother made you lie?"

I made us lie. I went to Vashathke. I cost us everything. "There's more, if you want to hear it. You probably don't. You should hate me for betraying you."

She sighed. "Part of me does. But I was wrong to rob Mofezo. So I'll forgive you, just this once, and take you back."

"You mean it?" I whispered. Tears slid down my cheeks—at last, the face I should show. But fear and desperation, not love, not grief, drew the shimmering pearls. "You still love me if I do bad things?" All my secret failings: ruining my betrothal to Iradz. Getting my mother branded. The dark truth of my own existence. Driving the one who loved me most to self-destruction.

"What you do doesn't matter." She stroked my hair. "You're pretty. Smart. Strong. Bright. That's what I need from you. You'll move in with my family. When I turn sixteen, we'll fake your age, get married, and invest your essence somewhere safe. I bet a baby would make you smile. We could name her after your mom."

Pretty. Smart. Strong. Bright. Neatly, she'd spelled out my value and the life she'd give me in exchange. Not the love I'd dreamed of, but I'd never been encouraged to dream for myself. This bargain would protect me.

I nodded. Gei-dzeo leant across the table and kissed my brow. Her sash slid. Metal glinted at her waist.

I rose so fast our table went flying. Coffee and kelp scattered to the floor. "Where'd you get that baton?"

"What?"

"That's hers!" Scallop-shell engravings lined the metal shaft. My bright mind whirled, matching the size of my mother's bruises to her fists. Essence turned my voice strong. "You killed her. You robbed her!"

"I only struck her once or twice!" Gei-dzeo shouted, blood rushing to her pale cheeks. The whole shop was staring at us. "She was lying under a panel, already dying. Why not get her back for humiliating me?"

"She loved me!" I said, though the cry felt hollow.

"I love you now. I'm saving you from the street." She grabbed my arm and wrenched me toward the door. I kept my bright feet planted. Voices rose around us. "You're making a scene. Be good and come home with me. Now."

I should have been on her side. She was all I had left. My last protector in a world where my own father had the power and will to destroy me. But anger screamed raw in my ears, more important than safety, more important than any other person but me. *Selfish. Needed.*

Gei-dzeo drew my mother's baton. The *shiki* sparked. "Don't make me start our marriage this way."

My roaring anger overwhelmed all. I forgot my virtues my mother and Gei-dzeo loved. I forgot to be a quiet, pleasing thing. My anger became me and, holding nothing back, I slammed my skull into her forehead.

It went... through.

Blood, muscle and brain made a red and squelching sound as I stumbled back, blinking like what I'd broken would piece itself back together. *That's not Gei-dzeo,* I thought as she fell. The streaming ruin of a skull belonged to no one at all.

The chef's scream "Murder!" brought back my senses. I grabbed my mother's baton and lunged for the door.

The walk upstreet took three days. I kept to the evershade, sleeping in cobblestone cracks, knocking back pickpockets with my mother's baton. Women asked if I was lost, or called crude propositions at my back. I ignored them, quietly crying for the dead I had no right to mourn, picking blood off my forehead with shaking hands.

At last, I came to the Palace of Ten Billion Swords.

The wings of the Palace, the traditional seat of our magistrates, enclosed the crest of Victory Street. Its high steel walls rippled with melted lines of weaponry. Spire after blocky spire lifted skyward. A glass dome crowned its center, great windows staring down like accusing eyes. Even the rubble Slatepile between it and the Surrender did nothing to mar its looming authority.

"*Dzaxa.*" The door guard bowed as I passed. My skin itched as I wandered through wrought-metal halls. Watching eyes found me. Once or twice, I heard my father's name. *Stop. Please.* I wanted no tie to him. I wanted to disappear. But would any place in War hide a monster like me?

At last, I stepped into a market atrium. The crowd swallowed me up. I swiped a candied plum and ate with my head lowered.

"Hello, *dzaxa.*" A short, round boy came up at my elbow. His brown curls made an untidy mop atop his head. "I haven't seen you before. I'm Zegakadze Kzagé. Call me Zega."

"I'm Koré. No *dzaxa.*"

"But you're so bright. And you have the Dzaxashigé eyes."

"I'm a bastard," I spat. It no longer hurt. *Bastard* was better than *monster*, and I had no need to please this strange boy. "All the essence and looks. None of the annoying family obligations."

He took my hand. His palm was warm. Soft. Welcoming. "Tell me more."

CHAPTER SIXTEEN
Border Ruins

25th *Dzeri*, Year 92 Rarafashi

"Ours is fire blood and brass bones. Engineers don't break easy. We rise, rebuild, and reshape the world back to wholeness."—Reve Raźa reru Mokli, third High Master of the Fire Weavers

"Today I executed three hundred Engineers who missed quota. My shoulders hurt and the screaming children give me migraines, but at least the survivors stepped up their production time on the new drones."—Varjthosheri the Dragon-Blessed, Shaper-Judge of War

EPRUE ZUCHO'S MOAN cut through my ringing ears. His head slammed back against the ground.

The shadow has him, I thought, crawling up through debris. Rubble slaked from my wings. Dying beams of sunset washed the rubble heap. Motes of light floated in evershade.

"Daddy?" Ria said. "Please. Fight back." She'd lifted some rubble from his chest, but left the collapsed hoverplatform atop the bloody, shredded mess of his legs.

I wrapped a shaking arm around her shoulders and breathed a stream of essence over Eprue Zucho. He relaxed, whispering, "My baby?"

Ria burst into tears.

"I'm sorry, sweetheart. I asked too much of you."

The smoking ruin of the tunnel snaked back to the Street of Inversions. Shattered brass marked where the Hive had stood. Unearthly shadows danced on the metal.

The Fire Weavers had fallen.

Not fair, whispered some selfish part of me. *They were supposed to be my fresh start.* But I couldn't mourn what wasn't mine. Not when Ria's world lay shattered.

Wordlessly, Faziz squeezed my hand and went to support Ria's other side.

"I should have realized they'd infected Päreshi," Eprue Zucho gasped. "A ploy... to trick out the password for the bombs. She must have discovered how to break the barrier, and they took her..." Blood pooled on his lips.

"You couldn't have known," Ria said. "We all trusted her."

"Protect your dragon," he breathed. "Use his power to heal the world."

"Don't talk like this, Daddy. You won't..."

"It's a poor High Master who outlives his own order."

I looked to where Päreshi's drained body lay, the undead army crumbling to dust around her. "*Dzkegé jekfik*. Tamadza didn't just want to kill the Fire Weavers. She's draining them to become a shadow-Shaper." She and Vashathke would conquer side-by-side.

"Rarafashi must be warned. The War District must fight Tamadza," Eprue Zucho whispered. "Cross the ruins to Armory Street. Ria, take my bracers and torc. You're the High Master now. Find the survivors and rebuild."

"I can't! Not me!"

He cupped her cheek. "You can do this. My baby..."

She grabbed his hand, sobbing as it went limp. I held her gently, my own chest twisting with every cry torn from her. *I'd rip out my bones to spare you this pain.* I could only brace her heartbreak on my flesh.

It felt like hours before Faziz spoke. "We have to seek cover."

Something shifted in Ria's face. Cracks ran through her concrete dust mask, a web of splintering stone. Her full lips narrowed with intent. The brass of her eyes went hard, and I shivered as they fell on me. I knew anger, hate and vengeance in my own soul, but her righteous force could shatter districts.

"Wait five minutes," Ria ordered. She stripped the bracers and torc from her father, replacing her own *opesero* with his. Metal crawled with living light as it adjusted to fit her. With a clenched fist, she poured flames over her father's body.

"Tamadza won't have him, and she won't have us." Ria shoved aside a boulder, revealing a downward staircase. "Let's go."

A waterproof pack marked with Voro's triceratops horns sat on the first landing. Ria grabbed it and drew out a holdlight lantern. "Southeast," she grunted, checking the compass in its grip. "Back to War. Follow me."

The staircase cut deep through rubble. Some steps were capped with white marble; others bare concrete. The mural-painted tunnel roof vanished into evershade. Holdair strips hissed with effort from making oxygen. Pockets of dry gas grew long. I watched Faziz's limping steps with sinking dread.

"Water break," Ria commanded as we reached the next landing.

Her pack held a holdwater-lined bottle that filled itself when you twisted the cap. I took a shallow sip and passed it to Faziz. "Are we staying on this stair? Armory Street is hundreds of stories above sea level. We can't go down forever."

"Tunnels are safer than the surface," Faziz said. "This

whole ruin is grey concrete. A Shaper will spot us. Their essence practically overflows, they hold so much of it. She'll sense us if we sneeze from a mile away."

Ria crossed the landing, her lantern held high. Sculptures swam into view: men, women, and dragons in weathered armor, throned on the bowed shoulders of giants. At last, the light hit a scree of fallen stones. "We'll gain height if we climb."

I met Faziz's eyes. "Can you make it?"

"Do you have a grappling hook, Ria?"

She pulled one from the pack, the same model she'd used to vault us into the Lost District's hovership, and pulled the trigger. The hook sailed up into evershade and struck concrete.

Faziz took the winch. "Do you need help, Koré? It can easily lift two."

Let him help me? After I'd exposed him to the mortal danger of Tamadza and my father's plot? "I'm fine," I snapped, and set myself to the climb.

Centuries of rain had worn the slope slippery. Some handholds crumbled at touch; others burned my palms with caustic rime. Ria climbed ahead, the lantern on her belt all the light in my world. Faziz slowed the winch's motor to keep pace with me.

"Sure you don't want a lift?" he asked. "Your hands are bleeding."

"I'll get used to it," I said, and reached for a higher stone.

Pain flickered across his face. I hated myself for inflicting it. *Climb faster. Punish yourself. You should have noticed Päreshi. You ruin everything. This is all your fault.*

Faziz gunned the winch and rose ahead.

Strain burned my shoulders. Blood and white power ran down my wrists. Nothing changed in the bobbing circle of light save the occasional flicker of falling scree. The winch engine creaked. Ria murmured quiet curses. Once, sparks hissed. Her light dropped ten feet.

"Careful of that black statue!" she shouted as the scent of burnt hair wafted down. "There's a holdspark defense mechanism. Dangerous!"

I clung to the strength in her voice. Ria had pulled the power of a giant from her soul. Her raw, heroic potential burned like her lantern. So long as she led, we had a chance.

At last, the climb opened onto night sky. We pulled ourselves up into the deep bowl of an amphitheater. White concrete arches framed dancing planets. The cruel-carved faces of War's soldiers stared down from every flat surface. Freezing wind painted goosebumps up my arms.

"We'll spend the night here," Ria said, burnt and tangled hair stirring around her dust-streaked face.

"Is that moon supposed to be so bright?" Faziz pointed up.

"It's the hovership," Ria said. The silver faces on its sides screamed quiet agony against stars. "It's getting closer."

"I'd rather have a ship after us than a shadow-Shaper on foot," he said. "My district's Shaper made horrors and marvels alike. When he disappeared, people mourned like the gods had fallen again—"

The air cracked in the wake of cutting sound. Faziz was thrown back into me. A birdlike violet form shot across the horizon, crossing the ruins in a heartbeat. Rubble in its path curled to powder. Cracks swarmed through the coliseum walls. One section broke and toppled towards us.

"Look out!" I screamed.

Ria lifted her hand. Air hissed. Space tightened. A bronto-sized wedge of ice cracked into existence. The wall slammed down across it.

"What was that?" I said as the dust settled.

"True Shapers build." Ria's voice shook as concrete dust swirled around her. "Their shadows destroy. We should get back underground."

We turned to find the tunnel had collapsed in Tamadza's wake.

"Shift rocks," Ria commanded, and we bent to the task. Faziz shifted loose shards, gasping as jagged concrete cut his palms. Ria and I hoisted boulders off into the night. Sweat rolled down my neck. My torn palms and aching back screamed curses at my nerves. Ria and Faziz spoke in low voices, but I tried to block them out. The weight of stone and failure made comfort feel like heresy to the moment. *I should suffer.*

With each piece of debris we moved, the tunnel groaned and collapsed further. "We'll never get back down," I declared.

"Then we find another route," Ria said.

"What if there is no other way and I've doomed us all?" Ria, with her fire and wisdom. Faziz, with his undying passion and secret smile. Two pillars I yearned to lean on. Two people I feared I'd destroy.

"This isn't your fault."

She wanted to make me feel better. I didn't deserve better or her. My presence ruined everything.

I turned and fled up the coliseum's side, leaping over fallen statues and wide cracks, desperately seeking distance. At last, I reached the upper tier and ducked inside an enclosed booth.

Millennia of scavengers had stripped the Dzaxashigé booth bare. Of furniture, only stone benches remained. Shadows on bleached concrete marked where curtains had hung. An exposed spur of holdfire poked up from the floor, and I held my hands to the orange substance, drinking in heat. Night wind poured through broken windows and down my white-streaked chest.

Outside, the intact pyramids of Armory Street rose high in the distance. Moon-washed miles of concrete wasteland surrounded me, broken brass and steel girders like aimless sentries. Fallen drops of holdlight cast eerie light below. *The perfect emptiness for me to lose myself forever.*

"Talk to me," Ria said, slipping inside. "What's going on in your head?"

A derecho. A firestorm. I ran a finger over a bare windowsill, saying the first thing I found. "We must have held amazing shows and races here. I wish I could have seen it then."

Ria lifted a crushed steel ring—part of an ancient handcuff—and flung it off into the night. "I read about this place. We built Skygarden nearby. The Dzaxashigé took Engineers who refused to work on it, tied them to posts, and made them watch our men and children fight raptors below. Your people called it *Fathj ka Eisha Zxo*. The Ring of Two Jokes. We called it *N Siate Żu Ru*."

"Where They Torture Us," I translated. "That's terrible."

"You don't know about this?"

"We don't talk about the Brass War, save to pity the gods' fall ended our conquests." The customs of my cruel lineage anchored deep in me. I remembered what Eprue Zucho had told me of the gods' fall, what Faziz had whispered in the night. *The Dzaxashigé have only one tactic to keep power: cutting through lives.*

Akizeké's campaign had pushed Vashathke to incite violence. To scream and shriek how the Treaty of Inversions unfairly restrained us. Ignorant, we'd convinced ourselves a war could never be. But no god nor Shaper enforced the ten thousand years' peace. Vashathke had allied with Tamadza. He'd attacked the Fire Weavers. He'd already broken the treaty. If I didn't enthrone Akizeké, he'd win the power to break the world. And he'd do so, because the monster in him was a thousand times darker than what lived in me.

"I'm sorry," I told Ria. "I've been moping and blaming myself for what happened, but I should have focused on your needs, not my own. How are you feeling? Do you want to talk to me?"

Ria studied an ancient control panel, its circuits melted within the black mark of a lightning strike, and touched the gold at her neck. "The *Sashua Vorona*. Voro's amulet. A High Master made this mark when she dismantled the stadium. My predecessor. She'd hate me if she knew what I'd let happen to the Fire Weavers."

"No one could hate you!" I gasped. The stab of her pain scarred my world.

She gave a small, hollow laugh. "Pure murder juice seeps up from the planet's foundations. Ancient bombs go off and buildings crumble because oligarchs hoard pennies instead of safeguarding lives. The Fire Weavers alone keep the city-planet intact. That responsibility is mine, now. I'm only twenty-three, I was never even formally initiated—I'm going to fail my father and my people. I might literally cause the apocalypse."

"You're my hero," I said. Silver spines ran down my back, marking my utter honesty. "You've saved me over and over. You can do this."

"A hero?" She shook her head. "If I'd just paid better attention in class, I would have realized what Tamadza wanted when we overheard her on the hovercraft."

"You can't blame a terrorist plot on some flicker of mistake you made in your childhood."

"What about what I did just hours ago? I didn't collapse the tunnel. I gave Päreshi and Tamadza an opening. Not because I was scared to die, but because of you. I saw you, my father, and my friends, and I couldn't... I couldn't... I failed." She broke into tears. "It's all my fault. How can I lead when I ruined everything?"

"You acted with love," I said. *Love fucks you up worse.*

She wrapped an arm around my waist and pulled me close. I brushed a kiss across her forehead. Her head tilted.

"Hold me," she said. "Please."

My arms slid around her, holding her like some precious glass charm. Her pendant crackled against my chest. Electric shivers ran down my spine. "I will. If you still want me after our fight."

"That small thing? I've forgotten all about it."

"Fights can be small?" Instincts drummed in me before I'd

learned my own name screamed every spark of anger could end me like Stonefire.

"Of course they can." Ria laughed, low, long and deep, the first I'd heard it all day. "Voro's mercy. I'm falling hard for you. You said you didn't understand your own feelings, but please. Tell me I'm not as alone as I feel."

"I don't know how real love feels," I confessed. Old memories prodded me like flint daggers. "My mother said she loved me, but she resented me and sold me into marriage. My betrotheds said they loved me and treated me like a toy. I don't know how I feel about you because I've never been loved as a person. Only as a living essence store."

"If you give me a chance," she whispered, breath hot on my chest, "I swear by the dead gods, by my honor as High Master, by my father's soul—I will love you as you deserve. Dull or bright, dragon or no. You make me laugh, you make me think, you forever surprise me. You hold me in the center of your heart."

"I'm afraid," I said. *I'm afraid I love you, too. I'm afraid I'll ruin this and you.*

"Me too," she said. "Let's be afraid together."

Her hungry, aching tongue forced my lips open. Her legs hooked around my waist as she slid herself up, plying kisses through my blond stubble. Scales swam down my chest as I surrendered to my wants. "Take me," I said between kisses. "I'm yours." She bent near-double, nuzzling my breastbone, licking my nipple. "Dzkegé's mercy, please…"

"Here!" She sat on a starlit windowsill. In one smooth motion, she undid the lace tying her jumpsuit shut. I nearly tripped over myself in my rush to meet her. My tongue unraveled the ties, sliding between her breasts, down her stomach, tasting dust and ink. Her feet curled against my back, guiding me forward. I buried my lips in her hair. With my every whispered breath, magic fell from my tongue on her pubis.

She clutched the tendrils floating free off my neck. "You're beautiful," she gasped as my tongue lapped inside her. Her sweet perfume washed out my world. Tension eased from her inner walls. "Mine, mine, mine. I have to take you."

Her hands traced my chest, pinioned my nipples, pushed me back onto a bench. The worn fabric of my skirt slid up beneath her desperate fingers. The length of me slid free. In a heartbeat, we were joined.

She straddled me, thrusting her hips in long, smooth passes. Her hands slid beneath me, exploring my back. I kissed the heavy miracle of her breast, pinching her flesh in my teeth, delighting in how well she used me. Essence flowed like a living river between our skin, weaving us together.

Gods have mercy. I'd never realized how good this felt. But I'd never made love to someone who loved me back.

Silver stars swam against the night sky. Not one shone brighter than she. My head tipped back as her soft, massaging rhythm tore me open. I throbbed inside her, spilling my seed. She shuddered, clenched tight, and gasped my name.

"I love you," she said, lying down beside me. "And I need you. Now more than ever."

This is bad, whispered a quiet part of me. *You can't risk this.*

But my fears lived far away, on the street that had raised me and taught me I was wrong. I tucked Ria's head against my chest and held her while she cried.

CHAPTER SEVENTEEN
Border Ruins

25th *Dzeri*, Year 92 Rarafashi

"I don't care what the magistrate does with the relics. We need her guards to chase undercroft dulls from our excavation site. They stand between us and the true history of War."—Professor Vodzkadziri Jorethox, Archeology Department, Armory Street Civic University

"I don't need a girlfriend to save me. I can save myself."—Hishura, Blood and Stone 4: The Quest to Save Hishura (Modern Jiké subtitles)

YOUNG, GHOSTLY VOICES rose in the ruins. "Lord Faziz!" they called, "You've come to save us!"

"Hurry!" I shouted to Ria, straightening my skirt as I sprinted outside.

Three small, bone-white figures ringed Faziz, eyes wide and hungry. *Children,* I told myself, forcing breath through my lungs. *Covered in concrete dust.* Faziz smiled at them, but my heart raced, untrusting. What were they doing out here?

"The Armory Street undercroft knows you," said a girl, her hair a ring-halo of white down one side. "The uncrowned lord of the Slatepile, who builds toys from foil and paper. The swordsman who smuggled fifty children from slavers. The builder who reinforced a collapsing cavern."

"We have lots of collapses," said the smallest boy. "Can you save us, Lord Faziz?"

The undercrofts. These children lived below the ruins, the rubble stacking down to the planet's core. *Folk of Faziz's dull world, though months of dull walking from his holdings.* Their Modern Jiké had an odd, archaic edge, vowels slicing like Old Jiké, 'r's touched with an Engineer's roll. A dialect from an isolated world, where essence and holdlife cost more than diamonds.

"Come with us," said another child. "We'll shelter you and your friends. We need…"

"Hope," Faziz finished, his accent shifting to match theirs. "Ria?"

"Yes," she said. "We can't sleep in the open."

Faziz cut me off as my lips opened. "We can trust them, Red Eyes. They're kids. You're much brighter than them. I promise it's safe."

Nothing keeps me safe. And I don't deserve your promise. My dark thoughts fought to surface. But my body still swam with the echoes of Ria's touch. *She loves me. I'm free to love her back.*

Victory Street lay whole lives away. My life rested in Ria and Faziz's hands. They were worthy to hold it. Maybe I was worthy of being held.

Now was time to trust.

The children led us to a tunnel not far from Tamadza's path of devastation. Down we slunk, past propped-up concrete locks, across a canvas bridge over sharp marble chips, through a dozen crumbling archways. Gradually, warm holdlight supplanted Ria's lantern. We stepped into a wide, low-roofed cavern, which must have once been a commercial office before it fell and lodged deep. Long shadows danced on white marble walls. Bodies shifted ghostlike as they moved through dark and light.

"A bright Engineer and a man of War?" called a technician dangling in a harness off the ceiling. A hazy holdlight sparked as she jabbed needles into a salvaged control panel. "Have the districts above resolved their differences?"

"Engineering's ready to reconcile." Ria laughed. "War's the pissy district."

A mason, plastering over a crumbling archway, shot Ria a fierce glare. Heavy iron jewelry clung to her lower jaw, an armoured plate engraved with fractal spirals. "Good to know the Fire Weavers serve as ambassadors of peace and reason, eh?" Sarcasm and anger fell from her pierced tongue.

My hand went for my baton. "I'll fight her," I murmured to Ria.

She shook her head. "Leave her be."

"Lord Faziz?" said a man with a toddler strapped to his chest. "Every day Zegakadze and Vashathke evict more ruins, driving folk deeper and closer to us. We've heard your legend. You bless us with your presence."

"A legend and a blessing," Ria mused. "The high *dzaxa* hate you, Faziz, but you might be the most popular man in War."

Faziz shrugged and lowered his voice. "I'll play that role for them. But I don't enjoy hero worship. Like taking too much essence, it makes me feel I'm not myself."

He's so honest and open. With me, with her, with everyone. Had I misread our moment of closeness in the Hive? It would be best if Faziz just saw me as an acquaintance. Falling for a High Master was complicated, but Ria didn't have a price on her head. Ria would never blackmail me to commit murder.

How dangerous would dating a criminal be?

The children led us to a vast communal hall. Dinner was served: thin lichen sheets grown in vanishing holdlife, fist-sized cabbages boiled with rock salt, skewered lizards. I attempted to pass the scant meat to the children, but Faziz murmured "don't insult our generous hosts," and so I ate, ravenously. After the meal, before the eager crowd, Ria shaped parading dinosaurs from flame bursts and Faziz folded lotus blossoms from salvaged newspaper.

Three women with iron jawplate jewelry and tear-reddened eyes approached Ria between demonstrations. "We're sorry for your loss," said one, her companions stiff and awkward as statues in the dark.

"I'm sorry for yours," Ria said. "I—we can make restitution—"

"Don't give us another broken promise to mourn." She shook her head. "A soul can only take so many cuts before it bleeds out. High Master, I pray you never know such pain."

"There's a lot of unmarked bottomless pits down here," Faziz murmured as they departed. "Be a shame if they went for a piss in the night and vanished, eh, Ria?"

"Let them be." Ria rubbed her neck, not yet used to the weight of the *Sashua Vorona*. "Five thousand years ago, a corrupt dynasty of judges ruled Engineering. Two women who called themselves the Iron Speakers declared dead Voro spoke to them through metal and abolished the very institution of judgeship. They built a faithful following, between those who hungered for meaning and those who hated the status quo, and constructed the Hive as their temple—a place where Voro could urge them all to overthrow the judge."

She sounded skeptical. "Dzkegé contacted me through a steel altar," I pointed out.

"I mean, maybe Voro did speak to them. I don't know. The Fire Weavers were little more than archivists back then. The judge and her heirs built us up as an alternative to the Iron Speakers. We offered faith in artifacts, history, and recovery from the Brass War—all good, all needed, and yet the path—" She bit her lip.

"Too many bloody paths in Jadzia," Faziz said.

Ria swallowed. "*We* installed those bombs in the Hive. To kill the Iron Speakers, if our judge ever commanded. And when she ordered them expelled from the district, and gave us their old home, we didn't remove the explosives. We couldn't face what we'd done. We told ourselves they protected us from the War District, but we ourselves were the ones we feared most. And that legacy caught up to us today."

Her face fell. Faziz pulled her into a one-armed hug. I didn't know what to say, so I murmured, "That happened so long ago. It's not your legacy. It wasn't your father's—"

"Yes, it is. And that coliseum is yours, the Surrender, the High Kiss and the dragon's sword. We all have our own history to carry. I just can't do it alone."

The hall holdlights dimmed. Faziz unpacked his sleeping roll near the wall, I unfolded mine beside his, and Ria lay on-guard outside us. Their twinned breathing, close in both my ears, filled me with soft, wondrous hush. Though I lay in a hall of strangers, I'd never felt so safe. Like I'd entered a world I'd dance in forever.

Once or twice, a distant shaking woke me. Voices rose, warm and welcome, as I dozed on sleep's edge.

"What is he to you?" Faziz murmured. "You're young and bright. You could have anyone. If this is a game, you should tell him."

"It's much more. I've never felt so whole around anyone. He sees all the best in me. He doesn't care I'm a two-legged disaster."

"Good. If you're taking him, you should treasure him."

"I'm not taking anyone. Love isn't ownership. That's the opposite of love."

"You're right." He chuckled. "Sorry. I don't have much experience with... relationships."

"It's cool," she said, and I could hear she meant it. "I think we three can make this work."

As the shaking world stilled, Ria yawned and pressed her face to my chest. Faziz rolled over, close to my back, and threw his arm over us both as we sank into sweeter dreams.

I woke to a dozen curious faces above me.

"Lord Faziz," said a dull man with a missing leg. "Bright guests. Our leader wants to meet you."

They led us down another wide, shattered corridor into a low-roofed cavern. Broken statues of sitting dragons lined the way to a throne rigged in the lap of the most intact. The woman sitting in it was old, by dull standards, grey hair knotted in braid-buns over her ears, a blasting pistol—dangerous, illegal, quick to backfire—in her sash.

"I am Thoshe," she said, "Judge of Nowhere. Why are you here?"

"Honored elder," Faziz replied. "I seek shelter for myself and my friends. In return, I'll send you two tons of holdlife and one of holdwater."

"You'll send them quick. We need fresh gardens."

Whispering counselors and guards paced behind her throne. My bright ears picked *"theshi sher gejé"* from their dialect's mélange.

We have lost. We will fall.

"A shadow-Shaper chased us here." Ria's voice wavered. "She attacked my home and killed my people. Your hospitality means a great deal after everything I've lost."

"We invited you for Faziz. Not out of pity. Dry your tears, Fire Weaver. Nothing brings back the dead. As someone who's about to join them, take my advice. Count gains, never losses. It keeps life palatable."

Ria's voice hardened. Anger stiffened her spine. "What do you know about loss?"

"Ria, please be careful—" Faziz started.

The ruins shook. Holdlight flickered. I grabbed Ria's arm. If the roof collapsed and buried us, I wanted her to be the last person I touched.

Thoshe rolled her eyes, as if the world was rude to interrupt her. "Send the last mapping crew," she said as all stilled. "Image that collapse and prepare the rescue team for when we reach stability."

"We're still waiting to send in rescue diggers?" said a guard.

"I won't lose diggers and essence by sending teams into unsettled ruins. We'll lose more lives than we save."

The floor stretched and cracked. Echoes traveled up the deep foundations, human voices warped to horrors by passage through metal and rock. Sounds from the Old Dread after a too-tall wave swept the ship. *Human lives too dull for the lady to bother saving.* "People are still alive down there," I said. "They need rescue."

"If a shadow-Shaper crosses a ruin while the crew's inside, we'll lose our chance to save anyone at all. We do nothing until that monster leaves. If the survivors have intact holdwater, some will last until we reach them."

"Tamadza's killing you," Ria said, stunned. "She's been killing you for hours. Why didn't you tell me when I arrived?"

"You're a stranger. Death has walked these tunnels since the gods fell. Child, will you duel with death? Give your bright life for the souls who live beneath you?"

Ria took a deep breath. Her fingers stroked the *Sashua Vorona*, like she sought Voro's blessing—or her father's. "I'm not a child. I'm the High Master of the Fire Weavers. It's my duty to protect and restore the city-planet. Whether you like me, whether you believe me, that doesn't matter." Her fists tightened. Lightning sparked on her chest. "I'll duel Tamadza."

Thoshe shrugged. "Good luck. It'll save us a ration."

"Ria," Faziz said. "Your courage is a credit to your integrity. But Shapers hold power beyond all others, and you're the last High Master of your order—"

"The Fire Weavers don't deserve to continue if I turn away," Ria said. "If my order dies with me, it dies well."

"I know, but—"

Ria took my hand. "I wish we'd had more time. If I fail, alert the judges of both districts about Tamadza. Tell them to fight back."

I bent and kissed her, like her lips could smother my doubts. She shone as brave and true as starlight. Not an ounce of bravado tainted her words. A soldier and a leader like nothing I'd ever seen. Risking her life for strangers came as naturally to her as breathing, and the thought of losing her ground like concrete on my skin.

"Come back to me," I whispered, and knew past all doubt I loved her.

Faziz took my hand, concealing the scales wrapping themselves around my wrist. Protecting me from watching eyes. "Ria. Let me help you."

"You can help me by protecting Koré," she said. Then she turned and ran up the tunnel in a bright blur. I stared until long past she was gone.

"Stop ogling air," Thoshe said. "Pick up a map, bright boy, and go join a collapse imaging team. Lord Faziz, if you want to talk diplomacy, I'm stuck here until I die."

"Later, Honored One. I need words with my companion." Faziz nodded, respectfully low, and tugged me from the hall.

"Go talk to Thoshe," I said as we walked through the marble dark. "I'm fine. Truly—"

"Ria isn't." He sighed, plowing a frustrated hand through his messy hair. "She's brave beyond measure, but she doesn't understand Shapers. I... *Miran nah mumiru,* I'm the only one of us who ever saw one! My district's Shaper was... unbeatable... alone. The High Scholars controlled him in teams. They overwhelmed his senses with alarms and lights, forcing him back into his cell."

"The Scholars kept their Shaper in a cell?"

"It's a cruel government. That doesn't matter. Ria needs help. She's fighting for my people, for the dulls of the ruins, and I should go to her. Can you fly me?"

Can I face a Shaper, you mean? She'd smash us both beneath her shadow. Break me worse than Victory Street had. *But what if I'm not broken? There's a world beyond Victory Street, where I can be good and love with people who care for me.*

Ria carried my heart with her. We had a chance at a future. If Faziz thought he could do this and knew it was needed, I would defy death for her.

We raced up the tunnels and into the light. When the pale sun hit my face, I offered him my shoulder. He squeezed it and drew the baton from my sash.

Happiness starts with opening up to people. I remembered how he'd welcomed me into his Slatepile sanctuary, and the gift of his acceptance filled my soul. Scales unfurled down my limbs like banners. I craned my neck and the sky opened wide.

In my swift kite form, it took all my strength to get Faziz airborne. But the wind caught my wings and slung us upwards. The clouds parted. Faziz gasped as the full sun lit me. His knees dug against my sides. His fists clutched tight at my tendrils and neck-fan.

"Didn't realize those scales had red flecks," he murmured. My skin hummed where his fingers ran. I narrowed my eyes and willed myself to concentrate.

Tamadza's chaotic wake had cut a straight gorge through rubble. Powdered concrete had tumbled into a ten-meter-deep trench. Wide craters pocked the ruins.

She'd done this just by running through.

"Tamadza of the Twelfth River! Face me!" Ria's high, confident voice carried up from a ruined pit. Her bracers were lifted. I readied to dive—

Purple light flashed. Tamadza blurred into stillness atop the concrete rubble. Ground gave with every step she took. Her pale, purple-tinted skin was liquid flawlessness; her black eyes deep as the planet's heart. A skeleton clothed in flesh, cheeks sunken with failing beauty, muscles lean and strong as the certainty of death.

Sunlight shied from her as she reached welcomingly for Ria.

Ria's knees trembled. Even aloft, I fought the urge to tremble. Dzkegé's shade hadn't matched the shadow-Shaper in dark glory. I wanted to bow and acknowledge her mastery. *I am nothing, and I will die.*

"Fuck off, murder asshole!" Ria shouted, and lifted her bracers.

Staff raised, cloaked in shadow, Tamadza flung herself at the High Master.

The *Sashua Vorona* pulsed. Lightning met Tamadza's chest. Thunder clapped. The scent of ozone leapt high.

"Now!" Faziz shouted, lifting his sword. "Hit the right angle!"

The air whistled around us as I dove. Faziz screamed, knocking sword against baton in discordant rhythm. I added my shriek to his as we shot past the pit in a torrent of sound.

Tamadza spun towards us, clasping her hands over her ears. Ria gasped and released an ice torrent, imprisoning the necromancer from the waist down. I twisted. Light glinted off my neck, flashing into Tamadza's eyes.

"What are you boys doing here?" Ria called.

"Helping!" Faziz said.

"Cool. Don't stop!"

I beat my wings hard, rising in a hot air stream. Faziz pressed low to my back. With a whip of my tail, I flipped downward for a second pass.

Tamadza fired.

The violet bolt caught my wing. The limb vanished into nothingness. I spun down like an unbalanced top, Faziz clinging to my neck. *Shield him.* My dragon's form dissolved human. I pinned him against my chest as I hit, back first.

Concrete cut my skin as I skidded. Stone broke under my head. Something cracked in my chest. I tasted blood.

Faziz took my hand and pulled me up. "Breathe. You're okay."

"Dzkegé's mercy. This is madness. How can you stay calm?"

"I've survived worse. At least Tamadza's not trying to collect late rent." Cool focus filled his eyes, courage forged in a thousand fearful nights, a survivor's knowledge they could walk through fire and find another side.

I knew that, too. No space for fear lived in this moment.

Lightning cracked. The *Sashua Vorona* pulsed at Ria's throat. Bolt after white-hot bolt leapt from her hand. Tamadza swept her staff in a loop, dissolving missiles into sparks. The ground shuddered as she stepped forward. Ria's ice shield cracked at the touch of her finger.

"No!" I shouted. Instinct drove me forward. Silk fire poured from my throat, washing the combatants. Ria grinned like a god, punching Tamadza with a sphere of lightning. The Shaper's corpselike beauty faded. She stumbled half a step at the blow.

"Keep hitting her!" Ria ordered, lifting both her arms. Waves of fire and lightning surged against Tamadza. The air boiled as I added my breath. Silver flame ate at her shadow store.

Tamadza howled. Her fierce visage wavered. For a moment, I wondered if enough essence would free her mind of whatever deeper darkness held it. *The power of my fire.* As I'd suspected. As Eprue Zucho had confirmed. The bright truth of dragon's fire broke destruction's hold. *The dragons before me stood against evil. I'm the one who can lift their standard today.*

But Tamadza's power ran deceptive and deep. Runes of liquid violet blossomed up her arms, freely spawning shadows. With a sweep of her staff, she knotted them into a cord and fired downward. Concrete shifted. Stones ground to powder. A tunnel opened below.

"No!" Ria shouted. Ice exploded beneath the shadow-Shaper, thick and unmelting, blocking her escape. "You'll pay for the Hive!"

I grabbed Ria's hand to steady myself. Her essence flowed until I could crush buildings. Two fresh wings, whole and healed, unfurled from my back. My breath pinned Tamadza down, draining her as she clawed my fire from her skin.

Faziz clambered across the crumbled stone behind Tamadza. *Too close.* My heart twisted. I summoned scales, letting them flash down my chest. Tamadza screamed, reaching to cover her eyes—

His sword flashed through bone. Tamadza's head dropped from her shoulders.

The shadow-Shaper fractured like glass. Her skin and bones crumbled into a billowing purple cloud. The holdshadow pulsed at the heart of her staff. The screaming remnants of her soul dissolved into its substance.

Ria caught the staff as it fell.

"Holy shit. I did it." A smile cracked the grime on her face. "I avenged them. I won."

Faziz wrapped an arm about her shoulders. "We make a pretty good hero team. Get over here, Red Eyes. Group hug."

Still stunned, I fell into their embrace. I couldn't quite remember how to stand. *A team?* On this nightmare adventure, we'd become that and more. *My bright fire. My dark flame. The two lights in my world. I barely know you. I can't live without you.* I nearly said as much, but a flicker of motion caught my eye.

My breath caught. I pointed up at the hovership.

Together, we watched it fall from the sky and crash into the ruins below.

CHAPTER EIGHTEEN

The High Kiss, within the eastern sculpture of The Surrender

14th *Reshi,* Year 92 Rarafashi

"Riot is second in disasters only to plague. The Pleasure District proved so when it died, as cries to dismantle the judgeship system provoked guards to raze buildings while hunting anarchists. War, Scholarly and Coldwater have all barely escaped fatal riots. Affordable housing policies in Engineering and Warmwater have minimized the contributing factors."—Urban Planning 202 lecture at the Archive University

"Our dragons are all dead."—gambling slang of upper Victory Street, expressing frustration at a run of bad luck

"THERE. RIGHT IN the—no, further."

I bit back a frustrated hiss. I'd left my good toys in Engineering, and my backup wand wasn't standard length. Worse, it was clenched between my teeth.

"Slower," Shethgefeo said. "I've had a stressful week."

I craned my neck, curling my tongue about the wand. The old wine importer was short. Trapped between her thighs and the bed, my cramping ankles cuffed to a post, I couldn't maneuver.

"Three of my suppliers want to bid for that cleared land in Engineering. The Judge and the High Master are feuding over who owns the site. They both want a bigger—ah, there!—payout. Vashathke's right to denounce greedy Engineers! Ow!"

I'd bitten her labia. Hard.

All legal records of the Hive's ownership had been destroyed during the genocide of the Iron Speakers, millennia ago. Ria insisted, following salvage and an independent investigation, the site be returned to their descendants, and Żeposháru Rena had written several strongly worded consolation letters to dissuade her.

"More than money," she'd said, "I need to do the right thing. And I need to know everyone involved in Tamadza's plot is caught. I need proof of what really happened."

I needed proof too. Vashathke's campaign momentum had slowed since Żeposháru Rena and Tożätupé endorsed Akizeké. Tamadza's choice of target reflected his hatred of the Fire Weavers. Hard evidence to implicate him in the Hive bombing would sink his campaign—Rarafashi might even bring criminal charges against him. He couldn't conquer the city-planet from inside a cell.

"You're a bad boy," Shethgefeo cooed. "Kiss me to apologize."

I should be happier, I thought, sucking the small slit toward the front of her. Akizeké's endorsement count had skyrocketed. *Eleven international and twenty-two domestic to Vashathke's thirteen and twenty-nine.* Seventeen and thirty-eight lay in grasping distance for both campaigns, but Akizeké was determined her fist would be first to grab the prize.

That's not it. Maybe I was irritated no one was investigating the crashed hovership. Tamadza's personal assets had to contain evidence against Vashathke, but Akizeké's guard had marched into the border ruins and barricaded the site. *No, that's not it either.* Akizeké would give me access if I asked.

"Don't you love me?" Shethgefeo asked. "Isn't this fun?"

"Yes, *dzaxa*," I muttered, trying not to drop the wand.

No. It wasn't politics that rankled. When I closed my eyes, I saw Ria and Faziz. Starlight and freedom. Electric fire filling me when we'd fought Tamadza, the sweet dreamlike moment I'd imagined a life outside War. Her kiss. His smile. *Love to open my soul and change everything inside it.*

The thought threatened to provoke scales down my spine. I recalled Vashathke's threats diminishing me at the state banquet and bit down feelings until my client left.

Evening wind from the balcony dried my freshly washed chest and hair as I sorted booking requests. A repeat client of Neza's needed entertainment at her daughter's birthday party, which sounded safe enough. An actor wanted Ruby after a party at the Entertainment District embassy, harmless. Bero, a *dzaxa* graduation party in the Archive... no, not with drugs and darkness.

With a hushed, pleading step, Ria slid through my door. I leapt down from my private nook to join her.

"Goodbye, Koré." A pack sat on her shoulders, topped by Tamadza's staff. She'd tried to burn it after the hovership crashed, but the fire hadn't caught. Ever since, she hadn't set it down. "Thanks for letting me stay with the other girls while I did legal stuff. But I'll be busy rebuilding my order, and you'll need space for a new hire, so I'm moving to a hotel in the Archive. Take care."

She turned. I caught her wrist, heart surging into my throat. *You fool*—but if she left, I'd unravel like torn crochet.

"Those Archive hotels are noisy," I stammered. "I have a giant bed."

Tears welled in her eyes. I kissed them away, grinning wide.

Wrapped in each other, we stumbled across the floor. Her pack hit the ground. My back hit the bed. Warm, soft, and smiling, she landed atop me.

"Thank you," she said, snuggling against my chest. "I couldn't bring myself to ask."

If you knew what I'd hidden from you, you'd leave. You should leave. "Please stay," I said. "Be my..." Words stuck in my throat. "You say the next thing. I'm not good at romance."

"You think I am?"

"You're amazing at everything you do."

"High praise, but fine, I'll say it. Will you be my boyfriend? Officially?"

I couldn't shake a yes loose. I nodded against her wash of dark curls.

She laughed. "It's official. A boyfriend. I'm a real adult now."

"Only now?" I teased. "Dueling Tamadza and saving every life in Jadzia didn't cut it?"

"Tamadza could only kill me. You could break my heart."

I most likely will. But I fought that fear with all the fire and light Dzkegé had seen in me. I'd never dared hope for this after Zega, but I'd found joy in the ruins. Once Vashathke was stopped, we could start a new life. Victory Street wouldn't define me forever. Ria would never learn what I'd left behind.

The High Kiss cheered when we came down for breakfast holding hands. Ruby passed Bero a silver *vodz*. Opal smiled like his parents had gotten back together. Kge clapped Ria on the back. I ordered my employees to keep her presence silent, lest a High Master attract unwanted attention from those who hated Engineers. But the *dzaxa* of War had their sources, and soon a letter arrived from Akizeké inviting the High Master and me to dine.

"She wants Ria's endorsement," I told Faziz during our sparring session the next morning. He waited at the far end of a catwalk, patient grace behind his blade. My wrists stung from a blow he'd landed. "What should I do? I've kept Ria from the campaign. We need her support to win, but I hate manipulating my girlfriend." Heat shivered through my chest at the last word. A promise of hope and sunshine.

Faziz's sword dropped. My bright brain suggested the perfect wrist-flick to disarm him, but the frown on his brow arrested me. "What's wrong?"

"Nothing. Look, just because you're not ready to share all yourself with Ria doesn't mean you should lie. Say Akizeké wants her endorsement and let her choose her path."

"Right." I laughed. "Sorry. I forget about honesty. I'm so used to people not caring, or even punishing me, when I don't tell them what they want to hear. I love sharing her trust."

A sneer weaved across his lips. He charged, pink neon holdlight flashing off leather-clad thighs, sword arching low. I pivoted, blocking—but he'd anticipated me. Our hips smashed together. Gasping from the blow, Faziz still danced in close and pressed my back against a catwalk railing. His blade rested in a cold line from my hip to my nipple.

"Practice honesty," he growled. "And turning left."

Something was off. "Does it bother you I'm dating Ria?"

"I like Ria. I'm happy for her."

"But are you happy for me?"

"I don't see why that matters."

"Because I value your opinion."

"My opinion is we're done for today." He fired a grappling hook into a slate stalactite, swung to the pillar his people were patching, and joined three grunting laborers forcing a holdweight brace into an opposing gravitational field. His thick, muscular shoulders trembled with strain. Sweat pooled in eddies of light down his back.

Had I done something wrong? Considering the matter with a practiced courtesan's eye, I might conclude Faziz was jealous. He'd certainly flirted with me before—I was fairly certain—and I'd sparred with him every morning since our return from Engineering. We'd built a pathway of ropes and grapples up the Surrender's side to connect his hideout and the High Kiss. But Ria's love already felt too great a miracle. Two people wouldn't want a monster—*no, hate yourself less, see yourself as they do*—wouldn't want an untrustworthy courtesan like me.

EVEN ARMED WITH his advice, I tripped on dry-throated nerves when Ria met me in our room after lunch. "Magistrate Akizeké of Armory Street has invited us to dinner in her private museum. She wants you to formally endorse her candidacy for Rarafashi's throne. She'll offer the Fire Weavers financial support in exchange."

"Sounds cool." Ria grinned. "If she isn't a terrible person, I'll do it."

Oh. Lightness bubbled up in my chest. Faziz had been right. Honesty worked.

"Boss?" Neza threw open the door. "Sorry. There's noise—bad noise."

With the door open, I heard footsteps pounding up the corridor outside the High Kiss. A roar of angry voices peaked near the entry arch. Calling my name.

Ria stood. The *Sashua Vorona* glinted at her throat. "Stay behind me, you two."

The mob, armed with steel pipes and cooking knives, packed the High Kiss's entry arch. Every hungry eye fell on me as we approached. Though my instincts screamed *run*, I tightened my fists and willed myself cool. My employees huddled in a nervous knot by the stairs. I had to protect them.

Greenwolf the baker headed the mob. Off-duty private guards massed behind her, some wearing the uniforms of employers I'd bribed to ignore my business. "Surrender, dragon," she said, "and we won't have to take you."

I froze. *Dzkegé's mercy. How do they know?*

"He's not going anywhere." Lightning gathered in Ria's fist. "*Sakri*, he isn't the dragon, he can't—"

"You've flown with him, here and in your own district. The district Koreshiza Brightstar just visited. It's greedy, keeping him all to yourself." Her tone was joking, but her smile was false. "Step aside and I'll split Vashathke's bounty with you. Victory Street needs fresh essence."

Ria raised both her bracers. Kge and Ruby lifted their batons. Opal trembled like a leaf. "No—" he said, his fear cutting like a whip.

The mob surged forward.

Curtains tore under their weight, ripping free in a gold and purple tide. Urns of flowers toppled, spilling dirt and blossoms. Hands reached for me, grabbing, pulling—

Ria's fire swept back the crowd as she pulled me behind her. "All of you, out!"

Her foot twisted. I caught her as we stumbled—and the mob flooded past us. One pale pack ran straight for the bar, shoving goblets into sashes, hoisting liquor casks on shoulders. Knives slashed embroidery from hangings. Fists dragged neon holdlights from their moorings.

My business. Ria and I pressed our backs to the fountain. *My haven. The thing I built for me.*

They'd come to tear me down. I wouldn't be so easily undone.

"Get the dragon!" called a high, clear voice. I flung a silver stool in the speaker's direction. My mother's baton flashed as I drew it free. *She'd hate seeing me wield this. Especially to defend a brothel. How terribly unmarriageable it would make me. Good.*

"Come and try!" I called.

Ria flung a wall of ice at the entry arch, knocking back invaders. Kge and Ruby hoisted a loveseat between them, ramming attackers off the bar. Bero's eyes met mine as he herded the boys toward my bedchamber. "Don't kill them!" he shouted before slamming the door.

He reads my true fury. No more hiding my fire. Hands seized my skirt. I shattered fingers and wrists with swirling loops of my baton. Rage bloomed as natural on my skin as silk and gentle touches.

"Whore!" spat an off-duty guard as I rammed my *shiki* into her shoulder. "Fucking essence thief!" I drove my foot into her stomach, knocking her back. *So sweet. So easy.* Scales prickled down my thighs, threatening to spread to my wrists and chest. Part of me fought to keep the dragon leashed, to center on cool logic—*is this all coincidence? Did someone send this mob?*—but my reason was vanishing into red.

"Stick close, Koré!" Ria flung sparks. A leaking barrel of alcohol—and the woman carrying it—ignited as a torch. I didn't care. *Burn them. They invaded my home to kidnap me.* I hammered one attacker until she fell unconscious, broke another's kneecap with a low blow, hoping my skirt hid my scales. *I won't be their prisoner. I won't be their pawn—*

A black glyph glittered on my wall. A bell-shaped poem, quickly drawn, the paint still fresh.

Faziz's emblem.

"Disperse!" Dzaro's voice rang over the mob. Her steel-armored guards pressed tight behind her, batons lifted behind silver shields. "Or I'll sentence you all to tithe dull!"

My goods dropped from grasping hands. The moaning, battered crowds flocked to the entry arch. Two abashed looters hoisted the burnt woman on their shoulders. "We need a dragon," Greenwolf muttered, limping out through spilled rum.

You're not entitled to make one of me. I spat at her feet.

"Rude slut," she gasped, and left.

Dzaro slid through the mess, her warhounds barking at anyone who got too close. "Are you hurt, Koré?"

I was... intact. Less could be said for the High Kiss. Gang sign on the wall, bar smashed and cut, shattered glass, alcohol flooding the dance floor, holdlights hanging loose. Four years I'd worked to build this. The damage felt like wounds to my own body. *A silly feeling.* My own mother would have ordered me ignore my distress. But Dzaro...

"This is my home," I whispered. Tears ran thick down my throat.

Her arms closed tight about me. "I'm sorry, sweetheart. I wish this didn't happen. Victory Street preys on boys who live outside its rules."

"I hate it here." For a handful of days, I'd tasted the outside world and felt the pull of other lives. But I was anchored, shaped and created by the yellow sandstone cobbles of Victory Street. A place I understood in my bones. A street that would devour itself to capture the power of my soul. The place I belonged.

"What if Lady Dzaroshardze hadn't come?" Opal whispered as he and other boys trickled back downstairs. "They wouldn't have stopped until they'd gotten what they'd come for."

They nearly did. The scales had faded from my thighs at the shock of Faziz's sigil. I wouldn't be so lucky again. My fingernails dug into my palms. I pulled back on my mask of a cool, stylish, in-control businessman. "I'll send a herald to the insurance agency. Bero, move our scheduled appointments for the next two days. I'll work double to cover overbookings."

"This won't go away," Bero said. "People need a dragon. Your name's been attached to the rumors."

I groaned.

"It's not all bad, boss," Opal said. "Most people wouldn't try to claim a dragon by force. They just want essence to be healthier, live longer lives, bear children. People need hope."

The locus of their dreams. The red eyes of their misery's architects. A boy to cut open with carving knives, take the parts you like and leave inconvenient ones behind. "I'm killing hope good and dead so we can work in peace."

Opal's soft brown eyes studied mine. "I need hope. Is there a chance... it's you?"

"If it is," Dzaro said, more carefully than I'd ever heard her speak, "you don't owe that truth to anyone. That secret would be yours. You don't belong to Victory Street."

I had nothing but rage for Greenwolf and her ilk. But my heart longed to comfort Bero, Opal, and my aunt. *Steady. Careful.* Even if it cost them the treaty, all the *dzaxa* hungered to capture the dragon and win her throne. I didn't count myself one of them, but my eyes already bore their mark.

"I have to belong to something," I said. "And Victory Street is a hard place to leave behind."

CHAPTER NINETEEN
The High Kiss, within the eastern sculpture of The Surrender

16ᵗʰ *Reshi*, Year 92 Rarafashi

"Common folk will spit at your back. Call you liar, seducer, whore. You've traded your goodness for essence. You're forever stained in their eyes. Ignore them. Get paid. We've ever been part of this city."—High Kiss employee handbook

"This accord is not drafted in a spirit of punishment, but of hope. The people of Jadzia have suffered enough through the War District's genocidal conquests. When we provide justice for the victims and restrain the destructive spirit of War, we may all move forward into a new and brighter future."—preamble to the Treaty of Inversions

FAZIZ DUCKED THROUGH my balcony curtains as the fourth bell pealed.

"Sun's high, Red Eyes." He snapped off the oxygen mask he used when ascending the Surrender. "I'm sorry about the mob. Was that why you missed practice this morning?"

"They left your symbol on my wall." I set down insurance reports and rose from my desk. He was already stepping back onto the balcony. Like he knew he'd done wrong and wanted distance. "Called me dragon and threatened to abduct me. The man I was a few months ago would have sent Dzaro's guards to arrest you. But you bid me trust, so I'll give you a chance to come clean. Did you incite the mob?"

"I'm blamed for half the crimes on Victory Street. The real inciter must have ordered it painted to cover their crime. I'd die before betraying your magic." Recovered from his first shock, he stood tall. The cool wind stirred his scent of sweat and ashes my way. "What makes you think I'd turn on you so crudely?"

"I'm also learning to trust myself." I bit my lip, aware I might blunder into a skyscraper-sized mistake. I feared not knowing more than I feared his laughter. *It could be possible.* "I thought you might be upset I chose Ria and not you."

"I'm not jealous," he said as my cheeks went red. "You and Ria make sense. You're both young, bright, full of fire. Plus, she's no criminal. She's exactly the partner I'd choose for you."

"I choose my own partners. How do you feel?"

"Like I need to hit something. Hard."

He'd dodged the question. But to hide emotions, not ill intent. Both of us were lashed to the wheel of Victory Street, fated to rise, fall, or be crushed as it turned. *Silk threads lie between us, easily torn.* In this moment, they wrapped us together.

I drew my baton. We stepped onto the balcony, where sunlight set the quartz to dancing. Baton flashed on sword. Metal sang, sweet and dangerous, as we cut and blocked in harmony. Starlings swirled about our dance. Faziz slid through his footwork, muscle memory smooth and practiced as paths worn through stone. Bright grace filled me as I mirrored him.

"Not bad!" he shouted as we came body-to-body. His arms strained. I levered my full height to force him down. His sword whipped free. He spun, lowering the blade at my bare stomach. "You'd be mesmerizing with a real sword."

"I'll have one made to match my eyes." I unfurled my wings. Lightness filled my limbs, lifting me onto a balcony rail. "A different scabbard for each skirt."

"You'll stun the necromancers with your fashion sense."

I leapt down and pressed him. *One. Two. Strike.* The *shiki* hissed towards his stomach. Faziz caught the baton, pulled it forward, and threw me over his hip. I locked my tail around his chest as I went down

Gravity ensued. I landed on top of us, grinning down into his dark eyes. His heart raced between my knees. "Mesmerized yet?"

"Strong form. You're getting good at this, Red Eyes." Sunlight winked off his chipped tooth—a souvenir from the fight with Tamadza. "Having fun?"

Too much. I slid off him, my whole heart aching as the knot of our bodies untangled. "Just how long have you been training with that sword?"

"Since my mid-teens, I assume. Twenty years or so."

"You assume? Don't you know?"

"Not the whole story." He touched the dark pockmarks on his chest. "The blue plague, remember? It put me in a coma. I woke in a dockside alley, no knowledge of who I was or how I got there, stray cats chewing on my face. Some guards threw trash at me. I stowed away on the first ship I saw. I found a sword below my robe, and my body could use it, so…"

The strange, fearful distance in his words shivered my soul. To lose everything you'd known, even yourself, and start over? "Dearest," I whispered, tears building in my eyes. "I'm so sorry. You've been alone for so long."

"It sucks. I won't pretend it doesn't. But I'm used to loneliness. And I built something good from that pain." His resignation put a brittle wall up against pain. I recognized the urge to push away the world before it hurt you. I couldn't let him suffer like I had.

"You're allowed to cry. Scream. Whatever you want." I squeezed his shoulder. "Don't be strong because it's convenient for others. Feel what you feel."

"I can't. Or—I shouldn't."

"Whyever not?"

He looked up at me, dark eyes blazing with a will to shape monuments. His fingers cupped my chin. "Because all I feel is wanting you."

A precipice opened, wind-swept and deep. I didn't care what lay at the bottom. I leapt. "You can have me."

Faziz drew me in. *Yes,* I thought. A light entered the world as his thin, chapped lips brushed mine, feather-light and tentative. For all his rough edges, the touch was so unexpectedly gentle I froze.

He started. "I'm sorry—"

"Don't be." I pressed my forehead to his. "It's okay."

"Was it?" His voice broke. "I'm not very good at kissing."

"I am." I brought my mouth down hard on his. My fingers twined through his long hair, pinning him to me. He tasted like sweat and straw, new life and old leather. His lips clashed against mine, tugging, gasping, goatee prickling my throat— and then the moment snapped. He buried his head against my chest. I held him steady.

For a heartbeat, the whole world spun around us.

Light feet landed. Settled starlings burst into flight. "I knew it!" Ria whistled. "Faziz, you beautiful genius, you finally made your move!"

He laughed. "Thanks for pushing me to do it."

"Ria encouraged you?" I stared at her. "You're okay with this?"

"I've got an order to rebuild and a world to defend. Someone's got to keep your bed warm when I'm working." She smiled. "I like Faziz. And I want you to be happy, Koré. I won't make you break anyone's heart."

Faziz hugged her. "You can have as much of us as you want, Red Eyes."

I can have this. By all the gods, I'm not a monster. I'm someone they can love.

I slid my baton through my sash and stepped back inside. Both Ria and Faziz yelped as my wings nearly knocked them over.

"Sorry!" I stammered, tossing seed to starlings with one hand, shaking out a wrinkled *thevé* with the other. "I've forgotten—everything, wow, everything—and I better go. I've got a meeting with the insurance company. I'll need to make it fast if I'm to dine with Akizeké tonight." The navy-and-gold cloth caught on my wing and slid off. "Dzkegé's tits!" A laugh sparkled up from low in my throat. *Please see how happy you two make me.*

"You're going with your wings out?" Ria joked.

My smile shrank as I remembered myself. *Come on, change back.* In the mirror, scales slunk further down my skin, the ruby roots of my neck-fan unfurling. A beautiful condemnation.

"Boss?" Kge stepped through the lower door. "Your *reja* is ready."

I flung myself against the back wall of my nook. Faziz and Ria stepped between me and Kge. But neither was tall enough to hide my wings. *My life ends if she looks up.* One shout would summon the mob. If I fled, I'd meet Akizeké's dragon-downing siege weapon. Even if I left War, I'd never escape my true self.

Ria's laughter. Faziz's hard-won smile.

Would living as myself, with them, be worth the danger?

"Is something wrong?" Ria asked.

"I'm… stuck." And I knew like poison in my veins. Eprue

Zucho had told me as much. *It takes an especially guarded soul to hide that magic.* I couldn't hide who I was around them. Even with Kge nearby. Even angry and afraid. They drew out the very best in me.

"If he can't pass, he's in danger," Ria told Faziz. "Can you hide him in the Slatepile?"

Faziz nodded. "Can you make a diversion?"

Ria charged out. Faziz threw a heavy, concealing cloak over my shoulders. Five minutes later, the scent of smoke wafted in. Every draper and carpenter in the main hall shouted as they searched for its source. Faziz rushed me through the chaos, lifting the hood over my cheeks as scales ran free. Ria drove us to the Slatepile at top speed.

As we emerged from the tunnel, Faziz's guards stared silently at the strange, distorted shape of me. Ria's eyes widened, drinking in their craft and architecture—but she stayed by my side as we climbed into the privacy of the old nightclub.

"What do we do?" I said, when at last I untied the cloak and stretched my wings.

"Your safety is our priority," Ria said. "Even if it means missing Akizeké's dinner tonight, or keeping you here longer."

Faziz nodded, squeezing her hand. The two made a wall, trapping me in. I didn't mind at all being caught by them. "You'll stay with me, if you're comfortable—"

"Always, with you."

"Use condoms, he's dull." Ria winked at us. "I'll dive into the Fire Weaver archives and research herald shapeshifting. It should only take a few months to find answers, if we salvaged the right sections."

Months. I bit my lip. Rarafashi didn't have months to live. Who would undo my father if I hid? But if I walked the streets like this, all flash and scale, I'd be spotted and caught. Rarafashi would give the throne to whichever *dzaxa* brought me before her and slice the treaty through its heart.

Just as the Hive had fallen, every foundation on the city-planet would tremble.

"What triggers your shapeshifting?" Faziz asked. "What stops you from turning back?"

"Happiness. Honest anger." Loathing Vashathke felt too clean and right to banish my scales. I tried remembering how worthless he'd made me feel at the state banquet—but I knew I had worth, for the two of them to stand beside me. "Being with you."

Faziz stepped back, his shadow blurring tall over the notches and pits in the slate. "If this is because I kissed you— say the word and I'll never touch you again."

"Me too," Ria said. "I love you, but your safety comes first. If you want me to leave, I understand."

Tears brimmed in my eyes. *How can I live without this, now I finally know how it feels?* But if I was with them, the whole world would see me as I truly was. I could picture them walking away—no more bad movies, no more sparring—but that wouldn't return me to who I'd been before. I'd always know I was worthy of love, so worthy they'd loved me enough to sacrifice their desires and step away. The hope they'd given me would shine out of my heart.

My secret form enveloped me, shifting my head and jaw as tears slid down my silver scales. The catwalk groaned under my weight. My neck brushed the tiny holdlights strung above.

Faziz's people looked up from the market atrium, pointing and squinting. They might not be able to make out my form, but they had to see my shadow. *They don't need to be dull. No one needs that on my street if they don't want it.* I breathed low across the ground. Delighted gasps rose as essence fell.

"That's nice," Faziz said. "You're a real sweetheart, Koré."

I am good. I pressed my head to his chest, coiling my neck around Ria. *I am loved.*

The bombs went off.

A resonant, shattering boom rattled through my eardrums. The pressure wave from a hundred holdfire charges slapped me like an invisible palm, flinging Faziz and Ria into my chest. Slate stirred. Catwalks trembled. Holdlights cracked and old speakers screamed feedback into a billow of heat.

The concrete-and-holdweight-patched column groaned as the cavern roof slid southward. Ria flung up her hands. Air cracked and hissed as her ice flew. Dark tendrils wove scaffolding from air. Screams rose as slate, concrete, and falling pulleys rained down from the collapsing pillar. A child cried.

Ria cursed, and spat, and a high brace of ice leapt into being. A tree-like pillar, branches spread wide, five brontos high, braced the whole cavern's roof as the last of the support column crumbled.

"*Miran mak darugi!*" Faziz spat in his birth tongue. "Zegakadze's doing. That fucking monster tried to bomb us out!"

His heartbreak cut deeper than a knife. My dragon's form dissolved into silver as Faziz leapt to the ground.

I donned my cloak and helped shaking, exhausted Ria follow him down. Faziz, surrounded by his people, didn't even look our way. All his eyes were for the crushed pulley and concrete chips he held.

He'd built a world for dulls. But the brights above could tear it down at their pleasure.

Falling stones had crushed the column worksite and half the market. Piece by piece, we excavated the debris, sorting through broken pottery, flickering holdlights and crushed food. Ria and I used our bright strength to push the largest fragments against a wall. The able carried the wounded off to the infirmary, but some were beyond saving. We laid twelve bodies in the cavern's central square.

My fault, hummed my nagging head as mourners' cries rose

high. Zega had ordered this. And I'd spared his life to give that order, so adrift in my own swirling feelings I'd spared no thought for the beating hearts Zega would still with a word.

I wasn't a monster for being born. But I'd tied myself to the *dzaxa* and their games. My need to hurt Vashathke pounded a second heartbeat beside my loves. *His power allows bombs on his street. Crushes souls and futures with batons and taxes.* The truth of his evil flooded me, filling my lungs, constricting my heart. No one else could finish this job. I'd pursue Vashathke's ruin until the bloody Dzaxashigé legacy defined me.

"Do you want me to stay here on guard?" Ria offered Faziz. "We can skip Magistrate Akizeké's banquet. She won't mind."

Faziz bit his lip at Akizeké's name. "Yes, she will. Go, the both of you. You're expected—and Koré, you have your power contained, right?"

I nodded. The knot tightened in my throat. The next thing I shattered would be human and warm. *Sadness. Darkness. Pain. My own and theirs.* I had to keep the slow *dzaxa* poison inside me from sloshing out and staining them. I couldn't just walk away, from them, from my father. I had to hurt them and myself so deeply the memory would forever lock up my light.

The hope I'd breathed in the ruins was sweet but fleeting. I couldn't be a Fire Weaver. I couldn't be War's dragon. I couldn't be anyone's boyfriend. I had to be the whore of Victory Street.

The monster Vashathke had created. The only one who could tear down his throne.

INTERLUDE: AGE EIGHTEEN
The Kzagé Hotel, in the Palace of Ten Billion Swords

9th *Verga,* Year 84 Rarafashi

"I know your secret. Give me what I want or I'll tell the world about the babies."—note delivered to Vashathke Faraakshgé Dzaxashigé during his magisterial coronation parade

"Gender: female (most likely)"—medical report for Najadziri Faraajzgé Dzaxashigé, age 52

THE WORST NIGHT of my life, I spent outside the Kzagé Hotel's wedding suite, on a cold floor shaped from dead Scholars' swords, envying them the deaf twilight of wandering spirits. My dull ears couldn't catch all sounds, but every laugh felt like a betrayal and every whimper tore me in two.

My fault. If I hadn't given all my essence to Zega, I'd be strong enough to charge in and push his new wife off him. If I hadn't given him all my essence, he never would have caught a Dzaxashigé's attention.

The eighth bell tolled through a sky I couldn't see, marking the day's end. Then the first. The second. The sun would be rising, beyond steel walls, but I hadn't seen it in years. I rested my cheek on cool metal, fighting sleep's fog, chewing my lip bloody. If I couldn't be in there with Zega, I would be awake when he emerged.

The third bell, high and swiftest in its peals, joined the low hum of the second. The fifth rattled like a broken drum. The eighth called the sweet lull of night's zenith. *They're not supposed to all ring together.* Shouts rose from below, rained from above. Footsteps clattered on steel. A river of sound poured through the Palace walls. My ears ached with the sense of broken time.

I didn't move. Everything I cared about had broken when the architect *dzaxa* Najadziri had signed the marriage contract for my sweet Zegakadze.

Steel hinges creaked. Zega stumbled out, wrapped in a disheveled swan-feather wedding skirt. Eyes wild and arms hugged tight about his chest.

"How are you?" I reached for him, then hesitated. "I asked if I could serve the high table at the wedding feast, but only the brightest servants were allowed. I'm sorry. I wanted to be near you.

Zega threw his bright arms around me, pulling me so tight I feared he'd snap my spine. His salt-streaked cheeks held the delicate, even white of magnolia petals. His bright beauty recalled statues carved by Shaper hands: torso unblemished and lithe, nose a gentle bow, full lashes fluttering over sapphire eyes. Our reflections entwined in the steel of dead armies, and I couldn't believe I was lucky enough to hold him. Myself, a plain, dull boy, hair in long tangles, yellow beard patchy, pimples down my cheeks and back, skirt worn to grey fringe. Smiling as the boy I loved kissed me hard enough to erase the world.

Fuck marriages, fuck customs, fuck traditions and gender roles. I had love. If the world wanted to take him from me, it could do so over my raging queer dead body.

"Get me out of here," Zega whispered. I took his hand and led him down to the stables.

"What are you doing here, Zega?" said Ironwhite as we entered. She and the other raptor handlers sat around a table, faces downcast, a sharp alcohol tang rising from their cups. Light thinned on the tall, narrow steel walls. "Doesn't your new wife want you with her?"

"*Dzaxa* Najadziri was too drunk last night to give orders," Zega said. "I'll see her enough when I move to her apartment."

"We still have time," I said. "Please. Let's not talk of that yet." I'd stay when he left, working for his mother in the Kzagé Hotel, as I had these past four years. Zega had taken me to Najadziri and told her he needed a male attendant. Her hungry eyes had crawled over my chest and face, leaving me guilty-glad when she'd declared my fate. *No scheming dull will seduce essence from my innocent young husband under my roof. I'll protect my family from his kind.*

No one would guess the truth: I was so hapless in bed I'd never drawn essence from my boyfriend. His touch undid me, soothing my aches, siphoning my power into him. Love, not my greed, bound us. Feelings the *dzaxa* didn't understand and yearned to destroy.

A breeding raptor, penned tight in a nesting cage, screeched like ripping metal. I winced. Zega, bright and vulnerable, clapped fists over his ears.

"It's the bells," Ironwhite said through grim lips. The back of my neck prickled. I knew before she spoke the news weighed heavy. "They play the mourning chimes. Sorry to ruin your special day, Zega, but the magistrate and her daughters are dead. Her apartment collapsed during a banquet."

How sad, I thought, my heart not in it. The old magistrate meant nothing to me.

"The street's crumbling," grumbled a stableworker. "We've lost our magistrate. Now our dignity. Rarafashi's appointed her husband to fill the empty seat. Vashathke will be crowned in a week. Her plaything, ruling the richest street in War?"

Vashathke. Magistrate of Victory Street. Something stirred in my breast, older than my love for Zega. *My father. Enthroned.* Magistrates ranked just below judges. As Rarafashi's husband, he could shape policies through pillow-talk—but as a magistrate, he could make his own.

He already loved his new title better than me.

"I'll need a new skirt for the coronation parade." Ironwhite tossed me a bolt of yellow cloth. "And a fresh cover for my old *fajix*. Ranking servants will stand with the household. You're not one, so don't steal any fabric."

I wouldn't even have new clothes for my father's coronation? Embers of my old, angry fire stirred to life. *No. Anger is trouble and death. Zega's all you need.*

I collected the others' measurements, and retreated with Zega to my little nook by the racing stables, where the walls rose higher than my dull eyes could see. Dark metal and narrow crannies, forged from the soft curves of melted chariots. I pricked my finger on a needle when I drew out my kit. Raptors howled at the blood-scent.

"I like you too." I scratched the plumes of the nearest beast, yanking my fingers back as she snapped at me. The raptors were my closest and only friends at the Kzagé Hotel.

"Koré," Zega whispered, breaking his uncharacteristic quiet. "I think I'm in danger. This accident..."

I wrapped cloth about my finger and took his hand. "It's a shame about the magistrate, but Najadziri lives far from her suite. You'll be safe from accidents when you move."

He lowered his head. Pressed his lips to my ear, and whispered. "I don't think it was an accident. I think Vashathke had her murdered. Najadziri told me terrible things last night. She knows your father. She's... bedded him, and made a game of telling me how poorly I compared. They've plotted something together."

"I'm so sorry," I whispered. From the wandering glint in Najadziri's eye when she'd seen me, I knew she'd never be faithful. But it was one thing to cheat on your husband, and another to fling the truth at him, like his inadequacy had driven you to do it.

"She's conceived a bastard with him. And she expects me to raise it."

My jaw dropped. Ice, cool and wet, slid down my spine. *Another bastard?* Women did as they chose with seed left in their bodies, but conceiving without the surety of a husband's essence store meant a financial risk. If Najadziri just wanted a child, she could have made one with Zega last night.

Zega paced across my nook, rumpled wedding skirt trailing in the dirt behind him. "She told me this like she expected me to be flattered. I'll be stepfather to the most important child in War—a daughter, most likely, the tests said. She and Vashathke would rise together, and carry me behind them like a tugboat in a dreadnought's wake. Like I've spent my life waiting for some *dzaxa* to lift me up and give me what I can't earn myself." Bitterness laced his words. "She's an architect; she'd know how to make a collapse look accidental. She's probably planning for her bastard to inherit Victory Street, since Vashathke's legitimate children are all boys."

"Whatever she's done," I said, "my father put the idea in her head. He would have asked her to conceive, as he asked my mother to make me." I'd told Zega the story years ago, but confessing hadn't drained the poison from the memory. *He flooded me with essence, flattered me, and asked me to conceive a child.* Why did my father want bastards? I'd been proof of his fertility—now well-established by his three sons with Rarafashi. His wife had slapped him when she saw me in the Prizeheron. Why deliberately provoke her?

Something screamed in the back of my dull brain.

"Is there a pattern in the women he lets bed him?" I said.

"My mother. Najadziri. Rarafashi. Pale, short, with dark hair—Rarafashi's was dark when she was younger."

"It's not about love," Zega said. "Men like Vashathke have outgrown love. Maybe he's punishing his wife. Seducing women who look like her, but younger, to give the knife an extra twist."

Outgrown love. My heart shivered. He'd said it like he admired that. I hoped my dull ears had misheard.

"Why the babies, then?" Gifts from unwitting women who thought they could master my father if they gave him this one thing. Vashathke wanted more than children. He'd killed to be crowned magistrate. His wants knew no limit. Darkness ran through his veins and mine.

He wouldn't stop at Victory Street. He'd set his eyes on a bigger throne.

"It wasn't Rarafashi's husbands who failed," I whispered. "It's her. Rarafashi is infertile."

With no close female relatives to inherit her store and throne, Rarafashi's legacy would be cast in shadow if the *dzaxa* fought to succeed her. She needed a daughter—no. She needed a female infant to pass as her own. A plump woman with a loose stomach, the judge could easily feign pregnancy. Vashathke's genes ran strong. A child with his face, lifted in the judge's arms... who would question that child's rights? *He wanted my mother silenced, not just because of me, but because she could figure out what he and Rarafashi planned. He's silenced every other woman he's seduced.*

Vashathke had given the judge three sons. But no daughters. *What happens to the girls?* My stomach twisted. *Dead babies. Dead sisters. His own children sacrifice to his ambition.* Rarafashi had bought herself children, but not a clear heir. The succession would be disputed.

A husband—and a magistrate—would be favored to ascend.

I told Zega my theory. "He's a monster," I whispered.

"He's murdered his lovers and babies—murdered everyone in the magistrate's apartment last night—to open his path to the judgeship."

"He had no choice," Zega said. "You're lucky to be dull and poor, Koré. People only take things from you. When you're pretty and rich, they tear out your soul."

You made me dull and poor. But saying that would offend him. "Vashathke tore out his own soul. There's a choice between being a monster and being devoured by one."

"Easy for you to say. You made that choice years ago, when you ran to me with a dead guard trainee's blood on your face. You're already a monster."

I winced. "But you're not." The truth dawned on me, with sickening, dull slowness. I'd need to break my heart for him. "You and Najadziri must leave Victory Street, or my father will kill her and the baby, if it's a girl. Go to Shadowcoin. Hire smugglers to take you to the Scholarly District, or further if you must."

"And leave you?" Something broke in his voice. "It's one thing to move apartments within the Palace. It's another to cross a world. I'll never see you again."

"It's the only way," I choked. "For your family."

"They forced this family on me!" He pulled me into his arms. His lips danced like lightning up my neck, over my cheek. His fists bunched in my long, unkempt hair. "I love you. I choose you."

He loves me. Essence leapt from my skin, flooding him. My palms went coarse and dry where they clutched his back. My vision swam, blurry and unfocused. I didn't care. I'd give him every piece of me he could carry, because when he left I'd have nothing at all.

"You'll need this." I slid from his arms, dug under my rag pillow, and drew out a scallop-shell-engraved baton. "This was my mother's. I want it to protect you when you—" I cut off. I was crying too hard to breathe.

Zega snatched the baton and squeezed my shoulder. His brown curls flopped over his face. I wanted to touch them. I didn't dare move, for fear the moment would turn to smoke around us. "I won't give you up because of Najadziri's mistake."

"It's okay," I whispered. "I understand. She's your wife. This is how it works."

"This isn't how it works for every man." He cupped my chin in his hands. Fingers tight on the rough scraps of my beard. "And I'm not like every man. Be brave for me, Koré, and I'll be bloody for you."

In a bright flash of motion, he vanished up the hall.

VASHATHKE'S CORONATION PARADE took days climbing Victory Street. Rarafashi crowned her husband on the Palace steps; his speech never alluded to the fact he was the fourth male magistrate in War's history. While the family and high servants watched, I mended raptor harnesses and chewed my lip bloody.

But when music rose from the corridor outside, I couldn't stay hidden. Mine was the life he'd created and shattered to reach this day. I crept out to join his moment, which I also belonged to.

The trumpets and drums played soft Warmwater jazz. Lilies poured off the magistrate's *reja*. A canopy of white feathers shaded him, rising about his platinum lace spire crown.

I pushed, past servants and other watching dulls, to the front of the crowd. The new magistrate's eyes drew me: a scarlet as shocking as the gems of his crown. My eyes.

His gaze flickered past me. Washing by. Not for a heartbeat did he stop to see his son.

In his wake, cheering spectators drifted back to their lives. I remained, alone, among petals and broken plumes.

He's getting away with it. Vashathke had destroyed my

mother and countless others. His evil would steal Zega from my side. He'd rule in luxury while I dwelt loveless in shadows. Knowledge, unwanted and aching, coiled through my bones: I was powerless to expose and punish him. He'd won the game between us.

He'd already ground me down to nothing.

No. Revelation unfurled in me, a flower stretching toward the sun. *He hasn't won yet.* Twice he'd tried to destroy me. I still lived.

I didn't have to stay dull. I didn't have to stay in the Kzagé Hotel, especially with Zega leaving. I could brighten. Move forward. Fight for my mother, my family, and my love. For myself. *Myself.* A word beautiful and taboo. *I have a self. I can choose things for me.* My soul, guilty and blood-soaked, reached to me like a firefighter's hand through smoke. *I will bring my father down. I will do the justice the law denies. And I will do it because I want it done.*

Instead of afternoon chores, I ran to Zega's suite.

"Koré!" He lowered his book as I burst through the entry curtains, sliding off his bed, still dressed for the parade. "I have good news—"

"I need my essence back." I slid through the maze of moving boxes and took his hands, alive with the anger inside me. "I'll punish Vashathke for what he's done to us. I'll stop him from becoming judge. But I can only do it bright."

"Vashathke isn't your concern. You don't need essence. You have me to take care of you." He kissed my cheek. "Smile, lay down, and let me talk."

He couldn't care for me from across the world. I needed this gift. Couldn't he see this wasn't about us as a couple, but me as a person?

A soft scraping irritation whittled itself from the burning scraps of me. "I listen when you talk about your dreams. Now I've a dream. I need power to claim it." I tried pulling on a flirtatious smile. Would it work from a dull face? "I

345

know I'm bad in bed. But could you please tithe me a little essence?"

"You don't need your essence back. It's all taken care of. I spoke to Vashathke at the coronation banquet. I told him I'd discovered his plot, and we made a deal. I'll keep Najadziri from bragging about bedding him. I'll bring her to him when she's ready to give birth. When he's finished with her, he'll make me the captain of his personal guard. I'll stay in the Palace. I'll be free of her. Free for you."

"You'll kill her," I said softly.

"I'll escape her. For you."

"For me?" My voice grew cold. "What if I asked for essence, not because I needed it, but because I also wanted to shine. For me. Would you do that for me?"

"Don't give me that line. If I'm to enter Vashathke's inner circle, I'll need every drop I can get. I'm not of Dzaxashigé blood. I can't let them look at me and see an imposter."

"But you'll let them look at me and see a dull they can hurt without consequence?" My voice rose, loosened by the shift in my world. I wanted something. I'd chosen a path because I wanted to choose it, because there was joy in the act of choosing. If he loved me, wouldn't he be glad for my happiness? "I didn't ask you to become a monster for me. Only to help me have a life of my own. Are you doing this all for me, Zega, or for you?"

"Stop being so selfish. Do you want my wife to hurt me?" A whine crept into his voice. A sound a child might make when snatching up their favorite toy. "You shouldn't deny me. You're part of me."

"I'm my own. I love you, but I'm my own, and I'm asking for my essence."

"And I'm saying no." His blue eyes—lovely as the noon sky, shining with the light he'd taken from me—went flat and cold. "You can't have your baton back either. So don't ask."

A soul can die in a moment. It doesn't make a sound. The

world doesn't dim as it dwindles. And War doesn't notice its passing. It skips over the dull men with empty eyes.

This is what love is worth. Love that tales and movies praise, love like devouring fire. Four years I'd given Zega. Every secret of my past, every forbidden longing. My beauty, dreams and strength—I hadn't wanted what I'd surrendered, but I'd needed it to survive. Zega had known that. He'd manipulated me to take it. He'd loved me, but he hadn't cared.

So I didn't care when I went to Najadziri's hotel room.

FIRST, I BATHED in the raptor trough, drenched myself in Zega's stolen plum perfume, and tied my hair with one of his pearl pins. I had no fine skirts shaped to fit me, but the stable windows still hung white tulle to herald Vashathke's ascension, and a few quick cuts let me fashion a loose wrap. A silk-flower harness strap locked around my neck like a choker. My legs, I shaved bare with a shaping knife.

I'll warn her, I told myself as I dressed, my spite shaping a darker plan. *She needs to know what Zega plans. And Zega needs to know I'm no pet. I've a will of my own, and it's bloody and dark.*

Najadziri had remained at the Kzagé Hotel for the coronation parade. The sword-shaped wedding suite lay darkly lit as I entered. Zega's bride was in her mid-forties, of medium brightness for a Dzaxashigé. Her eyes simmered cherry-red; tight, dark curls piled atop her head. She sat on her bed, *fajix* discarded and stomach swelling, reading by a single holdlight.

I hoped the shadows would hide my pimples.

Into the vast chamber I slunk, sitting beside her and taking her hand. She stiffened. "What brings my betrothed's little friend to my bedroom?"

"I want to help you," I said. "Look at me. Zega told me who you conceived from. I came the same way."

She stroked my cheek. A thick silver ring traced cool lines down my neck. "Another of my dear Vasha's mistakes."

"Vashathke doesn't make mistakes," I said. "You may think you've accomplished something, seducing him, but he's playing your lust against you. You and your baby are only his weapons to capture the throne. The judge's throne."

"Don't speak of things you don't understand." She pushed me away, so bright and strong her ring cut my cheek. I winced and kept smiling. "You might fear Vashathke, but I've got him on a leash."

He will strangle you with that leash. But no one would believe me. The *dzaxa* would paint my father a slut if they knew his indiscretions. But they'd never see the depth of his sins, never realize a young man had turned their expectations against them.

Time to see if I play his game.

"You're right. I'm afraid." I leant my head on her shoulder. The cut screamed on my cheek. "I need help."

"What help?"

I couldn't parse the interest in her voice, not dull as I was. But I had instincts. I let her stroke my hair. "Essence. Enough to get away from Zega so you two can start a new life, without me interfering."

"You want essence from me?" Her red eyes weighed me up. "Are you as skilled as your father in bed?"

Bed. She'd spoken what I feared. What I longed for. I'd only ever been with Zega, and never drawn essence from him. I doubted I'd please her. But I had to start somewhere, and if Zega had ever cared for me, this would cut him deep. "Tithe to me, *dzaxa,* and you'll learn I'm better."

A flutter of essence leapt from her to me, easy as a starling shocked into flight. Her gentle fingers guided me to her throat. Darkness turned her skin a dusky violet. "Start there."

I ran my lips along the smooth, graceful curve, marveling at its difference from Zega's. She moaned as my tongue cupped her breastbone, squeaked as my teeth found her nipple. *So responsive.* "Thank you," I whispered to her round stomach as my tongue washed down the orb. "My champion. My hero." I nuzzled the hair between her legs. The thicket of her mound was ripe with heat. Eager to be explored.

I all but drowned when I began to suck.

"Steady, boy!" Her high gasp echoed off steel. "Again. Again!"

I licked, and kissed, and she flowed into me. My senses rolled out like rain down a roof. I could feel the fine hairs on her thighs, taste the road's dust on her skin, hear every breathy grunt. A strange, electric arousal filled me. *I'm good at this.*

Zega had been holding back his pleasure. Robbing me with indifference. I could do the same by remembering my father's coronation parade. Vashathke's eyes, skipping over me in the crowd. Like I was nothing. Like he had won.

It hurt. But the pain brought me her power.

I swung her to the floor atop me, hiking up my makeshift skirt. Her lips tickled my ear. "There's my good boy. I've got you." She pulled me inside her, teaching my body the rhythm of her hips. *One. Two. Three.* She'd brag of having me if she lived long enough—but for now, all that mattered was us, connected and burning together.

I called her name as I crested. "My savior, my savior!" She arched back her head, shouting something like victory. It was silly, but I let her have it. The true triumph was mine.

Najadziri dragged me into bed beside her. When she fell snoring on my chest, I squirmed out from her grasp. The raptors clicked and spat as I slipped back into the stable, grabbed my rusted razor, and sliced through my matted hair. Blond clumps fell into straight trim.

Part of me wanted to fling the hair in Zega's bed. *Remember that little queer boy you thought you could control?* I'd fled my mother's dreams and my girlfriends' plans, but I'd only changed one set of rules for another.

A stranger with a nicked jawline stared back at me from the trough: pretty in a common way, with red eyes and an upturned nose, the promise of adult muscles finally filling in. I hadn't clearly seen myself in years. This would do nicely.

In clumsy, half-remembered glyphs, I wrote a note and left it by the harnesses. No matter who found it, the whole household would hear the gossiped message—*I fucked the bride and groom*. Maybe their marriage would sunder before Zega dragged Najadziri further into Vashathke's trap. Or maybe she'd think me a liar. Either way, I was done living only for the sake of others. I was ready to rise.

As the first bell rang, I snuck off downstairs.

The Palace had deep undercellars, roots where unused swords from its forging lay in rusty piles. Amidst the scrap, blemished silks and rotting wood built lopsided shacks. Music rose from every door and window. The air reeked of whiskey and cheap spirits.

I plodded along, legs aching, cut cheek burning. Najadziri's essence hadn't replaced a fraction of what I'd lost, and every shout from a drunk made me shudder. *My body has power over them. That scares them. They only harass to hold on to their might.*

At last, I came to the winding stair of the Bold Blades.

"What brings you here, boy?" shouted a bright, older woman with a tangle of red curls. The brothel's insignia marked her *fajix,* an Old Jiké glyph in a clumsy hand.

I bowed. "*Dzaxa.* I need work."

The old pimp grinned like a predator. I didn't mind. I knew what she was. From her, I could guard the parts of my soul that moved planets and wrecked families.

No one would break me again. I was done with love.

CHAPTER TWENTY
The Pyramid of Souls, Armory Street

16th *Reshi,* Year 92 Rarafashi

"Male representation in film can't stop at the unexamined presentation of male-identified bodies. We must ask ourselves what these fictional men say about how we expect men to behave and which male stories we value telling."—"Blood, Stone, and Gender," Journal of Film Study

RIA BORROWED DZARO'S helicopter for the evening, and the two of us flew to Armory Street in idle comfort. Part of me wished to spread my own wings, but I couldn't dare a full shapeshift. Not with the mob's shouts echoing in my head. Maybe not ever again.

Unlike Victory Street, with its eclectic trophy-buildings, Armory Street had been built around ancient Dzaxashigé factories. Broken pipes pocked the concrete. Blocky sculptures of armored soldiers listed and lay in ancient heaps. Snow-capped pyramids lined the street's northward curve, shaved off in a straight line at the ruins, where the hovership listed under heavy guard.

"Can I flirt with Akizeké?" I asked Ria as she landed us. "The better mood she's in, the more money she'll offer for your support."

"I don't mind, if you're comfortable," Ria said. "I look like a wise High Master and not some stupid party kid, right? I want Akizeké to respect me, not the title."

Between the *Sashua Vorona* and Tamadza's staff, Ria's red skirt and *fajix* were fittingly accessorized. I couldn't imagine anyone being unimpressed by her. "Absolutely. And if she insults you, we can always slice her throat and use the staff to raise her in thrall."

"Blessed Voro, I can't even get this thing to turn on." Ria poked the holdshadow node in the staff's crown and sighed. "A real Fire Weaver would have found out how to destroy it by now."

I laughed. "We don't even like Tamadza. Don't let her weird shadow magic get under your skin."

"It's not Tamadza in my head. I can't stop wondering what Dad might think of everything I'm doing, how Päreshi and the other Fire Weavers would react. It's like they're still weighing my words. Dad would have wanted me to remember happy things, but..."

"Perhaps the pressure you feel comes from here." I tapped her forehead. "You push yourself too hard."

"Someone has to push me. My too-nice boyfriend treats me like I shit gold."

"Your boyfriend draws a firm line at scatological fetishes. I dealt enough with that in my first job."

"Look at you, communicating your boundaries." She smiled. A glorious light, one I feared would vanish once I broke her heart. "We just might make this work after all."

I hung back as the herald announced Ria, not wanting Akizeké to see me enter on another woman's arm. By the time I made my bow, they were deep in conversation.

"You look lovely, Koré." Akizeké waved me over. I wore

the snow-white skirt she'd given me for the state banquet, with a storm-grey *thevé*, smoky trails leading back from my eyes. "I hope our tour won't bore you."

"Whatever interests you interests me." I dropped into her lap. *Please her. Control her. Bend her to your will like your father with Rarafashi.* Ria raised an eyebrow, but said nothing.

Akizeké had ordered her dining table set atop a *reja*, its wide hoverplatform sporting an enclosed kitchen and a dozen servants. Two brontos pulled us down the high-arched slate corridor. Snow fell outside holdlight-rimmed windows. Glass cases glittered in a thousand alcoves.

"The local universities curse me for keeping a private museum," Akizeké said, "but a ruler's entitled to private treasure."

An antique set of armor hung in the hall's center. Steel scales fell in a long skirt, the breastplate and pauldrons shaped like dragons' heads, bracers wreathed with electrum talons. A sword and shield hung where the hands would be, ruby-set and gold-rimmed.

"The armor of Varjthosheri the Dragon-Blessed." Akizeké chuckled. "An expensive purchase, but it fits me well. The sword isn't original. Shaper Varjthosheri carried the dragons' sword."

No. I remembered Eprue Zucho. Varjthosheri and my other Dzaxashigé ancestors hadn't lifted the dragons' sword. They'd never acknowledged the truth of their dark deeds. But reminding Akizeké of our family's taint would only anger her.

Supper came hearty and thick: duck-blood soup, brimming with noodles and apple slices. Roast bronto leg, stewed in red wine and its own juices, served atop potato puffs and pickled beets. Chocolate-dusted trenchers of bone marrow. Fried hazelnut-studded dough dipped in sugar. Vodka flights flavored with raspberries and dried plums. I drank as the wonders rolled by. Each new sight made me drink more.

"A holdfast automaton." Ria pointed to a blue-and-gold statue pacing across a cage. "*Rodi Vorona,* is that one a man? Do you ever let it out?"

"Of course not," Akizeké said. "It's too valuable. That one was excavated from a border ruin tunnel. Our university found it. I claimed eminent domain to take it."

"No wonder my father always complained about you!" Ria laughed. "You're cunning, Magistrate. I like that."

"I've always admired the Fire Weavers. If I'd been born in Engineering, I'd probably be High Master in your place."

"Voro knows you're qualified." Ria offered Akizeké a compact of firepowder. The magistrate breathed deep. Neither woman offered any to me. "But we're pacifists. It's odd to celebrate both us and your violent ancestors."

"A bold woman is virtuous, no matter her cause. I celebrate boldness." She winked at me as she spoke.

Ria frowned and took back her compact.

The brontos plodded through the private hall. Ancient robots spun in their chains. Screens and circuits flashed broken rhythm. Substance flickered on the lips of broken cannons. Flowers walked through holdlife trenchers, waving roots like feet.

"What was there?" I pointed at an empty rack.

"A giant *njiji* dart crossbow. Made to capture rebellious dragons. My guards are training for the next time it flies."

I shivered, desperately missing the safety of Engineering.

Ria shouted, "A containment chamber!" as a cylinder of swirling gas rolled past. She leapt off the *reja* and pressed her hand to the glass. "We had one in the Hive. They prevent dangerous artifacts from releasing energy."

Exactly what we needed. "Magistrate, Ria killed a powerful necromancer. That's why the hovership crashed on your border. The staff she carries is her trophy."

Ria's eyebrows shot up. "Koré! You can't—"

"You can trust Akizeké." For the endorsement to go through, she had to trust Akizeké. "*Dzaxa* Akizeké, will you lease us that chamber to securely store the staff?"

"I keep all my toys in one place." Akizeké squeezed my ass. "But you may use it, High Master. My museum is well-guarded, and you can visit your stick whenever you want."

Ria opened the cylinder's cap and dropped the staff inside. It sealed with a reassuring hiss. "Thanks, Akizeké."

"No problem. It's nice to have some life in my halls. Would you like to use this museum as the new base of the Fire Weavers?"

"That'd be awesome. I don't know how I'd repay you."

"I'm a candidate for Rarafashi's throne. I'd like a High Master's endorsement."

We'd reached the evening's purpose. I hadn't expected Akizeké's opening offer to go so high.

Ria nodded. "Of course I'll—"

"Magistrate Vashathke, the other candidate, hates your order. In exchange for my hosting, you'll accuse Vashathke of conspiring in the Hive attack and demand his arrest."

My jaw nearly fell into the mustard dish.

"Accuse Vashathke?" Ria said. "On what evidence?"

"He blames your people for his son's murder. He'll attack your district if he inherits. Who needs evidence? Help me win or risk ten thousand years' peace when he rises to the throne."

I'd made that same argument to Ria once. It hadn't gone well. Time to draw pleasantries over chaos, wield sweetness as my weapon. "High Master," I murmured, "we can settle this at length. Will you at least give the magistrate your endorsement?"

"Of course!" Ria smiled. "For a price."

She and Akizeké haggled for the rest of the dinner. I sat on the magistrate's lap, feigning the passivity of her imprisoned construct. By the time they settled on two hundred thousand *thera*, the brontos had stopped before a small, private staircase. Akizeké grabbed my wrist. "My servants will show you the guest rooms, High Master. Koreshiza will attend me."

My spine stiffened. It wasn't a request.

Ria looked to me. "Are you good?"

Akizeké is a piece in my game. I nodded to Ria. Fear fluttered in my chest as I followed the magistrate upstairs.

Akizeké's personal rooms, though spacious, lay unearthly still. She'd lived alone since her husband's death. I'd half-expected her to lead me to a sex dungeon; instead, she pulled me into her private theater and called for a movie.

"It's *Blood and Stone 5: The Reckoning.*" She pushed me down on a viewing couch. The projector light turned her hollow cheeks blade-sharp and her grey-blond hair to electrum. She laughed as the first extra died in a shower of fake blood. *Like Dzkegé herself. A god of War. Why am I the dragon and not you?*

"What's the plot?" I asked, lying back.

"A team of soldiers sneak past enemy lines." She pointed at the screen, which was half covered in subtitles and half in red goo, and dropped a hazelnut on my tongue. "That's Mesham. She struggles living up to her Shaper mother. That's Yan. She was a famous athlete until the enemy killed her husband. She's using her money and tech to get revenge. That's Hishura. His ex-girlfriend raped and castrated him. Now he's an assassin who seduces people to death."

Hishura's actor resembled Faziz, neat goatee and all. Stupid longing twisted my heart. *He's already lost enough this week. Now I plan to push him away.* "How awful."

"It's a war movie. They've got trauma. It's realistic." On screen, the loincloth-clad Hishura snapped a soldier's neck with his thighs. "Besides, it's not like he whines much. That's admirable."

"What a strong male character," I mused, tongue running away with me. "He's everything you think a man should be, minus trauma from living up to those expectations."

"Men don't suffer trauma. They raise babies while we risk ourselves to protect them."

"Have you ever been a man?"

"Have you ever been a woman?" She smiled. "It's all perspective."

No, it isn't! I thought, and immediately started questioning myself. *Be soft. Cushion your disagreement.* "Maybe it would be better if there was more than one man in the movie?"

"What, an army of men? They're so tall! No general could afford that much extra armor!" She laughed. "The Scholars scientifically proved men can't fight. Female hormones make us socially cohesive and protective—the perfect soldiers. Male hormones make you moody, isolated, and easily upset. Not fit for guard service." She kissed my neck. "There are exceptions. Like Hishura."

Onscreen, Hishura strangled a soldier with his loincloth. Strategic shadows covered his groin. "What is this rated?"

"Age twelve and up." She crushed a hazelnut in her fist and sprinkled powder from my breastbone to my navel. "You don't have to pay attention. I've seen this before." Her fingers slid down my skirt. Tightened around my shaft. "I knew you were liking the movie."

I wasn't under contract. I didn't love her. But I needed something from her, and letting her have me was easy. She would never drag out my true self.

Akizeké undid my skirt and mounted me, not looking away from the screen. A fistful of hazelnuts in my mouth kept me silent. She clenched whenever another character died. After my peak passed, she kept me inside her, pushing with her fingers until her final pleasure came. Essence flickered into me, sure and predictable as a bank deposit.

"Your Fire Weaver's killed your cunning," she said,

releasing me. "You could have convinced her to blame Vashathke. She's young, with a girl's desires."

My anger sparked at her dismissal of Ria. *Hide your feelings. Play her.* "Ria needs an extra push. The crashed hovership is on your land. Give me access to the site. I think there's evidence on board to prove Vashathke colluded in the attack."

She rolled her eyes. "You? Excavate a ruin? A boy your size would get stuck in a tunnel and endanger my crew saving him!"

"Trust me. You trusted me as your herald in Engineering."

"I sent you to Engineering so the judge would fuck you. I don't need you getting fucked by a hovership." She probed my ass. "You'd be ruined."

My stomach sank. "You told my father I'd speak on your behalf."

"Rarafashi didn't need to hear crudeness from her future heir."

She never believed in me. I bit my lip, covering disappointment with a neat plan that would also helpfully push Ria away. "I'll write a statement accusing Vashathke of conspiring in the bombing. You can send heralds to read it in each building in War, print it in a pamphlet, whatever you judge best. My word doesn't have Ria's power, but it'll help discredit him."

"Excellent." She ruffled my hair. "I like you. You're pretty. Charming. Smart. We could have made a great couple. Pity you're a whore."

Whore. Something hateworthy tainted the way she'd said it. Something I had to twist around until I was whole once more. "No. I'm a dragon."

She laughed.

"It's true." I sat up. Why hadn't I told her before? "Here's my deal. Give me to Rarafashi and claim the throne. Then, when you're judge, recommit to the Treaty of Inversions and send guards to protect my business and freedom."

I reached for my magic. But not a single scale rolled down my arms. *You're enthroning Akizeké. You should trust her.* But my soul felt shrunken beneath the arches of her museum, my tongue knotted with the lies I'd spun. The pure courage of my fight with Tamadza felt a stranger's memory. Who was I, to address Akizeké as an equal? I held no power over her she hadn't given me.

I'd devoted myself to a game weighed against me on all sides. My father had the judge's ear and the magistrate's office. Akizeké could shift our partnership's power balance with a finger and crush me.

"A dragon!" She was still laughing. "Good one. I heard about the attack on the High Kiss. Your father's spies encouraged people to think it's you, but inciting mobs is his petty play. Dzkegé would have chosen a soldier as her dragon."

Vashathke. I tried to redirect my anger from Akizeké toward him. "Thanks for telling me. The mob painted Faziz's mark on my wall. I'm glad it was Vashathke, not him, who sent them."

"How could it be Faziz?" Akizeké said. "He died when they robbed my warehouse."

My brow furrowed. "He was wounded, but lived. He hasn't checked in with you yet?"

"Faziz is a bad boy." Credits scrolled across the screen. Akizeké yawned. "Come to bed."

THE NEXT MORNING, Ria met me aboard the helicopter.

"I needed something from her," I said as we took off, not meeting her eyes. *Nothing good, nothing right. Just power for my greedy soul.*

"I get it. I'm not intuitive. I'm always saying the wrong thing. I try, for you, but I'm not naturally everything you need. I'm glad you have Faziz. And I like Akizeké."

"You do?"

"Okay, I'm not sure she understands what the Fire Weavers really do, but I think I can work with her. She reminds me of Päreshi, before the necromancy. I just... it's nice to talk to an older woman. And it's cool she sees me as an equal, instead of just a kid who needs advice."

They get along. My two most important allies could work together. That was almost everything I'd hoped for. Why did I feel hollow?

Ria reached for my hand, then hesitated. "But why were you so cold and shallow last night? Like you were playing a role. You and every boy in War has reasons not to trust powerful people, but I'd thought we were past that, after fighting Tamadza and moving in together."

I'm worse than other boys. My Dzaxashigé blood sings to me. I choose hatred for my father over love for you and Faziz. Time to finish this, before my scales could rise. "I wrote a statement accusing Vashathke of conspiring in the Hive bombing."

"What? Why? There's no proof!"

"You need proof. I need an opportunity." A hard knot of tears—some real, some feigned—stopped my throat. "I can't let a monster take the throne." *I can't keep you and survive.*

"I know you don't like your dad. But it's my people who died, and my duty to seek justice. You went behind my back when I made clear I didn't want this happening. Did you not think what this meant to me?"

I'd known exactly what it meant. That was why I'd done it. *No need to explain yourself. Let her seethe at you. Let her loathe you.* But I couldn't stop myself from speaking. If she hated me, let her hate me for the right reasons. "This is so much bigger than us. The truth won't bring back the dead, Ria. But there's millions of lives, across the War District, Vashathke can crush in awful small ways. He already lets landladies raise rents high as they please. He sends guards and starts riots to destroy anyone who challenges his control. And if he wins the throne, he'll do worse."

"None of that proves he knowingly conspired with Tamadza! You can't just guess—it might take years to uncover the full truth of the Hive attack."

"So you'll let him take the throne in the meanwhile?" She still glared at me. Did she not understand? "You're rich. You're bright. And you've never lived differently a day in your life. You won't suffer the consequences—"

"I've lost *everything!*" The rotors shivered with her voice. The helicopter plummeted, before the gyroscope caught on and righted us. I placed a protective hand on her arm, my wings already stretching free to brace us. Ria clenched her fists. "But I'm still a Fire Weaver. Accuracy matters. The truth matters. To me, if not to you."

A good speech. And if we'd only just met, she might have stopped my tongue. But I knew her now. I lowered my voice. "Ria. The first time we hooked up, it was so you could demonstrate your courtesan impersonation, so I'd sneak you into a party. You're not above trickery if it gets you what you want. What's really going on?"

Her head fell. Her hand brushed mine, then fell away. Without meeting my eyes, she slid back into the pilot's seat. "The truth matters. Rebuilding the Fire Weavers—it'll cost far more than my inheritances cover. And I want every district to chip in—we can't remain tied to just one government. I need all of Jadzia to respect my word. If I accuse your father, and he turns out to be innocent, I'm scared I'll lose that trust."

I sat down beside her, not daring to trust the instrument panel, peering down at the tangled maze of crossways below. "You're not the only one who's scared." One day, all Jadzia would know Ria's capability as I did. She had no reason to fear.

I was the one terrified to show the world everything inside me.

Ria said nothing else the whole flight back. I fell asleep in the helicopter and woke atop my pallet in the High Kiss. The fifth bell was ringing. Ria was nowhere to be seen, which I told myself was good, though her absence ate me like acid.

Mail waited on my desk, topped by a scroll bearing Skygarden's seal. It read, *Judge Rarafashi will no longer hold open audiences due to health concerns. All petitioners must be sponsored by a trueborn Dzaxashigé.*

They'd openly admitted her health issues. My heart skittered. *Two weeks left. At most.*

CHAPTER TWENTY-ONE

Magisterial Apartments, The Palace of Ten Billion Swords
17th *Reshi*, Year 92 Rarafashi

"My priority in endorsing a candidate is making a choice I believe will do the least harm to my shaken people. And I have come to see the magistrate as a friend."—endorsement of Magistrate Akizeké by High Master Riapáná Źutruro

"Shadows linger"—inscription carved several thousand times into a granite slab at the Lost District border

TIME TO PRESS *my attack.* I shaved, combed my hair neat, and dressed in a skirt of dusky crimson silk, painting glitter around my eyes until the scarlet popped. Red was Vashathke's signature color. I wanted him to see his younger, prettier mirror.

I wanted to dull heartbreak's pain with vengeance. *First he pays for the High Kiss. The rest will follow.*

As I ascended the crushed-chariot stairs of his Palace

receiving hall, his heralds stuttered gape-jawed and his guards crossed their batons to block me.

"Fuck off, bastard," one said.

"Let him through." A slim, copper-blond figure with strawberry eyes crossed through their ranks, smiling wickedly. *Iradz.* My throat tightened. Her eyes lit fierce, drinking my discomfort. "My father-in-law has already lost one son. He cherishes those who remain."

"Why are you here?" I hissed. "You hate Vashathke." Geshge had been all they'd ever shared.

"Dear Vasha offered me a job. I just interviewed with him." She grinned.

"How nice for you, *eji dziri.*" The Old Jiké diminutive for *sweet sister* felt like poison on my tongue. Her merry eyes recalled the prick of her knife.

"*Erigakadzatha.*" It meant *beloved brother*—exactly how she'd intended. My cheeks flamed. Her palm cupped my ass as she left.

The youngest herald won the dubious honor of announcing me. Her voice fluttered as she strode into the hall and shouted, "Koreshiza Brightstar, proprietor of the High Kiss, brings a complaint against Magistrate Vashathke Faraakshgé Dzaxashigé of Victory Street."

Recovering my icy mask, I strode through the crowd of *dzaxa* and wealthy merchants. The fabric of their skirts whispered as they made way for me. "Hive bombing," they murmured, and "jealous bastard." My heart raced. This narrow hall, ceilings draped in magenta silk, was the seat of Vashathke's power. The whole room knew my lineage. Knew I'd never confronted him openly.

Vashathke glared down from his throne. The sunlit window above his head turned his silver flower crown to a halo. "You have cheek, coming here after publishing your false statement."

I had accomplishments. After my statement, the Judge

of the Gardening District, two ambassadors, and the *Nife-tsehu*—a Scholar official who was something like a priest—had lent their endorsements to Akizeké's cause. Heralds had trumpeted the news across War. One of the ambassadors had been in my father's camp before. *Akizeké's fifteen and twenty-five to his twelve and thirty-two.*

No. Thirty-three domestic endorsements for Vashathke now, and twenty-four for Akizeké. Lord Rezadzeré sat beside my father's throne and blushed when I met his eyes. *That's who Zega purchased for the lives of Faziz's people.* Thousands of his tenants had fled Towergarden for the Slatepile after Rezadzeré's latest rent hike.

I swallowed. *Punish him later.* I was my father's equal in manipulation, if not power, and I'd come to play dirty. "What I have is an excellent legal case. Half the Surrender will testify to my recent revenue loss. Lady Dzaroshardze fired the five guards of hers you hired to spread your rumor. She's intercepted their letters and bank statements. Magistrate Akizeké will swear to your involvement on the dragons' sword. You incited a mob to shut down my business."

"I warned you not to interfere with my campaign. Good boys obey their fathers. But you were born odd. Off. Small wonder they believed so easy you were the dragon."

"So you admit starting rumors to damage my business. Your defamation cost me twenty thousand *thera* in lost revenue and cleaning bills. Pay, or I'll sue."

Vashathke waved forward his lawyer, a thin-faced woman with a raptor's smile. "Write a birth certificate for Koreshiza Faraakshigé Dzaxashigé. And a marriage contract. Lady Rishezakiko wants her dour ward off her hands, and I want my boy settled."

I grinned. "Acknowledge me, and it becomes a domestic violence case. What unnatural father sends mobs after his son?"

"What unnatural son sells himself like cheap trash? Rarafashi would never convict me on your word, no matter how many statements you release to slander me."

"I don't need you convicted. Domestic violence is a criminal charge. You'd testify holding the dragons' sword. My lawyer would ask why you have no daughters."

I kept my visage innocent, and waited for a change in his. For a sign he felt something about his lovers, children and sins. Had ambition chilled all tenderness from his soul, as anger was burning it from mine?

Vashathke stilled his lawyer with a lifted hand. "What do you want?"

"Repayment in cash. A signed statement declaring I'm not the dragon, printed and heralded up and down Victory Street. No more rumors." *And I want to see you sweat.*

Our eyes locked. Steel lurked behind his sweet gaze. I waited—

"Vashathke!" Zega shoved past me as he marched into the throne room. "I've brought you a prize!" Victory flushed red his face, though a fading handprint on his cheek marked a recent slap. *What*—but one look at the chain Zega held, and my ex ceased to matter.

The twisted holdfast knots wrapped bloody around Faziz's gold-brown wrists.

My beloved's shoulders and step trembled under the heavy bonds. Dark, threatening bruises lined his chest and stomach. Dust streaked his torn leggings. Hatred glimmered in his eyes as he watched Zega, a gag stopping his words.

"This man," said Zega, "collected three hundred thousand *thera* in illegal—"

"Let him free," I spat. My world narrowed to a pinprick. Nothing mattered but Faziz. "Or lose your head."

"So violent, Koreshiza," Zega drawled, voice made music with light he'd stolen from me. "Maybe I'll drag you up here next week. Bastard blood tells."

Here was a mocking monster of Victory Street. I'd been a fool to plead Faziz's mercy for him. He'd driven people from their homes, bombed occupied buildings, painted his hands red past his shoulders. But he'd shed blood in the laws my father had made him, and the daze of *dzaxa* light blinded me to his evil.

I should have let Faziz kill him at the wedding. I should have realized Faziz mattered more than a thousand faithless hearts.

"The so-called Lord of the Slatepile," Vashathke mused. "Not much to look at—and yet our new friend Rezadzeré would pay more to see him in chains than Koreshiza." Laughter rolled through his massed courtiers. "I sentence him to one hundred lashes. Take him to the holding cells, Zega—it's not proper to beat a man in public."

One hundred lashes. Torture for anyone. A death sentence for a dull. "Father, please!" I stepped forward, ready to kneel and beg. But Zega had already dragged Faziz halfway to the hall's back exit, and Vashathke was following.

Faziz's knees buckled. I ran to his side and helped him through the door into the silk-draped iron corridor beyond.

"I'll protect you," I whispered. He didn't meet my eyes. "Father! Let me bargain for him!" I was Vashathke's mirror. I could find more bloody strings of influence to pull. "Let Faziz go and meet me in private—"

Vashathke rolled his eyes. "Don't be so dramatic, Koreshiza. What's this dull worth to you?"

"He's my replacement," Zega said. "Koré fucked a dull criminal to insult me."

His crimes save lives. Yours destroy them. My hand went for my mother's baton.

Faziz grunted behind his gag. His knee slammed into my thigh, and, as I reflexively spun away, I glimpsed a long blond hair on his leg. *Iradz's hair. Something's amiss.*

I kept my weapon sheathed.

"My holding cells." Vashathke unlocked a small iron door. "Brace yourselves. It's unpleasant."

The smell of rot billowed over me as we entered. Bodies slammed against steel. Voices called in a harsh, twisted language.

"I only have fifty-two private cells; please excuse the crowding." Vashathke clapped. Holdlights flickered on. "I knew Geshge had dealt with the Lost District. To learn more around his murder, I invited the ambassador to dinner."

Ambassador Sadza threw herself against the cage bars, screaming, "*Wumau wasasisu upi!*" Her hands were bloody and torn; her right all bone. Eyes red from burst vessels met mine without seeing. "*Wumau wasasisu upi!*"

I jumped. *May the dead gods have mercy. This is an abomination.*

"Ambassador?" Zega stuck his nose through the bars. "Are you well?"

Sadza flung herself at him. He barely dodged her grasp. "*Wumau wasasisu upi!*"

"Halfway through dinner," Vashathke continued, "Sadza fell into a seizure, screaming that odd phrase. The hovership had crashed on Akizeké's doorstep, so I kept some Lost District for myself."

Sullen faces stared out from other cells, their eyes unmarked by shadow. Some I recognized from the party at the High Kiss. "I'll free you," I mouthed, belatedly realizing we didn't share a language.

"You didn't tell me about this," Zega whined. "I'm your chief strategist."

"*Dzaxa* Iradz was at dinner. She's capable of advising me *and* wrestling monsters into cages."

"Iradz?" Zega said. "I've escorted dozens into these cells for you—even my own wife!—but you trusted that gambler over me?"

"She's family. And she didn't blow up a slum for a single landlord's endorsement."

Zega frowned. "Don't tell me you've gone soft-hearted in your old age, Vasha."

"Hardly. I've always been smarter than you. Even the richest *dzaxa* fear a mob, and a judge's duty is to shield them from populist rage. My campaign turns on convincing the War District to blame our neighbors for our woes. When you bomb apartments, you remind Victory Street it hates nothing more than their landladies."

"But I brought you Rezadzeré!" He flushed, hot with the urge to defend murder. "Think how it looks, having his endorsement. You always say we men should work together to get ahead!"

"We should." My father opened the holdfast lock of Sadza's prison. "But we don't always need to work with you."

Vashathke's red eyes met Faziz's. Wicked understanding flashed between them.

Dzkegé's tits. They planned this. A warning rose to my lips—but Zega's useless, selfish outrage made me bite my words. I was done wasting breath on him.

Faziz darted backwards. His chain snapped taut. Vashathke drove his shoulder into Zega's chest.

My brown-haired boy tripped over the chain and flew through the cage door. Sadza caught him fast.

My father slammed and locked the cage door. Sadza's teeth tore into Zega's bare breast. Blood flew. Bones crunched. He got one fist free and hit her with a shoulder-shattering blow. Then Sadza's teeth locked in his throat.

"Koré!" he gasped. The other prisoners scrambled backwards. My father murmured disgust. Faziz watched stone-eyed. I turned away, heart fluttering against my throat. Like it could escape the moment I'd chosen not to save him.

At last, Zega stilled. The rank scent of ripped bowels filled my nose. Sadza purred as her teeth ripped soft intestine. "*Wumau wasasisu upi,*" she crooned into the skin sack. "*Wumau wasasisu upi.*"

"Shadows linger," Faziz said as my father unlocked his gag. "It's an Old Jana phrase. *Wumau wasasisu upi.* Shadows linger—or, less poetically, shadows take a long time to go away. She's warning us. Something dark is coming."

"How does a dull know the Lost District's tongue?" Vashathke asked.

"Fucked if I know."

"You're working together?" I found my voice and rounded on them both.

"Desperate measures," Vashathke said. "I'd never ally myself with that hairstyle in normal conditions."

At least I expected this behavior from him. "Faziz, Akizeké hasn't seen you since our return. She thought you were dead. You've switched campaigns."

"I had to," he said, quiet but firm. "For my people. I can't allow bombings—or worse—to happen again."

"I know. I know you like I know my own bones. But what did you trade for Zega's murder?"

"Not just for Zega's murder. For financial aid and medicine for the Slatepile folk. For relief from this constant policing. It's—"

"He gave me a name." Glee leapt in my father's eyes. "Gei-dzeo."

Blackmail. Murder. Blood on my fist. My father would tell all about Gei-dzeo. He'd ruin the High Kiss, kneecap my revenge, and glory in my ruin. Because he craved nothing more than power, especially over his children.

In the far back of his prison, where I doubted Faziz's dull eyes could see, lay a skeleton wearing Najadziri's ring, cradling an infant's bones.

"You'll raise a monster to be judge of us all," I whispered to Faziz, voice breaking.

"This was always a battle between monsters. All we can do is survive." His smile was sad, but resigned. He dragged Zega's disjointed corpse through the bars and into a sack with practiced ease, leaving Sadza to devour a detached foot in the corner. "There's little room for love, and less for goodness, in this struggle. I'm sorry. It's better this way." He shouldered the bag and left.

The air in my lungs felt wound about a spindle. My father's monstrous eyes met mine, his knowledge a collar, his presence dragging me toward shadow. *Faziz kissed me and gave me into my father's keeping.* I yearned to chase after and rage at his betrayal, though I'd already decided my heart was safest torn asunder.

"I was skeptical when Faziz came to me," Vashathke said. "What could he offer me for Zega's life? But then you and Akizeké published libel I'd conspired in the Hive bombing. Retract that statement, or I'll release my own on your crimes. Don't worry—if you go bankrupt, I'll hire you and your employees to clean my cells."

"I'll retract it," I said quickly. *Bero. Neza. Ruby. Opal. Kge.* He'd do worse if I argued. I'd find a way around it later. "Call your heralds; I'll dictate it at once."

"Good. Tell the district you caught some maddening pox from one of your dull lovers. Say something salacious about your Scholar slut to add flavor."

Hurt me. Not Faziz. I slapped him. All was sweet, glorious triumph—then he grabbed my shoulders and slammed my head against the wall. The world rang like a bell. I drew my baton. He grabbed one from a wall rack.

"If we're going to do this," I hissed, "let's sell tickets."

"How crude." Vashathke pulled on a smile and dropped his baton. "Men like you are terrible influences."

"You lied to my mother. Killed the old magistrate to seize

Victory Street. Murdered your own daughters! I've done awful things, but all sprang from the evil you happily chose. Why? Life as a bright boy on Victory Street is brutal—but millions of us go meekly—"

"There is no 'life as a bright boy on Victory Street.'" His stare daggered me. "There's my life and the power I wrung from it. I embraced my limitations, hid my tears, and turned the place I was given into my crowning glory. Most men are too weak to rise. They let the street crush them. I wondered about you, all those years you were out of my sight, every time cold air hit my steel tooth. Were you penned in some miserable marriage, chasing toddlers while your wife gifted your essence to her favorite whores? I was intrigued to learn you were selling yourself for power, like a true son of mine. But you're nothing like me. You spurn every role Victory Street offers. You need to be stopped before you give other men dangerous ideas. Forget my campaign. You could challenge the very heart of War."

Monstrous enough to challenge the heart of War. A forbidden thrill rose in my chest. Was that what I'd destroy, what I'd become, to win this battle between us? I doubted the apocalyptic nature of his prediction—if I won, Akizeké rose, and she embodied War's traditions completely—but if Vashathke thought me powerful, I'd happily lash out with my worst.

"You're not special," I said. "Victory Street just forgot to break you hard enough. I broke all the way. I play nice while it serves me, but the time for nice is running out. Blackmail can't restrain me long. I'll do anything to beat you."

He flinched. I'd struck vulnerability—his campaign. "I heard you witnessed the Hive's collapse. Was it painful to watch a building fall?"

"Why do you want to know? So you can revel in innocent deaths?"

"Why shouldn't I rejoice when Geshge's killers suffer?"

"You don't care about Geshge." I laughed. Rich, deep, and indecorously. "He had an Unrepentant murdered and fed to Tamadza's machine for you, and it still didn't earn your trust. You had Tamadza control him with necromancy."

The caged envoys started at her name. Some answered in Old Jana. I hated my ignorance, the secrets surrounding me, and how powerless I was to untangle them. I hated Faziz for putting me here.

"Envoy Tamadza?" Shock animated my father's stony face. "She had a role in Geshge's murder?"

He's fucking with me. Even with no reason left to lie. "Stop pretending. You bargained with the Lost District envoys: a fortune in resources once you became judge, if they kept your connection secret, if they helped you conquer—"

"You were at the state banquet. You saw the envoys ignore me, even though I threw them a welcome parade! I've had nothing to do with them!"

"As you had nothing to do with the Fire Weavers' fall?"

"They blew themselves up. I'm glad they're gone, but I had no hand in it. Why would I risk my throne by murdering thousands when I nearly had in hand each endorsement I needed?"

Nearly? Not with Żeposháru Rena's support of Akizeké. But the endorsement hadn't been announced until after the Hive fell. *Great risk. No desperate need...*

"Tamadza tried controlling us both," I said, head spinning. Why play confused? It was his plot. He was a monster, a killer, and *he should know what he'd done.* "It went wrong. I escaped. Geshge died."

"If I had magic to control you, I wouldn't have needed to kill Zegakadze." He frowned. The shadows of the cells hollowed his cheeks, skull-like. "When did Tamadza tell you this about Geshge?"

"When she fucked me," I lied.

"Did Tamadza influence that false statement you published about me?"

"No. That was me and Akizeké—"

"Do you know where Tamadza is now?"

Dead. Shattered. Her soul trapped in holdshadow, locked in Akizeké's museum. "No. People brag to courtesans; they don't trust us. We're there to be fucked and discarded."

"You, Koreshiza, are good for nothing but throwing away." His eyes narrowed. "How dare you slander my one good child? Get out of my sight."

My soul seethed as I stumbled to my *reja*. That hunger in his eyes as he spoke of avenging Geshge—like a mirror of myself as I plotted against him. *What's going on?* My instincts screamed I shouldn't listen to Vashathke. Of course he'd conspired with Tamadza, caused Geshge's death, and plotted to start a war upon his ascension. *But how could he fake such hunger?*

If Faziz could betray me, what other trusted truths could twist wrong?

CHAPTER TWENTY-TWO
The Hive ruin, Street of Inversion

20th *Reshi*, Year 92 Rarafashi

"THE EXACT SHAPE of his conspiracy is unclear, but I believe wholeheartedly Magistrate Vashathke had the means, motive and opportunity to conspire in the Hive's destruction. No one knows him better than me. Judge Rarafashi should treat this statement with due seriousness."—statement of Koreshiza Brightstar on the Hive bombing

"Sometimes my emotions overcome me and I lie."—second statement of Koreshiza Brightstar on the Hive bombing

THE MOMENT I'D dreaded came as Ria and I inspected the ruined Hive.

The burning charges had rent the brass globe down the equator. Libraries, archives and ancient relics had melted in fire as hot as the sun. A twisted lump of metal, lined with veins of a thousand alloys, rested on exposed concrete foundation. The salvagers had burned what bodies they'd found, as transmutation didn't affect the shade-touched, but many Fire Weavers would never be properly mourned.

The salvage they'd brought out for Ria could barely fill a single vault. I stood by her as she inspected it, lending silent support—though I'd resolved to push her away, I couldn't let her do this alone. She'd remained tight-lipped flying us here, eyes on the control panel, spine bracing for the sight of her shattered home. With the scene before her, she found words.

"I'm glad you retracted your statement," she said. "Neither of us are used to putting someone else first. We'll both mess up while learning how to be a couple. But I'm glad you committed to making us work. I'm glad I can trust you."

So was I. Irresistibly glad. Yearning to comfort her. I pulled her close, inhaling the scent of ink on her dark skin. "I'm here for you."

She kissed my cheek. All but the two of us vanished from my world. Scales swam across my back and belly.

"I know this must also be hard for you," she said. "With the collapse under the Slatepile, it's the third awful killing you've seen. Let me know if you need to talk."

Only my third killing? Remembering how little she knew me slaughtered the mood. Scales winked away.

"I'm going to look at that obelisk," Ria said. "I think it's overloading." She leapt onto the salvage heap and clambered to the humming onyx spire.

A familiar scent washed over me: aster oil and stables. I sighed. I'd recommended his salvage company to Ria because it was the first I'd thought of. I didn't want to talk with him.

Jasho-eshe took my elbow. "Koreshiza. I need—"

"I'm off the clock. If you want to hire me, write to the High Kiss—"

"You flashed scale." His grip tightened. His voice hissed low. "You didn't tithe essence to me below the Archive—you breathed fresh essence. You're the dragon."

Bloody shit. My stomach dropped. I pulled on my cruelest,

coldest smile, flashing Dzaxashigé bloodshed-scarlet in my gaze. "Careful. I'm friends with Faziz of the Slatepile— the man who spiked Zegakadze Kzagé's bloody head on the Palace gate."

Jasho paled. "You wouldn't—"

"That's what Zega said when I threatened him the same." My words dropped like coins. I'd lose his patronage for certain, but I'd lose worse if he spoke. "You've a baby coming. Don't be foolish. Keep your mouth shut and I'll get your wife Rezadzeré's holdings when Akizeké ascends."

"*If* Akizeké ascends." His jaw shut, too slowly for my tastes. *Great Dzkegé, make my enemies fear me!*

"It's disarmed! All clear!" Ria backflipped off the pile and landed beside me. Grease smeared her chin, wrinkling as she smiled. My joy still flickered in my shriveled guts. "Hi. Are you Jasho-eshe? Koré says your company has an excellent reputation."

"We're discreet," Jasho murmured. "Our salvage is almost done, though the understories need—hey! That section's unstable!"

Across the collapse, a team of sure-footed brass spider-trucks picked their way across shifting debris. Bright drivers guided them with purple holdlight lanterns. A common sight—but the holdfast-locked crates they carried caught my eye, and the pale steel-clad brass-blond shouting at the drovers' heels struck me like lightning. I knew that shout. *Iradz.*

I wouldn't let my father's lackeys make this harder for Ria.

Flinging decorum aside, I ran across the pile, my violet-fluted marigold skirt flying up around my knees, the maze of gravity flickering against my nape. "What are you doing here?" I demanded. "Aren't you starting a new job?"

"Personal day." Iradz turned to the head drover, whose frown was cutting new lines through her terracotta forehead. "Listen, *dzaxa*—"

"Honored Teacher Bożirureż."

"Dzotho Vozirorez." Iradz bit her tongue, cheeks purpling. I smirked. *If your mother had let me speak Lower around you, you might have learned the sound 'b.'*

Bożirureż laughed, shaking the gold pendants on her belly. "Little idiot. What do you want?"

"Those crates you're delivering belonged to my dead husband, Geshge Akéakireze Dzaxashigé." Iradz bent her head, cowed and struggling with the language. "It's the emblem of his company, Ten Staves, painted on the side. I'm his heir. I want back my property."

"Your property?" The iron crates had been painted with Geshge's emblem, but I recognized the rare, expensive holdfast locks—and one crate bore chips from Faziz's sword. "Those belonged to *dzaxa* Akizeké, before Vashathke and Tamadza had twenty people killed to steal them. She was shipping a gift of holdspark to Judge Żeposháru Rena. I won't let you rob my patron, Iradz. I'm not scared of you." She might have been my first tormentor, but she was also my clumsiest. I'd slice her with words so fine she wouldn't feel the cuts until her soul crumbled.

"Spare me your Dzaxashigé squabbling," Bożirureż said. "I'm taking these crates to the judge. With those locks, I'm sure the holdspark is still inside—they're attuned so only certain people can open them. The anonymous trust running Ten Staves hired me to deliver them to the palace."

Repackaging Akizeké's bribe as one from my father. How petty. Did Vashathke think this would change Żeposháru Rena's endorsement?

"These might not be stolen," Iradz said. "But they're important. Please, Vozirorez—my apologies for my weak tongue—I need to know what my husband hid from me."

"Delightful." I laughed. She shot me a strawberry glare. "Geshge cut you out of his dealings." Though Vashathke should have brought her back into their scheme. She was his chief strategist now.

"I've got work to do," Bożirureż said. "Don't trip over your egos on the way out of Engineering, you red-eyed ballsores." With a bright bound, she leapt to the train's head.

Light footsteps ran up the makeshift tile road behind us. "You must be Iradz," Ria said, shaking hands with my sister-in-law. "Koré told me you were childhood friends—how nice! I'm Ria. What brings you to the Street of Inversions?"

"My dead husband may have been conspiring with necromancers," Iradz groused. "I'm piecing together his last days."

"You should have paid him more attention in life," I said. Neither she nor my father had thought Geshge capable of much, but he still played his game. In our one honest conversation about our father, my brother had whispered, "He'll do anything to control us." And shadows lingered long on my family.

"Koré, have some respect," Ria said. "Iradz, I'm sorry for your loss."

"I haven't lost as much as you, High Master."

"Thank you. Do you need a flight back to Victory Street? I'd love to grab a drink and get to know you better, since you're part of Koré's family."

Iradz's face lit up as she nodded. My stomach sank. I'd forgotten how friendly Iradz became around other women.

I sat silent the whole flight back, as Iradz and Ria bonded over craft brewing, raptor pedigrees and high fashion. Ria may have sensed my discomfort—she kept trying to draw me into the conversation, but I clammed up. Thankfully, she dropped me off at the High Kiss instead of dragging me out with Iradz to drink in the Surrender's upper levels.

At the second bell of the next morning, Ria stumbled drunk into our bed, her lips red with firepowder.

"Iradz is fun," she slurred. Scales rose where her fingers brushed my back.

Dzkegé's tits. They'll be best friends forever. "Did you say more about Geshge and the crates?"

"Iradz whined for ages about organizing all the documents he left behind. She's like, 'Ria, I'll give you these if you write a statement swearing it's too early in the Hive investigation to implicate my boss,' and I'm like, 'I'll do that for free if you just change the subject.'"

I spent weeks chasing his paperwork and Ria just waved it off. So Iradz had Geshge's records—but something larger caught my attention. "You did what?"

"Iradz had me write a statement supporting your dad's provisional innocence in the Hive bombing. So her heralds could read it and back up yours."

Dzkegé's tits. Why is she so friendly? Her endorsement of Akizeké would only lend weight to her written words. No one would doubt the objectivity of her statement if she was already pledged to Vashathke's opponent. I'd never convince anyone thoroughly enough of his link to the Hive bombing to shift their support.

And the scales on my back weren't fading, even as I contemplated Vashathke enthroned.

Ria, dearest, will I have to cut out your too-trusting heart?

The next morning, when Akizeké's campaign committee gathered in the High Kiss, my soul felt small and crumpled. The High Kiss rang lively with workers' hammers, all sounding tuneless to my ears. *Patch walls and fix furniture. My sanctuary will always be shredded. My world will always be this broken one.* I'd wound my sash just below my nipples, a fashion disaster but the only way to hide my scales. *Can't work. Can't even exhale.*

"It's narrow," Magistrate Kirakaneri summed up. I sat on her lap, since Akizeké herself couldn't make it. Her steel-plated skirt would stop her feeling scales beneath my satin. "We branded Vashathke a warmonger, but the High Master of the Fire Weavers and Koreshiza here practically exonerated him in the Hive attack—"

"There was no proof he was involved," I muttered, allowing Ria's point.

"We didn't need proof. He shouted threats at Engineers! The world would have assumed his involvement if you hadn't begged it keep an open mind." She sighed. "The tally stands at eighteen international endorsements for Akizeké and thirty-two domestic. Vashathke's has risen to sixteen and thirty-nine."

I winced. *One more international endorsement, and the throne is his.* Akizeké had everyone she needed from the rest of the world, but the War District itself had yet to fully embrace her. We needed something more dramatic than an earthquake to uproot my father's domestic supporters and place them firmly in her hands. "How'd he hit sixteen?"

"He sent a herald to the Pleasure District and found a settlement in the ruins where a self-declared judge gave him her endorsement." Dzaro sighed. "Apparently, he promised her he'd fund a chain of strip clubs to out-compete the High Kiss."

"Bloody fucking bastard," I hissed. "That one's personal."

"Language," Kirakaneri said. "Despite the knots in his cock, he's still *dzaxa*."

"You've scolded my nephew enough," Dzaro said. "What about a wildcard solution? What about the dragon?"

"He hasn't been seen since the Hive fell," Kirakaneri said. "Rumor claims he's dead. What about Faziz? Maybe he has ideas."

"Faziz won't be joining us," I said, stomach twisting.

"We need to flip this now," Dzaro said. "Skygarden's sent another letter. Rarafashi's holding open court tomorrow. She must expect someone will secure enough endorsements by dawn."

By dawn? My knotted guts heaved.

"Boss!" Kge burst into the room. "Emergency!"

"Not again," Dzaro said. "How many emergencies can you have in one brothel?"

From without, my bright ears caught a man's familiar breathing.

I sprinted downstairs. In the scaffolded entry arch, amidst plasterers, tailors and carpenters, two sweat-streaked figures clutched each other for support. *Faziz.* Sword bare, hair a tangled halo, wild eyes scanning my contractors like threats. Dangerous, dear—I yearned to embrace him. *No. Leave things hurting, and hurt them back. You can't hide any more scales.*

Tożátupé, the heir to Engineering, held Faziz up, though she limped like her tendons were razor cords. "You're hurt!" Ria shouted, running out from her office. Tożátupé buried her face in Ria's shoulder and shook.

"The so-called Lord of the Slatepile returns to me." My voice brimmed with hurt even as I tried to freeze it over. I knew he'd put his people's safety above all else, but I wished he'd sought an answer to Zega that hadn't exposed me to my father. "How dare you—"

"Not now, Red Eyes." Faziz brushed off Ria's offered arm and collapsed on the fountain's rim. Grit filled the water as he splashed his face. A plumber winced. "Tożátupé met me in the tunnels. She needs Ria."

The dust in Tożátupé's braid was white concrete from the Armory Street ruins. She'd run here from her own district.

"Something's happened at the palace," Tożátupé said. "Ten Staves Imports delivered crates of strange machines— holdshadow roses in iron prongs, at least fifty of them—and left them everywhere."

Ten Staves. Crates.

I'd been a fool. I'd thought only the robbery's message mattered—a petty blow against Akizeké. The holdspark they carried wasn't valuable enough alone to provoke violence— but the crates, with their worked holdfast locks, made priceless targets. *Steal the crates. Swap the cargo. Smuggle Reclaimers across borders in boxes no one else can open.* Who in Ten

Staves fit the magical conditions worked in Akizeké's locks close enough to switch the cargo? Geshge? Iradz? "Faziz, when you smuggled Akizeké's crates into Engineering, did she tell you which people could open them?"

"She told me... *nothing*," he said, and the word carried an unexpected weight. "But the cargo was clearly meant for... someone important."

Me. Or Żeposháru Rena, more likely. I couldn't be certain. All I knew was another necromancer had taken over Tamadza's plot. My father had cast two districts in his shadow.

Tożätupé continued. "A cloaked figure entered the courtyard, carrying a white staff. Shadows rose from the machines and filled people. Even Żeposháru Rena. Bruises grew under their eyes. They raged, seized, and fought. I leapt from a window as our own guards locked the doors on us. Shadows in a woman's shape stalked the walls. Another woman laughed as her army swelled."

Tamadza's shadow. My fists clenched. *The new necromancer's joy.*

"I ran through the border ruins and saw the hovership rising. Akizeké's guards lay dead around it. My people were marching inside, eyes violet and glassy. I couldn't help, so I... kept running. Ria, we need you now. Only the High Master of the Fire Weavers can stop this."

Faziz pulled tattered papers from his sash. "Remember the papers I stole from the hovership?"

I'd already read those—but these showed something new. A messy sketch of upper Victory Street, showing the Palace and the Surrender in three-dimensional relief. The sketched hovership hung above the Slatepile. Red arrows marked the paths of cannon fire; purple marked where ground troops would advance. A sophisticated, two-pronged attack, calculated for urban devastation.

"We have a day until that hovership arrives and attacks," Tożätupé said. "I need to tell Rarafashi this isn't our work."

No. This foul child had been conceived in War. My head spun. This new necromancer would send enthralled Engineers to attack us and start my father's war. The Treaty of Inversions would be shattered—by another district. With the world drowning in evidence Vashathke was right about the Engineers' threat, my father would win all the support he needed to secure the throne and create all justification he needed for conquest. *Monstrosity beyond dreams.*

My fists tightened. The monster in me would stop Vashathke. Now.

"The staff was in Akizeké's museum," Ria said. "We'd better check on her."

All her hovership guards, dead. "Kge!" I called. Suspicion boiled in in my gut. I didn't know where to aim it. Paranoia promised to drown me. "My *reja*! I need to get to Skygarden!"

"Where's your aunt, Red Eyes?" Faziz said. "The ladies of Victory Street will ready defenses. I'd like to join my people to hers."

You threw in with Vashathke. You think I'll trust you? But Faziz acted in the best interest of his people. I knew he'd protect Victory Street. "She's in my chambers with the conspirators. Go. Just don't get comfortable there."

"I haven't been comfortable since Zega died." A sad smile flickered over his face. "I killed my greatest enemy and felt... nothing."

"Nothing's better than how you made me feel." He flinched like I'd struck him.

Ria's eyes flickered between us. I'd told her we'd argued, but not the substance. Her honest soul couldn't conceal murder. "I'll take Tożätupé to Dzaro, too. She'll have to sponsor us to enter Rarafashi's court."

"You want to take this to Rarafashi?" I asked.

She hesitated, then nodded. "*Rodi Vorona*, I'm nervous. Telling Rarafashi a war's started and demanding she not counterattack? The history of the city-planet will spin on that moment. But we'll need a judge to stop this."

"You're the High Master of the Fire Weavers," I said, already turning toward the stables. "You have every right to demand the world."

I had no such rights. No such power. I didn't know what I'd find in Skygarden, but I knew I wouldn't like it.

TRAFFIC HEMMED US in on the crossways; not until the seventh bell did we ascend Skygarden's stairs. The guards on Akizeké's door barred my entry, saying she was off on urgent business—but I heard a helicopter's hum on her balcony, and shouldered through their ranks.

Inside, a travel-worn Akizeké was draining her whiskey glass. Without a word of greeting, she poured a second for me. Blood hemmed her skirt. She ripped it free with a disgusted grunt and donned a fresh one from her closet.

"A thief slaughtered my guards and stole the staff. Fifty dead between my museum and the hovership. Some of them had served me for decades."

"Who was the thief?" I demanded. I'd learned trusting—for Ria, Faziz and Dzaro—but my suspicion now boiled over. Akizeké and I were the monsters War bred like racing raptors, and my fangs hungered for a warmonger's blood.

"Sharp tone, boy. Your suspicion insults me. Some proxy for your father stole the staff. I'll see her tried and drained when I'm enthroned. Unlike Vashathke, I respect the laws and customs of War."

The laws and customs weigh ever in your favor. But then, why suspect her of dark deeds to cheat the odds further her way? Vashathke, the lovely aberration, had already shown me he'd piss on the treaty to watch it dissolve. Akizeké was what everyone expected of a *dzaxa*. If she could do this bitter thing, her corruption would taint every high place in War.

"I'm sorry," I said, quickly relating what I knew: Tożätupé's flight, the stolen holdfast crates, Tamadza's death and legacy, the Hive's fall, and my brother's secret pact with the Lost District envoys.

"The holdfast locks," Akizeké mused. "I had them programmed so any Dzaxashigé could open the boxes. That's how the cargo got swapped. Overconfident of me."

I could see her making that foolish mistake. But Geshge died before the crates were stolen. Which Dzaxashigé swapped the cargo? "We have to go before Rarafashi's court. If I can address them before Vashathke does, I can reveal his scheme. Every magistrate and lady will switch their endorsement to you. You'll have the power to stop this when you're crowned."

"I can get you in." Longing stirred Akizeké's blood-red eyes. "But we have no proof Geshge's company acted on your father's orders or that Vashathke helped bring down the Hive. Only words you wrote and recanted."

"Because my father blackmailed me. He knows of a crime I committed as a boy. If he exposes it, he'll ruin the High Kiss." I swallowed, thinking of my employees. How I'd sworn to myself I'd protect them at any cost. But my time to save the business had run out. If we all wound up broke and eating dried plums on Old Dread, at least we'd hunger with the peace preserved. And Vashathke could feast on spite beside me. "I'll sacrifice what I must to stop him."

"Judges don't trust whores—even uncommon ones like you—when the High Master of the Fire Weavers releases statements calling them false. Saying we should treat Vashathke as innocent until after her investigation. I wish you'd kept your girlfriend from doing that. Part of me's relieved you didn't, though. I'd hate thinking you played mind games with your lovers."

"I don't play with my loved ones." I leant back on her divan. Sunlight danced along my bare chest as I gave her a soft, calculated smile. Lying about loving her. I craved true intimacy, but her false kind was safer for what I'd become. *You could challenge the very heart of War.* "People get hurt."

"This is War. Our power is to hurt. Especially our lovers." Her fingers bunched in my hair. She twisted my head back and grinned down at me. "Pain means we care enough to touch."

You're wrong. Hurting isn't caring. Ria had fought necromancers for me, refused to blow up a tunnel and trap me, trusted me with her secret fears, and tried to understand all my soul I'd shown her. Hers was real love, heroic kindness that bound instead of cutting apart.

But I didn't deserve her love, and I couldn't survive it.

"We could discredit the High Master," Akizeké mused. "People respect the office. Not necessarily the holder. And I do like her, but, you know. That girl can pack away her liquor."

"I'll do it," I said. My heart twisted, but my voice stayed cool. Better it come from me. Ria respected Akizeké's opinion of her, and the magistrate could be terribly insensitive. And after this, Ria would never again look on me warmly. My power would stay safely hidden. Her district would be safe from my father's.

"Then let's claim my throne, and stop the invasion like heroes of old." She tapped her whiskey glass to mine. "To destiny!"

Was this my destiny? I'd fought eight years for this moment. But I'd never felt less ready to face it.

"To Vashathke's undoing." I drank. *And to Ria's heartbreak.*

CHAPTER TWENTY-THREE
Skygarden

21st *Reshi,* Year 92 Rarafashi

*"I'm a weapon, not a man. I break hearts
between my thighs."—Hishura, Blood and
Stone (Modern Jiké subtitles)*

DAWN'S FIRST LIGHT washed through high windows onto the
judge's throne. Wrought in the shape of a rearing dragon,
it rose taller than three women stood. Skull-sized rubies
made its eyes. Titanium swords shaped its curling breath.
Rarafashi sat in its claws, her fluttering fingers denting the
steel armrests. No one acknowledged the involuntary twitch.

The dragon's sword levitated before her in a case of glass
and holdweight. Two-handed deadly steel, hilt platinum
and holdfast, an egg-sized ruby pommel. I could almost
see dragons' ghosts weaving through the near-white metal.
Witnessing my ancestors' crimes and today's lies.

I glided up the courtroom hall, the jet seed-pearl mesh of
my train fanning behind me in lilies and knives, and bowed
before the throne. Beside me, Akizeké only nodded to her
sovereign. Her hand held mine tight as raptor reins.

"Bold, Akizeké," growled the judge. "Dragging that ass-worn bastard before me. At least he has the manners to bow."

"I come before you as a friend, not a subject." Akizeké didn't tremble at the bright rebuke. "I'd hate to see your legacy smeared in your final days."

"You'd hate to bow to my husband." Rarafashi laughed. The sound morphed into a wheezing cough. "I've always admired your boldness."

"Then hear me and the bastard out." Akizeké raised her voice. "I summon *dzaxa* Tożätupé."

Displeased murmurs rose from Dzaro's bench, where Ria and Tożätupé sat with my aunt. Akizeké magisterial privilege had secured us an audience before theirs. I tried not to wonder what Ria thought about me pre-empting her invasion warning. Bad enough I'd stayed with Akizeké last night instead of comforting her. Worse still what I planned to do today.

"I am Tożätupé *reru* Żeposháru Rena," said the heir to Engineering as she stepped past Rarafashi's guards. Her sky-blue jumpsuit, cinched with bracelets and anklets of orange topaz, accented the cool tones of her pale cheek. Her brass tiara waved holdspark *shiki* arms at any who stepped too close. "I have never claimed the Dzaxashigé name."

"The sword will claim you." Akizeké snapped her fingers. Two guards lifted the weapon from its hovering case. "Speak true."

Tożätupé brushed a reluctant finger to the ruby pommel. Her spine arched. Tears rose in her eyes as her fist tightened on the hilt, but her clenched jaw kept in any pain.

I winced. *Sorry, Tożätupé.* War needed to hear pure truth to destroy today's wicked architect.

"Why did you flee Engineering?" I asked her.

The tale spilled out, wild and rapid, just as she'd recounted in the High Kiss. Watching eyes widened as she described the hovership and the attack plans; the hasty defenses Dzaro and Victory Street's other ladies had drawn up last night. Whispers spread like loose fire when she described the necromancer hidden under her white cloak.

"Do you believe the party responsible for the Hive bombing is also behind this atrocity?" I said.

She nodded. I was certain she'd rather spit in my face. "Someone's trying to break the Treaty of Inversions and restart the old wars."

"Do you believe it could be the judge's husband, Magistrate Vashathke?"

In the box behind the judge, my father mouthed, "Gei-dzeo." Like he thought I'd forgotten. I'd stopped caring.

"High Master Riapáná Żutruro released a statement maintaining Vashathke's presumed innocence unless evidence is found against him."

"The High Master was drunk when she wrote it." The hall fell silent. I winced. My bright ears caught Ria's gasp. I didn't look at her as I pressed on. "Do you know Ria has a drinking problem?"

Tożätupé's molten glare pierced me like a hunter's crossbow. "Unlike you, I protect Ria's secrets."

I stepped backwards in a clatter of pearls. The mesh netting across my left breast grew chill. Shame gripped my throat and locked up my words. In the sanctity of love, Ria had confided in me her shame. Now I'd feed her to the public.

"Answer!" Akizeké demanded. "Could the High Master's judgement have been impaired when she—at the request of *dzaxa* Iradz, Vashathke's chief strategist—signed a statement allowing Vashathke provisional innocence in the Hive bombing?"

"Yes," Tożätupé spat, the word dragged from her. "Light and shadows, yes! She's struggled with drinking since age fourteen. Can I put this sword down?"

The guards took it from her hands. She stumbled backwards. Blood ran from her nose.

"A cruel instrument," Rarafashi remarked. "I hope the men will answer without its weight. Koreshiza, you've called Tożátupé to warn us of invasion. Why does the High Master's private conduct matter?"

I pushed past the lump in my throat and spoke. "Ria holds her position because her mistakes destroyed her order—and her father, the last High Master. She missed a traitor in their ranks and gave their enemies an opening. She can't competently investigate the Hive bombing when her own failure caused it."

Ria's sharp sob cut the courtroom air. It took every instinct forged under a client's whip for me to smile and make my play. "Honored Rarafashi, your husband conspired in the Hive bombing because he hated the Fire Weavers. I spoke against him, but he blackmailed me to retract my statement. I'll swear on the dragon's sword if I must. Please, ignore what Ria and I have said before. Your husband should be arrested for murder. Not entrusted with your throne."

"How dare you address our judge?" At last, Vashathke strode down from his box. Guards stepped aside for him, a scarlet-eyed storm in silk. "Koreshiza, you killed—"

"A guard cadet," I finished. "I was fourteen. Newly flush with essence. My emotions overcame me and I struck her too hard. I'll pay the essence tithe to Gei-dzeo's next of kin. There. Matter settled. Now, Rarafashi, do justice for the Fire Weavers."

"This isn't justice!" Ria's jumpsuit brocade of golden planets flashed as she shoved through the guards and joined us on the floor. The hoops in her ears swung like fate's pendulums. "This is your dumb fucking family drama!"

"What sort of justice do you expect?" I snapped. Something broke in my voice. "Everyone in my family's a monster. It would always end like this." I'd tried to be better for her. To be loving and kind. But Victory Street had sunk its teeth deep inside me. My hate for Vashathke burned like an open flame. Maybe Dzkegé had only chosen me for my power to break things.

"I can't deal with you now." Ria turned to Rarafashi. "*Dzaxa—*"

"Enough!" Rarafashi's trumpet call echoed through the hall, ringing in my soul. A thousand courtiers and servants stilled at her power. "Vasha. Dearest. You didn't tell me about your bastard's crime. Or your blackmail."

My father flushed. "That's a private matter."

"You're my husband. You have no privacy from me. I know you blame the Engineers and the Fire Weavers for Geshge's death." Her eyebrows sharpened into ivory knives. "Answer, or I'll bring back the dragon's sword. Did your grief blind you to conspire in the bombing?"

Not grief, I thought. *Greed. Ambition. He feels no grief.* But he'd mourned Geshge—or the obedient son he'd thought Geshge was—when we'd been alone together.

A spark of wicked fire lit Vashathke's eyes. "This is about more than a conspiracy, *dzaxa* Rarafashi. More than our son. This is about your precious dragon. A boy last spotted in the Street of Inversions with this Fire Weaver on his back."

"What are you suggesting?" Rarafashi demanded.

"The truth. Engineering wants to conquer the city-planet. To do to us what we did to them. Flooding our markets with technology and infrastructure hasn't satisfied their vengeance. So the Fire Weavers stole our god's last gift. They abducted and murdered our dragon in their Hive!"

"Lies!" Ria said, and my clenching heart said the same. *My father speaks like all souls hold our evil.* How could anyone discredit claims so vast?

"The drunk calls me a liar?" Vashathke bowed his head, a master actor painting aching regret. "I sent my agents to investigate your Hive. You took a beautiful son of War and cut him open. Tortured him. Castrated him. My people fought to save him, but you cut open his throat yourself!"

"Are you confessing to ordering the Hive attack?" Rarafashi bellowed.

"I ordered a rescue!" my father snapped. Summoned tears brimmed in his eyes. "When that failed, I ordered vengeance. To uphold your legacy, *dzaxa* Rarafashi, and to respect the traditions of War."

My knees buckled. I nearly swooned. *He's confessed.* Without even the dragon's sword in his hands. *I'm right. He was involved.* But falsehoods knotted his story. Making the case for his ascension from a damning truth. The perfect husband, begging his wife not to condemn him for loving her too much. The perfect *dzaxa* man, viciously protecting customs that would devour him in the end. *He loves nothing but power and control.*

"Subpoena Vashathke under the dragon's sword," I suggested to Akizeké. Only she or Rarafashi had the rank to demand that.

"Why?" Akizeké grinned. "He's already talking his hopes to death."

Rarafashi drew a shuddering breath. "If this is true, Vasha, perhaps you are strong enough to rule." She turned to Ria. "My husband's accused you of murder. But he's also confessed to a crime. Was he justified in his deed? Accounts say you flew with the dragon, you even knew his name. If the dragon lives, where and who is he?"

My heart plummeted. I gripped my baton through my sash, though I couldn't fight my way out. My mother wasn't here to fight for me.

Ria stared at my father. Her lips moved in silent calculation. *Two red-eyed men dealt her a double blow.* Seconds of unknown anxiety ached by. *Get it over with.* My name would turn Vashathke's confession into murder. She'd win justice for the Fire Weavers and the judge's ear for her petition.

"You'll never lay a finger on the dragon." Ria knelt, lifting her arms in surrender. My memory flashed to our first conversation in the High Kiss. *The Fire Weavers protect everyone on the city-planet. Including courtesans.*

Including cruel boys who broke hearts.

"Koré was right," she said. I could hear the words biting under her strength. "I'm a drunk, a failure, and a coward. Unworthy to lead the Fire Weavers. I confess to murdering your dragon and surrender to your justice."

THE COURTROOM'S ROAR still rang in my ears as we retreated to Dzaro's Skygarden apartment.

Dzaxa had cursed Ria's name as the guards led her out. Cries of 'Vashathke, Judge Vashathke!' had risen as my father climbed to Rarafashi's side, smirking as she trustingly squeezed his hand. Akizeké had tried to lead me away, but I'd stayed frozen until they'd dragged Ria past me. I hadn't met her eyes. How could I begin thanking her for what she'd done?

Why had I chosen vengeance over her? Why had I chosen my terror?

Dzaro's guards knotted tight around her *reja* as it raced us up the steel halls. "I've called in all my debts and favors," my aunt said. "There's twenty thousand armed guards at my command, not counting Faziz's three thousand fighters. If those plans he found are accurate, we can resist the attack for a while."

My stomach flipped as I imagined the oncoming assault. I'd learned some military theory in the Prizeheron, but Iradz had grasped it better. "How long is 'a while'?"

"A few hours at best. We'll need Skygarden mobilized to support us. Only a judge can do that." She bit her lip. "But Rarafashi moves on her own time. Right now, we need to help the Engineers."

The Lost District envoys sat uneasily in the private solar of Dzaro's Skygarden apartment: a small space, lovingly decorated in Dusklily's taste. Gauzy curtains hid cold steel walls. Coral cushions heaped gilded chairs. A blue, cloudless sky shone beyond the balcony. A breeze wafted up from Victory Street, carrying the scent of beer and fried food.

It would have felt like any other diplomatic gathering, were it not for Sadza on the floor, thrashing against the heavy nets binding her. Hatred glimmered in her eyes. Dried blood covered her chin.

Faziz stood above her, sword ready to chop through her neck. "Hello, Red Eyes."

"After all you did to ally with my father, you help Dzaro raid his private cells? No matter who takes the throne, you're fucked."

"I certainly won't win lordships. But if we can't free the enthralled Engineers, the throne doesn't matter. The war won't end until the shadows take us all." Clearing his throat, he nodded to the envoys. "Hello, all. I... hmm. *Rusuchak vi suchasu?*"

"*Rusuchak chapudav suik suchasu, saki vavadyn.*" An envoy in soiled furs pressed her hands to her eyes. *A sign of respect?* Faziz flinched.

"Resourceful boy for a dull," Dzaro whispered. "A polyglot and an inventor. His net gun took Sadza down."

"He's smart. Too smart." I didn't look away from Faziz as I spoke. I didn't know if I should brace for him to backstab me or braid his loose hair off his shoulders.

"Is he why you pulled that cruel stunt with the High Master? If you wanted to break up with her, you should have just said so. Ria would have let you go."

And remembering her would always call scale to my skin. I bit my lip and said nothing.

"Or maybe you're playing another game. I love you, and I want to help, but I can't if you're not honest. You confessed to a murder—"

"That's true," I muttered.

"You never told me. Did you think it would go away if you lied? Secrets don't last forever."

My truth is too dangerous. Hiding a wince, I turned from my aunt.

Slowly, Faziz edged and stumbled through the conversation. The envoys animated, visibly grateful to share their stories. At last, Faziz nodded and stood.

"I think I got most of it," he said. "They're from a small building on the Lost District's borders. The necromancer Tamadza came from the high ruins and hired them as servants. She came south to find international allies to help her conquer. When Geshge approached them, they thought they'd found everything they needed. But he and Tamadza are dead, and they're terrified. They think another necromancer will bind Tamadza's soul and hunt them down."

"How do you bind a shadow-Shaper's soul?" I asked.

Faziz posed the question. The answer came whispered, fearful. "Tamadza's soul is linked to her staff, which links her to… the great shadow below, whatever that is. If another breaks Tamadza's will with her own, she'll control Tamadza's power while she holds the staff."

I laughed out a knife of frustrated pain. "If willpower's the key, any *dzaxa* could wield the staff for my father."

Faziz rephrased his question, asking different envoys, changing his verbs and salutations. The language unfolded. My understanding cleared. Each envoy spoke the same: willpower alone controlled the staff.

"Thank you for speaking with us," Dusklily sputtered, in halting phrasese he'd picked up from the envoys' conversation. "With your permission, Lady Dzaroshardze, I'll lead the envoys back to the Surrender."

My aunt nodded. "Bring a barrel. I'll stuff the dead one in."

The lady and her concubine shoved the thrashing Sadza in the barrel. Slayer the terrier sniffed greedily at the wooden slats. The living envoys nodded thanks as Dusklily led them to the waiting *reja*.

"As tradition dictates," Dzaro said gently, once the curtains closed, "the judge will consult her council before sentencing Ria. Once they finish talking, she'll be condemned and drained for murdering the dragon."

I remembered Bero, pale and shaking in the shattered High Kiss as Dzaro escorted out the mob. *People need a dragon. They won't stop looking for hope.* The *dzaxa* and their supporters should burn in their own violence, but my employees deserved better. Faziz's people deserved better. *Justice. Mercy. Vision.* Our district had a hole where our hopes for the future should live. A hole that needed filling.

War needed action. Ria needed action. But how could someone like me step forward without breaking everything?

"You have a few hours until court reconvenes," Dzaro said. "Now that everyone's decided Vashathke avenged the dragon, there's a line of *dzaxa* outside his quarters writing him endorsements. I'm going to try talking them down. Will you come with me?"

She studied my face, then shook her head and stepped back. Faziz took my arm. "I'll look after him," he promised.

I couldn't speak past the knot in my throat. Dzaro nodded at Faziz and left. I buried my head in my hands.

"This is all my fault," I whispered when we were alone. "She's going to die."

"This is a lot of people's fault. A lot of people are going to die." Faziz dropped onto the loveseat beside me. His court skirt, blush-blue and covered in a mesh of pale seed pearls, was stolen from my closet. "Ria's a natural hero. Challenged a shadow-Shaper alone. You couldn't have stopped her."

"I should have pushed you both away before things went this far."

"Both of us? I thought I removed myself from your favor when I went to Vashathke."

"I know why you did it. That blackmail's over. I don't have the energy to be mad at you now. I need someone to talk to." I couldn't keep the weakness from my voice. He drew me like a magnet.

Softly, he said, "You can always talk to me, Red Eyes. About Gei-dzeo? Ria?"

I turned away from him, peering over the balcony. Brass bands gathered on Victory Street, practicing parade formations on the bronto-sized sandstone cobbles. "They're practicing for the Festival of Ten Keys. Celebrating some atrocity my Dzaxashigé ancestors committed. I used to see these festivals as harmless. But what sort of people build streets from monuments to destruction? I wish we could change the past, but we can't. We can't separate the bad from the beautiful."

"Are you talking about this district, or yourself? They don't have to be the same thing. Does your aunt have any beer?"

I found a cask and poured. Fresh amber ale, dark malt with a slight cinnamon edge. Heat tingled through my fingers as he took the glass from me. "Of course they're the same. I'm what Victory Street made me. Bright. Desired. Monstrous."

He grinned. Still unafraid of me. That fuckhead. "It matters what you're a monster for."

I don't know what I'm fighting for. But my heart lifted that he recognized the fighter inside me. I dropped down on the couch beside him. "How do you do that? See past silk and steel to my soul?"

"I know there's something to look for." White foam gathered on his upper lip. "Wherever I got my sword, someone must have hurt me badly, to make me want to fight. It's not just my weapon. It's my scar, like the scar of that mask you wear. You play a role to protect yourself, and push people away when they get too close to your soul's truth." His fingers wrapped around mine, cold from the glass and sticky with beer. "Tell me everything you hid. Tell me about Gei-dzeo and your family. Tell me about Zegakadze. My spies gave me most, but I want to hear it from your lips."

"You won't like it," I warned. "It's a thousand times better for you not to know. I don't want to hurt you."

"I know who you are. The same stardust birthed both our souls. Nothing you do can hurt me, not in any way that lasts. You're all the healing I need." The force of him, deeper than essence, lit his onyx eyes. "Give me your secrets. Maybe then, when I say you're beautiful, you'll finally believe me."

I took one breath. Then another. And words spilled out like the tide.

I held nothing back. My betrothals and loves, my mother's shattered care, my father's shadow on my face. My sisters, dead and broken in the secret cells. The lies I'd told, the hearts I'd broken, the cadet I'd slain. The stain on my soul. *How I have nothing but wretchedness to offer you.*

"I've always feared I'm a monster," I confessed at the end. "I could have walked away, but I kept fighting for revenge. The Fire Weavers have fallen, an army flies to Victory Street, my business is ruined, and my father's won a throne. What have I gained? No revenge. No justice. I'm pushing my loved ones away because my own happiness threatens my freedom!"

I ached like I'd scaled a building. *Now he sees my anger. He sees all.* The power was in Faziz's hands. A sensible man would run screaming, before the toxic weight of me dragged him down. But Faziz courted danger like a lover. He could reach across our strained bond and make us whole.

He set down his beer. "It's been ten thousand years since the world's seen someone like you. Even a Shaper couldn't predict what would happen if you stepped into the light. All you know is what quiet will cost you. There's no right option when the world thinks you're wrong."

"I thought you'd just tell me I'm beautiful when I panic." I smiled. My chest felt lighter, now, and strange. He hadn't crushed me yet. Maybe that meant I could hold him.

"You're always beautiful." His thin lips arched into a smile, their deep, reddish brown smooth as fresh clay. "And you deserve to be who you are: the man I love."

He leant in. Pressed his ravenous lips to mine. His hair fell like a curtain, closing out the world, and I surrendered. Nothing remained but the force of his kiss.

"The world could strike us down whenever it chooses." His whisper brushed hot on my cheek. "Closing off your heart won't keep either of us safe. Stop caring what's safe, and love me."

His breath caught as he spoke, each gasp a revelation. *Love me.* Like a command. I wanted to cradle his impossible compassion against my heart, protect it from all harm. That was his beauty—his smile, the shining line of his sword. I wanted and needed him to be mine.

I slid up on my elbows and kissed him back.

"Make me whole," he gasped. Eager desire tensed every knot of his body. His hands trembled as they stroked my spine, spikes and scales tumbling free in their wake. "Fuck me. Complete me."

"Which position?" My lips lapped the rough edge of his jaw. My fingers tangled in his thick, dark hair. "You strike me as a top, but I don't assume—"

Had his eyes always sparked like they held secret stars? Faziz smiled, wild and fierce as a racing raptor, and I couldn't stop a smile from cracking my own face. "It's been a while. Show me how it's done."

I slid under him, my tongue lavishing his scarred chest. Salt, straw, and *him* hit the roof of my mouth. His cheeks flexed, eagerly, as my hands sank under his hem. My thumbs sank inward. He tensed like I'd struck him.

"I usually start new people on trainers." My breath came in quick, excited gasps. "Small ones. This will hurt. I'm much bigger than my thumbs."

"I've seen you." He kissed my eyelids as they fluttered shut, kissed like there wasn't an inch of me he could leave unexplored. "Not that much bigger."

I laughed and rolled atop him. Sunlight bathed the taut muscles of his back, casting his skin scarred gold. Scales turned my thighs to burnished silver. Magic and light. Matching us. I uncorked a vial of oil and purred, "Don't pretend to be tough," as I massaged it into him. "Scream if you need to. Scream my name."

"I can take it."

"Silly boy." I spread his asscheeks with the heel of one hand and pushed the head of my cock inside him.

His neck arched like I'd dragged back his hair. I pinned him with my full weight. Watched him flex as each thrust drove me deeper. My shaft pulsed in time with my heartbeat, the core of my body craving relief. But I clenched my jaw and held steady. I couldn't break until I'd pleased him.

"Koreshiza," he moaned, my name deep in his throat. I bent low and kissed his ear, tasting his sweat as he moved below and around me. Essence coursed between us, his ash to my burning blaze, pounding at our temples like the beat of invisible wings. Knotting our souls together. "I need—tell you—"

My hand ran between him and the cushions, curling around downy hair and the hard length of him. "Easy," I said, and stroked. *One. Two. Thrust.* He came undone in my palm. I abandoned myself in him. A low, pulsing shudder ran from my groin through my whole body.

The world faded away. My cheek came to rest on his shoulderblade. I lay atop him, letting myself for once do nothing but breathe.

At last, he reached up and brushed the sweaty hair from my brow. "We ruined your aunt's couch. She was so nice to give us some privacy."

"My aunt's ruined fifty couches like this. Trust me. I pick out her boyfriends."

"There's my Koré." His fingers curled around my hand. It grew into a ruby-flecked talon.

"You used my name. Not Red Eyes. Koreshiza. Did it take you this long to learn?"

"My guards say I've been calling your name in my sleep. I might have muttered it to myself a few times while awake, too. But it always sounds like 'I love you, more than I can stand.' 'Red Eyes' I can say without needing to kiss you."

I'd never think his name again without wanting to shatter. "I'm in love with you," I whispered into his neck. "Listen. Past my heartbeat, my soul sings to yours."

"It doesn't take much essence to hear that." He smiled, and I tried to memorize his face, because this happiness couldn't last the day. *No certainty. No right option.* I had a responsibility to the people I loved. Even if that meant risking the world would tear me from them.

We lay wrapped in each other until the cannons opened fire.

CHAPTER TWENTY-FOUR
Skygarden

23rd *Reshi*, Year 92 Rarafashi

"When a god's path leads into the shadows, her heralds must lift new hymns to the skies."— *verse of Dzkegé's Testament, Shadowcoin Street oral tradition*

FESTIVAL FIREWORKS, WAS my first thought as booms rattled the flying palace. *Why are they so close?*

Then Skygarden shuddered.

The loveseat tipped. I grabbed Faziz, but wasn't fast enough to pull him underneath me, and elbowed his gut as we hit the rug.

"My hero," he grunted, standing and drawing his sword. My bright fingers swiftly untangled the meshed netting of pearls over both our skirts.

"That sword won't help." Raw fear cracked my voice.

The hovership blocked a black bar across the sun. Its silver faces, screaming soundless agony, spat flame. Sulfur washed the air. Faziz took my arm, steadying himself—but I was shaking deep in my bones.

The attack had come. Now we lived in a world at war.

"Victory Street!" boomed the voice of Żeposháru Rena, "We've come for justice. Hand over the murderer Vashathke, and we'll leave your district unscathed."

The murderer Vashathke. At last, the world heard those words. They didn't sound the same from the judge Vashathke's necromancer had enthralled. *What does he gain from naming himself a murderer, even in starting the battle he craves?*

Skygarden hummed. Mechanisms clicked and whirled in the walls. Substance rolled, lit and livid, behind thin steel plate. Heat rolled though the ground, as if the metal dragon braced to breathe fire.

"We should go." Dzaro flung open the doors. Her *reja* awaited outside. "Hurry!"

"Good idea," Faziz said as we clambered aboard. "Get into the building's core, away from the bombardment."

She looked at him like he'd grown two heads. "What? There's nothing we can do about that. It's time for Ria's sentencing."

The corridors shook as we raced back to the courtroom. Raptors snarled, plumes erect. Servants rushed past us, dull and slow, scrambling for shelter. Fear marked every face. Even Faziz looked worried.

I bit my lip, searching for courage. *Ria.*

The law of War crushed souls in its teeth.

Minor bureaucrats, servants and guards packed the courtroom wall-to-wall. Their body scent overwhelmed my bright senses, but I bore them no ill will. All knew the safest place in Skygarden was at the judge's side.

Rarafashi trembled atop her throne, eyes fixed on the dragon's sword in its hovering case. Vashathke stood proud at her side, his hand on her shoulder, scarlet gaze dancing over the crowd. *He must have secured the final endorsements he needed,* buzzed an inconsequential thought in the back of my head. From the second tier of seats, a lonely Akizeké glared at him. Dzaro pulled us through the crowds to her private bench. Faziz tugged on my arm to remind me to sit.

Guards marched Ria in. Holdfast chains twined her wrists and ankles, covering bracers and torc in a gold-flecked blue cocoon. Though a Fire Weaver's weapons couldn't be removed without her consent, Skygarden's ancient armory held the tools to restrain her.

"It gives me no pleasure to be here." Rarafashi panted as she spoke. The hovership hung outside the tall windows behind her, blocking half the sun. "Battle awaits, and my district must be safely passed to another. But avenging Dzkegé's last gift is my sacred duty."

The dragon's sword was the true gift. A sacred calling to protect our world. *A gift this district has squandered and besmirched.* The best part of our legacy and our one chance to rebuild ourselves.

"The ancient law of War," continued the judge, "states a murderer must pay threefold essence of what they destroyed. But the accused, Riapáná Żutruro *reru* Päreshi —"

"Riapáná Żutruro *reru* Eprue Zucho," Ria corrected.

"The accused has slain something irreplaceable." Anger rolled through Rarafashi's frail frame. Her right fist curled. Her left lay unresponsive. "That dragon should have renewed our district for ten thousand years. All I wanted, before passing on my throne, was to give War a future."

"You've got a shit way to show it," Ria said. "You're under attack. Sentence me later. Let me help you now. Skygarden's lower levels are shaking. People will die down there!"

The hovership's screaming silver faces flashed. *Dzaxa* screamed and jumped as more shells struck home.

"Only dulls will die from a little shaking," Rarafashi said. I squeezed Faziz's hand, wishing those words hadn't been spoken, hating he'd heard them. "Your sentence—"

"Those are your people! Fuck you, Rarafashi. You're not

worthy of that throne or sword. None of the hypocrite liars in this district are."

Her words struck deep. A thrown knife at our district—and at me, smallest of the high monsters it bred. The fire in her eyes sang to my heart. Even a prisoner, she outshone the court. I couldn't let them make her drain herself. Not if I wanted to deserve her.

Time to see if Dzkegé chose right.

"Take Faziz back to the Surrender and prepare your ground defenses," I told Dzaro. "This will be... chaotic."

"What do you mean?" Her voice wavered. "Are you planning something stupid?"

"For Ria," I whispered to Faziz. Understanding flickered in his eyes.

"We need to trust him," he told Dzaro. I could hear his goodbye. He knew what I had to do. "For Ria."

Dzaro, still confused, rose and pushed her way towards the exit. With one last look back at Faziz, I slipped through the crowd and leapt from the nearest windowsill.

Wind wrapped around me. Gravity tugged me down.

I closed my eyes and pictured my loves. Banished all fears. At last, at last, I set my soul free.

My wings unfurled and bit the air. Light rolled through my skull and shoulders. My scales flashed the orange hues of sunset.

Dzkegé's martial instincts whispered in my ear. I flicked my tail and launched myself at the hovership.

Shocked gasps rose from the courtroom windows. Hovership cannons pounded staccato rhythm. Sulphur-tainted white fire streaked towards my chest. Heat kissed my talons as I leapt over the missiles.

Too bright for you. I fell on the ship's top deck. Perched starlings leapt from my onslaught. Iron buckled. Holdweight crackled and hissed. I drove the barbed tip of my tail through the ship's side.

I'd never summoned a larger, deadlier dragon form. Engineers raced towards me, batons, swords and axes lifted. Purple ringed their eyes; their hearts beat quick and vital. *Still living.* My fire caught them in a wave. They straightened, blinking like clouds had been lifted from their sight.

Be free, I willed. *Please.* And perhaps Dzkegé heard me. Light flickered in their eyes as they remembered themselves and charged back at their enthralled fellows. I raised my head and unleashed another wave of living flame.

Metal clashed. Blood flew against sunset iron. Screams of pain stabbed into me. I pressed towards the melee, struggling to help. The ground shifted.

I leapt airborne as the hovership twisted me off. Bodies tumbled from the decks. The hovership's cannons held their fire, engines whistling as the craft floated back towards Shadowcoin Street.

I braced myself. I'd bought us time. We could regroup. Fight off the necromancers and tear down my father.

I'd done what I could to save War. Now I needed to save Ria.

The window behind the throne shattered as I struck. Glass rained around me as I landed, light reshaping my head and figure human. Jaws dropped as I strode forward, servants and *dzaxa* silently parting in my wake. Resplendent in silver wings and silk fire, I swept out my taloned hands and bowed before my judge.

"Dzkegé's tits," my father sneered, his eyes livid coals. "It's fucking you, you unworthy bastard whore!"

"Aren't you happy to see your precious dragon alive?" I mocked, alive with the force of me. "After those awful things you did to protect him? No. Of course not. You've never cared for this district—for anything—more than for your fucking ego."

"What the fuck, Koré?" Ria gasped. "Why would you…"

I wrapped my wings around us, drawing us together into a private space. "I'm sorry for those awful things I said. I've broken everything between us. But I want you to know you're worthy to lead the Fire Weavers and more than worthy of anything I can sacrifice. I've done monstrous things, but I love you with my skin, bones, and soul."

"Enough!" Rarafashi shouted. I jumped back from Ria as the judge stood, swaying. "The accused murdered our dragon! She will tithe me her store and face the dead gods in justice!"

Dzkegé's mercy. She didn't understand what my wings and scales meant. All was slipping from her mind. "The dragon lives. It's me." I lowered my head. "Rarafashi, please. Ria's committed no crime. Let her go."

"It's okay, dearest," Vashathke told her. "We have a better prize. Secure the dragon first."

Slowly, Rarafashi nodded. Her guards tore the holdfasts chains free. Ria stumbled forward, rubbing her wrists.

"Bind him," Vashathke ordered. The guards turned to me.

"No!" Ria shouted. "He's innocent—well, he confessed to a murder, but you can't arrest him for being what he is!"

Meekly, I held up my hands. The substance chains closed heavy on my wrists and ankles. My scales vanished as the holdfast locked my power, bright beauty vanishing in silver light. They forced me down, nude, coughing and gagging, before the throne.

"I've given you a dragon, dear," said Vashathke.

"Ambassador Sadza signed my last international endorsement yesterday. All the *dzaxa* of War stand on my side. Remember your pledges and your obligations as judge. Lay down your burdens and pass me the rule of War."

Rarafashi's eyes danced over me. Old as she was, desire lit them. "My loyal Vasha. You've done well."

So had I. In this, at least.

"You monster!" Ria shouted, rounding on Vashathke. "You organized the Hive attack! The dragon lives. Will you spin another story to excuse yourself? Or will you own up to your hateful crimes?"

"She's right, Rarafashi." That was Akizeké's voice, high-pitched, powerful, and utterly welcome. More *dzaxa* voices rose across the courtroom, questioning and angry. "Vashathke started a war for a lie. Your district is being invaded. Millions will die. The world falls into chaos, and you'll let this headstrong fool lead us into this new era? No. You're wise, my judge. You know what you must do."

Rarafashi croaked, "You made this war, Vasha?"

My father purpled. I craned my neck. My chain-weighted throat ached for air, but I couldn't look away from his humiliation. *Sweet as a kiss.* "I confessed. But dearest, I never... I couldn't... please! I brought you a dragon! You promised!"

"A dragon means nothing if you lack discipline!" Akizeké pushed through the guards and took Rarafashi's hand. "You need to arrest your husband. He's betrayed his district and the world. I can't repair what he's broken, but I'll do my best to bring swift victory if you invest me as War's new judge."

"War's..." Rarafashi stuttered. "Yes. My promise... had conditions. That was clear."

"But I did everything you wanted." True heartbreak filled Vashathke's voice. Deeper and truer than it had even rung at Geshge's funeral. "I earned the throne. I played by the rules and fulfilled the conditions—"

"I'm changing my endorsement," called a *dzaxa* with spinning gears mounted on her *fajix*. "Akizeké's who we need."

"Me too," said another, leaning on a cane as she rose. "Akizeké is the future of War."

"Sadza is undead," Kirakaneri added. "Her endorsement doesn't count. Vashathke is still one short."

In a rippling line of silver and a high, strong chorus, they stood. My father's face fell further with each new voice, his blood-gathered power slipping through his fingers like diamonds ground to sand. I wanted to cheer. I wanted to

411

laugh in his face. *You're not special among men, Father. The laws of War cheat us all.*

"By my count," Akizeké said, "and I'm very good at math, Vashathke is one short in the tally. I'm at eighteen and forty-two—is that a record? That must be a record."

"Come here... Akizeké." Rarafashi grabbed her chest. "War's new..."

She collapsed. Steel dented beneath her.

That was when the screaming started.

Footsteps pounded. Bodies slammed together. The world roared with cutting, terrible fear. Guards streamed around me, blocking my view. I pressed my cheek to the floor, praying they wouldn't step on me. The uneven thud of the judge's dying heartbeat fluttered at the edge of my hearing.

Someone grabbed my neck and dragged me backwards. I gasped, wrenching at my bonds. The chains fell free.

"Easy, boy," Akizeké breathed in my ear. "I've got you."

"Unhand me!" Vashathke shouted as the guards cuffed him. "I still rule Victory Street! I'm—"

"Take him to the Dzaxashigé cells," Akizeké commanded. The guards dragged my stammering father from the room. I laughed, though my heart sank low. *Battle in the sky.* Had Faziz felt this empty beside Zega's body?

Ria summoned a wave of ice, knocking her way through the mob. "Koré! Are you hurt?" I shook my head. She turned from me. "Akizeké. What's your plan?"

Akizeké looked to the moaning Rarafashi, hoisted on her guards' shoulders. "Be invested with her essence. Arm Skygarden and fight off the attack. But Rarafashi might take all night dying. Stubborn judge."

"The Engineers on that ship aren't themselves. I'll get Toźätupé. We can explain everything to you. We still might prevent the slaughter and save the Treaty of Inversions."

"Done. Meet me in my apartment. Koré, fly back to your brothel and lock yourself in. Mobs will rise to take a dragon's power—I'll send guards to protect you. Gods, boy, why didn't you tell me the truth sooner?"

You didn't listen. Instead of speaking, I kissed her. Her soft lips bent beneath mine as I exhaled essence. Her grey-blond hair flashed like hammered white gold. The curved stretch marks on her stomach lay like veins through white marble. Every inch of her was perfect grace. Perfect power.

"How do I look?" She grinned like a wildfire.

"Like a judge of War." I bowed low. "Good luck. I'm honored to serve you."

CHAPTER TWENTY-FIVE
The High Kiss, within the eastern sculpture of the Surrender

24th *Reshi,* Year 92 Rarafashi

"A true daughter of War boldly seizes her rights.
Those who can't are crushed under history's
wheel. The world is a hard, dark, violent place.
Rise firm and violent within."—speech by
Varjthosheri the Dragon-Blessed, Shaper-Judge
of War, upon ascending to the throne

THE MOB ROARED outside the High Kiss. "Dragon," they
cried. "Essence!" Screams rose as Akizeké's guard beat back
any too close to the entry arch. Five snipers with tactical
crossbows waited on my balcony, knocking off climbers.

At every bell of the night, a guard had pulled me from
my lonely bed with updates: the hovership kept firing. My
father remained imprisoned. The people of Victory Street
were fleeing. Ten thousand Engineers were crossing the
treacherous Slatepile ground on foot.

At the third bell, I'd given up on sleep. Music and nervous
laughter rose from downstairs as my courtesans entertained
the waiting reinforcements—the first business the half-

demolished High Kiss had seen all week. I paced across my chamber, yearning to fly out and breathe essence for the desperate. But Akizeké had told me I'd help best by staying safe.

"Boss?" Bero opened my door, flinching as I met his eyes.

"Are you afraid of me?"

"What? Don't be ridiculous. I'm checking in. I'm worried, for you and for us."

I bit my cheek. "Sorry. I know. I'm fine, though—I'm sorry. You, Neza, Ruby, Kge and Opal—Opal most of all—you need the High Kiss, and my scandals could ruin the business. I don't know how I can salvage this for you."

"I've got some ideas. I'm your assistant manager, after all. But you've got to cut down on the dramatics ten, twenty percent. Your magic couldn't be easy to hide, but hiding's over. You have my support. Respect me in return with a fraction more maturity."

"Okay." To my surprise, a small, genuine smile slipped across my lips. "You're right. I've been acting foolishly." I didn't know whether to add *lately* or *my whole life,* and I wasn't sure if that mattered. "Thank you. I'm glad for your friendship."

"And I for yours." He glanced back over his shoulder. "You have a guest."

A guest? My spine stiffened.

Iradz pushed inside and embraced me. "Brother dearest!"

My bowels turned to water. It took all my strength to maintain my composure. "Bero. Check on our other guests. I'll speak with my sister-in-law in private."

He nodded and left. I pulled back from her arms.

"Countless fortunes have slipped through my fingers, but you—my priceless one—I lost you twice." Street dust lined her gold-and-ebony hem. She'd come in a hurry. "The dragon of War." Her eyes glittered mischief and threat. "Our god has a sick sense of irony.

"I was who Dzkegé could reach. Ria almost fell into that temple. I wish it was her."

"You must love her dearly, exposing your secret for her. You're more emotional than Geshge. Foolish, short-sighted, silly boy. Loving someone even I can manipulate with a jar of vodka and firepowder. Hilarious how you didn't tell her our history. You realize no one but me would like you, if they knew your perversions."

Faziz. His hands on my spine, my lips on his chest. His heart loving mine, though he knew the true darkness in me, deeper than the false sins Iradz assigned me at a glance. "You're wrong. Bullying me as a child. Joining my father's guards. You're on the wrong side of history."

"Am I?" She frowned. "I didn't come for you to accuse me. I came to bargain. I know you were investigating Ten Staves. My late, dear, stupid husband's shell company." She drew a folder from her sash. "The contract that killed him. Ria didn't find my offer of paperwork compelling. But you were always interested in the oddest things. Want to look?"

It felt lifetimes had passed since the state banquet where they'd signed it. I reached for the papers. She pulled them back.

"I don't just offer these for nothing. I want a rematch. Me and you in bed. Fuck to the first tithe. You win, you get the folder. I win, we marry, and I get dragon heirs of my own."

"How like a Dzaxashigé. You, me, and all our twisted kin seek conquest. Your pride prickles while I live free." But Ria needed truth. The real killers exposed and tried, not quick and angry vengeance. And I needed to do everything in my power to stop this.

I had to get those papers.

The hovership's cannons cracked against the morning sky. I bowed to Iradz. "Let's dance, and see who's the master."

She grabbed me before I finished speaking. Her thumb tore through my skirt and sank inside me. "Don't get cocky. I've known you longer than anyone." Kisses ran down my jaw in an overwhelming stream. "Breathe easy, sweetheart. I'm here for you. Where are your toys?"

"Back there," I gasped.

Iradz flung back the silk curtain. Instruments glittered wickedly. "This should help you focus on me."

Silver chain glittered in her hands. Rings winked as she rolled them across her fingers. *Dzkegé's mercy.*

"I want you to think about me. Only me and my love for you." She pressed me back against the bed and locked the clips around my nipples. Her brass curls spilled against my thighs. The ring slid around my cock. The connecting chain caught in her teeth. Silver tightened as her mouth worked me. "You must be so afraid. The last dragon of War. No man should carry that burden, especially not one as vulnerable as you."

Vulnerable. Shivers rolled down my spine. She hooked the chain down with her chin, tonguing my sack, cupping achingly delicate flesh in her mouth. *So vulnerable.* The chain twisted around her finger. Electric darts swam through my chest and struck in my groin.

"I'll protect you," she cooed. "Picture this: you're my husband, safe in my apartment. The judge's guard walks in, but they can't claim you. No one can challenge *dzaxa* marriage rights. Instead of the judge passing you around her favorites, you'd be with me every night. Like this, every night."

Give in, part of me urged, as the ring bit into my erection. *She can protect you. It would be easy.* If I belonged to Iradz, it wouldn't matter I'd shattered Ria's heart. It wouldn't matter who I'd killed. I could slip into the role I'd been promised as a child. Everything I did would be right and good—as long as I never questioned the *dzaxa* and their use of me. *Vashathke's lost his judgeship and his freedom. The High Kiss lies shattered and undone. What do I need choices for?* Her chain wrenched my nipples, and all contradiction slipped away. I could let my story end here.

"Wouldn't it be easy?" Her tongue lashed my navel. Twined through pale hair. "I've loved you since you were promised to me. So bright. So pretty. The world expects you on my arm. You're not fallen past redemption. You can still be the boy your mother wanted you to be."

The boy she wanted. The proper son, not a courtesan with a monster's face and heart. I'd tried to be that. But her idea of perfect, Victory Street's idea of perfect, had always been a mirage, and chasing it drained the life from me. Iradz wasn't my happiness. My happiness was my unnatural love. The truth for Ria. A safer world for Faziz.

They deserved the best. They'd chosen me.

To be who they needed, I'd lash out with all the monstrous defiance inside me.

"I made a mistake four years ago." My fingers brushed Iradz's brow. "I shouldn't have insulted you, humiliated you, or taken your rights. You earned the Surrender. You earned the Prizeheron. I cheated to rob you of your entitlements."

Her essence fluttered at my fingertips. "Say it again," she murmured.

I grinned and drove my foot into her forehead.

Chain tore. Silver links flew. I screamed as her teeth ripped clean across my flesh. But then she hit the ground—my opening, my chance. I flew across the room, clutched the folder to my chest, and raised my baton.

"Start talking," I threatened, gasping. If not for my lightning focus, I'd collapse in a ball. "What got my brother killed? What did my father do?"

She laughed, low in her throat. Blood trickled down her forehead. "You still think this revolves around you and your daddy issues? You're worse than my husband. Vashathke promised to give Geshge Victory Street's throne once he became judge. Restore our lost fortunes. But then Vashathke offered that position to Lady Xezkavodz of the Archive. My poor Geshge sought another candidate who'd reward his service. Instead—again—he lost out to his prettier brother."

My heart pounded hard. Blood trickled down my thigh. "You're not making sense."

"Look in the folder."

My instincts screamed no. But I grounded myself in Ria's need, and looked.

The long-sought trade contract's body listed the fortune in goods offered for Tamadza's Reclaimers. I flipped to the last page. Tamadza had signed with a thorny glyph. Geshge's signature flowed in intricate calligraphy, ending with a mark he served as an agent for another, whose signature was the snowflake-shaped poem at the bottom.

Akizeké Shikishashir Dzaxashigé.

I felt the weight of her brushstrokes. The same signature she'd put on our contracts and every letter she'd written me.

My knees gave. I slumped against the wall.

"Funny, isn't it? Since you fucked her?" Iradz laughed. "Geshge took me to dinner with her. Between her museum and those Lost District envoys, I was completely creeped out. I told Geshge to ditch her, but everyone at dinner was seduced. Your father offers compliments and false promises. Magistrate Akizeké offers power. If she rises to the judge's throne, she'll use this Engineering attack as justification to conquer the city-planet."

I remembered the conversation Ria had translated on the hovership. *Sadza says the magistrate is upset about Geshge's death.* But Sadza hadn't named the magistrate they'd struck their deal with. Vashathke had taken her prisoner in a futile attempt to find the truth. *It can't be.* "No. My father partnered with the necromancers. He confessed to ordering the Hive attack!"

"He took credit for the attack when it suited him politically. He never realized his boasts would be turned against him. Like all the men in your family, he's a fool. Akizeké and

Tamadza played you all against each other. Kept you too busy to see the truth. Your spat demonstrated for all Jadzia why men can't be trusted to rule."

"Vashathke hates the Engineers." *But every* dzaxa *envies our powerful neighbors.* My head spun as I worked it out. My father had called for violence after Geshge died. He hadn't known about the undead. He'd truly believed an Engineer had murdered his 'loyal' son. Only Akizeké's taunts had pushed him to endorse open war. *A man must fight twice as hard to prove his strength. And his fighting gave Akizeké ammunition to shoot him down as a warmonger. He could never win.*

When two districts lay decimated and Akizeké rose up as the new judge, the War District would fight for her without question.

She slaughtered her own guards. Stole the staff and the hovership. Enthralled thousands of Engineers. That's only the start of her plan.

I'd been a fool to assume her innocence. *The traditional candidate. Upholding the traditions of a leadership rotten to its core.*

Ria had been right to doubt my suspicions of Vashathke. That she'd also missed Akizeké was cold comfort. I wasn't the one who'd pay for my bloody mistakes. The world was falling into violence. Ria was trapped in Skygarden with a murderer-traitor. And it was all my fault.

I kept working it through. "On the hovership, Geshge was confused when I asked why he was working with Vashathke. He might have told me everything then, but the bombs interrupted us. Tamadza had stolen the detonator from my aunt, and…"

I paused. Tamadza hadn't known about the detonator. But one of Akizeké's supporters had.

A man with light-enough fingers to pickpocket the detonator undetected.

"Faziz knew," I whispered.

"The dull man? He was closer to them than Geshge. Well, before he joined Vashathke and helped me get my new job. Must have developed morals after the Hive fell."

Faziz knew everything. He'd slipped my allies into Akizeké's fist by connecting us at the state banquet. When we'd attended the Reclaimer demonstration, he hadn't sought a copy of Geshge's contract—he'd passed me near-worthless junk paper I now realized he'd scrawled on in his own hand. Tamadza had possessed Dzaro because he'd told her of our scheme. He'd been close enough to save me from Geshge because he'd known how the shadow would affect my brother. And the crates he'd smuggled into Engineering must have come from the hovership. Must have held Reclaimers from the start.

He'd told me he loved me. And he'd played me neater than I'd ever played anyone.

"Why are you telling me this?" I spat as she sauntered towards me. Tears rolled down my cheeks. My groin burned fire from the ring's strip and her teeth.

"These guards aren't protecting you." My spine stiffened as her lips brushed my ear. "They're imprisoning you. When she's judge, Akizeké will breed you as she pleases. No one gets to win you but me."

She kissed my forehead and walked out.

I re-dressed in numb confusion: sturdy sandals and a skirt of undyed linen, a silver sash thick enough to hold weapons. *Faziz. Akizeké. Ria.* Their faces spun circles through my head. Love, hate, and raw embarrassment sliding together and laughing at me. *All broken and torn. The fate of two districts at play.*

I had to warn Ria. I had to stop Akizeké. I had to do it myself.

Lifting my mother's baton, I marched out onto the balcony. Starlings whirled around my shadow.

"Stay inside, boy," said an older guard, her face kindly but stern. "It's not safe. Plenty of folk would harm a dragon."

"I'm done staying inside," I said, and fired a *njiji* dart into her stomach.

She dropped. The other guards lunged for me.

They expected this. I cursed and pressed my back to the wall. Bright essence fueled my blows. Spreading scales repelled a *njiji* dart. But it was four against one. I blocked two cuts, hit a throat with a dart—and dropped into a hissing ball as two *shikia* kissed my side. Arms seized my limbs and wrenched my head backward.

"Careful, boy," said another guard, helping her *njiji*-struck, stumbling colleague to sit. "Akizeké wants you safe. You're lucky to be hers."

I don't belong to her. Shadow flickered over the sun. Dark leather, a crow's flight, a figure sliding down a zipline from the statue of the triumphant soldier. My treacherous heart twisted. *Dzkegé's mercy, I still want to belong with him!*

A whistling throwing star sliced deep through a guard's spine. My captors cursed and spun to face him, dropping me. I lowered my shoulder and barreled into the nearest, knocking her off the balcony. My mother's baton flashed up to block a blow from their captain—who dropped, spitting blood, as Faziz flipped off the winch and ran her through.

"Didn't look like you wanted them touching you, Red Eyes. You okay?" He drew his sword free and flung the dying guard over the edge.

Blood streaked his dark smiling cheek. The sun's heat sparked off his naked sword. Sweat fanned his long hair into a cloud. Dressed for battle in an armored leather vest and black leggings, the world slowed around him. Beauty with power all its own.

He took my breath away.

"You're safe." He wrapped his arms around me, cupping my face to his shoulder. His breath washed my skin, ash, fire and concrete. A bandage on his wrist covered a new addition to his tattooed record of failings. "It's okay. If you're not safe here, I'll hide you in the Slatepile. If you're not safe there, I'll take you to the planet's edge and beyond."

He offers it so easy. And I so want to lean on him. Somehow, he made that easy. A tie lay between us, something cosmic and terrifying, that could carry love, rage, despair—but never scorn. Never condemnation. He touched my soul as deeply as my god.

He split me open.

"I spoke with Iradz," I said. "Akizeké was conspiring with Tamadza. You knew all along. You helped them."

He dropped me and stepped backwards. Sunlight dimmed from his eyes. "I didn't know about the Hive bombing. Or what Akizeké and Tamadza packed in those crates. They used me and my crew to run errands, spy on *dzaxa,* smuggle weapons—and then they tried to kill me to cover their sins!"

"So you confess?" I said, voice flat.

"The Slatepile folk are dying by the hundreds. Only power can protect them—and to take power in War means trading all you are. As the legitimate lord of the Slatepile, I could have pushed the *dzaxa* to restore rent control. That's millions spared from poverty's crush. I made a deal with Akizeké to transform Victory Street. I would have paid almost any price, but I draw the line at genocide. That's why I went to your father!"

He decided better Vashathke win than her. Answers fit. I didn't care. "So I'm also part of your acceptable price? You played with me, with my wanting to be loved! Like Zega, Iradz, and my mother. 'Happiness starts with opening up to people—' but you weren't open to me. Maybe you switched sides, and you didn't know about the Hive bombing, but you let me stumble around blind. Did you laugh to know you held power over me? Did Akizeké tell you to seduce me? Is our connection only a leash to control me? You said we were soulmates!"

"Then it shouldn't surprise you I played my own game!" He paused. Drew a deep breath. Unclenched his fists and continued. "I told myself I'd do whatever it took to enthrone Akizeké, and then that I'd pay any price to stop her. You swore you'd made those same sacrifices to stop your father. But loving you changed everything. I deceived you on Akizeké's orders—but I flirted with you because I liked you. Then you saved my life, forgave me against reason, and things changed. I wanted to fight for a better world, one where I could be with you. And I didn't know how to tell you without breaking your trust."

"Consider my trust broken." Blinking past tears, I pressed against the wall like the sandstone could protect me. Like anything could protect me from someone who could shred my heart with the lightest touch. "Gods, we're such wretched souls. How could we change the world, with such bile inside us?"

He recoiled. "Listen to me. The *dzaxa* deserve your hate. It's not evil to rage against real monsters, even if they're the pillars holding up your world. It's the noblest thing of all—if you bend that anger to the right cause. Help me stop Akizeké. She's the threat today, not your father. Help me reclaim Victory Street for its people."

"I can't be on the heroes' side." I laughed, my soul twisting like a banner on the wind. "I was wrong about Akizeké, about Zega, and innocent people have already died. I belong to my mistakes. They're written in my eyes, as yours are tallied on your skin."

"I did wrong," he whispered. "I'd give my soul to fix it."

Enough. Protect myself. I'd broken things with Ria. He'd broken things with me. Trusting only hurt me. No path led to my happiness. "Get out. Join Dzaro's defenders, or hide below the Slatepile. I never want to see your face again. I've got to help Ria."

CHAPTER TWENTY-SIX
Skygarden

23rd *Reshi*, Year 92

"The gods once gathered the worthy dead in their golden beyond, a realm of healing, light, and miracles. But now the souls of our loved ones flee into grey, lest the greatest shadow trap them in life."—Priesthood's End, a Scholarly District text reserved for philosophers

"Break my heart, leave my love dead/I'll wander forever away."—'Wanderer', by Fezeof, popular song of Year 82 Rarafashi

The stabbing loss in my chest—lodged beside the wound Zega had carved eight years ago—left my magic slipping from my grasp. *I showed Faziz my true self, and he turned my trust against me.* Fear kept me human, vulnerable and slow. Even cursing Vashathke didn't draw my power free in anger. Loathing for my own mistakes contaminated the swift purity of my rage.

I ran up Victory Street on foot, head tucked low, checking

for stalkers over my shoulder. Bitter irony made it safe for a man—a dragon—to walk out alone. Fear had emptied the great sandstone way. A crowd only gathered by the blockade at the Slatepile's foot, where Dzaro's guards and Faziz's undercroft folk joined uneasy ranks. Advancing Engineers stared them down with purple-rimmed eyes.

They needed their High Master.

My bright hands found hidden grips in the Palace's walls. I climbed through thin air, rising level with Skygarden's lowest talon. With a twist and grunt of effort, I leapt the gap. My fingernails sank into steel. I clambered into an entry port near the steel dragon's tail.

My heart aching with each hovership fusillade, I snuck through the corridors to Akizeké's apartment. One of her guards fell to my *njiji* dart, the other I dropped with a blow to the head. I rolled them into a maintenance shaft; then, on my knees, pushed a finger through the steel wall and peered in.

"I don't understand!" Ria twisted against the silk cords binding her. Relief spun my head at the sight of her. "You said you respected the Fire Weavers!" Her voice cracked. Strain greyed her face. Bruises lingered on her jaw and stomach.

She's been almost completely drained. My stomach flipped. *She's been fighting off shadow for hours.*

Akizeké jabbed Tamadza's staff in Ria's face. The purple holdshadow rose pulsed like an infected wound. A Reclaimer hummed in the corner. "I respect you deeply, High Master. Join me, and your order will prosper under my patronage."

"You expect my support? You allied with Tamadza to kill us!"

"The Fire Weavers discover and explore. You can do that still when I rule your district. But you'll stay within bounds. No calling debt collectors on me or building bridges and crossways on our streets. You'll fill my bank account, not the other way around. Jadzia's balance must be restored. I don't like violence, but the Treaty of Inversions has held us back too long. It's time we chose our own rulers once more. Leaders who can restore our former glory."

I would have laughed if I didn't need the silence to shield me. Akizeké was arrogant, as was I, as was every red-eyed *dzaxa* in War. So assured she was born for greatness that she'd never questioned her own value. But underneath her arrogance lay empty, hapless, din.

"War's glory," Tożätupé spat. Akizeké had bound her to the futon. The heir to Engineering lay half-drained of her essence, hair limp and voice wavering. "The world's better with War's glory dead."

"Shut your fucking mouth." Akizeké drove her foot into Tożätupé's chest. Bones broke. Tożätupé moaned. "I won't take orders from—damn you!" The staff spat radiant sparks, wrenching snakelike against Akizeké's grip as Tamadza's soul resisted. "Be still! You're mine to command. Bow, necromancer!"

The staff spat once more. Akizeké growled and struck it against the wall. Sweat glistened on her brow. She straightened and glowered at her prisoners. "Who's first for another taste of shadow?"

"Let them go, Akizeké." Faziz slid through a back entrance. Hope lit Ria's eyes as they found him. I wanted to scream a warning. *He'll break you.*

"My lost boy returns." Akizeké chuckled, and poked the staff into his jaw. "Missing my warm arms? Or still trying to glean a lordship?"

"I'm not fool enough to expect gifts or tenderness after you killed twenty of my people and nearly killed me."

"The world can't know who sent the Reclaimers to Engineering. I need it to look like Vashathke's people stole the crates and used Geshge's company to move them." Akizeké shrugged. "When I'm enthroned, I'll make Koreshiza breathe essence to replace what's destroyed on my rise."

At her promise to force me, Faziz tightened his jaw. "Let

Ria and Tożätupé go, and I'll withdraw my fighters from
the Slatepile. Lady Dzaroshardze's defenders will be easily
broken then. You'll have the massacre on Victory Street
you'll need to justify your conquest."

"Good to have you back, Faziz." Akizeké grinned. "But
I'm not Koreshiza. I'm not fool enough to trust you."

With a sweep of the staff, she knocked his legs from beneath
him. He fell on his back, cursing as his head struck steel.
Shadows wheeled from the Reclaimer, gathering around the
staff as Akizeké spun it like a spindle. With a triumphant
grin, she rammed its tip down his throat.

Faziz convulsed—once, sharply—as shadows tore through
his chest. Dark circles bloomed under his eyes. Cool amethyst
undertones crept beneath his gold, polishing old scars from
his chest and arms. The hard lines of his shoulders and
abdomen sharpened like chiseled onyx. His hair flowed back
like a river as he stood and bowed gracefully before her.

"*Dzaxa*," he breathed, his voice a whisper of brass and
calling bells. His eyes deep and unfathomable as endless
night. "What do you bid?"

She'd snuffed out his soul like a candle.

"Be mine." Akizeké wrapped her arms around his neck
and pulled him into a kiss. "Fight beside me. Be loyal. Be
everything I need." He melted unresisting into her. Fear and
sick loathing screamed in my ears. *I will break Akizeké for
this. I will shred her soul to ribbons.*

I'd told him I'd never wanted to see his face again, but
that hadn't been true. I'd done what trauma had trained me,
pushed away the author of my pain. If I'd had time, space,
one nerve left undamaged from this awful day, I would have
said what I meant: *Wait. This hurts me. To be together, we
must find a better way.*

I needed to stop this. I needed to save him. I wasn't ready
to let go.

"Fuck you," Ria spat. "This is sick."

"I didn't want your opinion," Akizeké said. "I'm going back to my hovership. Take this time to consider my offer, High Master. I've a throne to inherit and a conquest to plan." She forced Toźátupé off the couch, holding the staff to her neck. "Try anything funny and I'll force more shadow down your girlfriend's throat."

I scrambled back into shadows as Akizeké stalked past, her chin arched and proud, Faziz gliding by her side.

Shit. Shit. Shit. I scrambled through the door, heart leaping into my lungs. Ria sagged against the wall, panting, worn to her soul. My heart skipped.

"It's okay." I cupped my hand to her temple. She hiccupped a sob into my palm. "Let me tithe to you. Let me heal you."

"Please just hold me."

I did. My body shook with her every gasped cry. My lungs ached as she trembled in my arms. I should unbind her. I should help her to stand. But if I let go, I didn't think she'd ever touch me again.

"The shadow said it would show me my father. If I let it have me, it would weave me an eternal dream where the Hive never fell. Where I wasn't in charge. Where I hadn't failed anyone. I wanted it so bad. More than I wanted to be High Master. More than I wanted to fight back. I almost fell."

"You're still here." I stroked her hair. "It's okay."

"How can it be okay when what we had is broken? I fell in love with a caring, kindhearted boy. I tried to make him my anchor as the shadow ripped through my mind. But he was a façade, and the shadow struck deep, and... I remembered my father, and held on for the love of him, but he's gone. I need to love someone living, vital and real. I need you. And I'm not even sure who you are."

"I didn't know who I was. Not for a very long time." I worked the ties on her hands, letting essence fall from my tongue to her cheek. Filling her. Healing her. My life's tale came out as I unraveled the knots, every bloody footstep

I'd trodden from the Prizeheron to the Palace and beyond. I couldn't speak the truth and meet her eyes.

"So let me get this right," Ria said when I finished. "Your mom sells you into an engagement for a plush job when you're six years old. Rarafashi learns your mom is this loose end that could endanger her and Vashathke's baby-snatching plot, brands her to shut her up. Your ex-girlfriend beats you up, robs your dying mom, and tries to abduct you, and you accidentally kill her trying to get away. Your ex-boyfriend drains all your essence, and so you sleep with his wife—which is literally the only reaction any sensible person would expect eighteen-year-old Koré to have—and your ex-fiancée tries to coerce you into an abusive relationship, so you flip the tables on her and seize an opportunity to make your own life. Where in this story is the big, terrible thing that's all your fault?"

"I'm the thread that draws it together," I said. "I exist because my father hungers for power. I could never even make my own parents love me. How can so much be about me without it being my fault? I knew you'd leave me once you learned the truth, and yet I hid it from you. I exposed and mocked your deepest shame before the judge's court, and now Victory Street is on fire!"

"At least it helps me understand why you're being such an ass." Her hand slipped free and shoved my shoulder. Dulled as she was, I couldn't tell if she'd meant it to hurt. "Believe me, I wish we'd uncovered Akizeké's plot sooner, but what she's chosen to do is on her, not us."

"And what I've chosen to do is on me."

"Koré, I did everything in my power to earn the world's respect—and then the moment you needed protection, I humiliated myself before Rarafashi's court and confessed to a crime I never committed. Because I love you. And I understand now, even if you don't—you're not just involved in this because you hate your father. You love Victory Street.

You love Jadzia, and everyone in it, and you know they deserve better leaders than they have."

I bit my lip. "I never thought of it that way."

"I'm pissed and hurt—but that's on a personal level. The shit that's your fault, you did because you care about this place. I just want to know if you also care about me. Like, I'm still not sure if you got close to me because you liked me or because I could help you get endorsements for Akizeké."

"Both," I admitted. "I've felt so many heartbreaks. I could only bring myself to let you in by telling myself it was all a grand scheme. But I loved you from the first time we spoke. And that terrified me. Because love would mean showing the world my magic, and it would also mean showing you my shame."

"You think I'd ever be ashamed of you? The day we met, I threw up on your skirt!"

"But that's you, Ria. I'm just me."

"Yeah, because we're so damn different." She rolled her eyes. "We both expect way too much of ourselves. You're just better than me at hiding how that hurts. And I can't help if you're not open with me."

"Let me help you now." Regret stirred in me, damp and heavy, weakening my embers of power. My tongue shaped puffs of essence into tiny drifting clouds. *Too little.* But my own essence store glimmered like sunlight under my skin, and the bittersweet pleasure of holding her for one last time tugged on it.

I surrendered to the sheer joy of touching her. One last time. As my lips brushed her sweaty throat, I gave, and gave, and trusted she wouldn't abuse what I'd offered. Trusted my gentle, hesitant touches wouldn't sting like a monster's claws.

Magic swam between us, sure as sunrise, waking her flesh. At last, she grunted, and kicked through the ties on her ankles and knees. My bones cried in pain as she pulled away.

I might never touch her again. But I'd never stop loving her.

"What's going on out there?" She turned her *opesero* on Akizeké's Reclaimer, devouring it in flames.

I related everything. The defenders holding the Slatepile. The enthralled Engineers marching into battle against their will. What we'd learned from the Lost District envoys, especially the slim, unreliable hope Akizeké's will wouldn't completely break Tamadza's.

"The ground assault is bad enough," I finished, fighting to think of strategy instead of my fractured heart. "But that hovership's cannons could flatten Victory Street in a few hours. We need Skygarden to counter it. Only a judge can activate its weapons."

"Rarafashi's dying. She'll summon Akizeké soon." Ria straightened. "I have a plan."

I could sense where this was going. "Absolutely not."

"This is bigger than one throne. One street, one district. Our world is broken. No single step can fix it." She took my hands. "If we do this, we'll survive today. And we'll have the rest of our lives before us to change everything. Can you give me your trust?"

My fingers ran along the warm, ancient gold of her *opesero*. I remembered the weight of the one she'd offered me in the Surrender, months ago. *Trust.* The old knot of anger pulsed in my breastbone, demanding vengeance. But I clenched my fists and bade it quiet.

I knew what mattered most. I knew what I fought for.

And I would do anything to equal the love she'd shown me.

The Dzaxashigé family prison cells lay in the steel dragon's spine. Bolts from the hovership's cannons had chewed through the walls, leaving holes with red-hot shattered edges. The guards had fled, but electrum snakes still curled around woman-tall holdfast locks, judging us with slitted eyes.

"Stand back, asshole!" Ria shouted. An ice fist smashed the lock on my father's cell. The door swung free.

With a desperate shout, Vashathke flung himself towards the light.

"Nope!" Ria's bracers crackled. Manacles of ice locked around his lower body, pinning him still. "I don't want to deal with this gasbag any longer than I have to. He's all yours, Koré."

Soon I'll be all his. I stepped into the cell, my heart beating like it would leap from my throat. Ria closed the door.

"Hello, dragon." He spat at my feet. "Did you fuck Dzkegé's shade? That's the only reason she would have chosen you."

No. There's more. As broken as I was, I'd come to do right. *Maybe Dzkegé chose me because she knew how much I'd willingly give.*

I donned a courtly, mocking smile. Showing him I had leverage. "Hello, Father. This feels strange, but I'm here to bargain instead of breaking your teeth."

"A bargain?" His eyes glinted. "You'll consider it wasn't me who attacked the Hive?"

I rolled my eyes. *Classic Vashathke. Always striving to be trash.* "I'll consider you stood between Ria and her justice." Quickly, I outlined a plan more like madness than strategy. Sweat rolled down my neck with every passing second.

"You think I'll strike a bargain that requires I make peace with Engineering? They killed Geshge."

"I killed Geshge." I spat the confession like bile. *Geshge wasn't your precious obedient good son either.* "You'll always be free to take vengeance on me."

If rage had a face, it was his. Vashathke looked like he'd shatter the world for a handful of silver. I knew that feeling. I'd control him with it.

I'd accepted the consequences of shapeshifting before Rarafashi's court. My enslavement to the state was a foregone conclusion. But I could choose my master. And I could shield Ria from his wrath.

"Give me twenty-four hours to save Victory Street and

my dear ones," I said firmly. "Then my body and power are yours. As will be everything you've wished for."

His eyes narrowed. "Done. Though it kills me."

Vashathke didn't meet Ria's eyes as she unwove him from the ice. None of us spoke as we three raced to the courtroom. Guards jumped as we turned the corner. Ria clapped two in icy prisons, knocking back the third with a net of lightning. An alarm bell shrieked.

"I'll guard the door. Act fast, Koré." She pointed her *opesero* at my father. "Move, fuckhead, and I incinerate you."

"I lied about attacking the Hive," Vashathke said. "Didn't you hear?"

"Why do you think you're still alive? But you can't be trusted with power. Not where my district is concerned."

I ducked from the two of them and threw myself into the empty courtroom. *I need a weapon.* The dragons' sword hovered above the judge's throne. Patterns of light swam through its blade. A thousand shimmering scales. A hundred winking red eyes.

Be kind to me. I gathered all my strength and leapt. The glass case shattered under my fist. My blood washed my palm as I took the hilt.

Time froze. A thousand screams broke across my mind, howling and clawing for attention. *Thijo ka Dzkegé. Shiké nkzi. Fidzregé. Shiké fidzregé.* Dragon. Liar. Red-eyed liar. I hung mid-leap, electrocuted and erect, as spectral dragons punched through my chest, raising scale where they passed.

Then the world moved. I slammed into the steel seat of the judge. The sword burned in my hand, hot and punishing as an open flame. *Fidzregé. Liar.* Their words clawed with phantom talons. *Want to claim us? Pay the price.*

Faziz had taught me confidence with weapons, but this was nothing like my baton. *I'm one of you,* I thought, pleading against pain. *Ivé xefith xe. Ivé—*

Fidzregé. Voices coalesced into a shimmering whole. A soldier strode forward, carved from starlight and holdfast. Glaive held high, armored skirt battered and dented, eyes gold like rising planets. *A dragon and a Dzaxashigé both. Pay your bloodline's price. Admit and accept the truth of your soul.*

"Great Dzkegé," I gasped at the flickering icon. "Have mercy on me. I only need the blade for a trick. I don't want to fight."

Another lie. Strength and pity both swept her eyes. *I'm not the one who's hurting you, Koreshiza Brightstar. There's no middle ground left to clutch at. You can't both hide and live true. Be brave. You're the only one who can set himself free.*

In a wink of light, she dissolved back into the sword.

The burning ebbed, though the sword did try to jerk from my hand as I staggered out. Ria stood witness as my father gripped the hilt. His back arched in pain as his fingers met metal.

"Swear you'll uphold the Treaty of Inversions and never start a war, and I'll know it's true," Ria said. "Swear, or no deal."

"I swear." Vashathke's eyes bored into mine, hard and punishing as a whip's cut. "As long as I live, I'll uphold the treaty and never start a war. Can I put this thing down?"

A shout of 'thieves!' rolled down the corridor. Ria swore and kicked a hole in the wall. "Try to keep up, boys. We need to move fast."

Access tunnels and secret passageways riddled Skygarden's heart, known to servants and the Engineers who'd worked their blood into the metal beast. Ria led us through narrow paths lined with substance rainbows and cracked screens spilling readouts in Old Jiké. Her bracer blasted through debris and twisted metal blocking our way.

We stepped out into noon air flush with rose perfume. Gravel paths cut through the judge's garden, weaving elegant loops past holdlife trenchers of giant blossoms. Guards patrolled in tight courses, batons sparking bright. Ria ducked low, watching—then waved us forward. We sprinted down the tangled paths.

Rarafashi's private chamber lay at the garden's heart. Bronto-sized rose petals cast her bed in shade. Glass and copper fountains filled a moat about her. Beneath her brocades and silks, the judge looked small. Withered. Half-devoured. Her bronzework crown rested in her hands. Beneath her bare breasts, her chest fluttered with every labored breath.

"Honored Rarafashi," Ria said. "As High Master of the Fire Weavers, I withdraw my endorsement from Magistrate Akizeké and give it to your shithead husband. So, you know. She doesn't have enough to qualify anymore. You've been informed."

Rarafashi squinted at her. "Guards?" she called, a note as clear as crystal.

Ria shook her head and turned to me. "I'll hold them off. Five minutes max."

"Take this." I offered my mother's baton. She took the scallop-patterned shaft with a firm nod. Fire sprang into her palm as she strode back down the path.

"What are you doing here, Vasha?" Confused tears swam into Rarafashi's eyes as the two of us approached our judge. "I thought I chose Akizeké. Where is she? Why does your bastard have my sword?"

My father knelt and took her hand. "All's well, dearest. Your dragon lives. War will have its essence. Your legacy is secure."

"Stupid boy. I see that hovership off our bow. I hear cannons and fighting on the Slatepile. You brought this on us, Vasha, with your cruel and thoughtless words. You lacked the sense to step aside and let Akizeké claim her rightful place."

"I gave everything for a chance at your throne. My body.

My heart. My children. I painted my soul bloody. You knew so much of what I'd done, but you still thought me biddable. You should have known I would die before handing my reward to someone who had everything else given to her."

Rarafashi laughed, a sly chuckle like the pulse of a failing supernova. "This again. I should invest you as judge because you're a disadvantaged man?"

"You should invest me because I shaped my soul for this. My sex isn't the point in my favor—it's the one thing that blinds you—"

"You should invest him," I interrupted, "because he's the only qualified candidate now. I'm the herald of our god. I have a voice in this process. Vashathke has my endorsement, and more. Invest him, or War loses its last hope of essence." I propped the sword's pommel against my foot and rested its tip on my breastbone. "I only have to fall forward."

Her eyes narrowed. "A bluff."

"Is that what our ancestors said when they turned Skygarden's guns against the Temple District?" She flinched, vulnerable still to the sharp knife of truth. "The dragons of old didn't surrender, and neither will I. Better I bleed out on their blade than let Akizeké ascend. At least my blood will flow honestly."

"He's a loyal son," Vashathke said, a shushing, calming note hovering under his breath, "and his mind is breaking. He fears Akizeké will enslave him should she take the throne. She's already debased him just to throw his whoredom in my face."

"She knows I'm the dragon!" I wailed. I knew how Vashathke would spin this, and I knew how to sing harmony. *Dzkegé's mercy, if he wasn't such a monster, we could have changed the world together.* "If Akizeké has the judge's power, she'll breed me and never put my babies in my arms!"

"Akizeké's a well-respected magistrate," Rarafashi said. "Don't fear, Koreshiza. She'd never hurt a boy."

"He's hysterical," Vashathke said. "Spilling seed does that

to a fragile mind. I'm to blame for choosing my career over my firstborn."

"It's not your fault, Father!" I sobbed. "Rarafashi would have never let you choose me. She hurt you!"

"Rarafashi never hurt me. She and I are from different generations, but we've always been fond of each other. She's a better wife than I deserve." He stroked the judge's fingers. A single tear rose to his eye. I wondered how long he'd practiced that move. "You hear him, dearest? He's deluded. Petrified of all women. I've never asked you for anything. But here, at the end, I beg you ease my son's troubled mind."

"Your son?" The perfect, wizened arch of her lower lip faltered.

I bent forward, letting the sword prick my skin. Rivulets of blood trickled down my chest. My heart raced like a raptor's step. I didn't know if this would work, or what would happen after.

But only by enthroning Vashathke could we bring Skygarden to defend Victory Street and deny Akizeké her prize.

"My son," Vashathke repeated. "My baby. Dzkegé chose him. She saw the true light of his soul, the light I nearly crushed by my own ambition. Please, give me a chance to be the father I should have been all along. To him. To War. To our people."

Every syllable of his spiked into my angry breast. They were the words he might speak if he loved me. But alone, words were empty and dead. If Vashathke loved like true hearts should, I never would have drawn breath.

Rarafashi squeezed his hand until his bones moved. He didn't cry out. "Swear you'll protect the dragon. For War. For our future."

"I swear on the blood of my beloved Geshge."

My father's eyes flickered to mine. Pure scarlet triumph.

The air rang. A soundless note hit me like I stood inside

a bell. Rarafashi fell, dull, shriveled and lifeless. Vashathke raked me with the condemning glare of a judge.

It felt like stepping on the sun. The sword dropped from my hands. I collapsed to my knees, longing to kiss the gravel in supplication—but I couldn't take my eyes off him. His arms and back, corded with enough lean muscle to push the world off its axis. The chiseled lines of his abdomen and hips, flowing as he stepped towards me, like they were carved from liquid diamond. A smile so cool it sucked heat from the world. *Bow and worship the Judge of War.*

He caressed my forehead with fingers strong enough to push through to my brain. "Well," he said, his baritone a rich brass symphony. "Shall we begin?"

I stared up into my own cruel mirror. The only thing separating me from him was my own utter weakness.

In twenty-four hours, I'd be his forever.

CHAPTER TWENTY-SEVEN
The skies above Victory Street

1ˢᵗ *Zdz,* Year 1 Vashathke

"I have not gone, Dread Judge Below. Another wields my potent soul. A white-fisted soldier with closed ears and an iron will. She spreads our shadow, though she know it not. Forever may we reign."—words carved in the hovership's iron side by unknown enthralled Engineer

THE STEEL ORB of the war room, barely large enough for a thousand souls, lay beneath Skygarden's heart. Dust and ancient sorrows drifted in the air. Screens swam with Old Jiké glyph poems, so intricately knotted I could only read one word in ten. Cool quiet raised bumps up my arms.

Holdlights activated as my father crossed the floor. Battered diodes flashed red warning. He eyed screens, puzzling through instructions meant only for a bright judge, and sat on the steel wire throne. Ancient weapons systems threaded light into his skin, marking him with a mantle of spiraling curls. Skygarden, testing his mettle.

A silver and holdfast circlet sparkled on his golden brow.

Deep engines hummed as his fingers flew across controls. Guards bowed in silent supplication as they entered, taking defensive positions along the walls. No one could doubt Vashathke was the judge of us all.

Traitor, whispered my mother's memory. *You promised me this one thing—vengeance—and failed at the last.*

This is bigger than you, I told myself. *Bigger than me. This is about the world and the wonderful people I need to save it for.*

"Your dad looks comfy," Ria said at my elbow. "How are you doing?"

"Fine," I lied. The dragons' sword, tied over my back with my silver sash, whispered *fidzregé, fidzregé, untrue.* Its magic pricked needles down my spine. But I couldn't share this pain with Ria. I'd lost my right to ask for her comfort.

"*Jadzxo ijireja,*" Vashathke commanded. Pictures of the hovership flooded the screens. Quiet as death, it rested off the Surrender's shoulder, cannons firing at the defenders on the Slatepile. Electronic-edged screams filled the war room.

"Ensure the outer decks are clear before engaging battle mode," Ria told my father. "You swore on the sword. Don't fire on the innocent."

"I remember, High Master. Save your lectures for Akizeké." Vashathke scanned the images. "All clear. *Jaji, zrixo.*"

Skygarden purred. Screens showed the building flexing like flesh. The floor shook. Ria and I locked arms as holdweight strips kicked on, bracing us with artificial gravity.

The steel dragon spat fire.

I felt it in my bones as white fire bathed the hovership's hull. Heat washed back through the war room's walls. Metal cried Skygarden's release.

Vashathke grinned. "*Dzaz zrixo.*" *Again.*

Ria squeezed my arm tight. "What's happening on the Slatepile?"

"*Naxo jadzo!*" I called. Screens changed. Vashathke's glare hit me like a bullet.

Armies clashed on shattered slate, flowing around impact craters and the bodies of the fallen. At the battle's heart, Dzaro urged her guards forward. Gore-jawed hounds stalked her feet. Massive holes marked her lines where Faziz's folk had withdrawn. My breath caught.

"Dzaro will hold the assault off the street," Ria said. "If anyone can contain this, it's her."

Żeposháru Rena topped the Slatepile in a chariot pulled by metal insects. Blood spattered her clothes. Dark circles gleamed beneath uncomprehending bright eyes. Her whiplike arms swung a brass scythe.

Dzaro and her dogs charged to meet her.

My gut twisted. "I'll be right back."

Vashathke opened his mouth—but he must have remembered the twenty-four hours I'd bought, because he swiftly closed it. Ria's eyes found mine, welling with hurt, anger, and a thousand unsaid words.

"Don't die," was all she told me.

I ran from the chamber and leapt from the first balcony I found.

My wings threw sunlight as they bit the air. My long neck and tail arched like a bow. I soared into the swift upstreet wind, stroking against hot air, rising high and stiff. Shouts and pleas rose from the Slatepile. *Dragon! Thijo! Ferifo!* and *Koreshiza! Koreshiza!*

I roared bright defiance. Essence flooded from my throat, filling Dzaro's scattered defenders. They cheered, banging steel batons on their makeshift siege barricades. I shrieked a triumphant reply, whipped my tail, and spun against the sky.

"Koreshiza! Koreshiza! The young dragon!" Not a note rang false. *Cheering on a courtesan, a murderer, and a liar.* Because I was more. Their sign, hope, and promise. A chance for fresh essence and a world born anew.

I need to be worthy of their hopes.

A hot whistling rush tore the air. I pulled in my wings, spiraling down in a wide arch. The cannon bolt went wide. For one shimmering heartbeat, I rose effortlessly—and then came the dart. I backflapped. The sickly green missile fell short of my leg. *Njiji* toxin.

Akizeké was firing to tranquilize. She wanted me alive.

Steel clashed on bronze as Żeposháru Rena drove Dzaro backwards, her scythe blurring through close strikes my aunt sweated to block. A dog tore at the judge's hip. Żeposháru Rena cursed and swung at its neck. Bronze glinted. Dzaro screamed, throwing herself before the blow—

My fire bathed her side. Moving like lightning, Dzaro twisted the scythe from Żeposháru Rena's grip and locked the other woman in a wrestler's hold.

"Keep up the fight, kid!" she shouted as I pivoted past.

A phalanx of Engineers broke over a ridge. I filled their ranks with silver fire. Some shook free the shadow, purple rings shrinking beneath their eyes. They shouted reason; turned weapons to restrain their fellows. Enthralled ranks washed around them, knocking them down.

It's not enough, I thought, despairing.

"Take out the ship!" Dzaro shouted as a rain of iron cannonballs punched deep into slate. "It's ripping us apart!"

I mounted higher, my wings stroking strong as the thermals caught me up. The hovership's holdweight faces ran melted from Skygarden's breath, though the craft still defied gravity and the cannons still spat. Engineers, dead and living, crowded the upper deck. Crossbow bolts and bullets pinged off my scales, stinging where they hit flesh.

I clenched my jaw and rammed the ship's stern.

Iron creaked. Silver snowflakes and flowers swam through dark metal and vanished. I struck again, ramming my whole weight into a fractured divot. Substance cracked and hissed. The hovership faltered. I flapped backwards, bracing for a final strike.

Steel clicked at my back. Heat built. An electrum reflection swam through the dark iron.

Skygarden's fire. I pivoted left.

A crossbow thrummed as Vashathke released his own fire. A meter-length *njiji* dart sank into my chest.

Sedative flooded my veins. All went dark as I crashed into the deck.

VISIONS CLAWED THROUGH my head. Ria, turning away from me. My mother, slumped in an alley. Gei-dzeo's shattered skull. A red ocean running from the Slatepile onto Victory Street and down to the sea.

Sense returned with a cold pricking. My eyes fluttered open. A low-ceilinged chamber surrounded me, blue braziers lining its corrugated walls, silver snowflakes lacing its iron floor. My bare human back pressed against an ice pillar, to which holdfast chains bound me as fast as a caged starling. All I wore was the silver sash holding the dragons' sword.

Fidzregé, it whispered to my stuttering heart. *Dzzexoz.* Liar. Free yourself.

"I don't know how," I said.

Gold glinted. I turned my head.

Akizeké entered in the Shaper's ancient armor. Steel scales made her skirt; a roaring dragon's head wreathed her breastplate. She held the golden sword in one hand, the shield and Tamadza's staff in the other. Though she used the necromancer's tool, her eyes were unmarked by the shadow's kiss. Her grin, glorious triumph and mastery, was all her own. She controlled Tamadza like a raptor on a lead.

As she controlled the man walking behind her.

Demure and tamed like some heretic's image of a male god, Faziz stood with his head bowed, midnight-river hair sliding liquid past his shoulders. Kohl lined his long eyes; glitter washed the smooth-shaved hollows of his cheeks and neck.

The mesh of amber snowflakes draped across his violet silk skirt clattered with each step he took. His left breast bore Akizeké's snowflake seal, painted in bright gold.

He still held his sword, but his eyes didn't meet mine. His metallic lip paint was smeared half to the side.

"What have you done to him?" I spat.

"Not nearly as much as I'd like. Can't celebrate victory until the work's done."

"It's too late." I donned a savage grin, trying to draw her anger off him. "Rarafashi's dead. She invested Vashathke."

"So that's why Skygarden fired. It doesn't matter. Vashathke's a warmonger and a fool. War will plead for my leadership once I've brought him down." Her hand pressed against the exposed inside of my thigh. "I can give them dragons."

It felt like an enormous fist had flattened my heart. I bit my lip. Made myself go cold. "You plan to rape us both, Magistrate?"

For a heartbeat, she looked horrified. Then her brows knitted in anger. "Don't give me that. I've had Faziz before, had you half a dozen times."

"With consent. Breeding me—"

Her hand cracked across my face. I gasped and sputtered, fear stopping my words. "I won't hear moral lectures from a whore."

Faziz, still as a skyscraper, didn't react to the blow. But Tamadza's staff darkened, drawing shadows out of the air. I remembered Stonefire and laughed. If Akizeké shared one character with the dead necromancer, it was their hatred for sex objects who wouldn't shut up and be things.

I'd thought myself a monster because I couldn't please everyone who wanted me. I cared too little for what I should and too much for what I shouldn't. I'd inherited some sins, and chosen others myself. I had apologies to offer, debts to pay, and wrongs I'd never make right.

But I was no monster. Now I saw the path true monsters trod.

"Let Tożätupé go." I drew steel into my voice. "She means nothing to you."

"She'll stay in the prison cells. A daughter of a traitor's bloodline. Who would want her as their heir?"

Weakness slipped into her voice. I drove it forward to split her open. "Żeposháru Rena chose her. You couldn't make a dying woman commit to you. You hurt Tożätupé because she reminded you of your failure."

"I'm no failure. I'm a magistrate of War, and I earned that myself!"

Fool, hissed the staff. *You haven't even earned my power.*

"Die, necromancer whore!" Akizeké cracked the staff against the wall. Faziz leapt back from her rage. Shadows billowed from the holdshadow atop the staff, sinking into Akizeké's skin, all dying before they could grab her eyes. "I will break the world before my will!"

My blood went cold. Her words held nothing but iron belief in her own greatness. She needed that myth to live.

The shadow could offer nothing she wanted more than to believe she could conquer the world on her own.

The staff screamed, a jagged, high note running my bones. I craned back against the ice, fighting fruitlessly to block my ears—then the sound died. The staff stilled.

"I knew I could do it." Akizeké laughed. "Now, Tamadza. Down into the breach. Reap the dead from War and Engineering. Make them fight. I want casualties in the tens of thousands. War should win, but only just. They should be punished for millennia of softness."

The shadow of Tamadza's soul billowed free from the substance rose. She arched against the ceiling, spread through walls, monstrously tall. Akizeké swept the staff about her head. The shadow plummeted down to the conflict below.

The old necromancer's laughter died from the air. All that remained was Akizeké's grin.

"You think you're so great?" I spat. "You might have the will to break Shapers, but you can't face the truth about yourself. Draw the dragons' sword and tell me how righteous you are."

She stared at the hilt, hanging loose in the sash over my shoulder. Her hand reached out—and faltered, curling into a fist.

"Vashathke could touch it," I said. "He's braver than you. Smarter than you. He'll win."

She grabbed my hair and forced my eyes down to meet her own. "I didn't understand why Dzkegé chose you. But now I know. You're her coronation gift to me." The rim of her shield struck my stomach. Her fist coiled around my penis. I screamed. "Shut up!"

The ship lurched sideways. I swung in my chains. Akizeké slammed into the far wall beside Faziz. She hooked the staff around his chest.

"More Skygarden bombardment," she spat. "I'm going to the deck to shoot Vashathke's palace from the air." She marched through the door. Faziz followed, not meeting my eyes as he slammed the chamber door.

Shoot his palace from the air. Tears stung hot in my eyelids. My chest shook with useless rage. Akizeké meant it. She'd bring Skygarden down on Victory Street, killing millions, for a throne she'd destroy on impact. She'd send Tamadza's shadow to make the dead bow, an army of admiring puppets. Never before had the veins of anger run so swift and pure in me. I knew what I needed to do, what Victory Street needed me to be. Stopping Akizeké was my one path forward and I was chained in a cage.

"Koré!" The door rattled. Ria cursed. Ice laced through iron. The door exploded inward.

She was covered in bone ash and gunpowder residue. Her

hairbands were gone, and her curls floated in a burnt halo around her head. Bruises lined her round jaw; the hem of her skirt was shredded and singed. Her smile cut like the dragons' sword. I'd never seen anyone so beautiful. *The master of Jadzia's secrets. The fire of the new day.*

Her *riasero* flashed white-blue, and the ice pillar crumbled. I sank to my knees as the chains fell loose.

"Tożátupé's being held below," I said, guessing Ria had come after her.

"Okay. How are you?"

"Me?"

"Yes, you." She reached for my arm, then hesitated. "Can I touch you?"

I flung my arms around her. She hugged me back, holding me like a treasure, a trust. Like I deserved protection. *I do. I deserve to be kept safe. I'm not like my father and I never have to be.* "You came for me. After everything."

"Of course I did. I owe you for, like, a third of my best orgasms."

My laughter surged weakly and died. I couldn't squeeze words past the heavy block in my throat.

"I have to go kill Akizeké." Her voice wavered. "The fate of two districts rests on me. I'll do my best to also save Faziz."

"You can't go without me."

"It's dangerous." Her jaw set. "*Rodi Vorona,* you don't even have clothing on."

I slid the sash off my back, gripped the sword gingerly, and twisted the silver into a makeshift skirt. At least it fell past my ass. "You're worth the risk a thousand times over." *Here I go, bright Dzkegé. Stepping forward. Changing things. Guard me well, if you can see me from where dead gods go.*

She nodded and drew my mother's baton from her sash. "Stay behind me. If they start shooting, duck."

I pressed close to her as we ran up the iron corridor.

The clatter of bone feet and fur boots echoed around us. Protective scales washed across my arms and chest, but I knew they wouldn't stop more than a dart.

Skeletons flooded the hall, bones strung together by iron and string. Purple coal eyes stared blankly. Broken bronze swords rose high.

Ria lifted her arms. *Opesero* fire smashed the dead, a wave so hot the walls glowed orange in its wake. "Avoid melted metal," she called, and "living!" as three more Engineers rounded the corner, lowering a cannon. Fists of ice knocked them aside, though one lunged fast enough to graze her thigh with a knife. "Koré! Help!" she shouted as her blood spilled.

Dzkegé's mercy. I exhaled a puff of essence onto her, but she still looked exhausted—and worse, afraid.

"I'm with you." My lungs felt aching and empty. Dragons had limits to their fire, and Ria's cool distance strangled me. I braced myself and lifted the sword.

Liar! it screamed, thrashing against the essence tied to my soul. *Fidzregé! Liar!*

I bit my lip. *Please*, I thought. *I have a day until my father owns me. Punish me then.*

The blade's fierce howl dimmed to a chorus of taunts. As Faziz had taught, I swung it into the high cut position. Ria gave me a thumbs-up and stumbled forward once more.

Flickering braziers washed our skin lifeless blue. The chemical air was ripe with blood and fire. Muted screams echoed behind walls. The dead and living came in waves. Ria's fiery torrents turned to quick blasts; her ice fists crumbled on impact. I stabbed at skeletons that slipped into range, wedging the ancient sword through dried flesh and sinews, awkward with the long weapon in these low-roofed passages. *Not a place for a man to fight.*

"The deck's through here." Ria rapped a panel. Her voice, though worn, was commanding and firm. "I'll engage her. You'll stay behind me."

"I'm with you." Essence tuned my voice true. I meant it in my bones—if I had a choice, I'd follow her past the world's end. But the bargain I'd struck with Vashathke meant I'd linger in Skygarden's dark basements while she went on to shine. *If we even survive Akizeké's wrath.* But it had to be done, and so I'd done it. I'd chosen to do right.

Ria's fingers danced across iron. The panel dissolved. Together, we stepped onto the hovership's gore-streaked spine.

Akizeké grinned back at us. Her white-blond hair fluttered in the wind. Her armor flashed in the ship's holdlights, aloft weapons making her twin to the ancient, axe-wielding figureheads. The staff tethered her to the teeming cloud of shadows. Tamadza's laughing face swirled through the storm, lashing at the soldiers on the ground below. Her mass curtained the world in inky black, blurring the sight of damaged Skygarden listing to the hovership's side. Faziz stood still beside her, head lowered, wind stirring his hair and silken skirts. A portrait, an idol. Frozen from life.

"High Master." If Akizeké was shocked by Ria's presence, her curt nod didn't show it. "I appreciate your tenacity. This doesn't have to be ugly. Bow and acknowledge my rule."

"Fuck you." The *Sashua Vorona* glittered. Lightning tore across the sky and struck Akizeké's chest.

She took half a step backwards—then raised her sword. "Clever. But Tamadza told me how you beat her. I take a more direct approach to combat than spells and shadow."

Akizeké charged. Ria's hand arched right and left, summoning walls of ice. The magistrate's shield smashed them to glittering fragments. A second bolt of lightning cracked into Akizeké's sword arm. The air smoked. Grunting, Akizeké flung herself inside Ria's guard.

Weapons clashed with ringing power. *One. Two.* Frantic flames billowed as Ria fell back, pressed by Akizeké's bright speed. *Bright from the essence I gave her.* Fire washed off Akizeké's armored chest as her blade crashed down, deadly and powerful. My mother's baton flashed up in a last, desperate block—and shattered. Scalloped steel shards winked in the light.

Akizeké's sword scored down Ria's stomach. Red bloomed. The High Master fell.

"No!" I screamed, sweeping a clumsy cut at Akizeké's head. She parried with a flick of her wrist, laughed, and rammed her shield into my gut.

Bile flooded my throat. The world flashed red. I stumbled backward, almost tripping over Ria—and stood tall between her and the magistrate. The dragons' sword screamed in my palms. But I didn't let go.

"Koré," Ria grunted. Her blood painted the dark iron. Her hands slipped in it as she fought to stand. "Fuck off. This is between me and Akizeké." Fear wavered her voice—but it wasn't fear for herself.

"Put down the sword, boy," Akizeké said. "You've no right to it. I'll feed you shadow, and you'll join Faziz in my household."

"No." I met Akizeké's blood-red eyes and tightened my trembling grip on the sword.

"Get out of here!" Ria shouted. "Fly down!"

"No! I love you, and I'm staying." My voice broke. The sword drank truth like cool wine. All else faded save for Ria and her desperate cry. I wouldn't move. I hadn't promised my father a live dragon, anyway. Dzkegé's mercy, though—I didn't want to die. I wanted to live, for her, with her, with everyone I loved. I'd spent so long trying to hide, reject and obliterate my soul. I wanted to embrace it and live in the light.

Enough of the lies.

"I hated myself." My whisper fell on the blade, but I meant it for the world. "Victory Street taught me I was only loved for the power in my flesh. For what I could give others, not my true self. Love meant ripping out my own soul. But I'm sick of believing my abusers. I'm sick of thinking my own self wrong."

"We get it, Koré," Akizeké sighed. "You're pathetic. Be smart and give me the sword. Your petty secrets aren't a fit tithe for its power."

I grinned, my smile cracking through the debris lines on my face. "It's not secret I loathed myself, Akizeké. The sword knew that from the moment I drew it free. But here's another truth. I'm not broken. I'm terrifyingly whole, because I'm done living by the rules of monsters like you."

The blade came alive in my hands. Phantom dragons crawled up my wrist, sinking into my soul, showing me how to wield it. Wings spilled from my shoulders as I lifted the blade with practiced ease. *Ours*, it called, morphing longer to fit my grasp. *You are ours.*

Akizeké froze. After a heartbeat staring at the blade, she turned and sprinted to the ship's bow in a bright blur, dragging Faziz at her side.

"Are you okay?" I dropped down by Ria's side. *Dzkegé's mercy, so much blood!* Essence scoured my throat as I breathed on her wound. Red edges shimmered and drew together.

"I'll live," she grunted. "I know you meant it, since you were holding the sword, and it seems to be working for you. I'm sorry I made you feel you couldn't tell me the truth about what you'd been through."

"You weren't the one who made me feel that way. So many people broke my trust. So many voices told me everything I was, everything I did, was wrong. You showed me I could trust other people." As Faziz had urged me to trust my own desires. "I love you. I'm here if you want me. But I understand if you want to leave things... ended. I fucked up big."

Thought furrowed her brow. I held still. Waiting on the edge of a storm.

"You... absolutely raptor-brained fool. Why do you think I came to save you?"

"Because you're you. A champion. A hero—"

"An idiot. Chasing after a boy when neither of us know how to be a couple." She stepped over the shattered pieces of my mother's baton and took my hand. "I'm with you. We both need a shit-ton of relationship counseling, but I'm with you. Your parents and your exes treat you badly? Fuck those idiots. They're wrong. I love you. I love your laugh, your wit, your caring soul. I love how you make me feel I can do anything. I'll fight to make this work. I just need you to fight on my side."

"It's a deal," I said, and she pressed her lips to mine in a hot, blood-streaked kiss. I let myself lean into her, let her hold me up. For a blissful second, I let my fears go.

Ria bit my lip and broke backwards. Lightning flickered at her throat. Her smile mirrored mine. "Come on, baby. Let's save the world."

This is who I belong to. Not my father. Not Victory Street. I would break all the rules of law and nature to stand beside her. Half-mad with the sudden pulse of love in my chest, I followed her as she charged at Akizeké.

Across the dark iron we ran. Ria's fire streamed across the deck, skin-crisping lines locking the magistrate down on the bow. My sword swept in long, shimmering arcs. Akizeké's gold blade darted and flickered as she knocked me back, laughing as I pressed her. "What a long sword you have!" She spun behind Faziz and shoved him forward. "Let's see some hot boy-on-boy action!"

Faziz smirked at me—a sick parody of his thoughtful smile—and lunged.

Instinct he'd drummed into me, refined by the sword's power, sprang to life as I parried. Sparks flew as metal clashed on metal. Shadows swam through his blade, mirroring the light in mine—a thousand crows spiraling in flight. Wherever he'd gotten it, it had been crafted with a power to match the dragon's last gift.

He has all the power. The shadow in his veins sang to his strength and grace, forging a peerless weapon from years of training and street fights. The ancient dragons guided me through a thousand wheeling patterns—but against his unleashed mastery, I was like a lost ship in a world-storm. He struck at me in steel clamor, advancing hard and fast. *Relentless.* My arms and shoulders burned from his blows. Fear flooded my chest as my heels brushed the deck's edge. *I'll fall*—but the sky was my friend. I unfurled my wings, lightness lifting my bones, and leapt into open air.

You're learning, hummed the sword, approving, as I crashed down on Faziz from above.

Our blades locked together. We came body-to-body, sun painting liquid light from the sweat-streaked lines of our straining chests. "Please," I gasped, his breath hot on my skin, his eyes starless night. "Fight back. I don't know what the shadow promised you, but it's not worth letting Akizeké shell your home."

"The shadow promised redemption. How could I resist?" He laughed, sick and self-mocking. "Ten years, I fought to help Victory Street. It's only gotten worse. Then I made the mistake of wanting you. Someone who saw me as me, not a boss, or a symbol, or an enemy. I let my love burn me hollow."

"You didn't deceive me out of love. Only fear." All eloquence fled me. Only desperate need remained. "Please. Be brave. Don't give up."

Faziz grinned. "Who said I'm surrendering, Red Eyes?"

He punched the handle of his blade into my knuckles. Pain wrote scarlet lines through my sight. My left hand came off the hilt—but I still had a weapon. I reached over our crossed blades and locked my talons on his throat.

Faziz stilled. His pulse fluttered on my palm. "Don't, Koré. Trust me. I—" He gasped, spasmed. Like an invisible chain collar tied his throat. "It won't let me say—there's darker things than shadows. *Trust* me."

Trust him again? Let him go? *He'd hurt me.* I'd abandoned Iradz, shattered Gei-dzeo, and fled Zega's arms. *He's different.* But they'd all been different, in their own ways. No one would blame me if I opened his neck.

It's just that I love him. I couldn't be sure if love was enough. If the tie between our souls could do more than connect us— if it could bring us peace. But I had to decide. And I could trust the part of me that knew the cost of heartbreak. I would risk every betrayal before I spilled his blood.

"Take my trust," I whispered. "Take everything. Then come back to me, so we can work us out together."

I rammed my hip into his chest and flung him back down the deck. He tumbled, rolling over and over, skirt shredding on the iron hide. His sword screamed as he jammed it into the hovership's side, slowing his fall over forty feet away. Buying me an opening.

"I could use a little help here!" Ria shouted as Akizeké's sword swept inches from her neck. I screamed and charged forward. Akizeké pivoted to face me, and I hammered her until my arms burned with aftershocks. My steel clanged off her shield. Its metal rim ruptured.

"It pays to be gentle!" she shouted. "What have you learned in that brothel?"

"This!" My tail whipped behind her. The silver barb punched through the armor-joint at her elbow, piercing tender flesh below. Ria called my name. I let my tail dissolve and scrambled back as lightning lanced through the wound.

Akizeké howled, dropped her sword, and jumped backwards. Blood spattered onto metal—crimson as cheering as fine silk to my eyes. She lifted the staff. The holdshadow rose glimmered at its heart. Darkness uncoiled and serpent-struck at my chest.

"Ria!" I twisted, tried to run to her. Thick loops of smoke and shadow billowed alive around me. Like manacles, like omens, they locked around my wrists and ankles. Distant flashes of Ria's fire clawed against dark bastille. But the only soul I saw was Akizeké, grinning, as Tamadza's whispers sank inside me.

You are stronger and more cunning than Akizeké and your father combined. The shadow-Shaper's lips brushed my earlobe in a cold kiss. *Yours is the hand that shall sunder the foundations of Jadzia.*

"No," I growled. "I don't want your power."

Not power. Prophecy.

Akizeké's laughter drowned out the ghost. "I knew I'd win!" Her smile widened, white and blinding as thin-atmosphere snow. "I've trained with swords since girlhood. No filthy whore could beat me in a fair fight."

"This is war," Faziz said. I thought his voice a phantom until he strode up the deck, passing through shadows like mist. *Of course. Back to Akizeké's side.* "Only victory matters."

He cupped Akizeké's chin, pulling her lips toward his. She inhaled—readying for a kiss—and his sword flashed. A bloody line sliced down her hamstring.

The darkness encaging me vanished on the wind.

Redemption. The shadow's promise to him, fulfilled. *You magnificent trickster. You gambled your freedom for this chance.* He'd let her possess him. For the shadow to grant him one moment like this.

I could trust him. We could win.

"Bind him, Ria!" I shouted. She leveled her bracer. Chains of ice shot free and manacled Faziz. A wave of fire separated him from Akizeké's grabbing arm.

My eyes tracked the bob of Akizeké's staff. I grabbed my chance and dashed back in.

She swung. A rap to my blade's tang stung my hands. I pivoted, wheeling the sword into the overhead strike Faziz had taught me. Akizeké grinned, pain distorting her smile, and blocked. Her angle went steep. I twisted the sword as we collided, and the blade drove a split through the wood.

The holdshadow rose wavered. Phantom dragons swarmed from my blade into the staff.

Fight destruction, they whispered. *Fight the dead.*

"For my father!" Ria screamed. Spurs of ice lanced into the wood, driving deep, splitting every crevasse. The staff cracked and dissolved into the mass of Tamadza's shadow. The hovership trembled beneath me.

Akizeké tried to step backwards. Her wounded leg bucked. She fell to one knee. "Join me, Koré!" Her eyes were just starting to widen with fear. "Call off your Fire Weaver. I'll kill Vashathke, take the throne, and marry you. Your children will be the heirs to War."

"My children will live in a peaceful world," I said. "So will I."

She didn't seem to notice the blade until it was halfway through her neck.

We pressed body-to-body. I cradled her as blood flowed over us both. The arms that had held me so many times stilled. Light left her eyes, but not the confusion.

"Why?" she whispered, and died beneath the rising shadow storm.

CHAPTER TWENTY-EIGHT
The skies above Victory Street

1st Zdz, Year 1 Vashathke

"Let me remind every dreaming little boy in War. If you work hard, follow the rules, and expect nothing but perfection from yourself, you too can rise high."—inaugural speech of Judge Vashathke Faraakshgé Dzaxashigé

"Below is a list of Vashathke's officials one must never accept as a client."—High Kiss employee handbook

I DROPPED AKIZEKÉ'S body, my eyes empty of tears for her, and ran to Faziz's side.

"Kiss me," he growled. "Set me free."

I grabbed his long dark hair and forced back his head. He strained and thrashed against the manacles. Enemy blood washed our faces, slicked our hands. I tasted it as my lips swallowed his, power falling from my kiss like meteors from the sky.

I would take nothing less than all of him forever.

He changed under my touch, shadows dimming, strength draining away. A switch flipped in his soul, darkness changing to a normal, human, dull essence store. I tried to pull back then, but he bit my lip and held me close. Drinking my fire until my lungs ran out.

"*Sakriu su riu,*" Ria cursed, limping up beside us. "The shadow."

The roiling dark mass of Tamadza's soul stained the sky. Cloaking the Surrender, the Palace, the Slatepile. It seeped through tall windows and cracks in ancient stone. Wherever it touched, people convulsed and gasped beneath the shadow's thrall. The high street winds pulled at its seams. Dragging it up and out, fast and strong.

"We have to destroy it before it spreads." Ria hooked her arms around my neck. "Let's do this. All three of us, together. Faziz, hold on."

"I don't deserve—" he started.

"Either all of us do or none of us do. Come on."

He wrapped an arm around my shoulders. Her lips brushed my ear. "Come on, baby. Show them your fire."

I gave Akizeké's body one last look. What we had was false. Corrupted. Broken. What lived inside me was real.

I drew on that love and surrendered to my power.

Instinct, all my own, amplified my light. Their weights went from my anchors to a pinprick at my back. The hovership dug into my side; I nudged it off with a talon. My wings covered Victory Street as I furled them free.

I was as large and gleaming as Skygarden.

The shadow rose, a thousand faces screaming. I raised my neck and exhaled the tide.

Essence rolled through the hungry world. Women cheered as they drank, shadows falling from their eyes, wounds sealing as they brightened. My talons braced against the Surrender's shoulders. I opened a second blast, my fire white-hot and streaked blue, washing Tamadza's thousand laughing faces.

The shadow recoiled.

"There!" Ria screamed, tugging one giant neck tendril. My head turned. The Surrender trembled beneath me.

My dragon's sight found Dzaro. She winked and nodded.

I breathed pure power into the gap.

The dead fell as I descended, skeletons and mangled corpses tumbling to final rest. Weapons fell. Living hands lifted in confused surrender. Back behind Dzaro's lines, Żeposháru Rena slumped dull in her restraints. Dzaro grinned, bright as Dzkegé herself, cheering my name as my talons touched down.

My giant's form dissolved around me.

We three crashed together in a close embrace. Faziz held me so tight I thought his new, brighter strength would crack ribs. His lips pressed my collarbone, kissing the blood-streaked scales. Ria locked an arm around both our waists, holding us up.

"I love you," I told them both. My chest felt so light, I would have floated into space without them holding me down. "Those are the truest words I've ever spoken. I love you." Steel conviction rooted in my breast. Vashathke wouldn't have me. Forget our bargain and the power of a judge's throne.

I'd stay with them and lead the life I deserved.

Dzaro, ringed by exhausted dogs, tossed a guard uniform at my feet. A tall guard stood behind her, nude and disgruntled. "There. I won't have one of Victory Street's heroes naked before his fans."

"I'm a courtesan. It's what they'd expect."

"You're not a courtesan anymore."

Her words warned sharp of my truth's price. *I'm their dragon. Their hopes and dreams in my flesh.*

I reached for the uniform and found the dragons' sword still clutched in my hand. *At last*, it purred as I dressed, *an honest Dzaxashigé. As long as you need us, we're yours.*

"Koreshiza!" The cheer began in the front ranks of Dzaro's guard. "The young dragon!" Ten thousand battered faces, their eyes wide and smiling, turned to me. *I'm worthy of all their pride?* My heart stuttered. My chest tightened. I made myself suck down a shaking breath. *How can I evade my father's cage and get you all what you need?*

Dzaro bowed. A ripple swept through the crowd. The gathered Engineers, busy tithing their fresh essence to their fellows, whispered uncertainly as every guard of Victory Street fell to their knees.

"A schism in the making," Żeposháru Rena murmured. "You'll fall to riot."

They should only bow so deeply to a judge. "Dzaro, get up. I have to speak with you." I had to tell her the truth.

Behind a guard barricade, I recounted what I'd confessed to the sword. How I'd betrayed her cause and invested the brother who'd spurned her. The nature of his marriage to Rarafashi, the truth of her missing nieces. My aunt didn't protest Vashathke's virtue, or decry my betrayal. Her lips narrowed into thin lines. She walked away.

My heart fell. I'd hoped she'd take my truth easy.

But Ria had listened, the dark and all of it, not once insisting my senses had fooled me or a *dzaxa* would never. Clear-headed, I knew a High Master would trust me when I said War's rulers wove evil. *A lifetime of suspicion. Old habits, and bad ones now.* The district might doubt the full truth, but any who knew both me and my father would acknowledge my tale held weight.

With Faziz on my back, I followed the hovership as Ria and Tożätupé piloted it to safety. Stars and planets swam through skies freed from Tamadza's shadow. The ancient craft's agonized faces flickered silver and died as it landed in the Armory Street ruins, rolling onto its side and powering down. The last mangled skeletons in its halls were easily dispatched, the dragons' sword singing silver in my hands.

Faziz helped me cut them down with uncommon grace.

"I can take back that extra essence," I told him quietly.

"Not yet. I still have work to do."

How much can you work at the cost of your health? But I trusted he could make that choice himself.

"This whole section of Armory can rebuild," Ria mused as we met her and Tożätupé in the piloting chamber. "With fresh essence, we can make true Shapers and erect new buildings."

"You've done well," Tożätupé told her. "The old Fire Weavers are avenged. Their future is secure. Your father would be proud. Will you come home now? Help me and Żeposháru Rena heal our district from this crime?"

Ria shook her head. "I can't spend my life staring at the Hive's ruin. And I want to limit Żeposháru Rena's hand in our rebuilding. The Fire Weavers—and I—need a new start."

"My Muruná Davé." Tożätupé nodded sadly, running a finger along the *Sashua Vorona* at her throat. "Careful not to start too many fires. You don't want your grand ambitions to go up in smoke."

As we left the ship, and I took wing once more, concrete-dusted children climbed from the ruins to inspect the broken stern. *Thoshe's people.* The ruins folk could salvage a fortune in substance from the ship. It wouldn't bring back their dead—but the ancient Thoshe would laugh and take what she could get.

By the time we returned to the Surrender—Dzaro's well-guarded apartment, not the exposed High Kiss—I could barely lift my flagging wings. Ria and Faziz helped me to my bedroom. With a nod of silent agreement, they dropped down on either side of me.

Love all around me, precious and true. I wouldn't let Vashathke take this from me, not if all his bright strength bent to make me his prize.

When I woke, no one had arrived from Skygarden to

claim me. Dzaro was nowhere to be found. Quickly, I wrote papers to transfer ownership of the High Kiss to Bero. Signing tasted bittersweet, but it would keep my people safe. I couldn't go back to who I'd been. I had to make a future as strange and uniquely myself.

We returned to the Slatepile and the wounded, where I spent half the day returning an irate Źeposháru Rena to her prior brightness. Faziz and his Slatepile folk helped guards carry bodies to the waiting transmutationists. Ria disarmed unexploded cannon shells.

Dzaro returned, exhausted, at the eighth bell. The three of us sat around her dining table. Faziz gulped bronto dumplings like he had seconds left to live. Ria was building hers into a tower with toothpicks. I hadn't touched my plate.

"Koré," Dzaro said, and my stomach lurched. *Does she hate me?*

"I'm so sorry," I blurted. "I should have told you everything before. But these secrets—"

Her arms slid around my shoulders. Black fur tickled my nose on her *fajix*-strap. "Dzkegé's tits, you think you're the one I'm mad at? You had real reasons to fear the *dzaxa*, even more than anyone could guess. I know the difference between you and my brother, even if you don't. He's a monster. You're a slut with a big heart."

"I'm not the nephew you wanted me to be. I'm not—"

"I want you to be you. That's all. We're family, you, me, and these interesting partners you've found."

I'd have to get used to family not ripping me apart. "What next?" I pulled my hem from Slayer's jaws. "Vashathke's still distracted with the cleanup. But I know it won't be long before he comes for me."

"I spoke with Toźátupé, Źeposháru Rena, Kirakaneri, and all the ladies of Victory Street. We've told your father we won't let War re-institute slavery. He can't defy us without sinking the district's economy."

My heart skipped. *They stood up to a judge for me?* "He can't leave me in peace. He needs a leash on me." I could flee. Maybe Żeposháru Rena would find a place for me in Engineering, though she'd want essence in exchange for granting sanctuary. I'd still be a pawn. Once, I might have flown as far as Gardening or Husbandry, joining a brothel in a district where no one knew my name. But Ria wouldn't abandon her order, and Faziz wouldn't leave the Slatepile—

The air cracked and shattered. My ears popped as Vashathke blurred into sight. He stood tall, a sun that set sandstone walls to sparkling, his grin lovely, triumphant, and petty as shit.

"Very right, Koreshiza. I need that leash."

"You eavesdropped?" Dzaro's jaw dropped. "You've inherited a district reeling from a terrorist plot and you're spying on your family instead of salvaging our relationship with the Engineers?"

"I'm spying on my dragon. He's key to my plans."

"He's your son, and you've worse than abandoned him." My aunt's fists balled. "I've sworn I'd never punch a boy, but you—"

"I'm your sovereign!" His voice boomed, low and powerful enough to crush armies. Dumplings popped in their bowl. Faziz cringed. Dzaro stumbled back against the wall.

So small, in thoughts and heart. All fear fled me. Hate pulsed in my breast, twinned with contempt. How could I deal with such utter trash?

I'd bring him to heel.

"You want a leash on me?" I said. "Name me to your old seat. Make me magistrate of Victory Street and I'll be duty-bound to work beside you for War's greater good."

He glared at me with eyes to flatten phalanxes. "I can't let a whore rule."

"Why not?" My heart sped. I didn't know how to rule. Would the *dzaxa* who'd fucked me ever respect my lead?

But maybe I could do this. Take the crown, live safe and happy. Happiness came into the world every day. Why shouldn't I get some?

I continued. "I can show you the High Kiss's accounts—I built a business from nothing. I've treated with judges and the undercroft's rulers, I know every lady of Victory Street, and I helped Ria save us from Akizeké's attack. I can do this. Dzaro can teach me basics." I'd be a thousand times better than anyone Vashathke would choose. I wouldn't throw people flailing to the street. I could help Ria rebuild her order and Faziz repair his home.

"Take the deal, brother." Dzaro peeled herself off the wall. "I know your secrets. Enough words in the right ears and your judgeship will crumble before it's begun. The *dzaxa* will take any excuse to rip your scandalous ass from the throne."

"Take it," Ria said. "Or I'll have Żeposháru Rena raise tolls on every crossway in War. You'll start your judgeship paralyzing inter-building trade."

My heart leapt at their support. I'd worried so long what Vashathke would do with my secret revealed. I'd never realized I wouldn't face him alone.

"Fine," Vashathke snapped. "All hail the Magistrate of Victory Street, Koreshiza Brightstar Dzaxashigé. Long may he rule. Long enough to pay the full price of thrones."

He spat in my face, so quick his missile traced a bloody line on my cheek. Then he vanished in a bright blur.

I watched him go, stunned. I'd out-schemed my father. I'd talked myself into a throne. Everything would be different now. Strange, new, shifted—and open. A world-spanning rainbow of possibility, ready for me to grab, change and remake.

"I'm not calling you *dzaxa*," Faziz huffed.

"Never do." I looked to him and Ria. "Do you want me to take this?"

"Is this who you want to be?" Ria asked.

Koreshiza Brightstar Dzaxashigé. Magistrate of Victory Street. Another man's title. Another man's life. A pampered *dzaxa*, not a scheming courtesan. Someone I'd scorn behind their back. But it sounded better than enslavement. I could stay with my family. And—I chuckled deep in my throat—I could certainly look the part.

"Dzaro, I need a loan," I said. "For the biggest coronation parade Victory Street has ever seen."

ONE MONTH LATER, every trumpet and bell on Victory Street played brass defiance. Notes echoed from Old Dread to the Palace of Ten Billion Swords, rising skyward in a thousand blending harmonies. The sun beamed gold and cleansing through cloudless blue. Wind carried high the scent and flutter of rose petals.

A fleet of guard *reja* swept before my own, their raptors harnessed with garnet-crusted leads. Batons flashed, steel and green holdspark. Drummers beat a homecoming march; dancers spun in artful trios. As we passed the Surrender, Bero and Opal cheered behind guard barricades. I gave them a wink.

Faziz squeezed my shoulder. Though some of my guards frowned at the gesture, not one dared question his presence at my side, twisting foil sheets into lilies and throwing them as favors. "You'll miss your friends. I'm sorry."

"I'll see them soon." They'd contracted themselves for my coronation feast. And they'd all send me spy reports in the morning.

I'd hired fifty raptors to pull my hoverplatform, each with snow-white plumage and golden eyes. All along the electrum-plated lily where I perched, children flung coin to the cheering crowd. Poems glyphed on banners spelled my name. Each spectator wore scales.

Even Ria, in the float ahead with Toźätupé and the other

Engineering dignitaries, wore a *fajix* of sunset-colored scale mail. Sparks flew from the *Sashua Vorona* as she sipped her club soda. Attending singers proclaimed her victory over Akizeké in three languages. *The hero of two districts. The High Master who rose from the wreckage.* If anyone had heard of her drinking habits or wild past, they'd forgiven. Young women could get into trouble before growing up to lead.

Faziz had first come downstairs wearing my skirt of silk roses and enough jewelry to buy a building. Ria had cracked up. Embarrassed by how hard he'd tried to please me, I'd handed him my first gifts. Now he wore a soft wool skirt, green-black and shimmering with polished onyx beads. A jade pauldron, carved like a raptor's head and lined with holdweight, hovered above his shoulder. His sword hung in a holdfast-locked sheath, the twin of my own. Dark paint accented his long eyes, which, at last, curled up in a smile.

My own costume was suitably ornate. A red skirt embroidered with platinum-thread starlings, a steel dragon-wing *thevé* across my chest, diamonds glued about my eyes. Instead of a necklace, I'd unfurled my dragon's ruff, and the delicate tendrils floated back on the breeze. I'd combed hazelnut perfume through my hair and shaved my legs to best display gemmed slippers. The dragons' sword lay across my shoulders, in a ruby-studded sheath locked with holdfast.

The hip where my mother's baton once hung felt curiously bare. I didn't miss its weight. If she were watching, she wouldn't be able to tell me from Vashathke. But she'd never looked at me deeply enough.

A new age dawned in the plaza before the Palace of Ten Billion Swords, where I knelt and swore to govern Victory Street well. My knees hated bending to Vashathke, but my sweet mask didn't slip. I recited my vows almost perfectly, omitting only my oath of personal fealty to the judge.

As I rose, Vashathke's hungry eyes lingered on the dragons' sword.

I grinned. Quiet joy thrilled my heart. *Love hasn't blunted my edges. It's cast me wicked sharp where it matters most.* "Let me carry it, Father. I'm the dragon. Such a kind, calm, demure man as you would never be so unnatural as to draw a blade."

I turned my back on him. My wings spread wide before the cheering crowd. Liquid essence hummed in the back of my throat. I opened my lips, and, instead of a speech, I gave life.

CHEERS STILL ROSE from the brightened streets as I joined my guests in the glass dome atop the Palace. Outside, snowflakes blew into bronto-high drifts along the rooftop. Bero winked at me from Kirakaneri's arm. Dzaro and Dusklily embraced under the dome's apex, watching shooting stars. Iradz cheered as her dice came up lucky. The only absent members of high *dzaxa* society were Akizeké's daughters, no doubt hoping a disappearing act would make the Engineers forget reparations were due.

Ria bid Tožätupé farewell and came to join us.

"How's sobriety?" I asked.

"Painful. Worth it." Her eyes danced all over me. "I've earned a reward for my good behavior. Wear that crown between my legs tonight."

I nodded and pulled her onto my lap. Her hair spilled down my chest. Faziz sat beside us and started twisting it into braids.

"Want me to do yours later?" she offered.

He laughed. "Not my style."

I waved over a servant. She offered me a case heavy with treasures. "Is this your style?"

Inside lay a tiara carved from salvaged green slate, marked by silver spirals of holdweight and covered in jade chips shaped like drawn swords. Beneath lay a deed written in my own smooth calligraphy. My first official act as magistrate.

He swallowed. "You're naming me Lord of the Slatepile."

"If you accept. I've reincorporated it as a building. You'll have authority to set rents and receive common Victory Street funds to bring it up to code. It'll take years of work and effort, and it's a hard responsibility—there's four hundred thousand people down there. I wouldn't blame you for saying no and taking time to rest. No matter what, I'm moving forward with reforms. But you're the best person for this job, and you want it done."

"I'm honored. I'll probably fuck it up."

"I'll probably fuck up as magistrate." I took his hand. "Let's build a new and better world. Together. Please."

Ria dropped the tiara on his head. The stone circlet floated an inch above his hair. "Welcome to respectability."

"I'm going to hate it." His smile lit his face like starlight.

"Koreshiza." The bright blaze of my father strode toward us. "A private word?"

"If my girlfriend can spare me. And my boyfriend."

Vashathke's nose wrinkled.

"Your father doesn't seem to like us," Faziz said.

"I know." I didn't hold back my grin or the swimming scrim of scales up my chest. Let Vashathke see me shine and know he could never dim my fire. "Watch my ass. I'll be back."

"Gladly!" they chorused.

My father and I walked to the dome's edge and peered down at the street. I could pick out every dancing couple, every rising starling, every fluttering banner of my name. I'd never seen such a lively, hopeful crowd. Certainly not one of people with no red in their eyes. *Bright. Full. Celebrating a peaceful future, not a violent past.*

A dragon can change everything.

"I was the clever one in our household, growing up," Vashathke began. "Good at sums and diplomacy. I wasn't like other boys. I was beautiful, pleasant, but also smart, strong with a baton in my hands. When my mother tried to sell me like a prize raptor, it tore me apart. I knew I deserved better. I'm sorry I hurt Briza—"

"Shut the fuck up. I don't need to hear about my mother tonight. I don't need your justification." It was laughable how little I cared for him. *A sly subtle whip who's done nothing but strike me. I can go elsewhere for love.*

His perfect mask didn't slip. But he did change the subject. "When your mother escaped my assassins, I knew I'd made a mistake. But my mistake saved my district. Dzkegé chose you to help atone for my sins."

I laughed. "Do you know why I keep the name Koreshiza Brightstar? It makes no sense in Old Jiké. My mother took it from a dictionary—'ko re,' all this, 'shiza', essence. Advertising my brightness. But 'ko re' is adverbial. It should be 'dzga re.' *Dzgareshiza.* I keep it, and the Modern surname I made myself, because the world should know I won't fit their boxes. I define the nature of my soul. Dzkegé chose me for me. Who I am doesn't revolve around you."

"I'm your judge. You serve at my pleasure."

Ria and Faziz broke off their conversation.

"I serve Victory Street." I met his eyes, twin to my own, and grinned. My skin, bones, and soul hummed with pleasure. "I'll never forget what you did to me. You'll never forget what I did to Geshge. One day, we'll tear down each other's thrones. Until then, I'll do justice. I'll help heal the wounds our ancestors made. And I'll be happy. That's my sweetest revenge."

"You're a monster, Vashathke," Ria chimed at my elbow. "I'll see history condemns you and Akizeké both. The new Fire Weavers will rise at the heart of your district. And your legacy will be eclipsed by your son's."

Faziz only kissed me. By the time we looked up, Tożätupé had dragged my father away to present a bill for her district's damages. I laughed quietly. "Thanks. And sorry. I didn't want to get you both on his bad side."

"But we're all there together," Ria said. "So what does it matter?"

It doesn't. Not tonight. Nothing mattered but shooting stars and wheeling planets. Night air, streaked with rose and hazelnut. The rising voices of my friends and family, ushering in a new day.

Their arms holding me up under the weight of my crown.

The tease of my wings as my heart set them free.

ACKNOWLEDGEMENTS

WRITING MAY BE solitary, but publishing is a team sport.

First and foremost, I'm grateful to my agent, Kaitlyn Johnson, for her faith in me and this story. Her notes and encouragement carried this one across the finish line, and I couldn't ask for a better champion in the publishing trenches. Likewise, I'm so grateful for Kate Coe and Jim Killen, whose passion and editorial guidance brought this book to Solaris and shaped it into its final form, and to Jess Gofton, an extraordinary publicist!

To everyone who read and gave feedback on that first draft—Fallon, Briston, Tasha, Tiffany, Kindra, and more—your feedback sharpened the voice, worldbuilding, and themes immensely. And to everyone who's supported me and given advice through the publishing process—Ashley, AJ, Ally, Aster, Erin, Foz, Laura, Saint, Kat—thank you so much for kind words and encouragement when I needed it most. To the early reviewers—Lu, Katrina, Cristina, Lily—who gave it all their support, and to incredible booksellers, especially Kel, Sol, and Ally, who do so much to get queer books to readers.

Thank you so much to my readers, for helping make this book a reality.

Most of all, I'm grateful I kept going.

FIND US ONLINE!

www.rebellionpublishing.com

/rebellionpub   /rebellionpublishing /rebellionpublishing

SIGN UP TO OUR NEWSLETTER!

rebellionpublishing.com/newsletter

YOUR REVIEWS MATTER!

Enjoy this book? Got something to say?

Leave a review on Amazon, GoodReads or with your
favourite bookseller and let the world know!